The Sh!te Before Christmas

Comedian, writer and public speaker, Serena Terry, known as @MammyBanter, has taken the social media world by storm after her hilarious videos started going viral. Her debut novel, *Mammy Banter: The Secret Life of an Uncool Mum*, was an instant *Sunday Times* bestseller.

Serena's down-to-earth humour has resonated with fans around the world. She has well over 2 million followers across TikTok, Instagram and Facebook, with more than 35 million views across all platforms.

She lives in Derry with her husband and two kids.

🎵 @mammybanter
📷 @mammybanter
f /mammybanterfb
🐦 @MammyBanter
www.mammybanter.com

Also by Serena Terry

The Secret Life of an Uncool Mum

The Sh!te Before Christmas

SERENA TERRY

With Claire Allan

HarperCollins*Publishers*

HarperCollins*Publishers*
1 London Bridge Street
London SE1 9GF

www.harpercollins.co.uk

HarperCollins*Publishers*
Macken House, 39/40 Mayor Street Upper
Dublin 1, D01 C9W8

First published by HarperCollins*Publishers* 2022
This paperback edition published 2023
1

With thanks to Claire Allan

Lyric from 'Fairytale of New York' by Jem Finer and Shane MacGowan

A catalogue record for this book
is available from the British Library

ISBN: 978-0-00-857991-3 (PB)

Typeset in Berling LT Std by Palimpsest Book Production Ltd, Falkirk, Stirlingshire

Printed and Bound in the UK
using 100% Renewable Electricity at CPI Group (UK) Ltd

To Alfie

'I've learned that people will forget what you said, people will forget what you did, but people will never forget how you made them feel'

Maya Angelou

1

Ladies and gentlemen, introducing Miss Vape Blanchett

Thursday, 1 December

December has arrived, bringing with it the promise of peace and goodwill to all. It's the perfect time to remember what really matters in life, right? Friends, family, generosity and goodness. Making cherished memories with loved ones, carol singing, decorating gingerbread houses, cosy matching Christmas jammies, twinkling fairy lights, Christmas movies, open fires and the look of wonder and amazement in the eyes of children of all ages.

Or, in my case, it has arrived holding up the middle finger, and instead of sitting at home, drinking hot chocolate and planning a month of Christmas cheer for my family, I'm sitting in the reception of Gemma's school waiting to be called in to see the principal.

Did I mention that I am also thirty-five weeks pregnant,

resemble a hungover, back-alley Miss Piggy, am clutching a bottle of Gaviscon to my hugely inflated chest, and have had to cross my legs tightly for fear any sudden movement will cause me to wet myself?

I'd rather be anywhere but here, but Gemma, my darling eldest child (aged thirteen, who thinks she's eighteen), has been caught vaping. I'm pretty sure I detected a certain sense of smug satisfaction in the voice of Mrs Lynch, principal of St Anne's College, when she imparted the news to me over the phone earlier. In fact, I'd say she revelled in it.

Mrs Lynch, or 'The Undertaker' as we used to call her, has never been my biggest fan – not now, and certainly not twenty years ago when she was my year head, and told me I'd never amount to much in life. I've no doubt she considers Gemma's experimentation with vaping to be evidence that she was right all along.

Now I may be completely out of the 'cool' loop here, but I thought vaping was designed to help long-term smokers withdraw from the tarry nastiness of cigarettes, for God's sake, not to become a trendy new cool thing for teenagers to do. There's no way Gemma is getting away with this crap and if I don't come down on her hard and heavy, what will be next? Will she skip the marijuana stage and head directly for class A drugs? Will she end up shacked up with some junkie drummer while working the streets to feed their habit?

OK, breathe . . . in and out . . . in and out . . . in and out . . . and relax.

And of course, Gemma – or should I call her Vapey McVaperson, or Vape Blanchett – will no doubt blame this wee flight off the rails on me.

You see, she isn't exactly buzzing about the imminent arrival of her new wee brother or sister. In fact, 'pure disgusted' would be a better way of describing her feelings towards my pregnant state.

Paul and I knew she wasn't likely to be deliriously happy about our little surprise, but we hadn't really expected her to cry real tears and launch into phase two – this time it's serious – of being an obnoxious teenager.

'Eughhhhh you can't have a new baby, Mammy. You're too old. Oh my God, all my friends will know you had sex. Boke. I'm gonny die. Like literally die. Mammy! Seriously! You'll be like, ninety when the baby is starting secondary school and I'll be left to watch it all the time and I'll not be able to go to concerts or parties or have any kind of a life and you have totally ruined everything!' This came all in one breath, at great volume, on being told the news.

Paul, very naively, tried to tell me later that our daughter clearly has the same ability to catastrophize everything as I do. I cried, shouted at him, accused him of being sexist, and it was only in a mid-burning-my-bra rant that I realized . . . he might have a point.

A tiny first year who looks like she should still be in primary school walks up the corridor and passes me while offering me a pitying look.

'Good luck, missus,' she taunts as she wanders on

3

laughing and I'm not sure whether my urge to boke with nerves is now greater than the fear that I might actually pee myself.

In the distance, the school choir is singing 'Oh Holy Night'. The dramatically building piano soundtrack isn't helping with my anxiety as I'm sent back in time, like I'm fifteen again sitting outside the office, awaiting my penance, and just as they reach the painful crescendo of 'fall on your knees . . .' I want to fall on mine. But the door to the office opens and there stands Mrs Lynch inviting me into her lair. It's like I'm Kevin from *Home Alone* who's just seen Old Man Marley in the church. But Old Man Marley was a good soul, this ghost of Christmas Past in the form of my old teacher however, well . . . not so much.

Her office looks – and smells – just how I remember it. In fact, I'm pretty sure that's the same sad, dusty nativity scene I remember her setting up as a token nod to Christmas cheer each year.

Looking closer, my suspicion is confirmed. There are only two Wise Men. The third Wise Man *may* have been rescued out of there, in my blazer pocket, circa 2001 in a fairly timid act of rebellion.

I think I might still have him in the back of a drawer somewhere.

Mrs Lynch looks just as I remember her: terrifying, with the aura of a woman who knows how to kill any ounce of craic with a single look. She looks old, of course, but she looked old back then too, she just doesn't look any older, if that makes sense? Or any different at all, come to think of it. Her hair is cut in the exact same silver-grey pixie cut, and I'm pretty sure she is wearing the same beige trouser suit that she wore in my day. Does she have a time machine hidden in her storage cupboard that I could get a wee go in? Then again, it's more likely she has a coffin in there and is in fact one of the undead like me and Cat used to assume. Dracula never aged either, did he?

I sit down, awkwardly, on a carved wooden seat that was certainly not designed with an eight-month-pregnant woman with an arse the size of two arses in mind. My efforts are not pretty but if Mrs Lynch dares to pass judgement on how long it's taking me to get seated here I'll . . . I'll do absolutely nothing because she's still intimidating AF and I'm in a fragile state here.

'Mrs Gallagher,' Mrs Lynch says, 'thank you for coming in. You must know we take vaping very seriously here at St Anne's College, and it is not permitted for any of our girls. Not even for our oldest pupils who are over the required legal age, and certainly not for our Year Nines.'

'Yes, I know,' I mutter.

'I know some parents can be a little more lax about these matters,' she says with a slight sneer, 'but the law does state that vaping under the age of eighteen is illegal and of course, there are questions over the long-term effects of . . .'

Hold up. She thinks I'm a 'lax' parent. How could she really think I would be OK with my child vaping?

Admittedly, when I was the same age I took it upon

myself to be a smoker like all the other cool girls. I didn't quite pull it off though, and instead fainted after smoking eight cheap cigarettes back to back behind the sports hall. I managed to crack my head on the concrete, burn a hole in my new blazer and throw up in my own hair in the seconds that followed.

From that day on I was labelled. Branded. My card had been well and truly marked. You only got to slip up once at Catholic school and that was it, ironically; repenting and offering up your sins to God didn't mean you automatically got back into the 'good student' list.

A knock at the office door pulls me from my walk down misery lane, and in comes Gemma's year head, Miss Brown, with a defiant-looking Gemma trailing behind her. The 'I'm so over this' look is set firmly on her face, and she shows not one hint of the shame I'm feeling about her. She even rolls her eyes at Mrs Lynch! Does this child have a death wish? Not to mention no manners? How is she not afraid of The Undertaker? Have I failed at parenting? Was Mrs Lynch right all along?

My anxiety hits the 'Launch Missile' button on my emotional deck and I am off.

To Gemma's horror, and Mrs Lynch and Miss Brown's shock, I burst into tears: full-on hysterical convulsions of ugly crying complete with snotty nose and hiccupping gulps of air.

With my bottle of Gaviscon clutched to my chest, and my legs firmly crossed in fear of my bladder also starting to cry, I must look demented.

'I'm sorry,' I wail. 'I don't know what happened to my wee princess and *hiccup*, I swear I didn't know she was vaping and in fairness, how would you know? It's not *hiccup* like she comes home smelling like twenty Benson & Hedges – I mean, c'mon, *hiccup* it's all raspberry flavour, or candyfloss flavour and' – my left eye is twitching at this point and I'm getting angry – 'My Little fucking Pony flavours and, and I didn't know *hiccup* and' – now I'm back to being sad – 'it's probably a cry for help cos I've let her down *hiccup* and now I'm preeeeegggnn-naaaannnttt.' This is a particularly long and howling pronunciation of pregnant and I see Mrs Lynch and Miss Brown glance at each other with fear in their eyes.

'Mrs Gallagher,' Mrs Lynch says, and I stop crying immediately and blink at her as if I'm still that fourteen-year-old girl in her English class all those years ago who she told to 'stop talking at once'.

'I can see that this is distressing for you, in your condition, so let's not labour the point.' There's a slight glimmer of a smile on her face and I don't know if she's delighted that she has reduced me to a wreck with very little effort or if she's delighted at her own painful pun. 'Gemma is suspended from school for two weeks from today. We have a zero-tolerance policy when it comes to smoking in all its forms and we must make an example of offenders to stop this trend from taking hold.'

I glance at Gemma, whose expression has now changed from 'I'm so over this' to 'holy shit, this is bad'.

'OK, Mrs Lynch, I understand completely and I can

promise you that this will never happen again,' I say quietly, aware that my face is now blazing with the sheer mortification of the holy show I've just made of myself. I try to get up quickly but the fact I am wedged into this stupid bloody *Antiques Roadshow* chair makes that impossible.

In the end, Mrs Lynch literally has to hold the fucking chair down by the arms while Miss Brown heaves me to standing. At eight stone at the very most, this is no mean feat. Miss Brown must do CrossFit or some shit.

I mutter a quick thank you before grabbing Gemma by the arm and waddling out of the door as fast as I can. Which isn't fast, to be fair.

When I climb behind the steering wheel in my car, I am out of breath, out of patience and out of Kegel strength.

'Gemma,' I say, painfully.

'Mammy, please don't start here. Just wait till we get out of the school car park at least. Look, there's a classroom right there, OMG, people can see us and they all probably heard you screaming like a madwoman in Lynch's office!'

'Gemma,' I repeat.

'Mammy, please. If they see you giving out to me—'

'Gemma!' I shout, cutting her off because I need her to listen to me and realize her friends seeing her is the least of my worries right now. 'I think I've just peed myself.'

2

Have you any woom, please?

Our journey home is silent, apart from the swish of the windscreen wipers tackling the icy rain of a grey December day. Gemma does not so much as peek in my direction and I'm OK with that. My face is roaring red, my ass is wet, and my dignity has run for the Donegal hills. Never in my life have I ever been so embarrassed. Between my breakdown in front of Mrs Lynch and Miss Brown, getting wedged into a chair requiring a full-scale rescue operation and actually pissing myself in front of my thirteen-year-old I am very, very, very much #NotLivingMyBestLife, besties.

Gemma is somehow humiliated and angry at *me* for 'embarrassing the life outta her'. Never mind that this is all *her* bloody fault, not only for vaping in the first place but getting caught. We pull into the driveway, and it's as if she is the disgusted mother and I am the naughty child, because she huffs out of the car, slams the door, and storms into the house without so much as a word or a backward glance.

Meanwhile, I'm left behind the wheel, stripped of any emotional or physical energy and trying to come to terms with the fact that I'm going to have to spend a good ten minutes cleaning pee from a car seat. And I can't even blame Nathan, or Jax – who by the way is potty-training at the moment.

Reminding myself, once again, to just breathe, I try to psych myself up for the task ahead. If I can just get a little quiet time before tending to my mini Chuckle Brothers, even five minutes, I'll feel better. Even if it does mean sitting on a wet seat.

'Mammy!' I hear Nathan, my now six-year-old, call as he bombs out of the front door his sister left wide open and makes a run straight for my car. 'Mammy! Mammy! I've got a surprise! Open the door so I can give you a big love cuddle and you can come see my costume!' My hormones are clearly still rattling through me as tears sting my eyes again at the sight of his wee innocent, beautiful, precious face.

'Oh that sounds very exciting, pet,' I say, opening the door and letting him hug me from the shoulders up. 'Can you do me a favour, angel, and please go get Daddy to come and help me get out of the car?'

'OK, Mammy!' he shouts before darting back up the path like the great wee helper he is. OK, maybe I haven't messed all my children up. Maybe I might be a good mammy after all.

Paul appears a moment later, Nathan trailing after him. I can't help but spot the look of worry on his face. 'Are you OK, love?' he asks. 'Is it the baby?' If truth be told this is the most attention he's shown me in weeks – things with Paul haven't exactly been brilliant recently either. I feel like he's been distant with me, and sometimes I can't blame him, but the concern on his face is yet another thing to pull me to the brink of tears. Until, that is, I remember I'm sitting in my own piss and that knowledge isn't likely to reignite the fire of passion in him.

'The baby's fine,' I stutter. 'I just, erm, just spilled some water over myself and I want to clean it up before it gets into the electrics or anything. Could you go back inside and mix one tablespoon of dishwashing liquid with two cups of cold water in a bowl? Then add in a tablespoon of white vinegar – it's in the press under the sink – and bring it out to me with a couple of those microfibre cloths.' (This is not my first pee-cleansing rodeo. I know the magic formula – especially with Jax thinking he can just spray it wherever he stands – although it is the first time *I'm* responsible for the mess in the first place.)

'To clean up water?' Paul says, his brow crinkled with confusion. 'Sure all you need is a few towels and I'll whack the AC on every few hours. It will be dry in no time.'

Yeah maybe, I think in my exhausted state, but then the car will smell like the inside of a portable festival toilet forever more. I couldn't live with the shame. Oh, Jesus, I'm going to have to tell him. And I go from mildly hysterical to full-on meltdown central again.

'Look,' I say, 'the truth is I pissed myself, in front of Gemma, in the school car park, after I got stuck in the principal's chair and had a massive meltdown. Because that wee . . . wee . . . bit . . . madam was caught vaping, and I got lectured about it by the woman who told me I'd never amount to anything. It's as if she thought I'd bought the vape myself and forced it into Gemma's mouth.'

Paul just stares at me. I imagine he knows better than to interrupt me mid-rant at this stage.

'So then I had a full meltdown and sobbed like a fucking lunatic about how I'm a failure as a mother so, now I just want to fall into bed and pull the duvet over my head but instead I'm sitting here in my own piss, unable to get up, and now it's starting to smell . . . *hiccup* and it's all my fault that Gemma's going to be injecting heroin into her big toe and riding a smelly junkie drummer before we know it and—'

A wee hand on my hand stops me in my tracks. Blinking, I look around to see Nathan – that gorgeous angelic child of mine – his eyes full of concern for me. He starts to speak very sheepishly. 'Miss Rose says we're not apposed to say piss cos it's rude and we should say pee, but it's OK cos everyone has ackydents sometimes. Jax had a ackydent a wee while ago on your bed, but it's OK cos you and Daddy say we can just try again. You can just try again, Mammy. It's OK and you can sleep in my bed with me.'

I am locked in a mixture of emotions – on one hand

his reassuring words are just so lovely. And of course, that's exactly what we told him when he was potty-training, and what we're telling Jax now during his active campaign to piss everywhere. (Sorry, Miss Rose, desperate times call for desperate measures and I refuse to say pee – not when my child has just pissed all over my clean sheets – and they were my fancy sheets too.) But for now, I focus on Nathan and the look in his eyes that screams 'I hope I helped'.

'You're right, pet,' I tell him, while wiping away my tears. 'You are totally right – and you are the best big brother in the whole wide world.' I look to Paul, waiting for him to do what he does best and rescue us from the high emotion of this scene with a truly awful dad joke or something similar that makes us all laugh, but he doesn't. He doesn't offer me a reassuring smile, or call me pet, or tell me he still loves me even when I smell like a urinal. He simply quirks a smile-not-smile that doesn't reach his eyes and turns to Nathan.

'Inside now, son, and finish your dinner or there will be no ice cream for after.' Nathan Gallagher, lover of ice cream, does not need telling twice. He's up the garden path quicker than you can say raspberry ripple.

Then he turns to me. 'Here, I'll help you out. You go get a shower. I'll clean the car and the bed. Then you can put your feet up while the wee man shows you his costume for the nativity play. Thankfully Nathan has accepted that Captain America was not one of the first visitors to the Baby Jesus, and that he can't wear that particular costume.'

He smiles again, but I can see there's something else going on in his mind. He's looking a bit shifty, if the truth be told, and then, there it is. 'Actually, love, once I've done that, I think I'll head down to the driving range. Hit a few balls with the boys for an hour or two? I can't see it being much longer than that. Three hours at most.'

My mood swings again, with alarming efficiency this time, and I find myself death-glaring at him. 'You . . . you want to go out? And leave me to put the boys to bed? And deal with the she-devil herself who, for the record, despises my very guts right now? Ah sure, on you go,' I say, passive aggression seeping from my pores. 'I'm only heavily pregnant with your fourth child, exhausted, stressed and ready for the hills, but batter on. Don't worry about me.'

He glares back at me. 'Forget it. I won't bother if it annoys you that much,' he spits before turning on his heel and storming off to the house to get my piss-be-gone formula. (No, Miss Rose, I am not even one bit sorry for not saying pee again. In fact right now, along with Paul and Gemma, Miss Rose can go and take her face for a shite.)

I'm still trying to haul myself out of the car – having been abandoned mid exit – when Jax tumbles through the door, face covered in Petits Filous, wearing nothing but a Spider-Man T-shirt, a cowboy hat and his welly boots, and runs down the path to the car, his willy bouncing freely with every step. Dear Jesus . . . could there be any more proof that my children are neglected than a boggin' half-naked child running towards the street in the baltic winds of December? How is he not absolutely freezing?

'Mammeee!' he screeches, loud enough that I'm sure even the neighbours in the next street can hear him. 'Come see my poo poo! In the potty! I keeped it for you!'

'Tis the season to be jolly, my hole.

After a shower and a quick disco nap in Nathan's bed, I haul myself up to face my adulting duties head-on. As much as I'd love to just sleep right through, my levels of mammy guilt are already nearing their peak and I can't risk them getting any worse. Besides, it's entirely likely that Nathan will spontaneously combust if he doesn't get to show me his costume for the nativity play.

As I walk past Gemma's door, I can hear her watching TikToks. On any other day – maybe a day when I am feeling emotionally stronger and have not just pissed myself in front of her – I would be coming down on her like Luther himself. TikTok gone. Phone gone. Freedom gone. But this is not any other day, so I will keep a lid on my inner beast and come back to it in the morning when I'm less likely to cry again, mid 'no phone for two weeks' punishment speech.

When I get downstairs Nathan is strutting up and down the hall dressed as a very short, and very happy innkeeper. He is pure lured with himself as he spins around in his costume as if he is walking the Paris catwalks.

I'd love to say I'm one of those mammies who hand-makes their children's school costumes, but we all know

15

that's not true. I'm not even going to try and fake it. Every costume my children have worn has come courtesy of Amazon Prime – next day delivery, minimal effort, job done, everyone's happy. (Except the ghosts of my ancestors past who were all brilliant at making things out of nothing and whipping up a quick costume out of a pair of curtains and a tea towel. The sewing gene and the desire to be a 'crafty mum' skipped me entirely.)

'Do you want to hear me say my line, Mammy?' he asks, grabbing me by the hand and leading me through to the sofa. Already, he has most of his toys lined up as his very own audience and Jax is sitting (on his potty) awaiting the performance. Squeezing my sizeable pregnant arse down between Buzz Lightyear and the Hulk, I say, 'Yes, pet. Of course.'

The room falls silent and Nathan stands in front of the fireplace and takes a breath. 'No, we do not have any woom here!' he exclaims, in an extremely confident, albeit borderline aggressive tone.

Part of me knows I should correct his pronunciation and work on his R phonic delivery, but it's too cute to mess with and funny too, when I think not only of the immaculate conception but also of my own current predicament. We are very quickly running out of womb here too.

'Brilliant, pet!' I tell him, proudly. 'You look so professional in your wee costume! You'll be the best-looking innkeeper out of all the boys in all the schools in all of Derry this Christmas.'

He beams with pride back at me. 'Can I sing my song now, Mammy? Miss Rose says practice makes perfect.'

Right now I'd like to practise kicking Miss Rose square up the arse, but I smile sweetly. 'Yes, pet. Of course,' I say, hoping and praying he doesn't choose the most annoying song in the entire nativity, which happens to be called . . .

'Who's That Knocking at My Door!' Nathan proclaims. Fuck.

It's his 'favowit' song, but it is far from mine. Very far. I'd rather listen to 'Barbie Girl' on a loop for a fortnight, but I can't discourage the wain. Even though this particular festive favourite comes with its own percussion (cue a small wooden mallet and my good coffee table), and has been sung every night, multiple times, in this house for the last three weeks.

'Are you ready?' he screeches, and dear reader, no, I am not ready. But I will sit here, as I suffocate the Hulk under my left arse cheek(s), and I will nod and smile as if Nathan was Michael Bublé belting out hit after hit. And then I will applaud because that's what good mammies do and right now, I need to believe that I am a good mammy.

We spend some time cuddling on the sofa, Nathan repeating the story of the nativity for the six thousandth time – high-pitched, loud and extremely enthusiastic. 'And she just had the baby right there with the donkey and the chickens . . .' he says. 'Tell me again, Mammy, how do babies get out of their mammies' tummies?'

'Oh, well, pet, you know – magic is involved!' I can't

risk telling Nathan how it all actually happens for fear he'll try and explain cervix dilation and third-degree tears to Miss Rose and the rest of Primary 2 instead of doing his paired reading.

Paul, still in a huff, takes the boys to bed while I set about my favourite ever task (said no one ever) of making up tomorrow's lunches. One for Nathan. One for Paul. None for Gemma because she's in the gulag now and will be feasting on dry bread and water if she's lucky, and two lunches for me. Well, I say two lunches but really, it's more of a rolling buffet of carb-loaded snacks to get me through the day without stabbing anyone in the eye with my pen. I'm growing another human being here. Don't judge me.

With lunches made and packed, my work phone lights up on the worktop. Nope. I'm not falling for it. I am not *at* work. I refuse to be pulled into this trap while I'm pregnant and so close to finishing up. I don't care that a quick glance shows me there are six missed calls from ToteTech, all of which are probably from my absolute dose of a boss Mr Handley. They'll have to learn to manage without me. In precisely one week I will be on maternity leave and ToteTech will be the last thing on my mind.

In fact, I vow it will be the last thing on my mind for the rest of the evening as I make a couple of cups of tea, grab a family pack of KitKats and carry them through to the living room. This is where Paul and I should sit together, drink our tea, eat our biscuits and bitch along with *Selling Sunset*. (Yes, Paul watches it. Although I think his reasons for loving a show filled with beautiful women are a little different to mine.)

But when I walk into the living room, mug of tea in each hand, packet of KitKats dangling seductively from my mouth, Paul is doing a really theatrical yawn. 'God, I'm wrecked,' he says. 'I'm going to get an early night, babe.'

His acting is so bad, he makes Nathan look like the Leonardo DiCaprio of innkeepers.

'But I made tea,' I say (after spitting the KitKat packet onto the floor) 'and Chrishelle and Christine are proper ready to pull each other's weaves out. Rich beautiful people hairing each other, Paul. C'mon!'

'Ah but, pet, it was a tough day and I'm just done in.'

'But we need to talk about Gemma,' I say, pleading. Because we do need to talk about our eldest child. I need him to do a Paul and calm me the fuck down, because that's how we work. I freak out, he calms me down. It is the circle of life in the Gallagher household.

'She's a teenager,' he says. 'She's going to be up to all sorts, but hopefully the suspension and a good grounding will make her wise up. Look, love, I really need to get some sleep, I'm knackered.'

And that's him, gone before I've even asked him how we're going to deal with the junkie drummer. I can't help but feel something is badly wrong here. I feel so shit that not even the prospect of the entire packet of KitKats all to myself cheers me up.

I still eat them of course.

3

Full fat milk with your tea?

Friday, 2 December

The sound of Shane MacGowan declaring that it was Christmas Eve and calling me 'babe' hauls me from my sleep. Shane isn't in my bedroom, obviously, but his intoxicated tones are bellowing from my old clock radio, the one which replaces my usual phone alarm every December.

Why? Well because getting up in the morning is hard, and it's even harder when you feel like a beached whale lying on a bed of sinking sand, and because, well, I fucking love Christmas. Once December hits, I am Will Ferrell in *Elf* when he hears Santa is coming to the department store. I am Betty Lou Who from *The Grinch* who secretly wants to compete with her neighbours in the Christmas decoration stakes. I am Arthur from *Arthur Christmas* whose fierce love of Christmas grows stronger every single year. So, if there's anything that's going to assist in me hoisting my cankles out of bed, it's Christmas FM.

I will admit, though, that this year, I'm hitting the snooze button more times than Granny Sweeney used to hit a wee bottle of port and believe me, that's a lot. Not even Mickey Bubbles (or Michael Bublé, if you're not from Derry) dreaming of a white Christmas is shifting me this morning. I only give in and get up when I'm extremely close to risking yet another episode of 'Incontinence, sponsored by The Third Trimester'. I'm going to have to get some TENA Lady. And not the discreet slivers of things designed for the 'oops' moments. I need battle-grade absorption, for those 'oh fuck' moments instead.

It's three attempts at rolling over and sitting up before I can actually get out of bed, and I do so with a loud 'ahforJesussake'.

'You all right, love?' Paul asks.

'I'm grand,' I lie because as much as I'd love to launch into a tirade about all the many ways in which I am very much not all right, my laziness has meant we're cutting it fine on the morning routine and there just isn't enough time for Mammy's Meltdown Hour.

There are children to be dragged out of bed, washed, dressed, fed, dropped to school and childcare and, in the case of the Vape Artist formally known as Gemma, instructions to be given about today's penance, aka her chores. If she thinks she's going to have two weeks off school to lie in her pit scrolling TikTok and watching rich families that we'll never live up to on YouTube, she's in for a shock. Thinking on it, this two-week suspension of hers is probably perfectly timed. It's fair to say I've let my housekeeping standards slide a little in the last month or so. If I can't use pregnancy as an excuse to sit on my hole and eat biscuits then what's the point? Right?

So, my indisposed darling daughter will awaken to the sight of me handing her a list of chores that she has to complete before her daddy and I get home from work. And she'll get a new list every day until she has served her sentence. If I play this right I can get her to do all the big jobs I normally do in the run-up to Christmas – because it seems to be a firm belief in Derry that Santa will not arrive with gifts and Jesus will cancel his birthday if your windows aren't gleaming and your skirting boards aren't completely dust free. Some people go as far as to paint their houses and buy a new sofa; I'm more fond of a deep clean and spending money I don't have on copious amounts of new decorations every year, much to the dismay of my long-suffering husband who's convinced every December that I'm going to bankrupt us with my excessive Christmas spending.

But first, I must pee (for the fifth time since midnight), have a cup of coffee (the only cup of proper caffeinated stuff I allow myself in the day due to my extreme preggoness) and prepare myself for the chaos that is morning Chez Gallagher. Especially morning Chez Gallagher in the bleak midwinter, when it's still dark outside and the heating hasn't quite kicked in the way you'd like. (Must add getting the boiler serviced to the list of things which need doing. Must also add that I do not expect my mouthy teenager to service said boiler but simply google numbers of local services for Paul to ring.)

Before I wake the boys and have to wrestle/dress them and then chase them around the house with a face cloth and toothbrush, I pull my hair into a sleek loose bun at the back of my head, brush my lashes with a lick of mascara, conceal my pregnancy pimples and dust my cheeks with a little bit of bronzer. Minimalist make-up all the way for me these days. I stuff myself into a thick denier pair of maternity tights and pull on a black cotton maternity dress with a long grey pocketed cardi and my DMs, then I head downstairs for some Morning Mammy Alone Time. I flick the kettle on and I'm practically salivating at the thought of all that caffeiney goodness. This is my me time before the carnage, so I sit at the kitchen table and survey my kingdom. The fridge is clattered with appointment letters, photos of the kids and, I notice, a new picture, a drawing of Santa. Nathan must've brought one home from school yesterday. The wee dote. He's so clever. But then I look closer at his painting of a man in a red suit, with a huge tummy and rosy-red cheeks and . . . wait . . . why has he no hat on? And since when does Santa have black roots? I squint at the writing on the bottom of the page: 'My Mammy, by Nathan'.

FML.

My phone rings, belting out the opening bars of Mariah Carey's anthem 'All I Want for Christmas' (yes, I set this as my ringtone every Christmas) but what level of madness compels someone to phone at seven in the morning? That only happens if someone is dead. Oh shit, maybe someone is dead. Oh God, what if Cat or Amanda – my life-long friends – have been involved in some sort of horror crash or been electrocuted by dodgy Christmas lights . . . or what if . . .

Breathe . . . In and out . . . In . . . and out . . .

I look at the illuminated screen of doom on the table and, Christ . . . it's worse than my catastrophizing.

It's my mother.

And there's no way something bad has happened to my mother; she is bulletproof, she'll outlive us all, she just does this from time to time. We'll go for months not speaking then out of the blue she'll call, at some woefully unsuitable hour, and fill me in on her life – whether I have the time, patience or energy to listen or not. I could let it go to voicemail, but this is my ma, the one and only Pamela Sweeney, and she is a formidable force of nature who does not take well to being ghosted, even if she is in fact more or less a living ghost who decides to haunt me from time to time.

This is the woman who shocked the local Catholic church community when she was riding a man who was not my father when I was just eleven years old. Her affair with the milkman (yes, she wasn't even fucking original there) was the talk of not only every gossip circle in town, but also the source of much slagging to a very confused me at school.

I got called Semi-Skimmed for months. Which I suppose is better than full fat, but still.

My young heart was broken into pieces when my beloved daddy – who I hero-worshipped like the legend he was – moved out of our family home. Pamela, on the other hand, decided this was the time to live her very best life and became the life and soul of every party from The Bog to Buncrana.

Our relationship was extremely tense from that point, and it has never fully recovered. For the majority of my adult years, Pamela has swanned in and out of my life as she pleases, and I've had to get used to not having a mother I can rely on in a crisis, a constant doting grand-mother for the kids or even just someone to meet for a nice cup of tea and a chat when I need a hug or some good old motherly words of wisdom.

Things got harder when Daddy died just after Nathan was born and I honestly felt I'd been orphaned. I also felt acute loss on the part of Gemma and Nathan, and then for Jax, that neither of my parents were there for them.

Because my mother never has embraced being a granny. For the last thirteen years, she's been living the good life on the Costa del Sol singing dodgy covers of eighties power ballads in bars at night and bucking the rather sleazy Javier by day. He's my age. She's sixty-two (not that she would admit that to anyone). She says he's the love of her life – I can't see the appeal myself. Perma-tanned, horse-like teeth from a Turkish dentist, pure dying about himself and fond of wearing trousers that are def-initely too tight in the crotch area. How his balls aren't parboiled by now, I'll never know. Not that I want to think about his balls – boke – but you can't escape them when you see him. It's either the too-tight trousers or, worse still, Speedos (double boke).

I answer the phone because she's the type of woman who hunts people down for less than not answering their phone to her and it's better to just get whatever one-sided conversation she wants to have out of the way.

'Tara love?' she says in her thick Derry brogue before I've even had the chance to say hello.

'Yes, Mammy,' I say. 'How are you?' I shift in my seat to get comfortable but now I want toast so I put her on speaker.

'Ah good, love. Look I have the BEST news ever!' she declares.

Oh God, please don't let her tell me she's getting married to Javier.

'Are you sitting down?' she asks, and I wonder if it's too late for a 'New phone, who dis?'

'I'm making toast, Mammy. Just about to go and get the wains up for school,' I say, hoping she'll take the hint and keep her news short.

'Ach the wee dotes. I miss their faces so much. But that brings me to my news,' Pamela says. 'I'm coming home for Christmas! Well, for more than Christmas. I'm coming home for good! Won't it be brilliant, love? I'll be here to spend more time with my beautiful grandchildren, and when you have the new baby. Won't that be nice for you?'

I can't speak for a moment as I try to process what

she's just told me. My mother coming home *and* wanting to spend time with my children? Has she inhaled too much hairspray again? All that sun must have finally gone to her head. Or her and Javier have hit the sangria for breakfast. Jesus, what about Javier? Will he be looking to be welcomed into the Gallagher family home too? Imagine, Granda Javier beating about singing 'Feliz Navidad' with his blinding white teeth and his balls hanging out? No thank you.

'Erm . . . jeez, Mammy,' I eventually stutter, 'I wasn't expecting that. I thought Spain was your favourite place in the entire world?'

There's a beat before she speaks. 'Well, it is, kind of. But you know this Brexit madness has made things a wee bit tough . . . and I've realized I want to be more present for you and my grandchildren . . . and . . .'

There's a break in her voice. Is . . . is Pamela about to cry? What the actual fudge? Pamela Sweeney does not cry. She wouldn't waste the eyeliner, never mind let anyone witness a moment of weakness. Nope, Pamela puts two fingers up to the world, sprays her backcombed hair to within an inch of its life, pushes her tits up in an exceptionally low-cut top and gets on with things.

'Mammy, are you OK?' I ask.

She sniffs. 'The truth is, Tara, Javier and I have split up. I caught the dirty bastard riding a barmaid in one of the pubs I sing in. He says he loves her . . .' at this, I hear a sob before she pulls herself together. 'She's only thirty-five. Tan, dark hair, perky. Gorgeous wee bitch she is. But she's

27

definitely had work done, she can't not have . . . but . . . he says they're going to have a baby.' More sniffles.

Fuck. This is not a drill. This is serious.

'So I said to myself,' my mother continues, 'well, Pamela, you can stay here and cry about it, or you can go home to your family in Derry and have a lovely Christmas surrounded by love instead of a cheating bastard. And . . . well, long story short: I'm arriving tomorrow because really, what's the point in dragging things out, and I'm sure you could do with the help and . . .'

Truth be told, I've stopped listening because my brain is just imploding with the idea that Pamela is coming home. Pamela. My fucking bomb-scare of a mother. Tomorrow. And she clearly believes she will be welcomed warmly into the bosom of my family as if the last twenty-odd years have never happened.

Aye. Good luck with that, Pamela. You'll be about as welcome in my house as a donkey shitting in the stables just as the Baby Jesus is crowning.

4

No peeeeee!

I'm still processing the bombshell my mother just dropped as I get the wains dressed and washed, get their bags ready and try and avert their meltdowns when I inform them that no, they cannot have their advent calendar chocolate before breakfast. (They also can't have it because I inhaled right up until 21 December in a hormone-induced chocolate binge at about 3 a.m. this morning. I add buying replacement calendars to my list of things to do.)

There is an urgency about getting up the stairs because when Jax awakes, it's vital that we get to him as quickly as possible to check if he's had a 'dry night' (mammy code for 'not peed the bloody bed again') and to get him to the nearest toilet as quickly as possible before he sprays his wee pee pistol everywhere.

This morning though, when I stumble into his room – breathless and feeling as if this baby is now actually trying to burrow out of my vagina – Jax is grinning widely from his bed, while Nathan is hopping up and down and running around in circles (innkeeper headdress still on his head).

'No pee! No pee! No peeeeee!' Jax shouts.

'He's a good boy, Mammy!' Nathan chimes in. 'Can I choose his sticker for the chart?'

We bought a reward chart for Jax to incentivise him to pee in appropriate places. Every successful trip to the potty earns him a sticker, and very quickly Nathan managed to convince his baby brother that it was Nathan's big-brother duty to pick the right sticker and place it on the right square. As a favour to Jax. Obvs.

While I admire Nathan's enthusiasm and dedication to the anti-piss cause, it does sometimes slightly terrify me. When he himself was being potty-trained, we weren't so with it to go for a reward chart. Instead, we opted for bribery with chocolate buttons (one for a pee, a fun-size bag for a poo). It worked well until the day Nathan had a dodgy tummy and argued his case for eating ten fun-size bags of chocolate buttons over a three-hour period – because rules are rules. I'd had to run to the shops, between his toddler shitstorms, because I had also somewhere along the line taken to rewarding myself the same way and our stash had depleted quicker than expected. What, adults can't reward themselves for not pissing themselves? Of course, we can. In fairness, with my pee accident record these days, I really could be doing with my own reward chart as incentive.

'Yes, pet,' I tell my middle child. 'You can *help* Jax choose a sticker for *his* chart because he is a very, very clever boy!'

Nathan beams with pride. 'Now he's a big boy like me! Jax, I am very, very pwoud of you.' Jax, who has a serious case of hero worship going on when it comes to his brother, grins back and the two of them laugh and jump around together shouting 'Big boy! Big boy! Big boy!' until Paul walks in to see what all the fuss is about.

'Jax had his first dry night, Paul,' I say proudly. 'Our baby boy is growing up.' And as I get those last words out, I have to swallow a lump in my throat that feels the size of an apple. A big fat tear rolls down my cheek so fast it lands with a plop on my mahoosive tummy.

'Right,' says Paul, in a way that swiftly concludes my Jax love-in. 'Nathan, you can't wear your costume today. Let's go get some breakfast before we get you washed and dressed for school. Tara, are you OK to get Jax ready for Jo's and I'll drop him off on the way to work?'

'Sure.' Jax starts to pull at my hand to get him to the bathroom so he can release all that night-time wee. 'But aren't you proud of our wee boy?' I give him a hard stare, feeling like he's brushing past this momentous occasion for some reason.

'Of course.' He plasters a not-totally sincere smile on and crouches down to hug Jax. 'Well done, buddy, keep up the good work.'

'Thank you.' I squeeze Paul's hand as he stands up and give him another misty-eyed look, which he returns with a rather harassed grimace. 'Oh, and look, there's something we need to talk about.' I am dreading his reaction to my mother's return.

He glances at his watch. 'Pet, we're starting to run really late here, and I still have to defrost the cars, it froze hard out there last night, traffic will be mental. We can talk this evening?'

'Oh. OK grand.' Maybe putting off telling him until later isn't such a bad thing. I'm slightly weirded out by his uncharacteristically timid reaction to the big news of Jax's dry night, but I'm determined not to allow anything to burst this little happy bubble of Jax-induced pride, even though there is a sinking feeling in the pit of my stomach. I can't say for certain, but it feels like Paul's more concerned with the traffic and the ice than this usually momentous toddler milestone.

'Mammeeee! My pee is trying to get out!' Jax squeals, and I am jolted back to more urgent matters.

'OK, pet. Let's get you to the bathroom,' I say as Paul ferries Nathan downstairs for breakfast. I'll just have to tell him about Pamela later.

A shout comes from Gemma's room as we pass. 'Could youse ever be quiet, like? I'm trying to get some sleep and all I can hear is youse shouting about pee like it's actually the most amazing thing in the world!'

I can't see through the wood of her door but I can sense the eye-roll from here. You'd think she'd be on her very best behaviour after yesterday's shenanigans, but no. Not even the fear of two weeks of lockdown is enough to cool her teenage jets.

'Gemma is verwee angwy,' Jax says as he sits on the potty in the bathroom.

'Yep. But she better be careful,' I sing-song. 'Because Santa doesn't come to grumpy children, or boys and girls who are cheeky to their mammies and daddies.'

To a soundtrack of probably the longest pee in history, Jax assures me he knows the craic. 'Amma good boy, Mammy,' he says. 'I do my pees in the potty. Santa will come a me.'

'You do, pet, and you are the best boy. Gemma is just a grumpy teenager.'

He nods sagely in the manner of a wizened old man in the pub after a few pints of stout.

I try not to think about Gemma at the same age – delighted with herself that she was using the potty like a big girl. How we enjoyed those rose-tinted days of shopping together for multipacks of Disney Princess big girl pants. How she took to using the potty like a duck to water. How she made me think that I had this parenting craic all sorted and we were both clearly naturals at getting everything right.

And now look at us.

'Don't be sad,' Jax says, standing up so he can examine the volume, colour and smell of his own pee. ('Wow . . . thassa lot of pee!')

'I'm not sad, pet,' I tell him. Deep down, I'm just

wondering how I am going to cope with both Gemma and my mother existing in the same city at the same time – both of them adept at making me feel like a complete failure in their own special ways.

5

Say it, don't spray it

Overnight the foyer of ToteTech, the software company I work for, has been transformed into some sort of dystopian Christmas scene that makes Melania Trump's white Christmas twig/tree hellscape look warm and inviting.

It's corporate Christmas bullshit in all its corny glory. An imposing ToteTech on-brand black Christmas tree has been erected just inside the main foyer and instead of candy canes and twinkling coloured lights it has been decorated with baubles in the shape of mini laptops, tiny whiteboards and, Jesus, is that actually a bauble in the shape of a bar chart? Where would you even buy such a war crime of a decoration? Stark white lights that are so bright they could double job in an interrogation room adorn the branches and I can almost hear Ted Hastings from *Line of Duty* muttering 'Jesus, Mary,

Joseph and the wee donkey' in my ear. To be honest, I'm thinking the same thing myself, big man.

The decorations don't improve much as I walk through reception. Acrylic black and grey (not silver) atrocities in the shape of some sort of Christmas-esque thing (it might be a snowman, it might be Santa, it might in fact be a heavily pregnant Mary) rest on the high counter. As Kirsty MacColl (God rest her soul) would sing: 'Happy Christmas, your arse'.

I don't have time to stand and judge all the ways in which this particular display screams B2B bullshittery, because it turns out Paul was right and we were running late and I didn't even have time for my second breakfast (seems pregnant women and hobbits are very alike) before I left the house. But, I am here, at five to nine, by the very skin of my teeth.

Breathless, sweaty and inhaling a Nature Valley bar, already wondering if I could eat a second one, I walk through the inner office doors and into the heart of our soulless operation. My team are all already here, and I get a handful of muted 'morning's as I collapse into my desk chair.

The team, for the record, comprises of Luke – a youngster who was recently promoted over me because . . . well . . . patriarchy; a few other junior male account managers, a sub-team of predominantly male software developers, a guy who oversees software development delivery and the 'Ys' – Molly, Amy and Lucy, my three twenty-something colleagues who work in customer support, with not so much as a stretch mark between them, and whose names all end with Y.

The Ys were initially, predictably, overexcited at the news of baby Gallagher number four, and there is little as terrifying in this world as having three excited twenty-somethings do that squealing, jumping up and down, flappy thing that only women in their twenties do.

'Oh my actual God, Tara, I can't believe you're going to have another wee tiny baby,' Lucy had squealed. 'This is the best news. We'll have to do a special ToteTech baby shower for you – what do you think, girls?'

Molly and Amy had squealed back in agreement, and they had started talking about balloon arches, and champagne fountains (fuck that – if mamma ain't drinkin', ain't nobody drinkin'), not to mention the party games and sashes and – this is a direct quote – 'Oh my God, my friend just had a baby and she got the most gorgeous wee Dior onesie for it. Absolutely stunnin'! And a wee tiny pair of Gucci shoes, OMG, I was like nawww I'm dying!'

I'd smiled and nodded: anyone who puts a Dior onesie on a living, breathing constant vomit-and-shite machine needs their head looked at, and why in God's name would a newborn, who can't even walk, need Gucci trainers? Oh no . . . no designer gifts, thanks, give me a Boots voucher so I can avoid finding myself up baby shit creek without a nappy.

My heart sinks when I cop my boss, Mr Handley, pacing up and down past my desk.

'Morning, Tara, can you please pop into my office? I'd

like to have a word,' he barks, abruptly. For shite's sake, it's not even nine and he already wants to have 'a word'. This is rarely anything good. Then I remember the six missed calls from last night and realize it's quite likely to be something very bad.

'Take a seat, Tara,' he says, in his usual slimy manner after I follow him into his office. 'Now, I'm hoping you won't take this the wrong way, but I want to reimpress upon you that the Langsworth firm is one of our longest-standing and most profitable clients. It's imperative that I have my top guys on exceptional form at all times throughout their project delivery.'

The latest Langsworth project has been rumbling on for the last six months, coinciding almost perfectly with my notice that I'd be going on maternity leave at the end of the year. I could tell in the early days that Mr Handley had wanted to give the project to someone else to manage, but I've worked with the Langsworth team for years and I was damned if he'd take my favourite account away from me now. Not to mention, they were super generous as clients, loved me, my work ethic and the fact I didn't try and upsell everything but the kitchen sink to them, so I was pretty sure they'd send a lovely little treat for this mama once the baby arrived. I'd ignored Handley's hints about a change of hands for a few months and eventually had to explicitly tell him to stop – this was *my* project, *my* team, and I'd be delivering it successfully before I went off to deliver my new baby, end of story. Delivery of their project, which included a new all-singing, all-dancing online HR system, was delayed due to Handley being tight and refusing to bring in an extra software developer like I'd suggested, but we'd finally gotten it over the line at the start of this week, so I couldn't imagine what he had found to complain about.

'Of course, Mr Handley,' I said, stifling a sigh (we were done? What could I possibly have missed?), 'and you *have* had your top guys on this project even if we were a software developer short, we did it and Langsworth are delighted.' (I resist doing air quotes as I say 'guys,' no need to be pass-agg from the start is there?) 'And as you know, I am always on exceptional form.'

As I say the word 'form', a shower of Nature Valley oats bursts out of my mouth like confetti and lands all over Handley's shiny white desk. 'Sorry,' I say sheepishly, before I start sweeping the crumbs into my hand to clean up. I'm actually contemplating eating them when Handley interrupts this rock-bottom of greed thought.

'Leave that,' Handley says. 'I'll get the cleaner in to sort it in a minute.'

I glare at him while speeding up clearing the desk of my offending oat-spew in seconds. I've seen how Handley talks to Peggy, our very accommodating and lovely cleaner. And I'm not going to get her to do something I'm perfectly capable of. As I triumphantly drop the crumbs into his wastepaper bin, I smile sweetly.

'The fact of the matter is, Tara,' he says, in a tone not dissimilar to how The Undertaker spoke to me yesterday, 'I've noticed a certain drop-off in your productivity lately, which I'm sure is down to your condition.' He glances down at my stomach, and I am instantly furious and equally creeped out at him staring at my bump. Handley is known for being overly forward with the female members of staff (we don't call him 'Mr Handsy' for nothing) and there's something in the way he ogles my swollen body that makes my skin crawl.

'You don't seem to be as present as you used to be,' he continues, 'and certainly not as conscientious. I did try calling you multiple times yesterday after you left early, because the Langsworth team called – they couldn't find the data migration document which you apparently had promised you'd send over by end of day yesterday.'

'Oh.' I blinked. Six missed calls for one document? When the project is wrapped up anyway and the data has already been migrated? Hardly a crisis . . . but still. 'Well, I had the document ready, and just needed some numbers from the development team before I could send it out, but as you know, they are extremely under pressure and over capacity. I was going to let them know yesterday but then Gemma's school called. Sure, the Dev team will have sent the data to me last night, I can have it with them in five minutes. Is that all?'

'Well, OK, yes,' Mr Handley stuttered and twitched his brow, looking put out. 'But look, in these closing stages and before the retrospective early next week, I really need my team right on it. And it's clear that this type of project may be too much for you since you, um, since you became . . . um . . .'

'Pregnant?' I say. Why does it seem to be such a struggle for him to say it?

'Yes. Yes, that,' he mumbles. 'Anyway, look, all things considered, we think it would be beneficial all round that ToteTech allows you to wind down now and maybe spend this next week until your "mammy leave" doing something a little less taxing.' (And he *does* actually use air quotes as he says 'mammy leave' while offering a patronizing AF smile at the same time.) 'It's the second of December today, you were due to finish next Friday anyway. Why don't you take this week, let's call it holiday leave, and finish up today? And we can hand your accounts over to someone else, someone who can really get down with the details like they need to and prepare for the retrospective. And, of course, it will allow you to put your feet up properly without worrying about dropping any more balls.'

I can feel my face redden but it's not with shame at being accused of not pulling my weight. It's with anger. An anger so fierce that I fear the surge of rage-induced endorphins might just push me into labour, right here and right now. What in the Scrooge McFuck is this absolute gobshite trying to insinuate here?

'My condition? My' (fucking air quotes) '*condition*? I'm pregnant, I haven't got the plague, and let me remind you that I have been pregnant while working this job twice before and I have *never* dropped the ball with any of my clients. Not then and not now.' So far so good at keeping a lid on my explosive anger, not even any swears, good girl Tara. 'As for my mammy leave, did you mean to say maternity leave? You know, the legal entitlement a mother has following the birth of a child to both physically recover from the birth and to bond with the tiny new human she has responsibility for? I'm taking what is permitted to me by law and I've earned every last second of it. I work harder and smarter than anyone else in this office and if you think for one moment that you can take away my key client because I didn't answer a few calls last night about a document that was held up due to our well-known capacity issues – which by the way were outside of core working hours – or that you can imply I haven't been as committed to this job as usual because I took a day of annual leave, and shunt me off so that someone without my "condition" can take over, then let me tell you something—'

Handley shifts uncomfortably in his seat and his face starts to heat from the neck up. If I'm reading him right, it's possible he is either about to shit himself or cry. I am familiar with both expressions thanks to Jax and Nathan, and for the record neither prospect scares me. My inner 'fuck-it' demon will carry me through.

'This is a joke. Except it's not funny, is it? It's actually discrimination. I had planned to finish up weeks ago – which, need I remind you, I would've been legally entitled to do – but I stayed on and worked my ass off to get this Langsworth project over the line, which I *told* you months ago I would do. And which we did. Two days ago. I did that for you, and for ToteTech, and you sit there with a straight face and tell me I've not been present or conscientious and then patronize the absolute shite out of me with talk of winding down and relaxing as if this baby has actually leeched any form of intelligence out of my brain? Tell me, Mr Handley, should I call my union rep first or HR?'

He blinks at me, mouth gaping open as he tries to think of a response. Meanwhile, my rage is very quickly morphing into a hormonal overload of feeling utterly shite about myself, and to my shame I start to cry. Like uncontrollable ugly snotter cry with the occasional sob. Handley just stares at me as if he has no fucking idea how to deal with this . . . this . . . mess in front of him. To be fair to him, neither do I. I'm not sure which emotion is coming next, it's a hormonal lottery at this rate, lads.

All the humiliation I fought off with my rage comes flooding back. I shouldn't have expected anything more than this from Handley. He hasn't exactly been overly enthusiastic about my third request for maternity leave in six years. When I broke the news that I was pregnant you would have thought I'd literally sauntered into his office with Paul and begun shagging on his desk bare-back as he ate his granola.

'Look, Tara,' Mr Handley blurts, and his face is now sheet white. 'I don't think there's any need for talk of unions or HR, I'm sure we can talk this through. There's no need to get upset.'

Wiping my tears away and trying to get my just-been-sobbing breathing back under control with a few deep breaths, I realize I need to compose myself. While there is very much a need to get upset and angry again, I do have the law on my side.

I clear my throat and find a much calmer voice. 'Mr Handley, I have never taken a moment's leave that I have not been entitled to. In fact, I could've taken more, but I didn't, and I am quite concerned that you aren't recognizing that, considering the lengthy discussions we've had throughout about finishing this project. We've known the deadlines for months and even though you refused to hire another developer, I assured you *on multiple occasions* I was not going to let anyone, let alone myself, down before I left to have this baby. I am sure you are very much aware of all the legalities which offer protection to pregnant women in the workplace . . .' I pause, watching an actual bead of sweat break out on his forehead.

'Look,' he says, more flustered than I have ever seen him in his life, 'I am aware and maybe I worded it incorrectly. But as you said, you have been working extra hard to get this project over the line. And it's there now. It's completed. And ToteTech is very appreciative of the work you've done. So, erm . . . why not take some of that leave you didn't take, that you were perfectly legally and rightly entitled to take, and start your mam— maternity leave a little early? I mean . . . your leave will still officially start next week, but this week can be seen as time off in lieu . . . does that seem fair?'

Hmm. I sit back and let his offer sink in, conscious that every second I'm quiet feels like an eternity for him. It's a good start for now, but I will not let Handley or ToteTech think they can brush what's just happened under the HR carpet just by giving me some free paid time off. When I'm stronger and not pregnant, I can fight this properly. For now, though, I'm exhausted physically and emotionally and if I have to stay here any longer I fear ToteTech and their awful corporate Christmas décor and Handley and his disgusting sexism will force me to kick him right in those balls he accused me of dropping.

'Fine,' I say eventually. I lever myself out of the chair so that I can look down on him. 'However, I want to formally state that I'm not happy about the way this has been handled, this has to be recorded. I won't be drafting a note to HR *for now*, but between you and I, this shouldn't happen to any other woman here again. And if I hear it has . . .' I let the pause lengthen; Mr Handley gulps. 'Merry Christmas.'

Adios muthafuckas, big mamma has left the building.

6

Are you gaslighting me?

The rest of Friday morning passed in a blur. Once I'd composed myself and left Handley's office, I sat at my desk and wrote out a very vanilla email letting the wider team know I was downing tools a week early. I scheduled the email to go out one hour after I left the office, which once I'd grabbed anything I needed from my desk, was 10 a.m. Thankfully someone had ordered in ToteTech Christmas cupcakes, which created a convenient decoy of staff rushing to the kitchen and allowed me to sneak out the side door. While I wanted to tell everyone what had just happened, I also wanted to avoid any more drama and keep the knowledge of Handley's grand fuck-up safely in my back pocket for now.

Announcing my early leave from work to my family was met with mixed reactions. Paul replied to my text with a very underwhelming 'OK babe'. I'll tell the boys this evening, not that it will change anything for them of course. And needless to say, Gemma – as the only one actually in the house when I roll in – isn't exactly buzzing at the thought of her 'total control freak' of a ma being home during the first day of her suspension. I imagine she thought she was in for some kind of mid-term break, giving a half-assed effort at her chores before lying in her pit, scrolling her phone and binge-watching *Stranger Things* before complaining that she has to wait another year or two for the next season. (Bish, please! You'll never know the pain of waiting weeks in between episodes of *Dawson's Creek* to find out who Joey picked.)

Discovering Mammy Dearest will be here to keep her busy, her face sours even more than before. 'Can you not just ask Mrs Lynch to let me back into school?' she begs when I break the news. 'I'll even stay in the classroom during break and lunch and do extra work?'

As tempting as that is, I am not for going head-to-head with The Undertaker about anything just now or ever again, and besides, this wee madam has to learn her lesson so she never even contemplates pulling some sneaky vape-like shit again. Even if it means I have to go full-scale Miss Hannigan on her ass.

Stretching in my bed (I've about an hour before Paul gets home with the boys and I'll genuinely rip my own ears off if I have to listen to Gemma's moaning downstairs, so I sneak a quick disco nap), I decide I must text Cat and fill her in on the madness of the last two days. The prodigal mother's impending return, Handley's unholy

HR fuck-up that at least got me an extra week's paid leave, and Vapey McVaperson, which she'll more than likely have a reasonable 'you were her age too once upon a time, Tara' response to. It dawns on me that I've not actually heard from Cat in a few days. Admittedly I've been too busy/emotionally unstable/pregnant to get round to messaging her myself, but it's very unlike her not to at least bombard my WhatsApp with completely inappropriate memes several times a day.

I find myself in that sacred, comfortable position every eight-month pregnant woman searches for, and I don't want to move an inch for fear of arsing it all up, or waking Baby Gallagher and reminding him or her they haven't jumped on my bladder in a while. And it's becoming harder and harder to ignore the almighty clattering and banging Gemma is orchestrating as she makes it known to the world that she's enduring hard labour on her first day in 'prison,' as she calls it.

The noise is all for effect and part of her cunning plan to make me lose the plot listening to her swearing at the hoover and stomp down the stairs to rescue her from a life of skivvying. I know her game; I was a teenager once and clearly remember using the same tactic on Pamela. Well, it didn't work then and it sure as shit isn't going to work now. I work in an open-plan office with the Ys, and I've worked from home during the Pandemic with the boys. I have a remarkable tolerance for tantrums, overexcited squeals and pleading looks, so unless your limb has been severed, I'm staying where I am.

I'm way too pregnant to even care about the racket she's making or the huffs she's puffing. So I will lie here, and I will eat this Dairy Milk (share-sized bar, to share with the baby of course) and ignore the noise, safe in the knowledge that my floors are getting washed by someone who isn't me.

I do at least heave myself to a sitting position and grab my phone off my bedside locker to message Cat, but I'm quickly distracted by 157 new notifications from the Rebel Mums' group chat. I start to scroll through it, even though I know I shouldn't do it to myself. The girls – a group of mums who take life by the balls and who helped me overcome my complete meltdown earlier this year – will be wishing for an early death today after their big Christmas night out last night.

I was invited, of course, but it's zero craic sat in a crowded bar with everyone else lashing the drink into them, knowing that there will always be a mammoth queue for the toilets and that getting a taxi home in sub-zero temperatures is like Mission Impossible. Not to mention I'm at the stage of pregnancy where I refuse to wear anything other than loose-fit cotton clothing or pyjamas, and there isn't a hope of my swollen cankles fitting into a pair of 'going out-out' shoes. There's also a hormone-induced spot the size of Mount Errigal living rent-free on my chin.

Don't get me wrong, the Rebel Mums are the least judgemental people I know, but I am not for sitting watching them all sequins and stilettos downing shots of tequila while I take shots of Gaviscon wearing Paul's sliders because they're the only open-toe shoes my hooves fit into. It was a hard pass on the Christmas night out for this Rebel Mum.

Regrettably, I've found myself withdrawing more and more from them over the last few months as my pregnancy has progressed. It's not like in the advanced stage of my 'condition' (urgh, Handley), I could rock up and bust a few moves at the street dance class I'd once taught and loved. One slutdrop and I'd break my waters, pee myself, or finally cause that haemorrhoid that is threatening to make my life hell to pop out and do some twerking of its own.

I've turned down the last few activities all round, to be honest. Like go-kart racing, which looks amazing, but it's obviously a safety hazard and a definite no-no. Then rock-climbing because well, with a bump it's impossible and also seriously dangerous, another no-can-do from me. Obviously drinking like a fish and partying into the wee hours with them has also lost its appeal. When I was in the second trimester, God love them, they tried their best to think of less 'physical' activities but I refused to let them go against the grain of the Rebel Mums ethos, which is basically 'do crazy fun shit, regret it later'. I hated the thought of them trying to dilute their fearless spirit just to accommodate my impregnated ass. 'No way,' I told them, 'I'll be back to my best after the baby, and I'll be there first in line to take on every activity then.' I do miss those girls though, so so much, and I'm sniffling with just a smidge of self-pity and FOMO, scrolling through their pictures and seeing their shenanigans from last night. There's Eva looking fucking unreal in a red sequinned body-con dress cut down to her waist and up to her vagina. She has her hair done in loose fifties-style waves, and is looking all kinds of Jessica Rabbit sexy with a dash of red lipstick, red nails and a Santa hat perfectly positioned on top of her sleek, wavy head of hair. The woman is pin-up gorgeous. Like, film-star beautiful. (I look down at myself – at the chocolate that managed to escape my mouth as I inhaled the entire bar while scrolling, now scattered like my own type of edible chocolate sequins around my fleecy Christmas pyjamas, which themselves are straining around my bump, all the way down to my swollen ankles popping out of the top of fluffy bed socks. Urgh.)

Back to scrolling the debrief of the Rebel Mums' Christmas aftermath, I see a picture of Oonagh, who's wearing a hairband which is dangling mistletoe in front of her face, and sitting on the knee of some ridey young man who is probably about the same age as Luke and . . . oh shit! It *is* Luke and . . . fuck . . . Where did they meet Luke? And why is he looking so hot? No. No. I cannot allow my brain to go back to that place. I do not fancy Luke. Not one bit. Nope. He is a bit of a dick when all is said and done, and no. Just no.

I'm just a wee bit horny, that's all. Fucking pregnancy hormones. What kind of a sick joke is it to make you look and feel like a beached whale and give you a dose of the raging horn as well?

I wonder if I could seduce Paul into giving me a ride? Although thinking about that makes me sad too – it's been a while since he's even as much as begged me for a quickie. At least a month, maybe even six weeks, and that is not at all like Paul Gallagher. Normally I'm beating him off me with a stick. The only other times we have gone this long without even a half-hearted duty-of-care shag have been post-birth with the other children. And no, it's definitely not the case that he feels weird about having sex with a pregnant woman. I have been this pregnant three times before and it hasn't taken a wrinkle out of him to stand in front of me, lad in his hand, with a cheeky glint in his eye ready to give me the best three minutes of my life.

Unless . . . of course . . . I'm extra grotesque this time round. I glance down at my fluffy chocolate-sequinned pyjamas again. The chocolate has now melted as though fleecy Rudolph has shit himself.

I'm saved from going full fear and self-loathing when Gemma dramatically kicks open my door, like an FBI agent on a drugs bust, and stomps in looking like she's done three days straight in one of Derry's old shirt factories. 'Ehm, that's all the floors washed, the dishwasher emptied, the bathroom bleached, and the laundry put away. Can I please have my hour of phone time now, bestie?' she pleads.

'Make me a cup of tea and some toast first, love, then you can have your phone,' I say smugly. Because I have the power. Right here in my dressing gown pocket, nestled

52

beside my heartburn tablets, sits the key to Gemma's teenage kingdom. I am the keeper of the keys, the master of her universe, the protector of the portal to her digital dimension. What she herself calls 'her whole world' is encased inside the shiny plastic of her phone.

Isn't it a sad world we live in today when teenagers would literally sell their souls for their phones? Granted, I hate not having my phone either, but Gemma's withdrawals are so bad, and the meltdown she had this morning during our rush to get out of the door, meant that I have already caved on my original penance of an all-out, no phone for two weeks ban. I want my house to be still standing, my remaining children to be still alive, and for me not to be doing time for murder by the time these two weeks are up, so an hour a day of phone time seemed like a fair compromise.

'Are you serious, Mammy?' She groans. 'You're pregnant, not disabled, why can't you make your own tea and toast like? What you're doing to me here is actually slave labour, ye know. It's child cruelty and totally borderline abusive.'

'Abusive?' I ask her, gaping slightly. 'Are you for real, wee girl? You've mopped the floors, not done a twelve-hour shift in a sweat shop. You need a dose of reality, daughter, because making you take responsibility for your own actions is very far from cruelty.'

She tuts loudly, and the accompanying eye-roll would give anyone else a migraine.

'And no, I am not disabled but I am eight months pregnant, and asking my eldest child to make me a wee cup of tea and a slice of toast isn't asking the world, is it?' I say.

She blinks back at me, and I think for the smallest of moments that I've gotten through to her. That she might actually be sorry for spouting her 'cruel and abusive' accusations. But . . .

'Oh. My. God. Stop gaslighting me. Like seriously, this is having such a negative effect on my mental health.' She storms out, slamming the door behind her.

Chhhhrist. I am all for mental health awareness and ensuring my children are informed and able to normalize any feelings associated with their own mental health. God knows I have my own issues with anxiety, and I've needed the help of medication to get me on an even keel a few times now. I'm off them at the moment for obvious bump-related reasons, but this . . . this horseshit my daughter is coming out with? What is it with teenagers picking up buzzwords like gaslighting and throwing them around without fully understanding them?

It would be nice if teenagers could be a bit more level-headed, instead of throwing ludicrous, and in some cases, pretty serious accusations at their dear parents. Surely *I* wasn't like this as a teen? I didn't get the chance – even though I'm certain my mother *was* negatively affecting my mental health at the time – I was too busy being the parent to her or trying to keep up my relationship with my lovely daddy.

Gemma doesn't know the half of what I went through or missed out on because of my mother, she still has her mammy and her daddy around to lovingly parent her together.

God. No. I don't want to think about my daddy now. Or Pamela. (Shite, I *have* to tell Paul about Pamela arriving this weekend.) Or Gemma. Or the Rebel Mums. Or Paul. Or suddenly finding Luke ridey again.

As anxiety starts to well up inside me (real anxiety, not Gemma's gaslighted brand), I feel a wave of desire for the calm my meds bring: being able to take one of my anti-anxiety pills just to balance me out is even more appealing than an ice-cold G&T right now. But I've been doing so well, and I'm so close to the finish line and . . . Nope. I don't want to think about that either. I'll medicate with some more chocolate instead, as Vape Blanchett is refusing to make me some toast.

Except I've eaten the whole share bar, haven't I? That's it. It's time to bring out the big guns. It's time to raid the Christmas cupboard.

7

Flipping that Christmas bird

Saturday, 3 December

By the time the weekend has arrived, I have reached the limit of my ability to lie on my arse on the sofa eating only the 'nice' Quality Street and leaving the Strawberry Cremes in the tin. I have also reached my tolerance levels when it comes to listening to Gemma grunt and groan like a contestant in the World's Strongest Man competition while doing her 'slave labour', or complaining that she is 'soooooo boredahhhh', and I need to get out of the house to clear my head and also to let my heart and lungs know that no, I'm not dead, I'm just lazy as shit.

I haven't heard so much as a peep from Pamela since her early-morning phone call yesterday, and for all I know she changed her mind and is currently engaging in some kinky three-way with Javier of the too-tight trousers fame and his new lover. (What is my brain doing to me with these images!)

Paul was weird AF with me again this morning. Like not totally disconnected from me but something just doesn't feel right and I can't put my finger on it. With my pregnancy horn still blaring, I'd cuddled up behind him in bed, kissing his neck to try and wake him. I figured if he gets some action, he might be on a dopamine high when I break the news of Pamela's return. So really, I was trying to kill two birds with one shag. But he did a 'me' and said he had a headache and asked if I'd mind if he just got a wee lie-in instead, promising he'd make it up to me later. I have a feeling he won't, though.

I'm off to talk about all the above with my two 'besties' Amanda and Cat – we've arranged to meet for lunch and I have hunted out my best comfy, day-wear red and black plaid maternity dress and my 100-denier magic maternity tights, squeezed my feet into a pair of black knock-off UGG boots and I have even put on some make-up – although no amount of make-up can hide Mount Errigal on my chin which has now grown to Mount Everest status.

If I'm hoping for a confidence boost from my beloved family, I'm in for a let-down.

'Are you going out?' Gemma asks in such a disgusted tone of voice that you'd swear I was on my way out to slaughter some baby lambs or kick a few puppies.

'I'm going to meet Auntie Cat and Amanda,' I tell her.

She stomps her feet, totally raging at me. 'THIS, this is

sooooooooo not fair!' she barges. 'How come you get to go outahhhhh?'

'Erm, well for a start, cos I'm an adult, and also I'm not grounded for vaping in school. Will that do?'

'Seriously, Mammy. Do you think you're funny? It's the weekend. I'd not even be at school anyway, you really just want me to be depressed, don't ye?'

'You're grounded, love,' I say. 'That doesn't mean you get to have all the craic at the weekend. There's no time off for good behaviour here.'

'Aaaaarrrghhhh!' she screams before stomping up the stairs and slamming her bedroom door. I should probably be the bigger person (which physically I very, very much am at the moment) but fuck it. I can be petty when the need arises.

'Thanks, love,' I shout after her. 'I will have a lovely time and yes of course I'll tell your aunties you said hello.'

There's a creak as her bedroom door opens: 'Eughh, they're not even my real aunties!' she snipes before slamming the door again.

'And don't forget to get the Christmas decorations down from the attic!' I bellow. 'We need to do the house tomorrow, you don't want your wee brothers to miss out, do you?'

She opens the door again just so she can slam it back closed. It might not be very mature of me (I think we've established at this point that I'm long past that stage), but I send a middle finger up to her closed bedroom door before turning to spot Nathan – innkeeper costume still on – staring up at me.

'Mammy, look I can do dat too,' he says with glee, while doing his best to adjust the fingers on his own right hand so that when he raises it a perfect bird is flipped.

Great. That'll be another phone call from Miss Rose on Monday. I wonder who Nathan will give the 'bad finger' to first. One of his school friends, perhaps? Or, more likely, Mrs Logue, the primary school principal?

I've no time to worry about it now though. I need to be away. I call to Paul, who makes an indistinct grunting sound to acknowledge me without even raising his eyes from his phone. No 'have fun, love'. No 'do you want me to drive you?' Just a grunt.

Yup, something is definitely not right with him, but I've no time right now to ask. I leave the house to both Nathan and Jax giggling and giving me the finger out the living room window.

Of course, I'm late by the time I bustle out of the cold and into Primrose on the Quay to join Amanda and Cat, who thankfully already have a table as this place is jam-packed. The warmth inside is a blessed relief from the chill of the wind coming off the river, and the scents of cinnamon, hot chocolate and freshly baked scones have me salivating.

The windows are dressed with twinkling lights, Bing Crosby is crooning on the radio and every staff member is wearing a Santa hat. I can't help but smile as I squeeze my way through to my table. Christmas is my favourite!

'Sorry,' I say as I ease myself onto a chair. 'I couldn't get a parking spot and by the time I did and duckwalked over here . . . well, you know the craic. Have youse ordered yet?'

'Not yet,' says Amanda, who is looking particularly cheerful today. There's a glint in her eye and a blush to her cheeks. No sign of the usually uptight mother of twins juggling all of life's balls with perfect precision.

'Great,' I say, scanning the menu. 'Oooh, I think I'll have the Primrose Christmas Chicken Burger with chunky chips and maybe see if they can do me some garlic bread too? Although I definitely want to save some space for a mince pie and cream after.' I'm practically drooling at the thought, even though this baby is now so big there's little room for anything else in there, never mind a full dinner. But here, I'm never one to shy away from a challenge. 'What about you two?' I ask.

'I'm going to get the goat's cheese and cranberry salad,' Amanda says. 'I'm trying to watch the old figure, ye know.' I give her a shrewd glance; she is looking particularly svelte and toned right now. Never one to worry about her mummy tummy, Amanda has traditionally been quite happy to hide in clothes I always thought a little too dootsy and dated for her age, but here she is, in a cream body-hugging polo neck, an A-line leather mini skirt, fishnet tights (WTF?) and a pair of ridiculously high-heeled boots.

'Have you been working out? You look amazing,' I tell her, while I try to suck my tummy in before catching myself on.

'Aye, something like that,' she says, and that wee crafty glint is back in her eye.

'And what about you, Cat?' I ask, but she is in her own wee world, staring out at the River Foyle.

'Cat,' I say again. 'What are you having?'

'Um, shit. Sorry. I totally zoned out there. Work is mad at the minute. Total pre-Christmas insanity, so actually I've been working this morning and I need to go back in and clear a few things up so, um, I'll just have a glass of water or something.'

My heart sinks a little. I was so looking forward to catching up with the girls and God knows I could really do with their advice right now, but I also know Cat has just recently been promoted at work to a fancy new senior business analyst position, and good for her for wanting to excel in her career.

'You can't just have a glass of water!' Amanda says. 'What kind of Scrooge McDuck rubbish is that? It's Christmas! At least have a hot chocolate – they do the most amazing one here with cream and pieces of brownie and . . .'

'Are you sure you don't want to sack off that salad and get one of those brownie yokes for yourself?' I ask her, but she nods back.

'Perfectly sure,' she says. 'I just don't want Cat having only a glass of water after escaping from the office to see us!'

'Water is all I want, honest, I've one more analysis report to deliver for a company we're thinking of acquiring then I'm off for two weeks!' We're surrounded by the happy chatter of diners and Mickey Bubbles has taken up the reins from Bing Crosby and is crooning in the background.

'Are you OK, Cat?' I ask. 'I mean, go you, career boss bitch and all. You just seem to be flat out with work these days, and there haven't even been any night out retrospective voice notes in our group chat for about a week. Have you not been out at all? I'm supposed to be living vicariously through you right now, so please do not leave a preggo girl hanging.'

'No outs,' she says. 'Honestly, work is just that busy right now, so I'm just keeping the head down trying to smash my targets so that I get a cracker Christmas bonus and don't lose my new position if we do end up acquiring another firm with a team of young graduates.'

'I know that feeling, sister, you're right, keep the head down for now!' I nod along. 'You can party your wee socks off between Christmas and New Year.'

'Aye, that's it,' she says with a smile that is as fake as my old ma's boobs. (Yes, Pamela had them 'done' a few years back. There is something fucked up in the world when your ma has perkier tits than you, but here we are.)

It's clear something is off with Cat. Maybe being married to this new job is just too much? She isn't her usual firecracker, gossip-spouting, advice-giving self, but I know better than to push her to open up. My best friend is not a woman who likes to be pushed; she is a strict believer in delivering information only as and when she wants to, and it's not often she gets like this. So I don't pry, deciding this is the perfect time to launch into my own tale of woes.

'Anyway, girls,' I say, 'I have had the week from hell. A full-scale shitemare – between Gemma getting suspended, Jax peeing and pooing everywhere he shouldn't, an HR run-in with Handley – and that's not even the worst of it. First off, Big Pamela is leaving the Costa del Sol and returning to the Maiden City. Which I have to tell Paul about tonight. Or at least, I assume she's coming back. She called me to say she was moving back 'cause Javier was riding a waitress, but I've heard feck all since. And well . . . things with Paul—'

'Sorry, girls,' Cat says, cutting me off as she gets up from her seat, looking at her phone and tapping at the screen, although I didn't hear it ring or vibrate. 'Something's come up, I really do have to get back to work. I shouldn't have come out. I've so much to do. I'll text youse later.' She blows a kiss and, with an opening and closing of a door sending the icy December breeze scurrying around our feet, she is gone. She hasn't even managed to order her water, let alone drink it. My mouth is hanging slightly open, rant interrupted. As the surprise wears off, I can't help but feel a sting of rejection and my feathers are a bit ruffled, if I'm being completely honest. Here am I, opening up about the problems in my life, and she's outta here as if Tom Hardy just texted to say he's lying naked on her desk waiting for her to come back. If that were true, I'd forgive her hastiness – hell, I'd knock her over to try and get there first. 'Hey, Tom, so de ye like pregnant women, aye?'

'What's going on there?' Amanda asks.

I close my hanging jaw. 'I don't know, but something is. Why did she even bother to come in the first place if she was just going to clear off? I mean, I know she's really busy in her new role so I've been cutting her some slack when I don't hear from her. I get it – I've been busy too, which is why I wanted us all to get together to chat face to face. Because I need you girls . . . Can she not see her best friend needs her?' I mumble sadly. And then, of course, I start to cry. Just as Mickey Bubbles is singing his wee lungs out about having a holly, jolly Christmas.

Amanda slides over and awkwardly puts her arm around my shoulders. 'Aww, Tara, we all go through rough patches – and it's no wonder you're feeling all unsure of yourself. This is a time of transition, what with the new baby and your mammy and everything. It's not surprising you feel a bit overwhelmed by it all. It will pass in a week or two.' She pats my head like I'm a golden retriever who has just done a trick and then gestures for the waiter to come and, finally, take our order.

While Amanda is lovely – truly she is, would give you the shirt off her back if you needed it – she's not normally known for her emotional depth. That's what I use Cat for, but as Cat has so inconsiderately pissed off, I'll take what I can right now. So I take Amanda's 'good boy, Fido' pats and her clichéd platitudes until I'm no longer afraid of ugly crying all over my chunky cut chips.

'Now,' Amanda says, spearing a large piece of goat's cheese with her fork, 'before we get on to Pamela's return, tell me about what's going on with Paul.'

'I dunno,' I tell her. 'It's hard to put my finger on it. But *something* isn't right. He's acting a bit funny. Like not really present. Distant even. Like, even when he's in the room with me, he isn't really in the room with me.'

Amanda nods, takes a sip of her wine and leans forward. 'And how are things in the bedroom department?' she whispers.

'The bedroom department?' I laugh. 'We're a married couple not a section of IKEA! But since you ask, things there are pretty much non-existent.'

'Well, you are coming near to your due date,' Amanda says. 'Sean wouldn't so much as snog me when I was at that stage with the twins. Said he'd read somewhere that sex can bring on labour and I'd had to explain how kissing isn't actually sex as if he was twelve years old. I mean, of course he knew, but he was afraid he would get me too turned on and I wouldn't be able to stop myself from wanting his body all night long. The poor, deluded eejit. I was carrying twins like . . . I had enough bodies inside me without adding another to the mix.'

Amanda's confession shocks me. Not because I think it's particularly dirty or anything, but this is Amanda. Amanda does not talk about S.E.X. In fact, whenever Cat or I dish the dirt about any shenanigans we get up to, Amanda usually sits tight-lipped and visibly uncomfortable. She has never so much as hinted at the size of Sean's dick in all the years they have been together, nor has she revealed any of her kinks or anything that happens in their wee section of IKEA. Cat and I have kind of assumed she doesn't have sex, or we've been known to joke that they must be a once-a-month couple, who keep the lights off, her nightie on and say a decade of the rosary after.

'It's never bothered him in the past. None of the other three times anyway. But Amanda, it's been *weeks* since he so much as slipped the hand,' I whisper.

'Right,' she says, and she puts her fork down, so I know shit is about to get serious. 'Maybe you just need to shake things up a little. Being pregnant doesn't mean you can't get your freak on, as Cat would say. Maybe you just have to take the proverbial ball, or balls, into your own hands.'

OK, who is this imposter because it sure as shit isn't the Amanda I've known since school days. I'm actually a wee bit embarrassed, as if it's my mother talking to me about the birds and the bees, although Pamela didn't have the decency to use terms like 'birds' or 'bees', but that's a whole other, cringeworthy and trauma-inducing story.

'Experiment a wee bit. Dress up. Get kinky. What about a sexy Mrs Claus costume? Mistletoe hung in a very inviting place? You get my drift?' She picks up her fork and spears another piece of goat's cheese and some lettuce and pops it into her mouth as if she has just been discussing the twins' Christmas show and not how I could dangle some inviting festive foliage in my actual labial area.

'Amanda!' I say. 'What the hell has come over . . . no,

let me rephrase that. What has gotten into . . . nope. Still an innuendo. OK, stop laughing.' Amanda has actual tears glistening in her eyes as she cackles at my discomfort. 'Are you having some sort of midlife crisis or whatever because this is very, very unlike you?'

'Not so much a midlife crisis as a midlife reinvention. It worked for you and it's working for me, and Sean. You know, I realized we'd got stuck in our same old routine. You know the score. Sex once a month . . .'

I snort involuntarily and bite back the urge to ask if she keeps her nightie on and pulls the rosary beads out.

'And well, I'll be honest. It was boring. The same moves each time. I could do it in my sleep. I have done it in my sleep, if I'm being honest. Consensually, of course,' she adds with a wink. 'So we decided to make some changes because I swear to the Baby Jesus if I was going to have to spend the rest of my life with those same, tired moves I'd lose my mind, Tara. We talked it through, and the upshot is . . . we've been seeing a counsellor.'

'A marriage counsellor?' I ask.

She shakes her head. 'Oh no. A sex counsellor.'

OK, so I've officially stepped into the Twilight Zone here because Cat has become a workaholic who isn't drinking or going out, Paul Gallagher doesn't appear to have the slightest interest in getting the ride, and Amanda – *Amanda!* – is seeing a sex counsellor.

Stick a fork in me, I am done.

8

*Not the f**king Elf*

'A sex counsellor?' I splutter. 'Do we have those here in Derry?' It's not a stupid question. Ireland isn't exactly known for its forward-thinking when it comes to matters of a sexual nature. The nearest most people get to a sex counsellor is the pre-marriage course some priests in the Catholic Church insist on couples taking part in before their big day.

And that has never been about spicing things up. When we endured it, it was heavy on the acceptable forms of contraception for a good Irish Catholic. (Condoms equals bad. Rhythm method equals good.) I'll never forget Paul's redner as a man of faith in his early sixties started to talk about the importance of hygiene. ('If you can't get a bath beforehand, lads, sure just give it a wash in the sink . . .')

'Yes,' Amanda cuts in. 'We have those here and let me tell you, it has changed our lives. These toned thighs aren't from the gym, I'll have you know. I never realized sex could be such fun – or so incredible. The connection we have now . . .'

OK, so part of me wants to know more because I'd very much like that connection reignited with Paul, but I'm also feeling awkward AF listening to Amanda talk about her sexual awakening. I force myself to zone out a little, also acutely aware that this place is packed and people will be able to hear her and, dear God, is this the same woman who nearly had a stroke the time Cat said 'Vagina' in here at the top of her voice?

I zone back in just in time to hear, '. . . but not too tight. The last thing you want is to cut off the circulation down there.'

I blink at her, and mumble, 'Well, I am impressed, and I am really, really interested, but I'm not sure this is the perfect time for sexual experimentation,' while gesturing towards my stomach.

'Nonsense. This is *exactly* the perfect time. You are more feminine now than you will ever be . . . but you don't have to go full throttle yet. Just take the first steps? You'll thank me for it, I promise.' She says it with a wink and a naughty wee laugh.

I wonder if by 'full throttle' Amanda is making another reference to some sort of S&M kinkiness before I immediately kick the image from my mind. I kinda want to go back to thinking of Amanda in her nightie with the lights out instead of choking Sean to climax in some erotic-asphyxiation play, thank you very much. Cat's the dirty one, I'm in between, and Amanda is supposed to be our vocal conscience, who we never, ever listen to. But not today, especially with Cat not even here.

I arrive home still obsessing over Amanda's confessions. I'm looking forward to sitting down later with a big mug of hot chocolate and filling Paul in on my friend's quarter-life reinvention, just to see his reaction and maybe even open up those lines of communication again. You never know, I may even get a ride. Although, truth be told, I'm just looking forward to sitting down with Paul full stop. I feel like we've barely seen each other all week – and when we have, we've been tag-teaming on Operation Potty-training with Jax, acting as audience members for Nathan's at-home practice nativity, or listening to Gemma giving out about how we're the 'strictest parents everrrrr'. The thought of getting quality alone time with him in front of the TV makes me feel warm and fuzzy inside. Maybe we could stick on a Christmas movie and open the replacement tin of Quality Street. (Forgive me, Santa, for I have sinned.)

Even though lunch with the girls wasn't what I expected, and even though I am still raging with Cat, it actually lifted my mood and I feel more contented and relaxed than I have all week, because Amanda, in between the dirty details of her new kink-fest with Sean, made me feel a glimmer of hope that whatever is going on with Paul is just a blip and it'll all work out. We'll be back to normal in no time.

But I'm no sooner in the front door than I can hear Nathan squealing with excitement. 'Mammmmeeeee!' he shouts at ear-splitting level before thundering down the stairs. Jax, still bare-arsed of course, shuffles down the stairs on his bum after him and I pray to God above that there is no repeat of the 'skid marks all down my stairs' disaster of last week.

Thankfully, there isn't.

'Yes, pet?' I say, finding it impossible not to mirror his excitement.

'Maammmeeee! Gemma was getting the Christmas decormarations from the attic and look who me and Jax finded?'

Oh sweet mother of Jesus. I can feel my entire life switch to slow motion as Nathan produces, one gangly red limb peeping out at a time, the absolute bane of my life, the biggest pain in the hole to ever grace the Gallagher household, the ultimate fuck-up in all my parenting decisions – our Elf on the fucking Shelf.

I am screaming inwardly now, cursing myself for not burning that wee bastard last year when I had vowed never, ever again would I give into the peer pressure of partaking in the full-scale nightmare that is finding increasingly inventive ways to trick your children into believing an elf comes to life at night to get up to mischief while supposedly watching them to make sure they don't get up to mischief.

The whole concept doesn't even make sense. Surely the Scout Elf should behave himself, sit on his seat keeping an eye on the kids and do fuck all for the entire run-up to Christmas to encourage the wains to do the same? He's a gurny-faced wee hypocrite. I loathe him.

The whole shebang was good craic the first time. And by 'the first time' I don't mean the first year we did it. I mean the first night – two Christmases ago – when Paul and I had spent an hour setting up an elaborate scene whereby our elf had left a train of fake poo (chocolate chips) behind him, and we'd decorated the living room with toilet paper. Nathan had thought it was the funniest, most magical thing he had ever laid eyes on. We'd felt smug. Until later that night, when we'd both had a couple of glasses of wine and realized we had to clean up the mess from the night before, and come up with another brilliant, creative, Pinterest-inspired, brand-new, fucking idea . . .

Like other parents the world over, we are now assigned to Elf prison for the entire Christmas period. No matter how tired you are, no matter how much you argue with your significant other that it's their turn (even when it's not: believe me, I try that one all the time), no matter how little creativity you've got left inside your fried adult brain, you will google 'Elf on the Shelf' ideas dozens of times over the Christmas period and then you will execute that idea like the good little parent you are. Yes, you will.

'Mammeeee, issanelf!' Jax squeals, and he has that glazed, manic look about him that only two-year-olds can really master, which means he might actually vomit with excitement at any second. Because of course last year, and the year before, Jax was too tiny to take any notice, but this year – as he approaches his third birthday – he is fully batshit hyper-invested in it.

'So it is,' I say, through clenched teeth and an awkward smile. 'Well, isn't that just magical? Elfie is back.'

'Hmmmm,' Nathan says. 'I don't think that's the same elf as last year.'

'No?' I ask.

He looks up at me, his expression solemn. 'No, Mammy. Cos I 'member that last year you said Elf could fuck right off back to the North Pole and stay there.'

Does this child forget anything? In my defence it was Christmas Day, I'd had a couple of glasses of wine with dinner and I was ecstatic at the thought of not having to think of more inventive ways to move the wee bastard around.

'So I don't fink Elfie would come back, cos you said if he did you'd break his bastardin' wee legs for him,' Nathan adds, and I see a wee glint in his eye that he is just pure lured at being able to say two swearwords in quick succession.

'Nathan, we don't have to use the bad words Mammy used when she was very tired . . . Mammy made a mistake and was just worried that Elfie would come back and make loads of mess that Mammy would have to clean up,' I say in a sing-song tone, and then I pause to see if he buys it.

He nods, then pauses. 'Wine makes you very tired, doesn't it, Mammy?'

'Yes, darling,' I say, wishing I could have some wine to send me into a coma-like sleep about now.

'A lot of fings must make you very tired, Mammy. Cos you say bad words all the time.'

As he speaks, I realize I'm feeling 'tired' right now, but I swallow down the F-bomb on my tongue and just look at him.

He blinks before speaking. 'So I fink this is a new elf and we need a new name for him.'

'Poo Bum!' Jax shouts. Clearly the child is very focused on all matters of a toilet nature.

'I don't fink ats a good name, Jax,' Nathan tells his brother. 'Cos Christmas is about the Baby Jesus and not poos or bums. Mammy, can we call the elf Baby Jesus?' He nods his head solemnly at the word 'Jesus' in the overexaggerated manner primary school children carry off so well.

I shake my head. That's one conversation I don't need to be having with Miss Rose. (Picture the phone call: 'Mrs Gallagher, Nathan has told me the Baby Jesus pooed on your kitchen worktop and asked me did I know that Baby Jesus's poo tastes like chocolate?' Nope! Not happening!)

'I don't think so, pet. Can we think of something else? What about Tinseltoes? Or . . . or . . . Crackers . . . or Buddy Elf, like in the movie?'

At this precise moment Jax lets out a stream of urine not only all over my floor but over my boots too. 'Jesus, Mary and the wee donkey!' I swear, stepping back out of the spray zone.

'Aye, Mammy!' Nathan grins. 'The Wee Donkey! That's what we'll call him!' He hugs 'Wee Donkey' into his chest and turns to run into the kitchen, no doubt to fill Paul in on the return of Elfie who isn't Elfie who was nearly Poo Bum and Baby Jesus, and who is actually now called Wee Donkey. Meanwhile, I stand and wait until my youngest child lets out a satisfied sigh and a wee shiver of delight as he completes his pee. Give me strength.

I start the clean-up operation, which isn't as easy as you'd think, given my ginormous stomach and change of centre of balance. So I'm on my knees, the aroma of fresh pee assaulting my nose – and given that I am pregnant my sense of smell has heightened to that of a dog. Not gonna lie, there's a very big chance this is going to make me boke, and given my knackered pelvic floor there's a very good chance that if I boke I will also pee myself. It will be hard to persuade Paul to want to ride me into the middle of next week if I'm in a puddle of body-waste soup.

Maybe Gemma could take over? I'll promise her an extra hour of precious phone time if she does, she'd do anything for phone time, I just know it. Hoisting myself up to standing, I let out a desperate roar of 'GEMMMMMMAAAAAA.' I'm not surprised when there's no answer. It seems all teenagers are afflicted with selective deafness and can tune out at will whenever the feck they want.

'GEEMMAAAAA!' I roar again, causing Nathan – cradling Wee Donkey as if he was the most precious piece of tat the world has ever known – to appear from the kitchen.

'Mammy, Gemma's not in the house,' he says.

'What do you mean, she's not in the house?'

He looks at me as if I'm particularly stupid not realizing that 'not in the house' means 'outside the house'.

'Ahhhm . . . I don't fink I'm supposed to tell you but Miss Rose says not to tell lies afore Christmas cos then Santa will give your toys to good boys and girls.'

For once, I like Miss Rose. But that is fleeting as I wait for Nathan to tell me what in the Miracle on 34th Street is going on.

'She said she was going out to get some fresh air but I was apposed to keep it secret or she said she would put Elfie, I mean Wee Donkey, down the toilet, but I am a good boy so I have to tell you. And now you have to pwotect Wee Donkey from Gemma.'

His wee bottom lip wobbles, his gorgeous chocolate-brown eyes filling with tears, and he cuddles Wee Donkey close to him.

Now, I'm conscious that I'm seconds away from losing my actual shit over Gemma's sneakiness but I'm also conscious of not scaring seven shades of shite out of Nathan by letting a roar out in his direction.

'Nathan. Get. Your. Daddy,' I say, my voice as tight as ToteTech's Christmas bonus pot.

He nods, turns and runs, and a moment later Paul appears from the kitchen.

'Are you aware Gemma has gone out?'

He shakes his head. 'No. Has she? But she's grounded!' he says as if this isn't what is giving me devil rage in the first place.

'You were here all afternoon and you let her go out?' I ask, as Nathan stands, eyes on stalks ping-ponging between us and the high drama of Mammy and Daddy kicking off in front of him.

'No, of course not. I mean, yes, I was here. No, I did not let her go out. I didn't know she'd gone out. I've been busy. She must've bloody sneaked out,' he says.

Now, I'd like to say we live in a big fancy mansion off the Culmore Road (aka the posh part of Derry), but the truth is, we don't. We live in a fairly ordinary four-bedroom semi where I wouldn't even want to risk swinging a cat for fear of giving it concussion. It's impossible to be sneaky about anything here. Especially not for Gemma, who has all the grace of a baby elephant when wearing her DMs that she just HAD to get before Christmas, because, like, *everyone's* wearing them.

'Sneaked out?' I squeak, and I know my voice is so high now that perhaps only dogs can hear it. But I'm standing in a puddle of piss, the bastard elf has returned early, my teenager is an escaped convict, and it seems I can't even go for lunch with my friends without this house descending into anarchy.

'Look, love, I didn't know. Honestly. I'll ring her phone and tell her to get her hole back here right now,' he says, reaching for his own phone.

'That would be a cracker plan, if I didn't have her

phone in my bag. Oh she is dead! She is so dead!' I bark, and then I notice poor Nathan's eyes begin to water.

'Mammmeeeeeee,' he sobs, 'is she really, really dead? My sister?'

That's enough to stop me in my tracks as I haul Nathan to me and assure him that she's very much alive. 'It's just something we say when someone is in trouble pet, Gemma's OK, I promise,' I assure him. Of course, I don't tell him she'll wish she was dead by the time I'm done with her. Soon his sobs subside to the occasional wee gulping of breath.

Paul and I just look at each other. There's so much to say but we must be aware of Nathan being right here with us, hanging on our every word.

'Mammy,' he sniffs, rubbing his snotty nose along the front of my jumper. 'If she ever really is dead . . . can I have her woom?'

It's that precise moment, of course, we hear movement from the back of the house – the not-so-subtle sliding of a patio door – and Paul and I look at each other, for once on the same page as we contemplate the best way to tackle Gemma's rule-breaking.

Fast as lightning, Nathan is off down the hall into the kitchen where he starts to plead to his sister that he didn't tell us she went out.

Seems not even the fear of no toys from Santa is enough to stop him lying to his sister to save his own skin. I don't blame the kid. It's a smart move.

There's a huff of exhaled breath from Gemma before she appears shame-faced at the door.

'I was only out for like twenty minutes. You can't keep me locked up forever, it's cruelty. I need fresh air and vitamin D and stuff,' she mumbles.

'Where did you go?' Paul barks. 'And don't be giving me any oul shite about going for a walk because I know you, Gemma. You don't go for walks. It's not in your nature.'

She blinks before looking down at the ground, to where I'm standing in Jax's pee.

'Mammy . . . did you, erm . . . wet yourself again?' she asks.

'No. It's— Look, it doesn't matter if I wet myself,' I say, 'just tell us where you were.'

'That's disgustin',' she says, looking at the ground.

'Well, you're cleaning it up,' I tell her. 'And more besides. It'll be even worse if you don't tell me where you were.'

She stomps her foot. 'I just went to see Mia for like ten minutes. My mental health is really suffering, being isolated from my friends.'

God give me strength this day. 'Gemma, this is what being grounded is. And you still speak to them every day!' I say.

'For one crappy hour!' she shouts back. 'That's nothing. You don't understand, Mammy, you never ever will!' And here they come. The waterworks. Which of course have the required effect on her soft-as-shite, knight-in-shining-armour daddy.

'Ach, pet. Don't cry,' he soothes, pulling her into a hug.

While I stand there, my socks now wet from where Jax's pee has soaked through my boots, and I begin to cry myself. Not only does Paul not soothe me. He doesn't even notice that I'm crying too.

9

Don't shit on Santa!

Sunday, 4 December

I am still absolutely raging at Gemma after her Houdini act yesterday. Not only did she disregard any notion of how grounding works; disrespect me and any shred of authority I thought I had over her; then have the audacity to play the victim to her doting daddy, but she also prematurely exposed the one thing that I actually despise at Christmas. The bastarding elf, who for this year will be known as Wee Donkey.

I'm conscious that may make me sound like a shit mammy, but I despise the very sight of him and all the effort for me that his arrival entails. But that won't stop me making sure the wee dick has done something hilarious every night because Tara Gallagher does not fall at any Christmas hurdle.

Thankfully, like the consumer-driven fool and Amazon addict I am, I am prepared this year. Last night, Wee Donkey snuck into Jax and Nathan's bedroom and built himself his own wee bed underneath the lamp. Cost: £3.99, minimal effort, job done and two happy, excited boys when they woke this morning to find they had a new roommate.

The Wee Donkey also left a note to say, *It's time to get the decorations up, then you're going to see my friend Santa at the mall.* Which was also met with screams of excitement from Jax and Nathan. In fairness, this year I'm running behind schedule. Normally I have the decorations up by the first of December. One year, I even put them up on the last week of November. But this year I've been lazy on it, which is sad really. I'm usually Mrs Claus, an all-singing, all-dancing, big ball of Christmas fucking Spirit – this year I'm trying to be the same but wrapped up in an impregnated five-foot-eight-inch body of a very tired, but still Christmassy AF mammy.

I've been pregnant before at Christmas, but never this heavily, and dammit I'm tired but I'm telling myself today is the day to pull up my big girl pants and get this house looking like it's been spat out of a Christmas Pinterest page.

As the boys eat/mess about with their breakfast of Coco Pops, I call Gemma and Paul to help me move the decorations down to the living room. Gemma, surprisingly, doesn't morph into a fire-breathing dragon. Is it possible she's realized just how out of line she was yesterday? Let's hope so.

'OK Gallaghers,' I chirp, the boys having abandoned breakfast and followed us upstairs. 'It's time to officially kick off Christmas and get these decorations up.' The boys jump with delight, oblivious of the fact that the boxes I'm allocating them are full of old decorations and two small trees that will not grace my living room, or any room downstairs for that matter.

This is one of my better parenting hacks. I want Jax and Nathan to be part of the excitement of decorating days, but those boys are, quite frankly, a fucking liability. Putting them anywhere near a full-sized Christmas tree while they're armed with tinsel is a disaster waiting to happen. They'll likely electrocute themselves, break at least sixteen baubles, impale themselves on the star destined for the top of the tree and tangle any good wire they can get their hands on. Fail to prepare, prepare to fail, that's what I say, so I'm primed with a decoy, AKA old decorations and two cheap trees from the pound shop, exclusively for the boys' bedrooms.

I admire my previous year's self for being so organized. I've all the lights in one box, labelled and sorted without any tangles, my wreath and garland separated nicely, baubles organized by colours, and ornaments labelled in boxes for each room and any outdoor lights stored safely in large plastic containers. What I'm not bloody impressed with is the actual Christmas tree, a six-foot fake frosted spruce, that I only bought new last year, by the way, stuffed into four separate black bags.

'Whose job was it to put the tree away last year?' I

howl, looking at Paul because I clearly remember Gemma had to 'conveniently' go to Mia's when we were taking everything down.

'Erm . . . yours love,' Paul says with a smirk. 'Remember, you did all the kitchen stuff and the tree and I did the rest?' Wait, so I didn't organize all these boxes and wires and do all the detangling and sorting? Actually, that makes more sense.

'Oh aye, that's right,' I say looking coy. 'Baby brain, ha.'

'OMG,' Gemma teases, 'you were actually gonna start a fight there now with me or Daddy and blame us, weren't you?'

I blush, then decide to style it out. 'No, I was simply going to say that whoever packed this tree away did a great job. Prob the best tree putting away I've ever seen, in fact.'

'Dead on, Mammy, you're so full of sh—'

'Ah Gemma,' I interrupt, 'there are wee ears here listening to every word you say and you're still on probation, missus, OK.'

'Shit!' Nathan shouts. 'She was going to say you are full of shit, which Miss Rose says we can't say, but 'member I asked her why not acuz everyone really does have poos in their body.'

'Yes, Nathan, I remember,' I sigh. That particular phone call from Miss Rose actually made me laugh out loud, which of course Miss Rose didn't appreciate. 'But we don't say that word,' I remind him. 'We say poo, and technically we're not full of it, our intestines are, remember?'

'Oh yeah, I 'member,' he says, going back to his mini tree decorating.

'Me shit?' asks Jax quizzically, which sends Nathan into a fit of giggles.

'Do you have to poo, Jax?' I ask, internally praying that he hasn't already emptied his own intestines in his pants.

'No, me shit,' Jax replies, and he points to the box of baubles that I foolishly sat beside the TV.

'Oh no pet, don't sit there,' I shriek as I realize he's trying to say sit and not shit, and I rush to move the box before the thin glass of my best Dunnes Stores baubles is shattered by a mini Michelin Man. It seems my youngest is struggling with some of his word pronunciations, much to the delight of Nathan, who keeps asking him to say words like sit and Fire Truck. My youngest pronounces his Ts as Fs – I'll let you do the working out on that one.

As we get to work, I ask Alexa to play Christmas classics and I pop *The Christmas Chronicles* on the TV. I light my candy-cane-scented oil burner and Paul lights the fire. Ahhhh, there it is, that warm fuzzy Christmas feeling.

Four hours, at least three arguments between Paul and me, fourteen dud bulb changes, two huffs up and back downstairs by Gemma, an epic meltdown by Jax over him wanting a red tree and not a green one, and a surrender on all things decorating by Nathan because it's 'boring and Roblox is better'. I'm surprised I managed to deck the halls today and not my family. But it is done.

Our tree is lit with twinkling gold lights and adorned with golden ribbon and bows and shining gold baubles, including an assortment of musical instruments, mini sleighs, reindeer, bells and stars. A golden angel with a white lace dress sits on top, and at the bottom I've placed a golden tree skirt complete with white fluffy trimming. The pièce de résistance, however, is the Santa's Express train and track circling the floor at the bottom of the tree. It was one of my first Christmas purchases when Paul and I moved in together, and while it has lost more than a few carriages, and the track pieces even feature bite marks, both from Nathan and Jax, it holds a certain place in my heart.

A garland now elegantly dresses the fireplace, artificial fir branches scattered with holly and berries. Golden lights twinkle delicately in between each branch and a candelabra sits pride of place in the middle. Below are hooks holding red velvet stockings with initials for each of the children embroidered on the front.

The usual black metal fireguard has been replaced by an extending colourful Christmas scene guard. To each side are golden and red bow LED present boxes and a ceramic Santa ornament placed to the left.

Our window blinds have been swapped for golden net lights that sparkle and shimmer and leave the boys – and me, to be honest – in a daze of twinkling wonder.

To top it all, Paul has hung golden icicle lights outside under the eaves, a festive wreath on the front door and perched a family of golden LED reindeer underneath the living room window. There's also the new addition in the form of an eight-foot inflatable light-up snowman which

Paul reluctantly set up for me because well . . . remember I 'promised' not to buy any more decorations? Whoops, he's going to freak out when the eight-foot accompanying inflatable Santa arrives tomorrow. I couldn't help it. It appeared on my Facebook feed and my Insta like a sign from the consumer gods. I'm a marketer's dream, what can I say.

I could not love it more, and I'm on such a Christmas high I've even convinced myself this year's visit to see Santa at the mall will be magical and not disastrous like every other year, ever.

Maybe they'll have hired a more convincing Santa this year and not just whoever was willing to listen to wains bang on about Minecraft for eight hours a day. Last year, that was Big Tommy, one of our local milkmen (no, not *that* milkman) who really did sit on a throne of lies but rather than smell like beef and cheese à la the Santa in *Elf*, he smelled like tobacco and stale whiskey.

As we stand in a hustling, bustling line of excited children and drained parents, I notice that Jax is clinging to me more than usual.

'You OK, wee man?' I ask him.

'My scared,' he says.

Coming face to face with Santa can be quite scary, I suppose. We coach our kids about never talking to *strangers*, never mind sitting on their knees. But it's all different at Christmas when we expect our children to be comfortable talking to someone they've never met before who they believe can see their every move, and who holds the power over whether or not they go on the naughty or nice list and get any toys on Christmas morning. It's no wonder it's a shite-the-tights moment for so many of them.

When our turn comes, Jax wraps his arms tighter still around my neck and buries his wee curly head into my chest. Nathan of course makes a beeline up to Santa and begins to talk the head off him. I try to lower Jax down to the ground, but he clings to me like a wee baby monkey, and now has a death grip on my neck so I decide not push him further out of his comfort zone.

It appears that Big Tommy is indeed reprising his role as Santa and as Nathan continues to chatter to him about how he wants to be a YouTuber when he grows up, and how Wotsits are his favourite food, I feel Jax begin to relax his grip. It's a case of monkey-see, monkey-do with my youngest, and anything Nathan can do, Jax thinks he can do the same. To my surprise, he points to Santa and says, 'Me now.' So I bring Jax over to Santa and ask Nathan to stand beside him so that Santa's elf assistant (Big Tommy's cousin Majella) can get the money shot.

Jax shocks me again as he puts his arms out to Santa, ushering him to lift him up on his knee. As he does, Nathan decides that he too wants to sit on Santa's knee, so I help him up, thinking of all the lovely likes, I mean memories, I'll get from this gorgeous pic of my two boys and Santa.

I step back to get out of the shot then notice Jax has a familiar look on his face. Shit. Shit! Maybe I'm wrong? I hope I'm wrong. But then that hope leaches from my body when I see Jax give a wee shudder. Fuck. I know that shudder. He's just peed himself. I watch in horror as the colour of Santa's suit leg begins to darken with the soaking of Jax's urine.

Nathan doesn't even flinch as Jax calls out, 'I shit on Santa and I peed on Santa' and continues to tell Santa about why he needs a drum kit and a microphone, and also starts singing one of the songs from Nathan's nativity. Big Tommy, to give him his dues, doesn't bat an eyelid.

If it wasn't for Jax's mispronunciation of the word 'sit' earlier on at home I'd have fainted there and then thinking my youngest not only pissed all over Santa, but cacked himself too . . . I can't smell any poo, so I hope I'm safe, and it's just toddler pee running down Santa's leg. Nathan laughs and I swear he's going to implode in hysterics if Jax doesn't stop saying 'shit on Santa'.

All I can muster is a mouthing of the words 'I'm sorry' to Tommy, who now looks like he could be doing with a top-up of fresh tobacco and whiskey. As his elf assistant hands me the picture and two presents for the boys, which are no doubt made in some non-safety-regulation-compliant sweatshop and will break within the first six seconds, I feel the heat of stares from all the parents waiting in the queue who now have to wait even longer as Santa goes and changes his pissy trousers.

As he walks away from his grotto to get cleaned up, there is an ever-growing chorus of children crying and wailing in his wake, thinking he's gone back to the North Pole before they could see him.

I'm mortified, and scared some of those kids could turn ugly, so I quickly usher the boys down to Paul and we leave the mall quicker than Big Tommy has probably headed straight for the off-licence.

We head home and Paul thankfully offers to bath the boys and get them in their PJs. Gemma, who refused to attend the seeing of Santa at the mall, brings me a cup of tea which I'll assume is a peace offering after her antics yesterday and one that I will gladly accept. Thank God she didn't come with us; I can only imagine the rant I'd have to listen to from her on the way home about her brother peeing himself in front of everyone and 'ruining her lifeuhhhhh'.

All I want to do is relax and bask in the glory of our gorgeous golden lights and newly festive house.

'I hungray,' shouts Nathan, and of course Jax echoes, 'Me hungwee too.'

'Like seriously,' Gemma groans. 'You haven't fed us all day.'

And I would argue with her but I haven't the energy, plus I'm starving too.

'Takeaway?' I say, because I'm damned if I'm standing cooking anything.

'Yes!' they cry in unison.

Happy fucking Christmas to me, I think. Takeaway it is!

10

What a shitemare!

Monday morning. I wake to Nathan and Jax both far too close to my face, Jax prying my eyes open with his always sticky fingers.

'Maaaammmmmmmeeeee,' they scream at the very top of their lungs, scaring the living daylights (and a wee bit of pee) out of me.

'Wha? What is it? What?' I mutter, trying to fully wake up and forklift myself to sitting.

'Wee Donkey . . .' Nathan howls with laughter . . . 'Wee Donkey drewed on our faces!' I blink into consciousness and sure enough both my darling boys have been accessorized with Sharpie-drawn moustaches, beards and glasses. It is funny, but here's the thing: I didn't do it. I totally forgot about Wee Donkey and his antics and did

91

buck all. And I know Paul didn't do it because he was asleep (turned away from me, snoring, by the time I got to bed . . . sigh).

Then I notice that both the boys' eyebrows are particularly on fleek and I realize that it must have been Gemma who stepped up. My heart softens to her and a big part of me is relieved because since the sneaking-out row on Saturday, even with the lovely day we all had yesterday, things have been tense AF. Especially when we told her that her grounding was being extended by another four days.

'OMG, look at you two! That bold wee elf!' I laugh, hugging both my boys, who are amazed by Wee Donkey's second act of elf magic.

OK. Today is off to a good start. Thanks to Gemma, which is strange but, hey, we take the wins where we can these days. Today is also the first official day of my maternity leave and not just my extra holiday. It feels like everything is settling – well, apart from Paul still being a bit of a rare duck and Pamela still not having arrived at my front door despite all her talk of being back here to be closer to me and the children.

No. I don't want to think about Pamela, who has informed me via text that she is staying with her sister, Lily, but she has to sleep on a sofa and it's bloody uncomfortable. Especially 'at my age'. I know what she's hinting at but I would rather shite in my hands and clap than invite Mammy Dearest to come and stay here. Plus, I haven't even had the chance to tell Paul yet. (Yes, we have a spare box room, but it's currently home to all of the shite that comes with having three children and no utility room . . . think less the Room of Requirement and more the Room of Unrequirement.)

I banish a looming Pamela from my mind: today I want to think about nice things, like Gemma doing something lovely to help the Christmas magic grow for her brothers – and she didn't even have to be asked. OK then, so maybe I'll drop the grounding by a day or two.

'We're gonny show Gemma!' Nathan declares, jumping off the bed and hauling Jax after him.

'Brave souls, waking our Gemma,' Paul whispers, his voice still thick with sleep. We both hold our breath, waiting for the screams of 'Get outta my roooommmm-mahhh nowwwwww', but it's a different girl I hear responding.

'Oh my goodness! Who drew on your faces?' she asks them in an exaggerated voice.

'Wee Donkey!' Jax says.

'We were sleeping. He is so funny and bold, isn't he,' Nathan adds, and I hear him laugh as Gemma takes them into the bathroom to wash their faces.

'What is going on there?' Paul asks.

I shrug. Part of me is wise enough to know that it's probably a charm offensive to secure time off for good behaviour and nothing else, but a bigger part of me wants to believe that maybe, just maybe, we are finally getting through to her and that she is starting to realize that we're a family and we need to support each other. Perhaps this is our very own little Christmas miracle in the making!

I'm about to start levering myself out of bed when I hear an 'oh shit' from the bathroom.

There's a stampede of footsteps running back towards our bedroom before Gemma, face as white as a dried-out dogshite in summer, appears in the doorway.

'I swear I didn't do it on purpose. I didn't know. I thought it was just an ordinary marker. I swear . . .'

'Fuck,' Paul swears, his mind clearly working out the riddle before I do. It's not until the two boys appear, faces rubbed red but still decorated with drawn-on moustaches and beards, that it clicks.

'Oh Gemma,' I say, and she looks stricken.

'It was a mistake, Mammy. I swear.'

'Wasn't you, Gemma. Was Wee Donkey!' Nathan says.

But both Gemma and I know it was her. And that the marker she used was a permanent one.

Gemma is taking it bad, and switches back to her craic-killer personality, even though we assure her that she's not in trouble, that shit happens and that sure it makes for a hilarious story to tell everyone and even better photographs to pull out when they're eighteen. (Yes I will take pictures of them before they leave with Paul, it's my God-given right as a modern mother to store shit like this in the cloud for years.) But no . . . she forbids us from telling anyone. Apparently, 'it would only humiliate' her and her 'mental health is already fragile'. In fact she's insisting she feels so bad that she thinks she might actually be sick and her 'inner trauma is manifesting in a physical way'. (How in the actual fudge does a thirteen-year-old learn psychology chat like this?)

Paul thinks she looks a wee bit pale and upon touching her forehead claims that 'Jeez, Tara she is a wee bit warm'. But I take that with a pinch of salt because this is Paul and this is Gemma. I also have the thermostat up full whack, so of course she's bloody warm. She has him wrapped around her wee finger and if anyone will feel sorry for her, it's Paul.

'It's only a bit of permanent marker, Gemma!' I reassure her again. 'It's hardly a first-class trauma. Nobody died. Nobody lost a limb. The eyebrows are actually symmetrical, and that's a talent beauty therapists and MUAs would kill for!' I laugh, because I'm at the stage now where I fully believe that if I don't laugh, I'll cry. Gemma's face remains stormy.

'Stop taking the hannnnnndddeh!' she sobs and throws herself into Paul's chest as I sit watching the two boys made up like the Super Mario Brothers ready to go plumb through some pipes in search of Princess Peach. Christ, that could be my Instagram caption for the pictures!

'Maybe give her a break this morning, pet,' Paul says, looking at me and then nodding at the pathetic sight of our eldest daughter whimpering.

'Daddy, can I go back to bed?' she asks, all pouty-lipped with tear-filled eyes. Dear God, this is Oscar-worthy. Paul, of course, agrees that she can indeed go back to bed, so I give in too and decide to give the Vapester a break because she did try and do a very good thing and make sure her wee brothers weren't disappointed with a no-show from the Wee Donkey. And, she even made me tea and toast, and she didn't put rat poison in my tea or anything.

Paul left with the boys, promising me he would explain exactly what happened to both Nathan's teacher, Miss Rose, and Jo, Jax's childminder. I love him for doing this because I really didn't want to have to explain why my children both look like two baby Ricky Gervais impersonators. Thankfully, Nathan thinks it's hilarious and that Wee Donkey is the funniest, boldest elf in the entire world. Jax forgot it was on his face after about five minutes.

It's now after ten and surely the trauma has softened enough for me to be able to go wake up my darling daughter and set her to work. The thing with Gemma is that I must absolutely show no weakness or she will walk all over me. It would actually be easier for me to let her sleep. Quieter. Less chance of anyone getting murdered. Less chance of me ringing the school and begging them to take her back. But it wouldn't be the right thing to do – not if I want to get the message through to her that she has to catch herself on, serve her sentence and never again get into trouble at school. Or anywhere else for that matter.

Giving her door a gentle knock, I call her name in my best soothing, lovely mammy voice. 'Gemma, pet. Time to be getting up! There's loads to be done.'

I hear a groan from inside her lair, so I cautiously open

the door. I very rarely go into Gemma's room any more. It's just easier that way. The less I go in, the lower my blood pressure tends to be. The less she 'triggers' me (as she says), the less I 'trigger' her. No, ignorance is most certainly bliss, and my ignorance allows me to imagine that behind that door, everything is in its rightful place. There are not enough spoons and forks, cups and bowls to open her own homeware department in Tesco, and there are no pizza boxes with half-eaten slices from weeks ago, or washing that's ready to walk out the door itself.

Needs must though, because as she groans I have to take at least one step in to see her properly. I vow not to react to her surroundings in case I damage her mental health further.

'Gemma, c'mon love, wake up,' I say again.

'Mammy, I really don't feel good,' she says, and she actually sounds physically and emotionally drained.

'Look, we all make mistakes, Gemma, but the best thing you can do is try not to sweat the small stuff. Gain some perspective. You were so good to your brothers this morning, marker mix-up aside. They loved it, you saw how happy they were – you did that! Look, I'm actually going to cut a bit of time off your grounding, and if you promise not to take me from the feet up with your eyes today or judge my clothes, how I eat, speak or breathe, you might get an extra bit of phone time too.'

'I don't want my phone, Mammy. I just want to sleep. I really don't feel good.'

Now this has me shook. There has never, ever, been a

time before when Gemma Marie Gallagher has refused access to her phone. It unsettles me to my very core. Is she pulling some sort of reverse psychology shit on me? Did she learn this on TikTok?

'Well, that's up to you, dote,' I tell her. 'But you still have to get up. I need all these beds stripped so I can do some washing.'

'Mammy, please,' she groans. She's not making it easy for me to stay in my happy, encouraging mammy place, and I take what should be a calming breath.

'Gemma, come on, stop this crap now. You know I need help around the house. You can't use what happened this morning as an excuse to lay in bed all—'

'But Mammeeeeeuuuurrrggghhh!' And she erupts – no, she explodes, all over her duvet. I have never seen someone throw up with such force and or volume. And I've seen Cat after a five-hour sesh on Aftershock when we were teens (and as a result, I cannot even look at a bottle of Aftershock without dry-boking, never mind smell it).

Before I have time to fully process what is happening, she's retching again, and I swear the noises she is making are inhumane: as if she is actually trying to turn herself inside out with the force of it. And then the sour smell hits me and my own stomach threatens to escape my body through my throat too. She is sick again and again, with no rest in between, no chance to run to the bathroom or for me to grab a basin. Instead, I quickly empty her wastepaper bin and hold it under her chin.

Her duvet is covered, her walls, her curtains. The

multitude of outfits scattered on the floor, the make-up cases and scrunchies and other essential teenage accessories she's abandoned on the ground. Ah shite, her AirPods are even covered, but now is not the time for me to preach about how they should have been in their case.

Dear Jesus, where do I even start with this? Gemma is crying now, her face clammy with sweat and her hair covered in vomit. Her hands clasp at her stomach and her breath judders as she tries to control her own panic.

'Shush, love, it's OK,' I say, even though this abso-fricking-lutely does not feel OK.

'Mammmmeeeee,' she calls, before jumping out of bed at lightning speed and running past me, waste bin in her hand, howling as she closes the bathroom door.

Oh shit.

Literally.

Scanning the apocalyptic boke-fest that is in front of me, I try to figure out where to even begin and how in the name of *Home Alone* I am going to deal with this without vomiting myself. Gemma is crying in the bathroom and the noises coming from there are like something from a horror movie.

I want to cry too but I can't. I have to gather an armoury of cleaning materials, whatever basin or bucket I can find and strip everything off Gemma's bed, as well as take down her curtains. I need a fucking hazmat suit, why have I never bought a hazmat suit from Amazon? But first and foremost, I need to console her. Feck, why didn't I believe her? I'm a terrible mother.

Very gently I knock on the bathroom door. 'Are you OK, pet? Do you want me to come in?'

'Noooo!' she shouts between bodily explosions. 'Don't come in, Mammy!' I sense the teenage side of her is horrified, but the part of her who is just a thirteen-year-old wee girl desperately wants her mammy to hold her hair, rub her back and tell her everything will be OK between waves of stomach cramps. The teenage side always wins though.

'OK, pet,' I say. 'I'm going to go get some things to clean up. I'll bring you up a glass of water too.'

I turn to walk away and there is another scream of 'Maaammmmmeeeeee!' from the bathroom.

'I'm coming,' I shout.

'No, don't come in!' she shouts back and I'm starting to get whiplash from all this back and forth. Is it OK for me to just sit down on my fat, pregnant hole, cry and shout, 'I don't know what to do!'?

It's clear that I cannot handle this on my own – not at eight months pregnant. I need to call in the cavalry. I fish in my dressing gown pocket for my phone, only for it to start ringing just as I take it out.

It's Nathan's school. No doubt it's Miss Rose primed to launch into a preaching: *Mrs Gallagher, it's really not suitable to send your child into school with permanent marker on his face blah blah blah* . . . I am not in the form for it. She's judged me way too many times and has to stop calling me about this petty shit. Nobody is perfect.

Answering the phone, Gemma still howling in the

background, I launch straight into defence mode: 'Look, Miss Rose,' I say without even saying hello or giving her the chance to talk, 'shit happens. I apologize for my language but, it's true. There was a mix-up this morning with a marker and an elf, and we did our best to wash it off but we can't work miracles. And frankly—'

'Mrs Gallagher!' she cuts in, her voice loud and proper scary-teacher in tone. Who would have thought she had it in her? I shut up: I'm kind of scared now.

'This isn't about the marker incident – although we have had to reschedule taking the nativity class picture because of it and it is something I'd like to discuss at a later date – but look, Nathan is sick and we need you to come and pick him up. As soon as possible.'

My heart sinks. No. God no. Please don't let him be vomiting like a volcano too. Please let it just be a little cough or a cold or a mild dose of chicken pox or something – but not the vomiting and diarrhoea bug that seems to have possessed Gemma. I've been trying to kid myself that she must have eaten something funky and the rest of us will be OK – but here it is: evidence that we are all fucked. Might as well paint the black cross on the door right now.

'Erm, what's wrong with him?' I ask, crossing my fingers and clinging on to one last wee thread of hope. Miss Rose's words are drowned out by Nathan making the same noises Gemma has been making.

When he finishes, Miss Rose, her voice a bit shaky this time, says, 'I really think you need to get here as soon as possible, he seems to have the Norovirus; it's been going around all schools lately.'

I end the call. I'm still in my red and white Christmas snowflake jammies, with my Santa slippers on my feet and my hair shoved on top of my head like a broken bird's nest. Gemma is now wailing and the smell from her room seems to be getting stronger. I dial Paul's number: no answer. I call the garage directly, hoping I'll be able to get through on the landline. After what feels like forever, a voice I recognize as Gary, the junior mechanic, answers.

'Gary, it's Tara here. Can you get Paul for me? It's kind of an emergency.'

There's a pause and some muffled chat in the background before Gary speaks again. 'Erm, Paul's not here. He went out on a call or something.'

'Or something?' I ask. 'What kind of something?'

'No, it was a call. He went out on a call.' Gary sounds as if he is bricking himself. He also sounds like the shitest liar since Nadine Coyle balled up her age on *Irish Popstars*.

'Look,' I say, 'I've tried his phone and there's no answer. So if and when he comes back can you tell him I need him at home. Now.'

I hang up in despair and scan my fog-filled brain for alternatives on who to call. It's not as easy as it sounds when I've spent the last eight months cocooning myself into a complete hermit lifestyle.

Cat! I can always rely on Cat. She's my right-hand woman. The Thelma to my Louise. She has never let me down yet in a crisis. But her number too rings out, prompting me to do what I'm only ever supposed to do in an actual, genuine, life-or-death emergency (which I'm sure this is) – call her direct line at work. It rings out until I hear Cat's voice inform me she's off on annual leave today and I should direct all urgent business matters to her colleague, etc. etc.

Cat – who is so busy she couldn't stay long for lunch or call in for a cuppa to see who I am – is not in the office today. I don't know which feeling hits me hardest – is it the disappointment that she might have been lying to me, or avoiding me, or is it the ugly truth staring me in the face and telling me that I'm out of options? I'm going to have to leave Gemma to suffer alone, at least while I go and grab Nathan. I should probably pick Jax up too – damage limitation and all.

I swap my dressing gown for my coat. I keep the Santa slippers on because it's too much hard work to force my size-eight swollen hooves into anything else, and I hide my Edward Scissorhands hairstyle under a woolly bobbled hat. God help Miss Rose, or anyone for that matter, if they so much as attempt to judge how I look today.

By the time I get home again, with an increasingly pale-looking Jax, whose marker moustache is now making him look like a baby Charlie Chaplin, a very limp Nathan and a Tesco bag full of his sick, I'm starting to feel waves of nausea washing over me too. I try Paul again, and again, and again, but still no fucking answer. And I try Cat again and it goes straight to voicemail. Cat never switches her phone off – ever. Where the hell is she? And where is

Paul? I even try Amanda, who is the last person I'd ever ask to come help me in a vomit- and shit-infused disaster, but quickly hang up when I remember she and Sean are away on an 'adult retreat', the thought of which just makes my nausea worse.

Then it strikes me. There is one person. And as much as it kills me to do this – as much as I want to maintain making her think I don't need her and I've got a handle on everything – there are times when everyone needs a little help. There are times when everyone needs their mammy.

I scroll down my phone until I find Pamela's name and I tap on her number. As soon as I hear her voice, I totally show myself up by bursting into tears.

'Mammmeeeeee!'

11

The prodigal mother returns

Tuesday, 6 December

Two hours. Two fucking hours of uninterrupted sleep. That's what I got last night. A night that will go in the history books as the most traumatic time of my life to date.

At one stage I was rubbing Nathan's back as he vomited into the toilet, and I boked simultaneously into the bathroom sink. And while I probably shouldn't admit this, things got bad. Things got very, very bad. And unless you were there, you can't judge but when I felt my stomach bubble and my arse loosen, I had no choice. I could hardly drop kick my six-year-old from in front of the toilet, where he was also doubling up exits via Jax's borrowed potty.

Gemma had taken up permanent residence in the downstairs loo. I'm not sure how the poor child had any fluid left in her body, but she was still experiencing eruptions from both ends.

So I did what any decent mother/pregnant woman/ person in this type of shitemare would do.

I shat in my own bath.

It wasn't like I had a choice. It wasn't like I enjoyed the spaciousness and wanted to see what it felt like not being stuck to a bowl. This was a grade-A emergency and it was either crap in the bath or crap on the floor.

Paul, thankfully, was not awake to witness his wife in all her bath-shitting shame. He was bunking in with Jax, who, after an afternoon which required a temporary return to nappies as an emergency measure, now seems to be over the worst and sleeping soundly. Part of me envies Paul, who's still blissfully asleep, and part of me also wants to wring his neck for not being here yesterday, but a bigger part of me is glad he was nowhere near this literal shit-show of mine right now.

It would be abso-fuckin-lutely impossible for me to retain any air of sexual mystery and allure if my husband had seen the state of it: me vomiting over myself, the sink, the floor, while squatted over the bath, trying to hold my balance while I lost control of my bowels. Any judge in the land would see that as fair grounds for divorce.

The Gallagher household resembles a scene from a horror movie, and smells like someone dumped a hundred tonnes of slurry down the chimney instead of a jolly fat man in a red suit swinging by with presents.

At this time of year, I like my home to smell like

cinnamon and home-baked cookies. Perhaps with a faint whiff of pine and berries in the air. Instead, it's very much Eau de Shit, with a strong hint of gastric acid. Yankee Candles, eat your heart out.

Eventually, at around 5 a.m., Gemma, Nathan and I all fell asleep in my bed. After each of us had no more vomit or, literal, shits to give, we cuddled together like army vets bonding over a tour of duty in 'Nam. Each of us drained and forever scarred by the sights and sounds (and smells) we had just witnessed but finding comfort in each other, never to speak of it again. Until, that is, Bing Crosby wakes us from our PTSD comedown slumber crooning 'White Christmas' on the radio. I really should've turned that fecking alarm off at some stage last night.

'Oh my gooooddddaaaahhh,' Gemma moans. 'Can you seriously turn whatever that is off. I'm trying to sleep, ye know.'

I've never in my life cut Bing Crosby off mid-song – it feels like an anti-Christmas war crime – but this morning I'm tempted to throw Bing and his Christmas wishes out of the window. Instead, I just pull the lead from the wall. The room falls silent.

'Sorry, love,' I whisper to Gemma, who, praise the Lord, is too exhausted to launch into full teenage dirtbag mode just yet. Thankfully, Nathan has slept through it all, which is perfect because even though I am desperate to roll over and go back to sleep, I know I need to get to work cleaning up the besieged City of Bathroom. And it will be much easier to tackle that without a six-year-old asking as many questions as he can think of about poo and farts and vomit, and now that Mammy pooed in the bath does that mean he can poo in the bath too?

There may have been no lives lost last night but the remnants of my very own Battle of the Bog makes it look as if there was a full-blown massacre in there. God only knows what is waiting for me in the downstairs loo. Obviously, I'll need Paul to help me with the clean-up, but not before I have cleaned up all evidence of bath-gate. I have (some) dignity, after all.

I also need to fill him in on my conversation with Pamela yesterday. Suddenly I feel nauseous again, but I think it's the thought of that impending conversation because there is no way in hell my body has anything left to expel.

An hour later, and after multiple dry-boking sessions, the bath is empty but still needs a scrub and my shame has been washed down the drain along with any evidence from my CSI Shite Scene. I finally feel safe to wake Paul and put him to work sorting the rest of this shitstorm. Both he and Jax are still sound asleep when I creep into the boys' room, wrapped around each other in the most adorable hug. My breath catches, and happy tears prick at my eyes as I look at them both and think about the family we're building, and the bond they so clearly share – even though I still want to kick Paul in the dick for not being here when I needed him yesterday.

'Paul,' I whisper, nudging him gently on the shoulder.

He stirs, stretches and looks up at me. 'Morning, love,

how are you feeling? I never heard a thing last night so I'm assuming you all got a good rest. Best thing for you. A good sleep.'

He slips his arm out from under a still-sleeping Jax and pulls himself up to sitting. 'I went out like a light myself, as soon as my head hit the pillow.'

For the record, his head hit the pillow at around nine last night – and he'd only come in from work at half eight. Said he was exhausted from a busy day. Said he didn't realize his phone was off. Jobs all day off-site – cars breaking down because of the cold weather. He'd jumped at the chance to take Jax up to bed, and I'd been too sick and too busy consoling Nathan to fight him on it.

I stare at him, willing the pregnancy demon to stay quiet and not unleash the worst of her anger on this poor, unsuspecting, well-rested man. As he rubs the sleep from his eyes and stretches again, the pregnancy demon wins the battle.

'Are you taking the hand?' I hiss. 'We had the night from hell. All three of us. Gemma was in the loo downstairs with it coming out of her both ends. Nathan was sat on Jax's potty, boking into the toilet as it was coming out of him both ends, and I was in the bathroom with him with it coming out—' I realize I'm about to reveal my disgusting crap in the bath secret and stop myself just in time: '. . . Of my mouth. It was the worst night of my entire life, and that is saying something, Paul, because we both remember the night of Oktoberfest and the dirty glasses. Last night made that look like a walk in the park.

Like a mere blip. We didn't get to sleep until near five. Everywhere stinks. There's vomit in our room. In Gemma's room. The bathroom. The downstairs toilet. My . . . stairs . . . carpet . . .' I sob.

Paul leaps up and pulls me into a hug, stroking the side of my hair. 'Jesus, love. I didn't know. You should have woke me up,' he soothes, before taking a very quick step back and pulling his hand away from me.

'Pet,' he says, and I can tell it's taking all his willpower not to throw up.

'Please don't tell me you're getting sick too,' I wail, because I cannot handle it. I cannot handle another day of this. I cannot handle him being sick and my mother and . . .

'No,' he says, but he has covered his mouth with his hand and I can see his stomach muscles clenching with the effort of holding it in. 'There's some, erm . . . chunky vomit in your hair.'

Immediately my hand goes to my head. 'Where?' I ask him, even though I don't really want to pick chunks of regurgitated carrot or whatever it might be from my hair.

'Kinda all over the place,' he says. 'And don't take this the wrong way, but you've smelled better, love . . .'

My frosty glare silences him for a moment, then he speaks. 'Go and get a shower. Get some fresh clothes on. Wash your hair. I'll get started on the cleaning. This wee man will sleep for another hour if we're quiet.'

I nod in agreement because I'm just too tired and emotional to trust myself to speak, before grabbing some clean underwear and PJs (of course) and heading into the bathroom, where I do my best to ignore the mess that I have yet to clean up. I've done my poop duty, my shift is well and truly over at Hotel de Shitesville. Now I just need to be clean, to have a nice clean house and a nice long sleep in fresh bedsheets.

I feel about a million times better once my hair is silky and smooth instead of funky and chunky. I've put on my favourite Christmas-themed PJs – the ones with Buddy from *Elf* on the front. I've wrapped myself in my cosy chunky knit cardigan and swapped out the Santa slippers for fluffy white socks. I've sat and enjoyed the feeling of Baby Gallagher pummelling my insides, reassured by the amount of movement going on in there after such a rough stretch last night.

And when I make my way down the stairs (which have been cleansed of all bodily fluids), I catch sight of my husband, dressed in his finest Primark boxers and a plain white T-shirt, on his hands and knees scrubbing the downstairs toilet floor. The strong smell of our plague house is slowly, but surely, being replaced by the smell of bleach and pine disinfectant. OK, it's not a pine candle, but it's not Eau de Boke either: small wins.

When he spots me, he stands up and smiles: he's sporting a comical-looking pair of yellow Marigolds that actually make him look sexy. 'That's down here done now, love,' he says. 'And I've put fresh sheets on Gemma's bed and thrown the rest of her dirty stuff in the machine. I'm going to go and start on the bathroom, and you can stick the kettle on and make yourself a cup of tea. Put your feet up. I can take the morning off work if you want to go back to sleep for an hour or two. Sure, Gemma's bed is free.'

And there he is – my dote. My absolute ride-or-die other half. I do love him so much, I just don't understand what's going on with him at the moment. At times he is this incredible man – the man I have known and loved for fifteen years. And then, at other times, like yesterday, he's unreachable – emotionally and physically – and I don't know what the hell is going on in his mind. This is not how it should be. I'm the flaky one. I'm the one with multiple personalities. He's supposed to be my constant.

He's supposed to be there for me, so I don't do batshit crazy things like what I did yesterday and which I still have to tell him about, and actually, looking at the clock, fuck! I better say it quick.

'Paul,' I say, 'Thank you, love. Look, there's something I need to tell you. I should've last night but I was so distracted with everything and—'

The doorbell rings.

'Who'd be calling here at eight in the morning?' Paul asks, his face a picture of confusion because not even the Amazon man arrives that early in the morning, and at this time of year he's almost a daily visitor. Before I can stop him from opening the door in just his underbags and a pair of Marigolds, he has taken the safety chain off and pulled the handle.

'It's Pamela,' I blurt just as the door swings open and

there she is. The woman, the myth, the legend that is Pamela Sweeney. 'Well!' she howls in the strongest Derry accent known to man or woman, while taking in my husband from top to toe. 'Paul, if I were you, I wouldn't be opening the front door in your underpants in the middle of winter. You'll get a chill in your kidneys and God love ye, it looks like your wee willy is trying to shrivel up inside your body.' He immediately glances down to see if his boxers are unbuttoned or if the mouse is indeed poking out of the house. But he's fine – this is just Pamela and how she rolls. A sense of humour largely based on making people feel uncomfortable AF. Yes, she's a real character.

'Erm . . . well, what about ye, Pamela?' Paul stutters, covering his crotch with the Marigolds as Pamela pushes past him into the house leaving, if I'm not mistaken, two massive suitcases on the front path.

'Get them in off the street, would you, love?' Pamela says, but it's an order more than a request. Paul is standing stock-still. I wouldn't be surprised if this sight of his mother-in-law, heavily made up with a pair of sunglasses perched on top of her head (it's fucking December! It's still dark!), hasn't been enough to make his 'wee willy' want to shrivel up inside his body. Pamela can emasculate a man with a single glance.

'Ahm, Pamela. I thought you were in Spain?' Paul asks, and my stomach, which feels as if it is still in a washing machine, now also feels like it's on a rollercoaster – and spiralling downwards at record speed.

'Why would ye think that?' she asks. 'Sure it was Tara

who phoned me and asked me to come here. And my baby needs me. Isn't that right, pet?' Pamela pulls me into a giant hug, pressing my face into the fur collar of her coat. I can't see the look on Paul's face, and that's probably a good thing.

'I told you,' I say, pulling back. 'I told you Paul, that Mammy has split up with Javier and has to come back from Spain for a while.'

'I need family around me while I nurse my poor wee broken heart,' Pamela says, dramatically clutching her chest. I resist the urge to roll my eyes. Pamela has never needed her family. Nor has she ever in her life adopted a 'my baby needs me' approach to parenting. With Javier? Yes. That man-child got everything and more. But me? Nope.

'You didn't tell me,' Paul says in a small, tight voice. 'I think I'd have remembered.'

'No, I did tell you. Or at least I think I did.' Shit, can I blame this on baby brain? 'I meant to,' I mumble, my face now roaring red. 'And I was just about to tell you she was coming to help for a couple of days when the door went and . . .'

'Yep,' Pamela says. 'Tara called me yesterday. Said everyone was sick and she was getting it rough and sure, you were nowhere to be found. From what I gather, that seems to be the case a lot of the time these days.' She walks into the living room, taking in everything as she goes, before sweeping her hand across the mantelpiece and looking at her fingers in disgust. 'Tara, being pregnant is no excuse to let the dusting go to the dogs, and here, what have I told you about too many bright colours? Those curtains clash with your cushions.'

'Hang on,' Paul says. 'I'm not around? I'm always around!'

'I didn't say you weren't,' I plead, turning to my mother. 'Can you please tell him that's not what I said?'

She shrugs.

'Paul, I told her . . . well yesterday on the phone I was so sick and I couldn't get a hold of you, and I was really upset. You have been kinda distant lately,' I say.

'What is that godawful smell?' Pamela interrupts, her nose in the air. She's only been here a minute and I'm already wishing she was gone again.

'It's shite, Mammy,' I snap, too tired for politeness. 'And vomit. We've all been sick. I told you that. Look, why don't you go and make yourself a cup of tea and let me talk to Paul here in private for a moment?'

Paul looks as if I have slapped him, hard, across the face and I want to switch to damage-control mode as quickly as possible.

'Well, excuse me for breathing,' Pamela snaps back. 'And here I am, putting all my plans to one side to be here with you in your time of need, and you are snapping at me, then telling me to go and make my own cup of tea? What kind of a welcome is that? Although, with the state and the smell of this place, I'm not sure I'd be wise to even accept a cup of tea. Have you not been cleaning this place, Tara? I'm surprised Social Services haven't been at your door before now if this is what things are usually like here.'

'Mammy, we've been sick,' I say again, and I don't know whether I want to cry or scream. I can feel Paul's eyes on me, feel his hurt radiating from across the room. But of course, Pamela is paying no attention to what I'm saying or the look on Paul's face. She is off on a Pamela special – putting herself front and centre in every drama. 'Tara, I know you told me things were bad—'

'I did not tell you things were bad,' I jump in. Because I didn't. I mean, I did – but I meant the vomit, not *everything* in my entire life.

'Well don't you worry, love. Mammy is here now, and I'll put some manners on this house in no time.' She casts another glance around the living room, judging every item we own from under her heavily lined eyes. Full make-up first thing in the morning, complete with false eyelashes and a heavy wing eyeliner. My lovely mammy, ladies and gentlemen.

Paul glares at me. His body language screaming 'What. The. Actual. Fuck. Tara.' I need to take action quick – so I guide my mother through the double doors into the kitchen.

'Make yourself a cup of tea,' I order. 'There's biscuits in the cupboard. I will make you loads of cups of tea later right, but for now, please, just make your own. I need to talk to Paul.'

'He's gotten wile crabbit,' she says, lifting a cup from the drainer, looking at it, wrinkling her nose and replacing it. 'Have you bleach, love? I'll just give these cups a quick clean for you, sure.'

I nod to the table where Paul has left his cleaning supplies and walk back towards the living room closing the double doors behind me for all the good it will do.

'This better be good, Tara,' he says, and I see a real flash of anger in his eyes – and believe me, Paul Gallagher is not an angry man. It takes a lot to wind him up, and God knows I have tested him in the past, but this is different.

'Look, Paul,' I start, now ready to word-vomit all the things I've been wanting to say for weeks but unable to find the time, energy or nerve to do so. 'I have been up to my eyes lately. What with work, and the kids and being pregnant again. Mammy rang me a few days ago, crying and telling me she had split up with Javier.

'She told me she wanted to come back and spend more time with us, get to know our kids more. And I was like, "Aye right, Pamela. Dead on. You almost got me there." But it wasn't another one of her stupid wind-ups. She *had* split up with him and she was coming home, and I absolutely meant to tell you. My head is just so far up my arse, I'm sorry. But you've been so off with me lately, and Cat is basically ghosting me and I've no idea why. I don't even have the Rebel Mums to lean on right now because they are all past this pregnancy shit and I don't want to spoil their buzz. So yes, I did call my mother. I rang Pamela for help because I was just desperate and . . . if it's any consolation to you at all, I'm already massively regretting it.'

Of course, I whisper the last line because Pamela has ears like a bat, and you can bet your last mince pie that she has one of them pressed up against that door right now.

Paul stares at me for a moment and shakes his head slowly like he can't believe what he is seeing or hearing. 'You've done some random, crazy shit and made some really mad and questionable decisions when you've been pregnant before, but this . . . this wins, Tara. This is the most epically fucked-up thing you have ever done. You asked *Pamela* for help. Your ma! The woman who left you just before you gave birth to Gemma so she could go to Spain and ride some slimy pool boy she met on her holidays. Your ma, who wasn't even a good ma before she met Javier. She hurt you so much Tara.' He paces the room, flapping his Marigolds at me. 'She has barely seen our children. Has she even met Jax yet? I don't think so. She only contacts you when she wants something, be it to listen to the sound of her own voice or to belittle you just to make her feel better about herself. How many times have I picked you up again after another disappointment? And you . . . you welcome her back to Derry and not only that, you invite her into our house! The woman who you describe as the source of your anxiety in the first place!?' He's not even trying to whisper now; this is coming out loud and clear and there is no way Pamela doesn't hear every single word. I imagine the entire street hears every single word.

I have never seen Paul so enraged about anything, and

the thing is: everything he says is true. I know that in my heart.

'Look,' I stutter, completely on the defensive now, 'I only asked her to come and help out while we were all sick. I was desperate, Paul.' Dropping my voice to a whisper, I add: 'She'll probably be gone in a few days anyway.'

He rolls his eyes in a way that is pure Gemma, before pointing to the hall. 'There's two big black suitcases out there which would say different.'

'Tara, love, is there a good hairdresser nearby?' Pamela emerges from the kitchen, not giving two shits about interrupting us. 'And I mean a *good* hairdresser, not one of those hipster ones who charge an arm and a leg for a blow-dry and look like they haven't even washed their own hair never mind styled it? Is Majella Lynch still alive? God, she did the best blow-dries in Derry . . . but then again if you believed the gossip at the time she also gave the best blow jobs in Derry. It was more than a short back and sides her male clients were after, if ye know what I mean.'

'To be fair, Pamela, I think it would be hard not to get your meaning with that one,' Paul says, before giving me another utterly disgusted look. 'You were never famous for your subtlety.'

I brace myself for a full onslaught from Pamela, only to find she continues speaking as if Paul hasn't so much as opened his mouth. 'But I would pay good money for her to get her hands on my hair right now. The sun is amazing and all, but it sure dries out the auld hair.'

Just when I think this lovely Christmas family reunion can't get any worse, Gemma herself stomps down the stairs looking like an extra from *The Walking Dead*, and an angry one at that.

'Does nobody in this bloody house have any respect for people who are trying to sleepahhh! I've been up all night and yeese don't even care . . .' She stops before getting into the full flow of her rant when she spots Pamela standing in the middle of the living room.

'Granny? Is that you?' she asks, and a small voice from the top of the stairs chimes in: 'Gwanny? Who's dat?' Nathan walks down the stairs and takes his sister's hand. Together in their pale and frail state they look like ghosts, absolutely boggin', disgusting, malnourished abused ghosts. And of course where two go, the third is bound to follow and Jax bum-shuffles his way down the stairs behind them.

I'm surprised Gemma recognizes my mother. God knows, they've not spent much time together. Nathan and Jax, on the other hand, have not a baldy notion who this person in front of them is.

'Yes,' Paul says, disgust oozing out of every pore. 'Your granny has come to visit.'

Pamela doesn't rush to them. There is no hugging or lavishing of affection. It makes me sad in a way that instead of pulling them into her arms my mother simply stands and stares before speaking. 'Hello there, wains. I'm your granny, but if you don't mind, I'd prefer it if you called me Pammy.'

Paul actually chokes at this but settles himself. Our

children nod. Even Gemma, who seems to be in some sort of trance.

'Tara,' Pammy says to me, 'these wains are boggin'. Dear God, have you no self-respect?' She shakes her head sadly as if she has just wandered upon a group of starving and sickly puppies in a box by the side of the road.

I can't speak, and Paul is about ready to explode.

'Take those children upstairs and get the wee ones in the bath,' Pamela drones on. 'Dear God, if anyone was to arrive here now and see the state of this place . . .'

'Gwanny . . . I mean Pammy,' Nathan says, sticking his hand in the air as if he's wanting to tell Miss Rose someone has just stolen his favourite pencil. 'We can't go in the bath acuz my mammy did her poos in it last night . . .'

12

The best calves in Derry

My humiliation in full effect – with everyone but the two boys looking at me like I am the most disgusting creature that ever lived – I want to go to bed. I want to go directly to bed and go to sleep and wake up in a few hours to find this has all been a terrible nightmare and Paul doesn't detest me, my mother hasn't moved in, and my six-year-old hasn't just gone on to out me as a bath-shitter by describing in detail what went on in the bathroom, complete with sound effects and scarily accurate facial expressions. Jax has found the whole thing hilarious. Gemma is looking at me as if I've just posted the video of it on her Snapchat, and Paul is storming about gathering his cleaning products as if it's the only thing to stop him losing his shit altogether.

'Right,' says Pamela. 'Well, since it seems the boys can't be bathed just yet – how about you two get on with cleaning and I'll make us all some breakfast. Gemma love, c'mon, you can help me.'

To my amazement, Gemma does not sulk or stomp her feet or go into her monologue about child labour. She smiles. 'Aye, Granny,' she says, while the gruesome twosome, who still have grey tracks on their faces from whatever industrial strength marker Gemma used on them yesterday, grab their iPads and clamber up on the sofa, ready to fill their wee YouTube boots.

'Grand,' Pamela says. 'We'll make some toast once I'm done with these cups. But love, remember, it's Pammy, not Granny. I don't want any of that granny craic. Grannies have permed grey hair, smell like fig rolls and wear godawful flower-patterned slips and skirts to their ankles. And we'll not even get started on those ortho-paedic shoes they walk about in.' She laughs and screws up her perma-tanned nose while her speech has been enough to distract the boys from their iPads.

'I mean have you seen my calves, wains?' she asks, and now she's playing to the room – enjoying having an audi-ence. 'I've got the best calves in Derry. Always did, so if you've got it, flaunt it, that's what I always say. And you'll never see me with a perm again – this is not 1982 any more. As for that purple rinse carry-on? Not a chance! I'll rather be dead, aye just euthanize me, wains, if youse ever see me with a purple rinse, right? There's nothing graceful about growing old gracefully, I'm in me prime, ye know.'

Her grandchildren just watch her, mouths open, not

quite sure what's going on in front of them and what this mahogany-coloured woman in heels higher than Mammy has ever worn in her life is talking about.

Except, of course, for Gemma, who is looking at my mother as if she is the second coming of Christ.

'Erm, I'm just going to go and get upstairs sorted now,' I say, but no one is really listening. The boys have returned their attention to their iPads and Gemma is following her granny around like an adoring puppy. Pamela is lapping it up, revelling in the attention. I watch as she takes her jacket off, revealing two toned bronze arms which look even darker against her white dress. As for 'the best calves in Derry', it's like looking at the legs of the antique chair I got stuck in at Gemma's school.

'Right, Gemma my love. Let's get to work,' Pamela says, opening and closing cupboards. 'It seems your mammy has things all wrong in here. *Dear God.* Why is the ketchup here and not in the fridge? And here, you don't keep coffee on one shelf and your tea on another. How any of youse find anything you're looking for here is beyond me. It seems I taught your mammy nothing,' she says with a laugh, talking about me as if I'm not even in the room – as if I don't matter enough to have this conversation with.

I want to interrupt. I want to tell her she taught me loads – like how to have an affair with the milkman, and break my daddy's heart. How to sneak a bottle of vodka into a wedding at the age of thirteen because 'they never search the wains'. How to get free gravy rings from creepy

124

Johnny in the bakery by wearing my skirts short and flashing my cleavage. How to walk out on my only child weeks before she became a mother herself, leaving her feeling completely abandoned and terrified . . . and . . .

I don't speak. I can't. Because if I started right now, I wouldn't stop and I would say things that can never, ever be taken back. Instead, I bite everything back as Gemma (the traitor) speaks: 'I'm always telling her this, ye know. We need a pantry, and loads of those wee organization drawers and glass jars so we can stack the cookies really neatly . . . you know, like the Kardashians have?'

Jesus Christ – if I have to hear about the Kardashians and their perfect pantries which their servants decorate with jars of cookies not a one of them ever eats, I will hit the roof. I leave, and go upstairs because cleaning up explosive diarrhoea is preferable to listening to verbal diarrhoea.

'OMG, the Kardashians! Yes! I love them. Kim is my fave,' I hear Pamela squeal from the kitchen.

Shoot me in the face. Just do it.

I make my way into the bathroom beside Paul who has a face on him like Jax just used his new Arsenal top to wipe his arse on.

He's angry, and I feel a sudden urge to make it all better. There are only two problems.

The first is that when Paul is angry he becomes extra productive, like superhuman-level get-shit-done productive and the result is that the bathroom is now just about back to its previous state. Actually, it might be cleaner than it was before the bug threatened to take us all out. The tiles are gleaming. Chase and Marshall are smiling from Jax's potty, no longer obscured by things we really don't need to talk about. The toilet looks as if you could eat your dinner off it. I'm impressed at just how good his angry-cleaning is.

The second problem is I haven't the first notion how to make it better. I opt for flattery. 'Love, this is brilliant. I would be lost without you. Now Gemma can get a shower and then we can get the boys bathed and . . .'

He gives me a look that could curdle milk as he stands up. 'And what about *her*?' he barks, storming past me into the bedroom, where he starts getting dressed for work. It doesn't look like he'll be taking the morning off after all – it looks very much like he can't wait to get the hell out of here.

'Paul, you know Pamela. She'll be out of here in a few days. This will all be some big drama she has created in her own head to get Javier to come crawling back to her. A couple of days here and she'll be back on a plane to Spain and her life in the sun. She'll realize playing the role of the doting granny – sorry, Pammy – isn't for her.' I give a little smile when I stop talking, hoping it's enough to get him onside, but no, his angry-cleaning has become angry-dressing. I've blinked and he has his overalls on and is lacing his shoes.

'You called her here because you think I'm never around,' he says. 'Never around? Are you for real? Is this what happens when, God forbid, I take some time to

126

myself to do something I want to do after all these years of doing everything to keep you and our wains happy? To make sure youse have had everything you need and more? OK, so I've had a wee bit more time out of the house than I normally do, and there have been a few late nights, but Jesus, Tara . . . it's hardly the case that I'm never here! I just need some time for me. Is that hard to believe? You really don't realize how hard it is for me at times, and I love you, pet, but sometimes it's just too much. It's draining trying to keep you happy all the time.'

It's like I've been punched. His eyes widen and he looks as shocked as I am that those words just came out of his mouth and didn't stay in his head. I don't speak because I can't speak. If I so much as open my mouth right now I will cry all over him and it won't be pretty and the words I say might not be kind.

I expect him to take the words back. To say he doesn't mean it. But he doesn't. He stands, lost in the moment, before he checks himself and gets on with getting ready for work. Before I can say a word, he's kissed me on the cheek (a ballsy move, given what he has just said) and heads for the door. 'I'll be late home tonight. Big job on. But sure you have company now to keep you entertained.'

I slump onto the bed. Draining him? I'm draining him. I AM DRAINING HIM!? It's all too much. *I'm* too much. A solo tear escapes and slides down my face onto my lip, where I can't taste its salty residue. Yes, like any couple, Paul and I have had our bumps along the way, but for him to say I'm draining him? It reinforces every insecurity

I have ever had about myself and then some. Did Pamela leave for Spain because I was too much to deal with? Is he getting tired of me – of my drama – and he will leave me too? I know I'm not always easy to live with, but he always said he loved all of me, even the dark bits. That life with me kept him on his toes, yet here he is, essentially telling me he's done with that. Done with me. My stomach twists with a whole new kind of grief mixed with fear. I don't want to lose Paul. I can't lose Paul. But maybe I really am too draining for anyone to want to stay in my life long-term. Maybe that's why Cat is ghosting me too. I feel sick, and this time I know it's not the Norovirus.

I've two options here. I can curl up into a ball and cry until I (once again) vomit, or I can take Paul's lead and get angry. Two can play at angry-cleaning. So I set to work putting our house back in order while pushing down the sadness that is threatening to choke me.

It turns out if you get angry enough, and you angry-clean enough – especially after you've spent the better part of twelve hours worried you might throw up some of your vital organs – you will leave yourself so exhausted you will fall into a deep, deep sleep.

The best thing about that, of course, was that I didn't have to think about how potentially fucked my marriage was, or berate myself for being 'draining'. So I took full advantage of it. Just as I took full advantage of Pamela's declaration she was here to help.

I had neither the emotional or physical energy to do

anything else. I slept the day away, occasionally woken by Nathan or Jax coming in to ask for a cuddle, or Gemma bringing me a cup of tea and toast before telling me that 'Pammy' was 'just so class'.

Pamela however was not 'class' enough to actually try and have any kind of an in-depth conversation with me, or spend any meaningful time in my company.

'Pammy says you're to stay in bed and rest in case you're contagious still and give her the shits,' Gemma said.

'Gemma my dear, everyone else in this house has been just as ill and Pammy doesn't seem to mind spending time with them.'

Gemma just shrugged and left. Perhaps another version of me would've asked my mother what she was doing, but it turns out being draining also results in feeling drained. So I slept some more, right through to the next morning in fact.

13

Santa Claus is coming to town

Thursday, 8 December

By Thursday afternoon, we're all a bit stir crazy and cabin fever has well and truly set in. The boys had to go a full forty-eight hours after being sick before they could return to school or creche, so Wednesday was mostly a write-off even though they were jumping off the sofa and swinging from the lampshades like two feral chimpanzees. I actually thought about sending video evidence of their recovery to Miss Rose and Jo but I quickly reneged against the idea and instead convinced them to lie on the sofa with me in exchange for stickers and a few extra advent chocolates.

This morning, Paul got up and left for work before I was even out of bed, citing, once again, 'a big job' he was working on.

'I'll see you in town for the big Christmas switch-on,'

he said. 'Text me to let me know where youse are standing.' There was no kiss on the cheek. No 'I love you'. Just family admin. I felt deflated about what is normally one of my favourite days in the build-up to Christmas knowing that, instead of a happy family showing up en masse to ooh and aah at the lights, we'd be there in three generations of dysfunctional glory.

Pamela and Gemma did me the hugest favour for most of today by keeping the boys entertained while I did a bit of resting, tidying and life admin – but mostly resting. In Pammy's own words, 'youse better get some rest because there is no way in heaven or hell I'm taking those wains to the Christmas lights switch-on without you.'

I was pathetically grateful, but by late afternoon, it's dark and I too am ready to leave the house. I'm just finishing putting a wee bit of slap on to disguise my grey skin and dark circles when I hear the front door go.

'Pammy, I'm back,' shouts Gemma. 'They didn't have any onion rings, so they gave us extra chips.'

Gemma sounds almost happy. Enthusiastic. Normal. Maybe I'm still asleep, and this is a dream?

'Good girl, Gemmy,' I hear my mother sing-song. 'Why don't you go and get your mammy? Right, boys, let's get some food in us before we go see Santa! And boys, we eat our dinner at the table and not on the floor in front of the TV.'

My children parrot a good, strong 'OK, Pammy.'

I'm pulling myself up to sitting when Gemma (or Gemmy – Jesus Christ, she'd phone Childline if I called her that) opens the door. 'Erm . . . bestie, Pammy has dinner downstairs. Chips, peas and gravy from the chippy down the street. I told her to get you two sausages as well,' she says, all her teenager 'IDGAF' attitude back. But she doesn't fool me. I can tell she's had a good day and she's delighted with herself.

'So I'm allowed out of quarantine now, am I?' I ask, keeping the sarkiness to a minimum because nothing is going to keep me from eating those sausages and chips.

'Aye, and she says you better hurry up or we'll end up missing the switch-on altogether.' The smirk is still there on my daughter's face and she's clearly loving seeing Pamela put me in my place.

But she also seems determined to stay on her granny's good side and that means, smirks and cheeky winks aside, she is behaving like an actual human being and not a teenage mutant ninja asshole.

Maybe she thinks Granny has thousands in the bank she can inherit? I'll not burst her bubble just yet and tell her Pammy lives off the motto 'Ye canny get knickers off a bare arse' and is likely to outlive every single one of us.

When I follow the scent of deep-fried food downstairs, I see that Pamela has been busy.

'Ah love, that's you up. Here, tell me, when was the last time the inside of those windows were cleaned? Sweet living divine, I had a wee swipe with the Windolene and we had to turn the lights off in here it got so bright,' she says with a cackle.

'Mammy, Gemma made us toasties wiv cheese and ham

for lunch. They were lovely and not even burnt like your toasties.' Nathan smiles, and I add him to the traitor list too.

'That was very lovely of Gemma,' I say and smile at my daughter, who is giving Pammy her best, most angelic smile. The poor girl is in for a quare shock when she realizes the only thing she'll inherit is a collection of knock-off handbags and sunglasses sold in the Irish pub in Spain where Pammy performs on a Tuesday night. Guchi anyone? Or a little Channel?

'Now, sit you down and eat up,' Pamela says. 'We want to make sure we get the best spot to see Santa, don't we, boys?'

Both Nathan and Jax nod in perfect unison. 'Pammy says Santa throws sweets to the good boys and girls and I'm going to get dem all and share them wif Jax, acuz he's a good boy who used his potty all day with no ackydents at all,' Nathan says.

'He's a great wee boy,' Pammy adds. 'Although, I'd potty-trained you well before that age. It's all about priorities, I suppose?'

I take a deep breath and focus, not on telling this woman she is a godawful hypocrite of the highest order, but instead on being grateful for the gravy-covered chip I'm inhaling which tastes like the food of the actual gods.

By five thirty we have parked and are moving en masse amid the crowds into a festively decorated Guildhall Square. The air is crisp, the night dry. Stars are twinkling overhead and 'Silent Night' is being sung on stage by a choir wearing Santa hats. The boys are wrapped up in their coats, gloves and scarves, and Jax has agreed to sit in his buggy even though he is a 'big boy now'. That he may well be, but this is the ultimate Christmas event in the Derry parenting calendar and I no longer have the agility to chase a hyper two-year-old through the crowds when he spots someone selling those light-up things that cost a small fortune.

Even though the lights have not yet been lit, Nathan is saucer-eyed with wonder. 'Mammy, look!' he exclaims over and over again while Pamela splurges on two light-up wands for the kids to wave, before noticing that Gemma has a longing in her eyes and buys three more so we have one each. Before I know it, I'm watching Gemma and my ma pouting and posing together while Gemma takes selfies for her Snapchat. That anxiety knot twists even tighter, and the nagging voice that I'm not good enough to be loved by my family grows louder.

But I push the sad feelings down, determined to get lost in the magic of the moment – to feel the excitement building not only with Nathan and Jax but all the other children, and quite a few of the grown-ups too.

With the glittering lights and crisp cold air, not to mention the building buzz of anticipation for the imminent display, I'm finally starting to feel that warm fuzzy Christmas feeling. I send a quick message to Paul – the first I've sent since he left for work this morning – telling him we're close to the Christmas tree. I won't let the tension between us take away from this moment because it's bigger than that. It's our family, and our community all coming together. It's choirs of all ages, bands and dodgy Christmas music. It's a compere making cheesy jokes and winding the children up with rumours of Santa sightings. It's Derry & Strabane District Council's way to show everyone there ain't no party like a Derry party, and I love every single moment of it. The atmosphere and the noise, the competition to catch the sweets that Santa lobs out into the crowd (I swear I once saw a five-year-old punch a grown man square in the throat for trying to grab a packet of Haribo she'd her eyes on). And if Paul does not get his ass here very bloody quickly he's going to miss every moment of it. It won't be long now till the countdown begins and the lights come on – the tree first, festooned in green, reds and golds before spreading across the town. Damn it, Paul, where are you? The boys haven't clicked yet that he's not here, but it won't be long.

I feel a tug at my hand and look down to Nathan who is pointing to the side of the stage. 'Daddy!' he shouts. 'Mammy, it's Daddy!'

I feel a wave of relief – it is Daddy. Deep in conversation with some woman, but I can't see her face, only the top of the fuzzy pink pom-pom on top of her hat. I ask Pamela and Gemma, who is now lifting Jax out of the buggy, to keep an eye on the boys while I go and fetch Paul, because clearly he hasn't gotten my text message yet and the compere is whipping the wains into such a frenzy there isn't a chance he'll hear his phone if I try calling it.

I wave to try and get his attention but Pink Bobble Hat, who now has her back to me, seems to be saying something very interesting and funny because he is laughing. A full head-thrown-back performative laugh, until he catches sight of me. I see him speak to the woman again, ending the conversation abruptly just as I'm getting close enough that I might actually see who he's talking to.

But off she goes, her pink bobble hat soon lost in a sea of bobble hats and excited parents holding their children up for optimal Santa-sighting.

'Who was that you were talking to?' I ask as I get close. 'I messaged you – the boys are over by the tree with Gemma and Pamela.'

'Ah, I didn't get the message,' he says. 'That was just a customer. Had her car through the garage a couple of weeks ago. I was just checking if she got it through the MOT OK.' I don't have time to say anything else before he takes me by the hand and walks as fast as he can towards the boys, as I try to push down the bobble-related wobble I can feel inside. I will not cry. I will not look sad. I will be fucking happy. OK? I will not have my children see me and see a hint of pain on my face. I remember all too well how it used to break me to see my daddy look sad after Pamela left him.

Paul scoops both boys up into his arms, giving them a perfect view of proceedings. 'Have you seen him yet?' he asks. 'Or the reindeers or the sleigh?'

'No, Daddy!' Nathan shouts while Jax just shakes his head as if he can't believe the magic all around him. I huddle close to my family and add the woman with the pink bobble hat to the list of things I cannot think about if I don't want to have a full-on breakdown.

Thankfully I'm distracted by a wall of noise as the Guildhall Square erupts at the sight of a jolly fat man in a big red suit being lifted above the crowd in a cherry picker.

'Saaaannnntttaaaaaa!' Nathan and Jax scream in unison.

I look at their faces, the joy and the wonder writ large across them, and my heart swells: this is it. This is the magic.

And this is all that matters.

14

Casa del Gemmy and Pammy

The excitement of seeing Santa and the Christmas light switch-on in town today exhausted the boys, and they fell sound asleep in the car on the way home. It exhausted me too, if the truth be told. All I wanted to do was get home, throw back a couple of shots of Gaviscon (those battered sausages may not have been such a good idea after all), and go to bed. And definitely not think about the woman in the pink bobble hat.

Pamela kept throwing me funny looks on the way home. She knows something isn't quite right. She is clearly busting her hole to ask me, but something is holding her back. Maybe it's the realization that we are not close and I'm not likely to use her as a shoulder to cry on any time soon. Or maybe she knows if she pokes this particular preggo bear too much, I'll lose my shit and she might end up homeless for the night.

Either way, she is another person I don't have the energy for right now. So, if Gemma and Pamela want to be 'besties', good luck to them; knock yourselves out, besties. It keeps them both out of my hair for a bit, and God knows that's a blessing in itself.

'I'm going to bunk in with Gemmy again tonight,' Pamela says once we're back. 'Maybe tomorrow, you can get all of that junk out of the spare room. You wouldn't expect anyone to sleep in there with all that rubbish and dust, for God's sake. I'd even be a wee bit feared of a touch of carbon monoxide poisoning in thon room.'

I swallow down my rage and the urge to tell her that maybe she could shove all that 'junk' up her arse. But I'm not so much upset about her insulting my shitemare of a spare room as jealous at the thought of them having a wee girly sleepover. For a third night. And Gemma appears absolutely OK with it.

She doesn't roll her eyes or stomp her feet or let out any *Exorcist*-type shrieks at the thought of having her granny share a room with her. In fact, Gemma smiles angelically at Pamela. Then she looks at me. 'That's right, Mammy. Granny is going to sleep in my bed tonight and I'll use the fold-down bed we got for sleepovers.'

'We'll have to have a wee midnight feast again, love,' Pamela smirks. 'Aw, it'll be so much fun.' I wonder if they'll paint each other's nails and braid each other's hair too? The jealousy is eating me alive.

'Pamela, Gemma is thirteen and she needs her sleep,' I say, earning a look that would kill from my darling daughter.

'Hardly, Mammy,' she says, smile tighter now. 'It's not like I have to go to school in the morning.'

'Aye, but you do have chores don't ye, love?' I smile back, my jaw aching from trying to appear completely cool with the situation. My head is starting to throb now too.

'Sure, we'll do those together, won't we?' Pamela links arms with Gemma and leads her up the stairs. 'Let's get our own wee Casa del Gemmy and Pammy set up!' she chirps as tears I refuse to let fall bubble at my eyes.

I am a sorry sight as I climb the stairs, alone, to get into my jammies. Every movement takes all my effort, and I'm glad to climb into bed and sink under the covers and into oblivion again. I stir when Paul comes to bed later, but I don't have the energy to chat to him and he doesn't seem to be particularly keen to talk to me either. I listen as he slumps into bed, sighs, turns his back to me and falls asleep.

Friday, 9 December

When I wake up, Paul has already left for work, somehow having managed to get the boys out of here without waking me. That would've required a mammoth effort, which of course makes me feel crap that he went to said mammoth effort to avoid talking to me.

'Pammy sent me up with this,' Gemma says, bustling into my room with a tray of tea and toast. As she sits the tray on the bed, she adds, 'And Daddy said that Miss Rose might ring today because there was no fruit left for Nathan's snack so he had to give him a KitKat.'

Christ.

'If she rings, I'm not here,' I say, grabbing the piece of toast with the most butter on it.

'You're looking grumpy,' Gemma says. 'Pammy says you always were a bit grumpy. A pure craic killer when you were younger.'

I don't bite. No. I just watch as Gemma turns and walks out of the room, a spring in her step as she heads back down to Pammy.

I was never a craic killer! There were just times when I had to be the parent because my mother was acting like a child.

I feel an imminent 'woe the fuck is me' pity party when my phone pings. I lift it, taking a sip of tea at the same time, and my heart does a wee jig when I see Cat's name.

Don't forget Tits McGee! Your baby shower is on Sunday! It's all in hand – all you have to do is show up and eat cake. How easy is that? So excited for you!

I have the hugest grin on my face. Cat is back on form and I get to see her and eat loads of cake very soon. Hallelujah, there is some good in the world.

I'm in a much better mood when I wander downstairs. In fact, I'm in such good form that instead of going apeshit that Pamela has decided to 'declutter' the living room and kitchen by boxing up a lot of family photos, art by the children and books I was absolutely intending to read, and packed them into the understairs cupboard, I simply take a deep breath and admire the minimalist vibe in the living room, which is probably – no, definitely – tidier than it has ever been.

'There's no need for half of this clutter,' she says, eyeing a picture of my daddy. 'It just gathers dust.' I nod, because if I start to speak, I will end up murdering her and I really don't want to have to give birth handcuffed to a prison guard. I do however lift the picture from the mantelpiece, give it a little rub and put it right back where it was, hoping Pamela gets the message. But as always, my mother exists in her own world and moves on to the next topic without breaking a sweat.

'Now that you're up, Gemma and I are going to go into town to get a few wee things,' she says.

'Mammy,' I groan, 'you know Gemma's grounded. We made an exception for the Christmas lights but . . .'

'Tara love, she's coming with me to help. It's not like it's a girly day *out* or anything,' Pamela says. I have a feeling they are both taking the piss out of me here, but I fear I'll be fighting a losing battle if I come right out and call her a liar.

'You know, someone is having a baby shower on Sunday and we have some arranging to do, don't we Gemmy?' Pamela says.

Oh this bitch is clever, very clever.

'Gemma is really creative, you know,' Pamela continues. 'She has some class ideas. You should be very proud.'

Gemma beams at me and it looks like a genuine smile, not the fake one she puts on when she's trying to get me to buy her a top that looks like it's size 12–18 months from Shein. As if I don't know how creative my daughter is, and she's beautiful and could genuinely be anything she wants to be? I tell her this all the time!

But I can't deny that it warms my heart, and threatens to make me cry yet again as I process the fact that Gemma is actually getting involved. Could she finally be coming to terms with the idea of a new baby brother or sister?

'You're coming to the baby shower?' I ask Gemma, with a genuine, albeit needy AF, smile of my own.

Gemma pauses and stares at me. I can almost hear her thought process as she tries to find a way to say, 'As if, are you actually serious?' without showing Pamela her true teenage dirtbag colours. But before she has the chance to speak, Pamela cuts in.

'Of course she is. We're both looking forward to it so much.'

The horror on Gemma's face is momentary but it's there all the same. Still, she's caught rightly and there'll be no getting out of it now that she's Pamela's Plus One. My mother gives me a knowing smile; she might just be more clued in than I thought.

I'm not ready to open my arms and welcome her back into my heart as Mother of the Year just yet, but hey, small steps are what big journeys begin with, and if she keeps pulling wee twists like this in my favour, then you never know. She might be the key to bridging this awful gap between Gemma and me.

'So Mammy, are you thinking you'll still be with us for Christmas?' I ask, because we actually never talked about arrangements, and I did assume she'd have had enough of acting World's Greatest Granny after a few hours.

'I'm not sure, love. I've no plans to go back to Spain, if that's what you're asking. But I got in touch with Sheila Campbell, you remember Sheila? Massive tits and a set of ears to match, God love her. Anyway, she thinks she might have a room free in one of her wee Airbnbs from next week, just until after Christmas, so sure I'll decide then what I'm doing.'

'No, Mammy,' I say, a pang of guilt gnawing at my stomach (or is that heartburn?). 'You should stay and have Christmas with us.' I say it without thinking for a second about the repercussions of my words or how Paul is going to feel. But I can hardly leave my mother to spend Christmas alone in some bedsit or houseshare.

'Are you sure?' she asks, eyebrows sky-high.

'I'm sure, Mammy. It'll be one big happy family Christmas,' I say. As I say it, I think it, which means I'm manifesting it and it has to happen. Or so Gemma tells me – she learned it on TikTok.

Pamela gives me a quick but tight hug, and so does Gemma. It feels weird, but not bad weird. Good weird.

OK, so Paul is going to be absolutely raging, but I need someone right now who can make my life just a little easier. And yes, she might be full of passive-aggressive jibes, and judgement, but she's keeping Gemma in line, and that's a huge deal right now. Especially as it's Christmas and especially in the run-up to the baby arriving.

How am I going to break the news to Paul, though? He won't be happy. But then again, nothing I do seems to make him happy at the moment. Why do I feel like I can't win – no matter what I do, someone's annoyed with me.

I fret about telling him for the rest of the day. There's no such thing as the perfect moment to tell Paul, but the least I can do is actually fucking tell him this time. He's still reeling from her unexpected return as it is, and now I'm going to blow up his Christmas with news she'll be here to help him pull his cracker.

When he climbs into bed that night, I realize I can't put it off and blame baby brain again in a few days' time.

'Erm, love, Pamela is going to stay here for a while,' I blurt. 'I've said she can spend Christmas with us.'

There is a deep sigh and instead of launching into one of his 'Tara you're not thinking straight' lectures or even asking me why, he stays silent, turns off his lamp and rolls over so his back's to me. With the room now in darkness, I'm once again alone with my thoughts and right now, that isn't a nice place to be. Into the wee hours I lie awake alone, spiralling into the pit of marital insecurity.

15

That jingle bell bitch!

Saturday, 10 December

Paul's 'all picture – no sound' routine doesn't last. By the time we've got to the weekend, I'm woken by the sound of him doing a first-class demolition job in our bedroom. He is banging about like an elephant in a china shop, opening and closing every door, rummaging around our wardrobes, making sure to rattle every hanger off one another and sighing heavily as he goes. He'd make a shite burglar.

'What are you doing, Paul?' I groan. 'It's only seven o'clock and it's Saturday. Come back to bed.'

But he doesn't answer me, or even look in my direction. He just carries on wrecking the place as he searches for God knows what.

'Paul,' I say, with a little more urgency in my voice. It's

a miracle the wains are still asleep, and I want to make the goddamn most of it and enjoy a lie-in. But if he keeps on the way he is going – pa-rump-pa-pa-pumping about like a fucking Little Drummer Boy – then the whole house will be up.

'I'm just grabbing my golf stuff,' he says. 'I'll be out of your way in a couple of minutes. Calm yourself.'

If there is one thing that I, in the words of the Grinch, 'loathe entirely', it is being told to 'calm down'. Like most people, it tends to have the completely opposite effect.

'Calm myself? I'm not the one stomping about trying my best to wake the whole house, am I? Why are you even looking for your golf stuff anyway? It's still dark. It's December. It's winter. And you do remember I have an appointment with the hairdresser and need to hit the shops before my baby shower tomorrow?'

'I'll be back around twelve, if you don't mind me having one morning in a week to myself? Your appointment isn't until two, but even if things do run on a bit you always have your ma here to take care of things. Don't you, love?' He looks like the cat who got the cream as that last line rolls off his tongue. Touché, Paul. Touché.

'Well . . .' I mumble. 'Enjoy your me time.'

'Oh don't worry,' he says, 'I will.' And with that he leaves the room (and the wardrobe doors hanging open). What the fuck is going on with him?

That's me awake for the morning now. I've no chance of getting to sleep after that wee episode of *Real Housewives of Derry*, along with Baby Gallagher deciding to stick one

147

very bony elbow right into my pelvic floor, unceremoniously waking my bladder up.

I heave myself out of bed to go to the bathroom, stopping to close the wardrobes as I go. I spot the bag of golf balls Paul normally takes with him when he's golfing. There's no way he could've missed them? Except . . . of course he *was* angry, and it *is* still dark. I might be raging with him, but I don't want him to have to drive the whole way back once he realizes he's forgotten them. I lift the bag and hustle down the stairs, where I can hear the car engine running outside. The front door is half open and I can see Paul, his breath like smoke in the crisp winter air, pouring a kettle of hot water over the windscreen to clear it.

'You forgot your balls,' I say drily. Normally he'd make a joke now. Something rude but funny. He doesn't though. He just nods, says thanks, exchanges the kettle he's holding for the bag of balls I have and gets into the car as if he hasn't a solitary care in the world.

What is happening to us? Does he really hate me that much? He doesn't give his pregnant wife, who just got out of her nice warm bed and came down here in the freezing cold to give him his golf balls, even as much as a kiss on the forehead?

My eyes begin to prickle, but NO, it's just the cold air. I will not stress about this today. I'm getting my hair done and buying myself something nice to wear and since I can't do either just yet, I'll make myself a cup of tea, curl up on the sofa and do some online shopping to pass the time. Money can't buy happiness, but it can buy a six-foot inflatable light-up outdoor reindeer, and right now it feels like the same thing – plus the inflatable snowman and Santa are incomplete without a reindeer. Add to cart.

I must drift off because I wake to a familiar pain in my neck which immediately tells me I've slept on the sofa. It's bright outside now and I can hear someone rustling about in the kitchen, Bing Crosby and David Bowie's 'Little Drummer Boy' playing on the radio. A familiar, nostalgic scent sweetly stings my nostrils.

'Breakfast is ready,' Pamela bellows in her pure Derry accent, and a flurry of footsteps rush down the stairs.

'Mornin', Mammy,' Jax says as he burrows his scruffy little bedhead into my chest. His big-boy pants are dry – I am impressed. Nathan is hot on his heels.

'Mornin' Mammy. I checked Jax's pants and his bed and he didn't do any pees, so I can go and pick his sticker now, can't I, Mammy?' He's doing a little jump of joy at the thought. It must be so magical to be six when a small piece of paper with glue on the back of it can get you so *excited*.

'Yes you can, Nathan. And you can even pick an extra one each for being such good boys.'

'Yesss!' Nathan shouts, punching the air triumphantly, which Jax immediately tries to copy and narrowly misses punching himself in the face. They both help haul me off the sofa and pull me towards the kitchen where the stickers live, and where Pamela has prepared one of my favourite foods from childhood.

'Pammy's French toast is served, everyone,' Pamela announces proudly, gesturing towards the kitchen table. Gemma, who by some miracle is awake on a Saturday morning, is looking proud as punch as she opens the cupboards and drawers and starts telling me that everything has 'a new organized place, like, because Pammy worked in a restaurant and this is how things are supposed to be, ye see'.

Christ on a bike, the 'restaurant' Pamela worked in was a fish and chip shop in the nineties, and I wouldn't mind, but she only lasted about three weeks because in her words 'the grease was no good for my pores'. But aye, fill your boots, Gemma, you believe whatever you want. If I wasn't so hungry right now, I'd feel more annoyed about the rearranged cupboards, but the smell of French toast is so irresistible that I inhale two pieces then ask for more.

My mother didn't cook much when I was a child, but she used to take notions and some days she'd cook things which were considered very fancy in Derry back then. Other people's mothers made a full Irish breakfast, my ma made French toast and bacon. Other people's mothers made a big pot of Derry stew, with Doherty's mince. My mother made creamed potatoes, steak mince and steamed veg, and you were swiftly clipped around the ear if you dared to call it 'stew'. Pamela had it in her head that if *she* cooked something then it had to be better than whatever the other mammies on our council estate cooked. It was all about appearances with Pamela. All fur coat and no knickers.

I have to admit that her French toast is the bomb, always was. It's a simple delicacy but maybe I loved it so much, and still love it now, because it was a rarity. Bread, dipped in egg yolk, fried and then topped with a sprinkle of icing sugar. In the words of Joey Tribbiani, 'What's not to like?'

'How come you've never made us French toast, Mammy?' Gemma asks.

To be honest, I'm not entirely sure. Maybe I subconsciously erased Pamela's little breakfast tradition from my memory on account of her absolutely smashing my heart to smithereens by abandoning me for a life in the sun. Call it PTSD or just being brutally broken, but it was easier to forget all about her.

However, I realize that this is probably a wee bit intense to get into with Gemma and the boys in front of Pamela, so I just shrug. 'Not sure, pet. But if you all like it, I'm sure I can make it another time.'

'We do like it!' Nathan says, taking another huge bite. 'And Wee Donkey helped to make 'em too, look!' He points to the worktop where the artist formerly known as Elfie appears to have been making snow angels out of icing sugar and has his very own mixing bowl, complete with a cracked egg in it.

'That's amazing!' I say. 'I wonder how he did that?' and I really do wonder because neither I, nor Paul, were in the form for any elf-related magic last night.

'I think he had some help,' Pamela says, nodding towards Gemma, who smiles broadly.

'Well, that was very thoughtful of whoever it was to help him,' I say, smiling at Gemma.

Never one to miss an opportunity to indulge in her favourite activity – chancing her arm – Gemma sits down beside me and briefly lays her head on my shoulder for a quick hug.

'Mammy?' she wheedles, all sweetness and light.

'I already ordered your Shein stuff.'

'It's not that, but thanks, bestie . . . Mia and the girls are going up the town today to do some Christmas shopping and I was wondering, maybe, since I've been doing my chores all week, if I could, ye know, go with them?' She is giving me the puppy-dog eyes to try and look cute, but I can see through her. I can see her left eye twitching as if she's David Banner trying to stop the Hulk from escaping.

'I'm sorry, pet,' I tell her. 'But rules are rules. You've only done one week's suspension and there's one more to go. You don't get a break from being grounded just because it's a Saturday. You know that. I want to make sure you never ever think about vaping again.'

I hear a snort of laughter from Pamela. 'Dear God, Tara, is that what this is all about? Vaping? Sure, that's nothing compared to the carry-on you got up to at that age.'

I throw her a death stare, inwardly pleading with her not to go any further with this story. But Pamela is oblivious.

'Gemma, did you know when your mammy was your age, Mrs Lynch had to call an ambulance to the school after she smoked eight cigarettes, one after the other, in school? She fainted, and even managed to burn a hole in her new blazer – and I'd not long finished paying up for it in Ferguson's either.'

Fuck. Pamela has completely sunk me. I look at Gemma, watching in fear as she processes this brand-new information. I glance at Pamela, who's wearing a smug, self-satisfied expression of 'And I have plenty more stories to tell . . .' and then I look back to Gemma: shit is about to go sideways.

'You got caught *smoking*?' she asks, her voice growing louder with every word. 'And you fainted, in school? OMG, maybe you are human after all,' she scoffs angrily. 'You had the cheek to tell me how "disappointed" you were in me, even though you'd done the exact same thing? Except it wasn't the same thing, was it? You were more disgusting. At least I didn't buy actual cigarettes or burn anything. OMG, this is priceless! Talk about double standards!'

She stands up and storms from the room and up the stairs.

I turn to look at Pamela, who seems quite amused by the whole thing.

'Mammy, why?' I gasp. 'Do you know what you've just done for my parenting credibility?'

'Ach, calm down, Tara,' she says, and now I can feel *my* inner Hulk threatening to escape. 'It doesn't do wains any harm to realize their parents make mistakes too. And to be honest, I think you're being a wee bit harsh on her. It's not like she robbed a bank or something.'

'Jesus Christ, that's not the point!'

'Mammmeee,' Nathan says, cutting in. 'Remember Miss Rose says you're not apposed to say Jesus's name unless it is in a prayer and if you do say Jesus's name you have to bow your head.' He bows his head solemnly and icing sugar floats from his nose to the table.

I don't want to go full Nicolas Rage in front of the boys, so I take a deep breath. 'You're right, pet. Thanks for reminding me.'

'You is welcome, Mammy,' he says as Jax takes the opportunity to say Jesus a couple of times, head banging as if he's at an Iron Maiden concert.

'Right,' I say, trying to work out how to fix this mess. 'You sit with the boys, Mammy, and start their crafts with them. They want to make paper chains to hang on the tree, and maybe some cards. I'll go talk to Gemma.'

Pamela looks back at me as if I'm speaking a whole new language. 'Love, I don't think arts and crafts are my strong suit. Do they not do enough of all that craic in school, like?'

'Mammy, just sit with them and make sure they don't sniff the glue or stick sequins up their noses. It's not hard. They'll let you know what they want to do.'

Nathan nods enthusiastically. 'I will help you, Pammy. Just remember don't paint the walls acuz my mammy doesn't like that.'

The unbreakable Pamela suddenly looks very breakable indeed. 'But, love,' she says, eyes slightly wild now. 'I haven't a notion half the time what they're talking about and the younger one just seems to make noises.'

'Jax,' I say. 'The younger one is called Jax. The older one is called Nathan.' I swallow what I want to say: she doesn't understand their references because she hasn't taken the time to get to know them. While it is a messy shitemare, doing arts and crafts with the boys, it can also actually be fun and qualifies as quality time, something she knows nothing about. I want to ask her why she needs me to remind her of the names of her own fucking grandchildren. I want to tell her they are amazing and funny, and yes, insane, but that's what makes them so loveable. I want to tell her she is not going to reject my children the way she rejected me.

'I can talk to Gemma,' she squawks, clearly in plea-bargaining mode. 'I'll tell her I got confused, that you were older when you were caught smoking. And that you were a good child. Never gave me a moment's trouble.' Desperation is clear in every word.

Now that might be a good idea. Yes, I could stomp up the stairs and talk to the Devil wears Converse, but she would likely just block me out. Her darling 'Pammy' might be in with a chance of getting her to listen though.

I think of their relationship and I remind myself why I asked Pamela to stay for Christmas in the first place – because it seems she can get through to my daughter.

'OK,' I say, before turning to my boys. 'Let's put these dishes in the sink and get our arts and craft stuff out.'

They both cheer and I refocus on them, this moment, and how cute they are.

We sit and stick, cut, and colour while the Geneva

Peace Talks continue upstairs. I don't hear shouting, which must be a good thing. The boys want to draw, and I watch as Jax draws (well, scribbles) all over a page with a green crayon before telling me it's a 'kwissmass tree'. I declare it the prettiest tree I have ever seen – it deserves a place on the much-coveted 'Le Fridge Door Gallery'.

'Can my picture go on the fridge too?' Nathan asks, pushing his page under my nose. At first glance it looks as if he has drawn a nativity scene, but on closer inspection it's actually a brown woman standing with two cows.

'Who's that, pet?' I ask.

'It's Pammy and her bestest calves in Derry,' he says earnestly. I have to stifle my laughter – this is priceless.

'Oh this is going on the fridge, dote,' I tell him. 'This is a masterpiece.'

'What's a masterpiece?' Pamela says, walking back into the kitchen, hopefully having successfully brokered the Good Gallagher Agreement.

'Look,' I say smiling, 'Nathan drew a picture of you!' I wave the page in front of her face and she looks at it, confused.

'And them's your two bestest calves in the whole of Derry!' Nathan says proudly.

I expect her to laugh, or at least crack a smile. She doesn't. She just nods and says a very insincere 'Well done, very good,' before adding under her breath, 'I don't think that really looks like me though.'

I watch as Nathan's smile falters.

'Well done, pet,' I announce loudly to cover the

awkward moment. 'Maybe Pammy needs glasses because it is pure class.' He smiles again and I stick the boys' pictures on the fridge.

'How did it go with Gemma?' I ask sternly, turning back to Pamela. 'Is it safe for me to go up there and talk to her?'

'Well you could try,' Pamela says. 'But she's not there. I asked her to go into Boots and pick me up a few things. Thought it would do her some good to get fresh air.'

I close my eyes and take a deep breath.

'Hold on, let me get this straight. You asked Gemma to go into town, because she was annoyed that I wouldn't let her go into town?' I can feel a twitch developing in my right eye.

'Aye,' Pamela says, dismissively. 'She's doing a chore, and if she meets up with her pals while she's there, well, sure that's just a coincidence. Everyone's happy, and no harm done.'

Before I can open my mouth, she claps her hands. 'Right, boys, will we tidy up all this crap, I mean crafts?' My boys do as they are told and I seethe at just how much Pamela disregards my parenting style.

Paul was right. In every way. But I don't know where I stand with him right now, so I'm not going to tell him he was right. Not yet anyway.

16

It's my baby shower, and I'll cry if I want to

Sunday, 11 December

Sunday dawns and I am still fuming with Pamela's antics yesterday, not to mention feeling completely in the dark about Paul's coldness towards me. But I have vowed to push any negativity aside because today is the day of the baby shower and, as Lizzo would say, I'm feeling good as hell. It really is amazing what a little Saturday afternoon pampering and getting changed out of your Christmas jammies can do to lift your spirits.

My nails are festively shimmering thanks to a fresh nail polish in the shade Christmas Crimson. My crooked crown of black roots has been banished and a silky tiara of ash blonde now sits in its place, blow-dried, teased and curled. I've dusted my eyes with a mauve shadow and my lashes are lifted and curled with mascara, giving me a doe-eyed vixen look, and I've even managed a little contouring, which isn't easy on my pregnancy-puffy face. But it works. Just about . . . I finish the look off with a slick of nude gloss. It's the first time I've worn full make-up in months and although I barely recognize myself in the mirror, I feel like me again.

Dressed in a cream and black floral tiered maternity dress, with 100 denier opaque tights and my trusty and comfortable as hell black Doc Martens, I am a MILF today, even if I say so myself. But, as it happens, I'm not the only one to think I'm looking all milfy.

'Wow,' Paul says, with a deep intake of breath. The kind of intake of breath that only comes when there is blood rushing to a certain part of the body. 'You look amazing.'

I revel in his gaze, even though I'm still thrown by his shifty and shitty behaviour yesterday. It's so lovely to see him look at me in a way he hasn't for a long time; I want to enjoy it, and moreover to pull him close and snog the face off him. But we're not in that place and it would feel awkward. Plus, I don't want to wreck this make-up because the chances of me getting to go full glam again any time in the next six months are pretty minimal. New baby and contouring? Hell to the no.

The plan is for Paul to drop me off at the Bishop's Gate Hotel and take the boys to Brunswick Moviebowl while I spend time with 'the girls'. I admire his bravery because the Moviebowl (which encompasses a huge soft play area, restaurant, café, pool tables, amusements and a cinema) is insanely busy at the best of times. A couple of weeks before Christmas? It's next-level nuts. Great for small kids, minus craic for parents of small kids who have to accompany said small children through ball pits and tunnels and foam-covered obstacle courses. Hordes of families enjoying quality time together mixed with people out for Christmas lunch, or early drinks before their Christmas parties? My idea of hell right now. The boys, of course, are insane with excitement at the prospect, and that's before they've even had any sugar.

Then again, faced with a choice between the Moviebowl on one of the busiest days of the year and my mother in full party mode . . . it's hard to know which has the most potential to go spectacularly tits-up.

Still, I thank Paul for his compliment – push his unusual behaviour of late out of my mind – and get ready to enjoy my day. And this is *my* day. This is the bit where I get to be treated like the queen I am, where I get to enjoy the fun side of an impending new arrival. You know, before the contractions and the tearing and the . . . Yes, well, the less said about that side of things today, the better.

I've not been told much about what to expect, except that Amanda and Cat have worked together on the arrangements. They've invited the Rebel Mums, and the Ys from work and a few of my cousins. Gemma and Pamela are both coming, of course. They've been getting ready since 9 a.m. and you'd swear they were the ones about to deliver a baby and not me.

When we arrive at the hotel, a smart woman in a strong

trouser suit leads us through a huge arch of blue, yellow and pink balloons, laced together with golden ribbon, into a private function room. A central table is scattered with blue and pink confetti in the shape of bottles and dummies. Each place setting is perfectly laid out for afternoon tea with fine bone china plates, cups and saucers, and to add to that little bit of magic, in the corner of the room is a ceiling-height Christmas tree festooned with delicate glass baubles in frosted green and gold. Fairy lights twinkle from the ceiling and are also artfully displayed around a beautiful floral centre, surrounded by silver-framed pictures of Gemma, Nathan and Jax as babies printed off in sepia tones. A fourth frame, with the image of a question mark, sits alongside them. I listen as Gemma and my mother 'ooh' and 'aah' in approval. Gemma doesn't even kick off at her baby picture being on show – possibly because Pamela is telling her what a beautiful baby she was.

A bubble of emotion (and snot) rises up in me. This is beautiful. My girls have never let me down before and I knew they wouldn't today. Amanda is waiting for me at the head of the table.

'Awww Tara, you look stunning,' she wails, crushing me into a tight hug, and I have to grin at her like a madwoman or I'll ruin my make-up with tears.

'Aw pet, don't cry.' She squeezes my hand (when did she get so bloody perceptive?) and ushers me to my seat at the top of the table, where the most extravagant bouquet of flowers I think I have ever seen is waiting for me on my chair. This is no £20 from M&S effort. Serious money has been spent here, and for a moment my heart lifts, wondering if Paul is declaring a truce through the medium of flowers. But when I glance at the card, I see it's addressed to 'Tara The Ride' and I know they can only be from one person.

Cat has been calling me 'Tara The Ride' for the last fifteen years, occasionally shortening it to TTR in text messages when she wants to remind me I still have it. As I open the card I look around the room, expecting to see her watching my reaction like a hawk. But she's not there. And when I start to read, my heart sinks to my boots.

Tara, I'm so sorry to miss your big day. Please forgive me? Love you, Cat xxx

'Who are they from?' calls Amanda as she shuffles some stuff around further down the table. She's looking extremely ridey in a slinky body-con frock, a cream clutch bag tucked under her arm, and a white 'Tara's Baby Shower' sash.

'Cat,' I say, my voice cracking. I stop and take a deep breath. 'They're from Cat. She's not coming. Did you know? What's going on, Amanda?'

Amanda looks as confused as I feel, and I know that reaction is genuine. Amanda has always been the worst liar in the world.

'I haven't a clue,' she says, taking the card and reading it as if she expects it to say 'only joking, bish!' at the end. 'She must've been here earlier – because this wasn't me.

She was in charge of decorations. Maybe I should phone her and see what's up?' She hands me back the card and reaches in her bag for her phone.

'No,' I say. 'Don't. She's not coming, let her just get on with whatever it is in her life that is more important than twenty-odd years of friendship.' I know I sound like a brat, but Jesus Christ, I'm not sure I can take another rejection, and especially not from Cat on today of all days. She should be here. I need her. I need to talk to her about Paul, and Gemma and oh my God, do I need to talk to her about my mother. But more than that, she's my best friend. She should be here. Instead she's sent flowers, and not even bothered to phone me and tell me why. Well, if I'm not worthy of her company then that's her loss, my anger surfacing to keep the hurt away. Fuck her. I'm going to enjoy this day with the people who can be bothered to show up for me when I need them.

'I'm ready for my sash,' I say to Amanda with a sniff, and she drapes it over my shoulders. I'm pretty sure Beyoncé would keep her queen energy and get on with her day with dignity if Kelly Rowland didn't attend her baby shower. So that's what I'm going to do.

When the door next opens, the Rebel Mums, led by Eva, parade in carrying gift bags, balloons and flowers.

'There she is,' shrieks Eva, a gorgeous, incredible woman who invited me to be part of the Rebel Mums all those months ago. She has her arms wide open as she walks across the room. 'Queen T! Look at you! It's been too long, Tara, but I have to say, pregnancy suits you. You're a total RIDE!' She laughs and I allow her to envelop me in a giant hug, breathing in a lungful of her expensive perfume as I do so. As the others take turns to hug me and hand over presents – for me as well as for the baby – I find myself once again getting emotional. These girls have made such a massive effort when Cat can't even be here.

'Girls, this is amazing,' I sniff. 'I can't believe you've gone to all this trouble when I've been so rubbish at keeping in touch. It's just, with being pregnant, I didn't want to hold you all back from your usual adventures. And then there was just so much going on and it's been tough and I didn't want to be a craic killer with all my melodramatics . . .' I tail off at a tearful pitch only dogs can hear.

If Eva is taken aback by my crying, she doesn't let it show. She just pulls me into another hug and gently rubs my back. 'We are always here to listen. To the good stuff and the bad stuff. That's what we're about. All us mammies – all in this same leaking boat together. We've been there, love. Pregnancy sucks balls and anyone who tells you otherwise is a liar. You're a Rebel Mum, Tara, and don't forget it. You're with us for life and you can't get away that easy!'

'Exactly,' Kerry chimes in, to a chorus of 'For defs' and 'Yups' from the other mammies. 'You're our Beyoncé. We'd be lost without you, so cut yourself some slack. You've three wains and you're knocked up again. That would fry anyone's head.'

She joins in the hug, and then I feel another set of arms around me. And another. And another. Until I am surrounded by love, support, understanding and solidarity. Not to mention a mix of umpteen different perfumes which become a little too strong for my pregnancy nose sense of smell, so I break free. I would be absolutely showed if I boked at my own baby shower. Not when I'm wearing a sash and looking this good.

Next to arrive are the Ys, who I can hear coming before the door opens – their high-pitched squeaks of excitement travelling down the hall in front of them. Dressed like they're on their way to a club in super-short skirts and six-inch heels, they come bearing gifts. Not so much the Three Wise Men, as the Three Not-Wise Work Colleagues.

I'm presented with a large card which they tell me is from all at ToteTech. I'd love to open it and see if it contains a generous monetary gift for Baby Gallagher, but as I've always told my kids as they tear through cards in search of cash on their birthdays, it's rude to make it all about the money. (But what's a card without money, eh?)

'You are looking pure class,' Amy gushes.

'Yep. I can't get over it. You look amazing, especially considering the fact you're about to pop,' Molly adds.

'And at your age,' Lucy chimes in. I'd be offended if I didn't know these girls better. They're not bitchy as I'd once thought, they are just incredibly young and equally immature. To them, thirty-six is old. I just smile and nod, knowing that all this is waiting for them later in life.

'We got you a wee something just from us,' Amy says,

pushing a beautifully wrapped gift box in my direction. Buried beneath layers of tissue paper are perhaps the most gorgeously dinky and perfect ivory Dior baby booties. I imagine them on the feet of this tiny baby currently inside me and once again my eyes fill up with tears. Lawdy me, but I opened a gate earlier.

Amanda arrives on cue to hand them glasses of Nosecco (Amanda decreed there was to be no alcohol because if I can't drink, it's only right that no one else can – solidarity, yo!). Just as she goes to show them to their seats, Amy asks: 'How come you left work early? We thought you'd another week to go and then you just, like disappeared?'

So, Handley hasn't admitted his dickish behaviour then? Although I suppose I can understand why he'd want to keep that particular HR blunder under his hat. I could throw him under the bus right now, but I remind myself that I'm anti-negativity today so I hold my tongue.

'I, umm, well I was just starting to feel really tired and I had some holiday time still owed so I decided to take some extra days.'

Molly and Lucy glance at each other before Molly speaks in a whisper, 'We heard you flipped out in his office the last day you were in.'

I feel my cheeks rush red. 'Well, I wouldn't say flipped out, but . . . look, I'll fill you in another time, OK?' I really don't want to get into ToteTech's massive misogyny problem here and now. Not when there is Nosecco to be drunk and cake to be eaten.

'Well, look, if he was messing you around or anything,

we've got your back,' Lucy says, and the other two Ys nod in agreement.

'Thanks, girls,' I say. 'Now, who wants to sniff a chocolate-filled nappy and guess which type of chocolate it is?'

Their eyes pop, but they giggle and nod anyway, lifting their glasses of non-alcoholic fizz to their lips and drinking. 'This isn't too bad, actually,' Amy says.

I take a sip and grimace. It's not great either. 'It'll do,' I say, 'but let me tell you, I am so looking forward to a bottle of the real deal as soon as this baby is delivered. I'm not even going to wait for the placenta to arrive before I'm cracking open a bottle!'

They give me that look. The one that lets me know once again that I have managed to completely horrify them with any mention of birth.

'Does the placenta not come out with the baby?' Molly asks, bravely. But before I have the chance to answer, the doors slam open and there stands Pamela, bottle of definitely-not-Nosecco raised above her head. I hadn't even realized she had left the room, but clearly she had found a bar.

There's a familiar stagger to her walk.

She's monkeyed. Absolutely steamboat drunk and as she climbs on a chair, brandishing a hairbrush as a make-shift microphone, it's clear that Pammy has come to party.

17

Total eclipse of the Pamela

There is nothing quite like the sight of Pamela Sweeney, hair backcombed to within an inch of its life, wobbling on a chair with one eye in town and the other eye away home.

'Quiet, everyone!' she booms.

'Mammy,' I hiss. 'Get down! Are you drunk? How are you drunk?'

'Well,' she says, taking a slug from her Prosecco bottle. 'It turns out there's a bar in this hotel and they sell alcohol to adults who want a drink! Hahaha.' She hiccups loudly.

I grab the bottle from her hand, noticing a waitress in the corner of the room watching intently, obviously starting to wonder if she should go and get a manager. I raise my hand and nod to her in universal sign language for 'It's OK, I'll sort this' and thankfully she nods back.

'God, Tara, when did you get so boring!' Pamela says,

before addressing the crowd. 'Don't worry, ladies. I have a sneaky bottle of vodka in my bag. Who wants to pay hotel prices?' The waitress no longer seems assured that I will indeed sort this.

'Mammy, for God's sake get down!'

I can hear awkward, embarrassed giggles from the Ys and some of my cousins, who will no doubt be sending videos of the returned prodigal mother to all of our relatives. Gemma is watching intently, her eyes wide.

'I will get down,' Pamela says, adopting a fake cockney English accent. 'But first, I want to sing a song for my baby girl, Tara, on her shower baby . . . baby shower . . .' She takes a deep breath and then starts to sing 'Total Eclipse of the Heart' – flipping between singing the turn around bit and the verse in different keys. She has just reached the third turn around when I lose my shit. I am humiliated, angry and reminded of just how selfish Pamela Sweeney can be. This is the straw that breaks my back.

'Mammy!' I shout, loud enough to silence the room – and I think the bar next door. 'Would you stop embarrassing me, and yourself. Standing there in your sixties, like the oldest swinger in town, drunk on a chair trying to sing – you sound more like a banshee trying to yodel. Stop trying to be a cool pub singer. You have never been cool and you certainly aren't now. You're an embarrassment and I wish to God you'd never come back!'

The room is silent, apart from a loud intake of breath as Pamela sheepishly steps down off the chair and hands me the hairbrush/microphone. The look in her eyes is one of pure hurt, and I think I might have gone too far, but this is Pamela we're talking about. She always has to swan in wherever she is and make *everything* about her. Was it too much to ask that she didn't drink? Was it too much to ask that she didn't stand on a chair and sing a cheesy eighties power ballad while pissed as a fart? At my baby shower!

'Mammy,' I hear Gemma say, and turn to see her looking absolutely disgusted. And not fake teenage 'I'm a wee shite' disgusted but actually, properly disgusted at me.

'OMG, that's awful talking to your own mother like that. I can't believe you just did it!' She reaches a hand out to a now tearful Pamela, who grabs on to her as if she is Jack and Gemma is Rose on top of the wooden door. Right now though, Pamela more resembles Jack Sparrow than Jack Dawson, and she's had more than a mega-pint.

'C'mon, Pammy,' Gemma says, 'Let's get a taxi home.'

She throws me the most filthy look I have ever seen in my life. The kind of look that brings a sting with it. Just before they turn to leave, Pamela looks at me, mascara-tracked tears streaming through her heavily applied foundation.

'I'm sorry I embarrassed you, love. I was just trying to make things *hiccup* a bit more fun, you know *hiccup*. Liven it up a bit. No offence to tea and all like but tea is boring.' She sniffs at Amanda, and then, arm now linked with Gemma's, they leave.

Fuck my actual life.

I feel a hand take mine, and give it a squeeze. It's

Amanda, and I know Amanda gets it because Amanda knows what Pamela is really like. Amanda, along with Cat and Paul, has been there to pick up the pieces time and time again when Pamela pulled a Pamela.

'Right,' Amanda says brightly, bringing the room's attention back to her. 'I think maybe it's time we had some tea and sandwiches.'

Maybe other women would say their appetite had disappeared at this stage, but not me. I'm always hungry. Even when I'm not gestating a baby elephant, I eat my feelings on a regular basis, so I lunge for the sandwiches while everyone else makes awkward conversation.

#BabyShowerFail.

'Everyone will think I'm the biggest bitch that ever walked the face of the planet now, won't they?' I whisper to Amanda, through a mouthful of chicken salad sandwich. I'm not even trying to display good table manners any more.

'Sweetheart, you can't control what other people think or do, only how you react to it. But that said, I'm sure they realize there must be something more going on behind the scenes that caused you to lose the head that way. They'd have to be emotionally stunted not to.'

I nod, as if I understand Amanda's psychobabble. When did she become so in tune with feelings and emotional growth? Surely this isn't related to the sex counselling? I wince at the thought, then remember how Paul looked at me before I left the house today and wonder should I find out more about it. But no, not now. Now I have tiny pastries of perfection to shovel into my face as fast as I can, and before everyone else tries to eat them, or worse, the staff take them away.

With filo pastry flaking and falling from my mouth on to my hugely enlarged boobs, I say, 'Amanda. I just don't know how to take her. She's moved in. Paul is losing the bap over it. Gemma is so pleased with herself that she has a new bestie who isn't afraid to put me in my place, and the boys haven't really a scooby who this woman is. Did I tell you she doesn't let them call her Granny? It's Pammy. Like she's that doll out of *Baywatch* that runs up the beach in slow motion, threatening to have someone's eye out with her knockers?'

'Pamela Anderson?' Amanda says.

'Aye, didn't she get people to call her Pammy too? I mean I don't mind that she doesn't want to be called Granny, but I do mind that she walks in and takes over as if I haven't been running my own life perfectly well for the last twenty-odd years since she fucked off to Costa del Buck a Pool Boy.'

'I'm sensing a lot of pain here,' Amanda says. 'Have you spoken to her about how you feel?'

I snort, and a bit of pastry flies out of my nose but I'm past being embarrassed by myself.

'Talk to Pamela? Are you wise? We don't do heart-to-hearts, you know that. Everything with Pammy is strictly on the superficial level. We don't have that kind of a relationship.'

Amanda raises her eyebrows and stays quiet while I

wait for her words of wisdom. But she just keeps looking at me like she's my therapist and I'm lying on one of those leather couches. It's starting to get a bit awkward.

'Well,' she says eventually, 'there's your answer. You need to have the conversation. Even if it's uncomfortable. That's the only way to lance the emotional boil.'

I look at the egg mayonnaise sandwich I was about to eat and feel my stomach turn. The thought of having a deep and meaningful with Pamela has turned me, and I put the sandwich back on my plate. I think I'm done.

18

I came here to sleigh

Monday, 12 December

It's the morning after the baby shower and even though not one drop of alcohol touched my lips, I have the fear. This, I suspect, is what Amanda would call 'an emotional hangover'. (Seriously, she's full-on into all this analyst bullshit. I'm not knocking it, it suits her and look, at least one of us is getting the ride on a regular basis.)

Yesterday had loads of nice parts, but the not so nice parts keep repeating on me – much like the three apple puff pastries I inhaled.

It's 6 a.m. and I'm wide awake, but not because there's a child requiring my attention, or someone has peed the bed, or projectile vomited everywhere. It's because there's a wee guilt demon gnawing away at my very soul and it's related to every single member of my family.

Pamela stayed in her room when I got home last night, so we still haven't addressed the karaoke meltdown, but to be honest, I feel awful for how I spoke to her, even though she absolutely did make a complete hallion of herself. Gemma, more overtly on no-speakies with me last night as she huffed around the house, has clearly lost what little respect she had left for me. And Paul is . . . well, Paul was exhausted after a day at the Moviebowl with the boys and wasn't in the form for talking when I got home. Nor was I, if the truth be told. I was exhausted and feeling just as drained as Paul claimed he was feeling.

As for the boys themselves? Well, I can't help but feel I'm heading for a crisis in the mammy department. I'm acutely aware that in a few short weeks, there will be another baby in the house who will demand the lion's share of my attention for quite some time. What if my boys feel rejected? Jax is only two. He's still a baby too.

Mammy guilt (the bastard!) pokes at me until I decide it's time to do what I do best, and that's deck the halls and not my mother. It is, after all, the most wonderful time of the year and normally I totally sleigh it (not even one bit sorry for that pun) when it comes to making Christmas come alive for my family. There's still time to rescue this year – pregnancy or not. It's time for me to get my festive shit together and turn this nightmare before Christmas around.

I sneak out of bed (no easy feat when you're 'built like a house', as my Granny Sweeney would say). I'm determined not to wake anyone, least of all Paul. I want him to remember how class I am and how I'm not always a snot-filled emotional bag of dramatics. I want him to feel loved: not just appreciated but loved, for ensuring all of our happiness while neglecting his own. So I let him sleep. When he gets up later, I want him to have nothing to worry about except getting himself to work. I'll do the school run. I'll make the breakfasts. I'll write the note to Miss Rose apologizing that Nathan hasn't done his homework (again) and apologizing in advance for whatever he is likely to say or do this week.

Creeping downstairs, I formulate a plan to make today the day that Christmas magic arrives at our home. I want Paul to know that his Mrs Claus is back in action and committed to creating the most magical family Christmas ever.

There's been another heavy frost overnight and while it is really pretty to look out and see the sparkle on the grass and pavements, it means this house is absolutely bloody baltic. I ignore my screaming purse strings and the stark rise in heating prices, and I whack the heating on full blast. Warmth is needed for this cosy morning scene that I'm about to create. I circle the living room and hall, lighting my cinnamon- and vanilla-scented candles to fill the air with festive Christmas aromas.

Now, to breakfast. I'm not a complete martyr: I do boil the kettle to make myself a cup of coffee first. As I reach for the coffee canister, I spot my nemesis – Wee Donkey – grinning at me like a Chucky doll from the worktop where he was left yesterday after Pammy's French toast feast. I'm committed to the cause here, so I'm going to have to think of something epic to do with the wee shite before the boys get up. I sip my coffee and have a good look around me. I want it to be something that will blow their minds. Think, Tara. Think!

Then I remember their craft stuff from Saturday and a thought comes to mind. This might just work. Pulling out a box of art materials, I find the packet of googly eye stickers the boys insisted I buy months ago but have never used. I'm sure I've seen Amanda do this one with her girls.

I open the fridge, and set about giving every single item, even the out-of-date block of parmesan cheese that might be older than Jax himself, a set of eyes. Then I grab the Wee Donkey and a face cloth from the hot press. I wrap that smug little elf bastard up as if he's freezing and in need of a blanket and I hide him on the top shelf of the fridge, right beside a tray of strawberries.

I give him the finger before closing the door. Because I'm petty and he deserves it for appearing early.

I fetch the children's bags and coats and make sure they have everything they need for school. I even iron Paul's work overalls, which is extremely domesticated even for me because I don't iron anything if I can get away with it. I'm an anti-iron mammy and proud of it, sure that's what tumble dryers are for.

I'm feeling Christmassy AF now, and have even got Alexa to blast me some festive classics. As Wham! start singing 'Last Christmas', I bop (well it's more of a shuffle) around the kitchen, using a wooden spoon for a microphone as I set the table with all my best Christmas necessities, including a holly jolly tablecloth, placemats and centrepiece, and matching plates and cups with wee candy canes dancing around the edges. I have it all.

Then I go to work popping some sweet waffles in the toaster and setting out a selection of sprinkles, syrup, chopped strawberries and the boys' favourite, Nutella, ready for them to help themselves. It looks so class when I'm done that I snap a picture for Instagram and plan to completely smug-mammy post the shit out of it once the boys are at school. Hashtag making memories.

For my final trick before I brave waking the children, I fill a large glass with water and ice and grab a couple of paracetamol. It's not much of a peace offering but it's a start. I climb the stairs, open Pamela's door (because we finally cleared her space in the spare room) just a crack and leave the water and tablets on the chest of drawers by the bed. I sneak out as quietly as I can before crossing the hall and into Gemma's room, but clearly I'm not as quiet as I thought as she wakes with her usual grace and joy at a brand-new day.

'Eugh! Do I have to get up already? It's still dark outside. That's child abuse. I hate my life!' she moans.

I smile as sweetly as I can and rest my hand gently on her shoulder. 'No, love. You don't *have* to get up. But if you're hungry, there's waffles with Nutella and fresh strawberries downstairs on the table. But if you want to lie in, then feel free, pet.'

At the very mention of food she comes to life, sitting up fast enough that I move just in time to avoid getting head-butted right in the nose. 'Is that what that smell is? OMG, I'm starving now.'

'OK,' I say, 'and if you want to go back to bed for a wee while after you've eaten, that's grand too.'

She eyes me suspiciously. 'I'm not being cheeky or anything, Mammy. But are you OK? Did you have a wee stroke, or have you been sniffing glue or something? I've my chores to do. I can't go back to bed.'

'You can today. I think you've earned a wee lazy day.'

She grins at me, but I haven't even played my winning hand yet. I reach into my pocket and take out her phone, handing it to her. 'I think you've earned this bad boy for a bit too,' I say.

She bounces out of bed and wraps her arms around me tightly, just like she used to when she was wee. It's enough to bring a lump to my throat and a tear to my eye.

'OMG, bestie! Thank you soooooo much!' she shrieks, directly into my ear, almost bursting my eardrum, but I'm enjoying the closeness with her too much to care.

When I do pull away, I take her hand. 'Listen, Gemma. I wanted to talk to you about yesterday with Pammy. I know I shouldn't have spoken to her like that, and especially not in front of everyone. But I was so embarrassed at her getting drunk at my baby shower, and then her starting to sing. Can you imagine how you would feel if I pulled a stunt like that on you?'

Gemma snorts. 'Uhhh, Mammy, what about my thirteenth birthday party and the Steps routine? Or my last sleepover with Mia and the Spice Girls routine? Or the St Patrick's Day parade and the B*Witched routine? I mean I could go on, bro.' She rolls her eyes so far back it feels like a solid six seconds before they come round to centre.

'It's not the same,' I tell her; denial is a lovely place to live.

'If you say so, bestie,' she laughs and hugs me again. I want to tell her just how complicated my relationship with Pamela really is, but she's happy and it's a joy to see, and I am not going to piss on her chips.

'Mammy!' she blurts, all of a sudden, her eyes stark with panic. 'The Wee Donkey! I forgot to do something with him last night. Let me do it quick before you wake the boys.'

'It's OK, love,' I say, and that bloody lump is back in my throat as I see how she has taken on responsibility for making sure the boys retain that sense of Christmas magic in my selfish absence. It's a lot of responsibility on young shoulders and I know how hard that can be. 'I did something earlier,' I tell her.

'Will we go wake them then?' Gemma says, and I nod. Although a part of me doesn't want to wake them yet. A part of me wants to sit here and enjoy this closeness with my beautiful daughter. These moments are few and far between these days and yes, while I know I have bought her affection with a day off her chores and use of her phone, I don't feel bad. I will enjoy it for as long as I possibly can.

I'm just about to go in for another hug when the boys burst out of their room, hair sticking in every direction, eyes sleepy and, in Nathan's case, with a serious PJ bum wedgie.

'I smell Nutella,' Nathan says. When it comes to chocolate, he's like a sniffer dog, that one.

'My smell it too,' Jax says, stumbling towards me. 'Mammy, Gemma, no pee in my bed today!'

'Good boy!' Gemma chimes. 'Will we go use the potty, wash our hands and go and find the Nutella?'

Nathan looks at Gemma suspiciously. 'Gemma, I don't fink you should use the potty. Your bum is way too big and I fink you would break it.'

'You're such a wee asshole,' Gemma snaps, and I brace myself for my blissful, Hallmark Christmas movie moment to disappear in a tsunami of teenage rage while at the same time shooting her a look that says, 'What did I tell you about calling your brothers assholes?' Maybe she sees the fear in my eyes, or maybe she wants to hang on to the perfect morning too because she takes a deep breath and stands up, taking her brothers by the hands. 'I still love you though, Nathan,' she says.

He smiles. 'S'OK. I love you too and sometimes Mammy says you're an asshole too.'

Thankfully she laughs, and I offer up a wee prayer to the ghost of Christmas present that I have dodged another couple of bullets.

My darling offspring are all seated at the table tucking into their breakfast when Jax shifts a little in his seat.

'What is it, pet? Do you need to use your potty again?' I ask.

'Nope,' he says. 'Where is the Wee Donkey? My can't see him!'

This sparks Inspector Nathan's detective skills and he glances every which way around the kitchen, trying to find him. Thankfully the Wee Donkey is not covered in Nutella, or Nathan would be able to sniff him out quicker than a German shepherd would find a kilo of cocaine in customs. Even Gemma looks confused. Is she doubting my amazing Elf-related organizational skills?

'Mammmmeeee,' Nathan says. 'I can't find him!'

I stand, back against the counter, and tap my finger on my lip. 'Hmmmm. Maybe he's having a wee day off?'

The boys' faces fall.

'That's cwap,' Nathan says, spearing the last of his strawberries and taking a big bite.

'We don't say cwap, I mean crap,' Gemma says. 'It's rude.'

Jesus, is this wee girl going for a sainthood? Not that I'm knocking it or anything.

'You just said it,' Nathan says, defiantly. 'And Mammy says it all the time.'

He's not lying, but now is not time for a further discussion about age-appropriate language. 'Nathan,' I say, 'Can you get me some more strawberries from the fridge? Please?'

'OK den,' he says and gets off his chair, his head lowered as if he is a condemned man walking the Green Mile, muttering about the Wee Donkey being 'cwap' and 'an asshole' in a whisper that isn't quite quiet enough to go unheard. I say nothing, and just wait until he opens the fridge door and is greeted by the sight of twenty pairs of googly eyes and a rather chilled Wee Donkey peeking out at him.

There is a moment's pause before he bursts into uncontrollable laughter, prompting Jax to jump off his seat to see what all the fuss is about.

'Mammy! Gemma! Come see!' Nathan calls. 'The Wee Donkey is sooooo funny!'

Gemma gives me a wee smile, and says, quiet enough that the boys can't hear her, 'Good job, Ma!' just as Nathan lifts the Wee Donkey from the shelf in the fridge and says: 'You're not cwap. I'm sowwy.'

Once the boys have finished breakfast, I hurry them upstairs to get washed and changed. This is the week of the big nativity play (after which I will ceremoniously burn the innkeeper costume and ban all singing of songs which require percussion accompaniment). Their excitement is at fever pitch, which makes keeping them focused on such basics as putting their pants on the right way round and brushing more than one tooth at the front of their mouth difficult. But I do it, and Gemma even helps.

We're just about ready when Paul emerges from our bedroom looking dishevelled and mega confused. 'Did I

19

Put me on the naughty list, please

'Are you OK?' Paul asks, one eyebrow raised.

'Yes,' I tell him, reaching over and giving him a peck on the cheek. 'I just thought it was time I got my shit together and kicked off Christmas properly in this house. Things with Handley being a dick and Cat being MIA have had me moping around, and I realized I need to focus on what I can control, and that's making things special for the wains and us.' I swear I hear Amanda's voice in my head urging me on. I'm sure that after the dramatics of the baby shower yesterday, he will have assumed I'd be in self-destruct pity-party mode all day. Can't lie – normally that's exactly how things would play out. He must be delighted to know he won't have to spend the day talking me down, and it dawns on me that maybe that's what he meant when he said I was draining.

Paul smiles, and for a change it is genuine and lovely and more than a little bit sexy. 'No one brings Christmas magic the way you do, Tara.'

He pulls me into a hug and, even though there's a faint whiff of morning breath in the air, I revel in the manliness of him as he holds me. I can feel that he loves me. This hug isn't forced or out of duty, it's one top-quality, all-in hug and I sink into it, not remembering the last time we hugged this way. I've missed it. And I've missed him. Yes, he's been here, and we've slept in the same bed every night, but I don't think either of us have been particularly present. And that might be more down to me than I've previously considered. Even I know I can be a total pain in the hole when I'm in my worst tired and needy mode.

I pull back and look up at him. 'And you, Paul, are you OK?'

He nods. 'Aye, love. I've had a lot on my mind, but it's so good to see you smiling this morning.'

Our hug is hijacked by the two very excited boys (Nutella and sprinkles for breakfast equals sugar rush equals good luck, Miss Rose, I'll no doubt be speaking to you later).

'Daddeeeeeee,' Jax squeals. 'The Wee Donkey was hiding in the fridge with funny eyes.'

'Was he now?' Paul asks, hunkering down to eye level with the boys.

'He was,' Nathan says, butting in with a more corrective analysis. 'He put googly eyes on all the fings like this.' He

186

makes his eyes go cross-eyed, which Jax tries to copy and they both look so ridiculous I can't help but laugh.

'Well, I can't wait to see what the wee rascal has done,' Paul says.

'He's a wee asshole,' Jax parrots, clearly inspired by his big sister, and Paul tries to hold in his laughter and gives me a 'WTF' look. I mouth the word 'Gemma' at him and he nods, knowingly.

'Jax, you know that's not a nice word,' I say softly.

'Oh cwap,' he says, wandering back into his room, his eyes still crossed.

I'm still smiling as I change from my pyjamas into my maternity cotton joggers and one of Paul's old gym hoodies (which smells all manly and dear Jesus, I think my libido is back). I bundle my hair into a messy bun on top of my head, and squeeze my feet into my battered but comfy 'walking shoes'. I'm in no way entering the school gate style awards, but I don't care. Today isn't about me. It's about my family and continuing my mission to be the bringer of Christmas joy. It's also about me trying my best not to think about the fact there's a big conversation looming with Pamela. No . . . I will focus on the here and now.

When I get downstairs the boys have emptied most of the googly-eyed contents of the fridge onto the table to show Paul just how hilarious the Wee Donkey is. Paul is cutting up the last of his waffles and his coffee cup is almost empty. It's warm and cosy and there is a hint of domestic bliss (and cinnamon) about it all. If I could bottle this moment and keep it to bring out every time something goes exceptionally wrong (as it frequently does in this house), I would.

'I'll help the boys get their coats on,' Paul says, getting up from the table and pulling me into another hug. 'You never lose it, do you?'

'Lose what?' I ask.

'Your ability to make our wains feel the magic of Christmas. It's class, Tara. You're class.' He plants a soft kiss on my lips. It's not a full-on snog. There's not even a hint of open mouth, never mind tongues, but it's enough to make my legs shake and my vagina flutter. I need to get this man naked tonight if it is the last thing I do. Yep, my libido has landed and brought all her friends.

'Eeeeeuuugh boke, you two,' Gemma says as she pulls on her coat. 'Get a room. Or maybe don't. Could youse just stop, like? There's wains in the room and you're pregnant.' I can't help but notice her tone is light, though.

'Eeeeeughh!' the boys repeat, and Gemma chases after them down the hall, leaving them in fits of laughter.

Why is Gemma putting on her coat, though? Didn't she say she wanted to go back to bed? She has her phone and full permission to lie in her pit. What more could a thirteen-year-old want?'

'Gemma,' I call. 'Why do you have your coat on?'

She rolls her eyes. 'Because I'm coming with you to drop the boys off,' she declares. 'Can't have you driving about on your own. What if you wet yourself again, bestie?' She laughs before lifting my car keys and saying she'll get the boys in their car seats – knowing full well that trying to wrestle two hyper wains into restraints in a confined space isn't a task I cherish as my stomach grows ever larger.

Paul and I are left standing together in the hall, and he takes my hand. 'This is amazing. This is the happiest I've seen everyone, including you, in a long time.'

I push down the self-destructive voice in my head that is trying to whisper to me that he must think I'm a saggy sack of misery most of the time, and revel in what we have at this very moment.

Pulling him towards me, I look up at him. 'I want us all to be happy, Paul. Especially you. How about we stay up a bit later tonight?' I say with a wink.

'Past nine?' he teases.

'Past ten,' I whisper with a seductive smile.

'Oh baby,' he groans with a sexy laugh that I swear would be enough to make me pregnant if I wasn't already heavy with child. 'Roll on ten!'

'Oi! Sickos!' Gemma calls from the car. 'Get a move on!'

The boys break into a chorus of 'sickos, sickos, sickos' from their seats where they are sitting with their matching hats and gloves and my heart is full to bursting.

We drop Jax off first, and then take Nathan to school. Gemma insists on walking her brother into his classroom, insisting it's because she doesn't want me to slip on any ice. It's lovely, and sweet and thoughtful, but it's not quite that cold and I think it's more that she doesn't want anyone to see me looking full scummy mummy in public. I let her do it though, because any day I don't have to smile at the school gate mafia is a good day in my books.

But I should know better than to be alone with my thoughts. I start to play over the conversation we had this morning, when she compared my dance routine fails to Pamela's drunken performance at the baby shower. Am I really that embarrassing? I've never been drunk in front of Gemma's friends, and it's not to say I'm a bad dancer. I have led the Rebel Mums in a dance class, of course. I'm pure class. But then again, Pamela isn't a bad singer. She can actually be quite good, but Jesus, the state she used to get into in front of my friends. Yesterday brought it all back and I can just imagine what the Ys are saying in work today.

If only Cat had been there to defuse the whole situation, things would've been different. She's a queen at crisis management and she'd have had Pamela off that chair and in a taxi before the first 'Turn around', never mind the third. Then she'd have spoken to me about it all in a way that somehow transformed it into a funny story and all would've been right with the world. But she wasn't there, and even though Amanda was, and was brilliant, Cat's absence still stings, and it most certainly doesn't make sense.

I see Gemma walk back towards the car, smiling, and I take a deep breath. I will not think about Cat. I will stay firmly in my happy, magical Christmassy family love bubble.

On our way home we swing by Doherty's bakery for

some of the finest buns in the entire world. There ain't nothing quite like a Derry bakery and I decide to err on the side of absolute greed (the baby needs what the baby needs) and send Gemma in with instructions to buy two snowballs, two cream horns, two chocolate gravy rings, and two turnovers for good measure.

When we get home, I put a selection of the buns on a plate, make a huge mug of tea and make my way up the stairs with stage two of my peace offering to Pamela. I know I need to take Amanda's advice here and 'open the lines of communication' between us, but when I get to the top of the stairs I see the door to Pamela's room is wide open. Her bed is made and there's a note left on top of her freshly shaken duvet. For a second I hope the note is to tell me she's gone back to Spain and reconciled with Javier after all – or preferably found a non-cheating Spaniard to ride instead. But no. I'm not getting out of my big apology that easy. It reads, *Tara love, I'm away for a blow-dry and I've a few messages to run.*

I feel a strange mix of disappointment and relief that leaves me feeling really confused.

'Pammy hasn't left, has she?'

Gemma's come up behind me, and I turn to see her face, pale and worried. I think of how they've bonded and I know she would be devastated if Pamela cleared out on her so soon – not least because I remember how *I* felt when I was her age and Pamela cleared out on me. I never ever want her to experience that same feeling of rejection. And they have made a good team . . .

191

'No, dote,' I say. 'She's just gone to get her hair done and run a few wee messages.'

The look of relief on Gemma's face is instant. She nods. 'Cool. Good. OK, bestie. In that case, I'm going back to bed.' She grabs a snowball, a shower of desiccated coconut falling to the floor as she walks away. I say nothing. I have succeeded in having a lovely morning with my eldest child and one wrong move could wake her inner asshole.

Back downstairs, I clean up from breakfast. My candles are still burning but I've had to knock the heating off. 'Cosy' and eight months pregnant has me sweating like a vegetarian in a butcher's shop. Tidying up is not easy. Especially not with the new 'organized' pantry system which Pamela and Gemma set up. The whole set-up is making me twitchy and, damn it, I really do think that nesting carry-on is kicking in, so I set about moving everything back to exactly how I like it. Fuck you, Pamela, and the Kardashians and your pantries. Nothing wrong with using an old Roses tin to hold the biscuits, thank you very much.

I'm just putting the finishing touches to my kitchen when Pamela arrives home, her hair now sleek and freshly coloured. To my annoyance, it suits her. She drops shopping bags from at least six different stores on the floor and pulls out a chair, sits down and pulls off her high-heeled boots. How she wears them at all is beyond me. Surely that's a broken hip waiting to happen.

'Stick the kettle on, would ye, love,' she says. 'My stomach thinks my throat's been cut. Maybe I'll have a wee slice of toast too.'

'There's some buns from Doherty's if you want,' I say before she can speak. Baked goods are always a good distraction.

'Ah lovely,' she says. 'Butter me a turnover, will ye? God, that's one thing I missed about Spain. A dirty big turnover. Not too much butter though, love. And give me the one with the most icing on it. Cheers!'

She's talking to me as if I actually work in Doherty's, but I let it slide and don't chime in to ask what her last slave died from because I know this is the perfect time to be a grown-up and have a proper conversation about yesterday.

I pop two teabags into a mug (Pamela likes tea that a spoon could stand up in) and butter the bun while the kettle boils. 'Mammy,' I say. 'About yesterday . . .'

'Don't worry,' she says. 'It's done.'

'But, Mammy, I think we should talk . . . don't you?'

'What about?' she says.

'About yesterday, and how I reacted. And maybe why I reacted the way I did?' I say, pouring the boiling water into the mug and trying to push down the sick feeling in the pit of my stomach. This could be one fucker of a conversation.

'I get it,' she says, as she watches me add milk to her tea. 'You're pregnant, and hormonal and I was drunk. But it's in the past. No point in carrying on about it. It's no big deal.'

Argh, she's missing the point. For me, it actually *is* a big deal and if she wants to have any kind of a relationship with me going forward, we need to look at the whole fucking herd of elephants who live in the room with us. But Pamela has the emotional intelligence of a spoon, and before I can open my mouth to remonstrate, she takes the mug from me, sips from it and makes a face that would sour milk.

'Jesus, I can't believe my own wain can't even make a proper cup of tea. Love, this is dishwater.' She gets up and pours it down the sink. 'I'm going to get a proper teapot for Christmas so you can learn once and for all how to do this properly. You young ones and your notions. Making tea in a cup, like a heathen.'

Picking up her shopping bags, she bustles out of the kitchen.

'I'm away to see Gemma,' she calls back over her shoulder. 'I picked up a few bits for her. Don't touch that turnover. And I'll make my own tea when I come down, that way I'll know it's done right.'

I try not to give in to the urge to throw the turnover at the back of her head as she walks away.

20

That's not Santa's sack!

I can't lie. I'm feeling smug AF right now, even though I've woken up at stupid o'clock again and I know there is feck all chance I'm getting back to sleep. I'm feeling smug because, Pamela's continued emotional fuckery aside, yesterday was a good day.

No, yesterday was a great day. And today is going to be just as good. Before I went to bed last night, I totally smashed it, setting the Wee Donkey up for today. I laid out A4 sheets personalized with each of my children's names and embossed with a gold shellac holly and mistletoe border. Beside them I left red envelopes, each addressed – in white ink – to 'Santa, The North Pole'. Each child has also got a glittery gold gel pen, and in the middle of the table the Wee Donkey is holding his own pen, and a note which says *After school we will write our letters to Santa*.

See, Amazon moms can smash it just as much as Pinterest moms, and without all the home-made mess to clean up. In your face, Kirstie Allsopp!

I'd packed the boys' lunches – added a Christmas cookie as a treat – and even left a flirty note in Paul's lunch box.

And then, dear reader, I set about doing the almost impossible: seducing my husband. I had a shower – obvs I forsook shaving my legs or any other hair removal because I can no longer reach to do that but, look, body hair landscaping was the least of my notions. I felt unusually nervous for some reason. This was my husband, who I love and who loves me but still I felt vulnerable; exposed even. And it wasn't because I'd traded in my usual fluffy PJs for just a towel and a smile.

I switched off the lights, aware I have become so big and feeling very body-conscious, and slipped into bed beside Paul, who was only too happy to get close to me. He started with gentle kisses down my neck, around my breasts (which, thanks to pregnancy are super sensitive – win!) and back up to my mouth, where his tongue lightly grazed against mine. By that stage I was putty in his very manly, incredibly sexy hands and then he . . . well, I'll save you the details but once we found a position that accommodated my stomach, we had the best two and a half minutes of our life.

'Jesus,' Paul moaned after.

'I know,' I said, my body still shaking from the most

epic orgasm in a decade. 'I'd forgotten how intense things can get when all those hormones are running wild. Wow!'

'Yes, that's a part of pregnancy I fully support.' Paul smiled.

'You're still getting the snip once this one is born,' I told him. 'We'll have to find other ways to rock our worlds.'

'Challenge accepted,' he grinned, pulling me close to him again.

Needless to say, we were both in the best of form when we woke up this morning, and once the boys have come down from orbit at the thought of writing those all-important Santa letters, Paul takes them to school while I set about continuing my reign of Queen of All Things Christmas.

Not only are we are going to write those letters tonight, I am also going to go full-on Operation Christmas Transformation and have my house looking like it just vomited itself out of a Christmas catalogue. There is not one room that will be left untouched. Christmas bathmats? Check. Santa Toilet Seat Cover? Check. Christmas table-cloth? Of course! Santa-themed duvet covers? You do know me, right? I have several sets.

First, though, I have to battle the toughest of all mother-hood challenges. I have to tidy the room my two boys share. A wasteland of colourful plastic toys, grubby plushies, Lego bricks just waiting to dig their way into my feet like little cheerful landmines and Play-Doh mushed into the carpet in a congealed brown mess. (At least I really, really hope it's Play-Doh . . .)

Every year I take on the annual declutter – packing up the toys they have outgrown or broken and taking them to the charity shop or the dump, respectively. (We shall never again speak of the year Paul mixed the bags up and some poor charity was 'gifted' a bag of chewed action figures, wheel-less toy trucks and some teddies with questionable stains that no amount of washing could take out. The shame was real, fam!)

Last week I made the baby-brained mistake of trying to undertake this task while the boys were still in the house. I even asked them to help me. I can only surmise that I was suffering from some sort of short-lived brain damage to even suggest such a thing. Needless to say, they laid claim to every toy in that room – broken or not – crying when I tried to box stuff up, claiming it was their most 'favowit toy ever'.

Today, they are not here and I'm a woman on a mission. A full bin bag for the dump and two charity boxes later, I'm feeling super smug. I've even boxed some items to store in our attic until Baby Gallagher is old enough to play with them. I change the bedsheets, run the hoover around and marvel at how lovely and cosy their room looks.

'Mammy! Seriously!' a sleepy Gemma says, stretching as she walks out of her room in her PJs. 'Did you have to hoover? It's keeping me awake!'

'It's after ten, love,' I tell her. 'Count yourself lucky you got a lie-in after all. Now, it's your turn.' I hand her a bin bag, polish and a duster. 'I want all those broken pieces of make-up, and manky Starbucks cups and torn school tights bagged up for the dump. Pack up another bag with any clothes which you don't wear any more or have outgrown. They're going to the charity shop and, so help me, Gemma, if I see a pile of stuff with labels still on that you just can't be arsed to put away properly, I will lose my shit.'

She rolls her eyes, but she knows she's caught. It's only recently I cottoned on to the fact I was washing the same jeans and sweaters over and over again without her having worn them in between times. Seems it's easier to throw stuff back in the laundry hamper than to put it away in her wardrobe. I don't want to break our uneasy peace though, so I smile. 'I'm going to tackle my wardrobe. How about we go out and get a hot chocolate when we're done?'

'Can we get one of those big ones with cream and bits of brownie and Flake in them?' she asks, her voice as excited as the boys were earlier.

'For defs,' I tell her.

'Cool, bestie! Thank you! By the way, Mammy, only losers say "for defs" any more.'

'Well, I'm the coolest loser I know,' I say with a smile and head off to tackle my own Everest.

I don't have a shopping 'problem' as such. I mean, like everyone I developed repetitive strain injury from clicking 'Add to Cart' during lockdown, and I am on first-name terms with all the local couriers (which reminds me, I must write them Christmas cards) but it's not an 'issue'.

When I am done wearing stuff, I donate it to charity. Yes, I have a fairly sizeable 'labels still on' section in my wardrobe – but that's all stuff that I love and may have bought on sale and in a smaller size, and I'm hell-bent on fitting into every single item once Baby Gallagher has exited through my vagina in an orderly fashion (no tearing, thank you very much). Yes, some of those clothes didn't actually fit me before I got pregnant, but I am determined that they will grace my body once I get back to spin class and dancing with the Rebel Mums. I'm also going to be one of those total MILFs who jogs to pick up her kids from school, wearing Lycra, pushing a buggy and with a fancy wee baseball cap and sunglasses. But for now, in the interests of Christmas harmony, creating space for stuff for the baby, and compelled by my nesting instinct, I fill a bag for charity, and two vacuum bags with spring/ summer clothes and a few 'not likely to fit unless I chop a limb off' items which I just can't bear to part with.

As I ungracefully bend down to store the bags under the bed, I notice clutter in the form of wrapping paper tubes, empty chocolate bars (for the baby, I swear!) and several empty Amazon packages which I know aren't from items I've ordered. Sure enough, when I pull the empty boxes out, they are addressed to Paul, and I get a warm and fuzzy feeling that he has taken my (completely not subtle) hints and ordered my presents early and not just done a quick dive around Foyleside on Christmas Eve afternoon.

Maybe I should leave it at this, content to know he

is in control, and satisfied to get a big surprise as to which of the many hints he has picked up on. But no. I am a nosy bitch and I have to look. I investigate the shipping stickers for clues. The first reads 'DeWEISN Vanity Mirror'. Yes! Good man, Paul. You've ordered me the trifold mirror I desperately want. Maybe this is where I should stop – but then again maybe Paul should've found a more Tara-proof hiding spot, like in his garage or his ma's house. Anything that comes within these four walls is fair game as far as I'm concerned – although maybe he didn't think, in my current state, I'd be hoking and poking under the bed.

Look, I'll just nosy at one more and leave the other two. That's fair, isn't it? I mean, that's a solid compromise in anyone's book.

The label on this one is harder to read. It has obviously gotten wet at some stage and the print is a bit blurry, but I'm not one to shy away from a challenge. But . . . Jesus . . . OK . . . what? I feel my heart flutter and I don't know if it's in a good way or a bad way. But I am definitely a little confused. The label reads 'Eight-inch Purple-Eyed Warrior Leather' and it looks like the label says 'Dom Fun'.

If I were Fleabag and this was a TV programme, I'd totally be side-eyeing the audience now. What in the actual fifty shades of kinky fuck is this? Eight-inch PURPLE-EYED WARRIOR? Is that some sort of name for a penis? Like one-eyed trouser snake? Why is my husband buying a penis? Or is it something for *his* penis? Neither answer makes me feel good, if I'm being honest. Is it a dildo? Is it a dildo for me? For him? Does he want to boldly go where no man has gone before and try some butt stuff? Does he want me to try butt stuff on *him*? I feel my half-digested snowball from Doherty's bakery like lead in my stomach. As the song says, I would do anything for love, but I sure as shite am not going to do that – plenty of people would, and you do youse, but it's not one that revs my engine. Sweet Baby Jesus.

And 'Dom Fun' – is that as in dominatrix? Trying to catch my breath, I grab my phone and type 'Dom Fun purple-eyed warrior leather' into the search bar and the first result is for BDSM accessories. Then I start to message Cat to ask her what BDSM actually is, because even though I'm thirty-six I really don't know too much about it. Cat, I imagine, knows it all.

Then I remember Cat has ghosted me, so I search Google instead, which doesn't pull any punches. 'Bondage, Discipline (or Domination), Sadism and Masochism – as a form of sexual practice'. Now I'm all up for a pair of fluffy handcuffs on Valentine's Day for a laugh, but this does not sound like a laugh. Not to kink-shame anyone – whatever floats your boat, lads – but at eight months pregnant the thought of my previously very vanilla husband suddenly buying kinky sex toys and showing an interest in discipline and sadism makes my heart sink. I am raging that there are only empty packages because I don't care what he might say later, I would tear that bad boy open and get to the bottom of this as quick as possible.

I need to know what all this means for us. Is he going to arrive home next with nipple clamps? I swear I feel my nips invert at the very thought.

I stem the incoming panic attack by doing my breathing exercises, in . . . and out . . . Is this for someone else? A lover? Wait . . . No. Paul would never have an affair. Not my Paul. I mean, OK, he has been working more late nights and going to golf more, and saying he finds me draining, and he needs some time to himself, but no. That's just because things have been stressful at home with three children, one on the way and now Pamela under our roof as well. And that's before we even get to my relentless meltdowns.

Right?

I know this man. I love this man and he loves me. He would never do the dirty. But this has to mean something. Does he have a fetish? Is he bored with our sex life? Does he want to spice it up with some BDSM-type play? Why doesn't he talk to me about it? It's not like I'm a prude. I'm open to a lot of things. And if he's not talking to me about it, who is he talking to and why is he buying sex toys and hiding them from me? Because I know there is no way he'd have decided to surprise me with a Purple-Eyed Warrior Leather vibrator under the tree on Christmas morning.

The world spins around me, zooming in and out like a special effect in a cheap TV show. Life doesn't make much sense at the moment, that's for sure.

I need to talk to someone. I need Cat, I think again,

and this time that realization comes with a tear tracing its way down my cheek. I can't have Cat right now. She has made that clear. I suppose Amanda is open to all that sexual counselling stuff; I could talk to her, but we've just never had that type of relationship. It would feel awkward. A headache starts to build behind my eyes. From the elation of last night's orgasm to the confusion over my husband buying sex toys is quite the come-down.

21

Dear Santa . . . Help!

I spared Amanda the details, typing a quick how would I know if Paul is into some kinky stuff? message to her after I'd picked myself up off the floor and flattened the boxes ready to be put out for recycling. (Not before taking a picture of the shipping label for reference, mind you!)

Her reply had been simple. Just two words in fact: Ask him.

So that was my plan – but obviously I wasn't going to rock up at the garage and ask him outright what the actual fudge was going on and why is he buying eight-inch purple penis extenders, or whatever it is? And I still had to pick Nathan up from school, and Jax from the childminder's, and I think both would look badly on me turning up late because I was off trying to find out if their daddy is some sort of sexual deviant.

I do what we mammies do best and I put on my best

perfectly normal(ish) mammy face and keep that Christmas train on track. We will have a fucking fabulously festive day, so help me God. I conduct the boys in a fairly tuneless rendition of 'Rudolph the Red-Nosed Reindeer' and 'Jingle Bells' in the car on the way home. They chat excitedly about what they are going to put in their letters to Santa, and Nathan promises to help Jax as obviously Jax can't write yet. I smile inwardly at his sweetness until he says, 'Jax, acuz I'm gonna help you write your letter, you have to give me one of your presents.'

Jax nods, as though it's a fair enough deal. He'll learn in time that his brother has been fleecing him all these years and I've a feeling poor Nathan will be in the shit when that happens.

As we pull up outside the house, Paul's car is parked in the driveway. A mixture of emotions washes over me. Affection for him. Love for our family. Appreciation that he has done what he said he would and finished work early to be home for letter-writing duties. It allows me to push my worries about his newfound inclinations to the back of my head, and when I walk into the hall to find Paul wearing a Santa hat, with a bunch of red roses for me, I feel only good things – a little flutter in my tummy, a wave of love for him. The fire is lit, as are the Yankee Candles, and our home feels cosy, warm and Christmassy.

'These are for you, Mrs Claus,' he says, handing me the roses, and then fixing a Santa hat on top of my head. Then he looks to the boys, 'And these are for you!' and he hands them both an elf hat to wear. 'Why don't you get Gemma to help you put them on?' The boys scamper down the hall in search of their big sister as Paul pulls me in for a snog.

'I love you, Mrs Claus,' he says, once the boys are out of earshot. 'But I might have to put you on the naughty list later tonight.'

Now normally I'd reply with some equally awful Santa-themed innuendo ('Can I have a ride on your sleigh?') but all I can think about when he says 'naughty list' is his recent interest BDSM. Is Mrs Claus in for a bit of disciplining? I swear to Christ, if he brings out a whip or a paddle, he'll find it very quickly inserted up his arse. Then again . . . maybe he'd like that. SCREAM. So I just kiss him back, chastely, and brush past him.

'Gemma,' I call. 'It's letter-writing time, pet. C'mon.'

'Mammy, I can't find her,' Nathan says, walking out of the kitchen with both Jax and the Wee Donkey in tow. 'I fink she might be in her bed.'

So help me, but that child better be in her (freshly cleaned) bed and not out on another secret mission for Pamela. I don't want anything to ruin this illusion that all is well in the Gallagher household.

I call her from the bottom of the stairs but there is no answer, so I call again. Louder this time. And then I hear her get out of bed, followed by a series of thuds as she stomps across her bedroom. When her bedroom door opens it does so with an almighty bang as it hits the wall. We all stand in a state of fear as she stomps down the stairs. You know the scene in *Jurassic Park* where they all try and stay really quiet so the dinosaurs don't pick them as their afternoon snack? Yeah, that.

'You don't seriously expect me to write a letter to Santa, do you?' she huffs. 'That's for wains, Mammy. Santa's not even re—'

I interject as if my life depends on it as the boys are staring at her, hanging on to her every asshole word. 'Really accepting letters after today. Yes, I know, Gemma. Which is why we have to do it now.'

If looks could kill, Paul would be picking out a coffin for me as we speak. But that child doesn't get her resting bitch face from Paul – I throw as filthy a look back at her. She looks to him for support, but he's on the side of Team Gallagher and Festive Magic with this one.

'Gemma,' I say. 'Just do this, for the boys. Please?'

'Finnneeee theeeennnah,' she sighs, her body tense with teenage aggression. 'I was just watching a really good episode of *Stranger Things* and this is so annooyiinnngah!'

And there she is, Gemma McAsshole is back in the building. It was bound to happen sometime.

Determined not to let the return of the teenage beast ruin the mood, I instruct Alexa to play Christmas classics and direct the children to their seats at the table before grabbing my phone and snapping a quick picture for Insta.

I fix my sweetest smile to my face. 'I am going to help Jax. Daddy will help Nathan and, Gemma, I think we can trust you to write your own.'

She rolls her eyes.

'Then we're going to read them out, put them in their

envelopes and pop them in the fire where they will shoot up the chimney in magic smoke and arrive at the North Pole by bedtime.' The boys are in extreme hyper mode, buoyed not only by the thought of writing their letters to Santa but also from the sugar in the candy canes I gave them on the drive home. (It is Christmas . . .)

'OK, Jax,' I say, snuggling in beside my beautiful baby. 'Let's see! What would you like to ask Santa for?'

'Erm . . . I would like Paw 'Atrol toys . . . and . . . and . . . a banana!'

'Darling, you can have a banana any day of the year,' I tell him, but he just crinkles his nose and crosses his arms. 'I want a banana from Santa!' he says. I write it down. I'm not brave enough to fight with a two-year-old, and it will save on our spending.

'Anything else?' I ask. 'You can ask Santa for three things.'

He looks at the page, then around the room, and then at me – his pupils dilated with the sugar high. 'I, uhm, want a willy,' he says, voice serious. Nathan erupts into a fit of giggles. Paul and I look at each other while we try not to laugh and Gemma, the original craic killer, just tuts.

'This is so stupidahhhhh,' she says, rolling her eyes.

'Jax, pet,' I say, trying to keep my face straight. 'You already have a willy.'

He keeps his expression deadpan and looks at me as if the frustration is leaping out of him that I'm not cart-wheeling with joy over his choices. 'OK den,' he says. 'I will have a twee.'

'A tree?' I ask as Nathan almost turns blue from the laughing fit he has wound himself up into.

'Yes. I want a twee,' he nods, and just like with the banana I decide there are more important things to be getting annoyed about in my life than the insanity of a two-year-old off his tits on sugar.

'OK so,' I tell him. 'I will write down a tree.'

'That's so stupidaaahhh,' Gemma adds again. I know it would be immature of me to answer her with a quick 'your face is so stuppppiddaaah', but God am I tempted.

'Now, Nathan,' Paul says. 'It's your turn. Here we go, Dear Santa, I have been a good boy and I would like . . .' He pauses for Nathan to list his three choices. Nathan isn't about to have his creativity clipped though. Oh no, he sits up straight in his chair, takes a deep breath and starts to speak. 'I want a drum kit, a microphone and a camera, acuz I am going to be a YouTuber. And I want some Minecraft toys, and Roblox toys and a Super Mario game and—'

'Nathan,' Paul cuts in. 'Hold your horses there, wee man. That's already six things and you know the rules. You can only ask Santa for three things.'

Nathan looks disgusted, but the child is smart enough to know that acting like a brat will get you on the naughty list with the promise of a lump of coal on Christmas morning. (Used to be a bag of coal, but you know, with the cost of living crisis that's probably more than I was hoping to spend on the entire house . . .)

He sighs. 'OK, den. I will have a drum kit and a microphone and a camera.'

'My want a drum kit and a mi-cara-phone and a camberra too,' Jax squeals – the desire for a banana and a tree clearly having worn off.

Paul looks at me. He knows I already have purchased said YouTuber's kit for Nathan, complete with a pretend camera that he will think is uploading him directly to the internet. I'm a smart mammy, I had his presents nailed down in October. Jax, on the other hand, he changes his mind approximately as often as he changes his pants. Which, given that we're potty-training, is several times a day. I've learned to just nod and tell him he's great and have faith that my incredible Mrs Claus skills means he doesn't Hulk out on Christmas morning when Santa leaves him a selection of Paw Patrol toys.

'OK, Gemma,' I say, my voice light and smile bright. 'What are you asking Santa for?'

She mutters that I'm 'so annoyingahhhhh' under her breath before she speaks. 'My list is on Snapchat. It's called a Snaplist,' she says with a cheeky smile. 'And when you're older, boys, you just snap it to Santa.'

A Snaplist? Is she serious? I have heard it all now.

'Anyway, I asked him for three crop-tops from Shein, a skincare fridge, a Nomination bracelet with six charms, a new laptop, a new iPhone, a pair of high-top Converse, a pair of Nike Dunks, a pair of DMs—'

'Whoa there, Gemma,' I bark. 'That's way more than three things and you know the rules.'

'Aye, love,' Paul says. 'Your mammy is right.' I'm delighted that Paul, who would go into debt and danger

211

to spoil his 'wee doll', is on my side. Gemma is, unsur-prisingly, disgusted at his treachery.

'But, Mammy,' Gemma says, fixing me with a stare so glacial I swear the temperature drops a few degrees. I shiver. 'When you're a teenager, Santa says you can ask for as much as you want. And if that's not true, then maybe there is no such thing as Santa . . .'

I hear a sharp intake of breath from both Jax and Nathan, who are staring at us wide-eyed. Everything moves in slow motion. I want to wipe that smug smile off my darling daughter's face but I'm not quite that petty and I am not going to let her ruin our lovely day.

'You're right, Gemma,' I say through a forced smile. 'Teenagers can ask for whatever they want, but that's only if they aren't on the naughty list for, say, getting caught vaping at school.'

The expression on her face says it all. She has been bested by Mrs Claus – the Mrs Claus who she knows is half responsible for buying her Christmas presents. This ain't my first rodeo, kid.

After the boys have finally succumbed to sleep, Gemma has returned to her pit and Pamela breezed in and breezed out again on a date (a date! Boke!), I cuddle up beside Paul on the sofa. I'd love to just snuggle into him and stick on a cheesy Christmas movie but there are other matters at hand.

'Paul,' I say coyly. 'Can I ask you a question?'

'I was wondering when you would,' he smiles. 'And the

answer is yes, I am indeed the ridiest man you have ever known and not even Jamie Dornan could steal you from me.'

'No Paul, this is serious,' making sure my tone is measured enough that he doesn't think crackpot Tara has ridden in on the same bus as Teenage Asshole Gemma. 'But not too serious,' I tell him. I can feel the colour start to build in my cheeks and I can't believe I am taking a redner in front of my husband. I am such a dick.

'Well, what is it?' he asks.

'Well, I was just wondering if you, you know, had any fetishes.' The word fetishes comes out like a squeak.

He raises an eyebrow. 'If you're asking if I want you to take the whole Mrs Claus thing to the next level and hang tinsel from your tits, then no,' he smiles.

'Naw, seriously, Paul. Is there nothing a bit, like, kinky that you want to try but haven't told me about? Anything you want me to try in the bedroom, because if you want to keep things fresh and . . .'

He takes my hand and rubs it gently as he looks me straight in the eye. Oh God, this man makes me melt just as he is. We don't need whips and chains, we just need us. I will him to be open with me and to tell me it is all OK.

'Tara, I know this is a tough time for you and you have all sorts of insecurities, and your body doesn't feel like your own, but you are always enough for me. Those few minutes last night? They were enough for me. More than enough. They were fucking amazing,' he says, grinning like a horny teenager. 'Don't get me wrong, I'm never going to say no to more than a few minutes, and once this baby is born and—'

'You've had the snip?' I interject.

He sighs. '. . . And I've had the snip. Well, once that is out of the way I am going to be flinging into multiple positions, multiple times. But see for now? Stop putting pressure on yourself. You, Tara Gallagher, are my fetish. Just you and nothing else.'

I want to believe him. It would be easier to believe him, but none of that explains what I found or why he hasn't told me about it. I kiss him.

'OK then love. I'm away to bed now, I've got a head-ache.'

I head upstairs. It's time to swallow my pride and bring out the big guns. I open the group chat and type in a message. SOS girls. Found this under our bed with Paul's name on it. Please can we meet for lunch tomorrow? I attach a picture of the shipping label and press send.

22

Nathan's time to shine

Thursday, 15 December

The girls have promised me an urgent meeting, but life is insane and the closest they can do is Saturday, which is still two days away from today. And today is the biggest, most important day in the Gallagher Christmas calendar.

It's the day we find out if there is any room at the inn as Nathan takes to the stage for his big theatrical debut playing the role of Innkeeper Number Three in the Primary 2 nativity show.

Keeping the 'talent' happy and calm and reassuring him he will 'smash it' has been a welcome distraction from thinking of all things BDSM/purple-eyed/kinky as hell.

The girls – yes, even Cat, much to my relief – have been amazing and reassuring via text since I sent out my SOS though. Cat actually seems a little more like her old self, so

I wonder has she just been really stressed with work after all and not ghosting me for some unknown reason. I can't wait to see her on Saturday and give her the biggest hug – and have her tell me how I cope with Paul's secret desires.

For now I have to make do with her support via completely inappropriate memes and GIFS, along with Amanda sending me recommendations for self-help books, and academic articles (snore!) about communication and sexual desire in marriage. I've had to clear my phone of messages, and my browser history more times in the last two days than I have my purse of receipts – I live in fear of Nathan getting a hold of my phone and accidentally catching sight of a GIF of a grown man having his bare arse spanked.

I give myself a shake and slip some Christmas bauble earrings into my ears. Mrs Claus has a proud mammy routine to maintain and Nathan's big moment is what really matters right now. Paul is going to meet us at the school, which means I just have to get Gemma and Pamela into the car, pick up Jax from the childminder and be seated at least half an hour before the nativity begins so we can get good seats. I want to be front and centre, playing the role of a good Feis mammy. (The Feis – pronounced fesh – is a yearly event where Irish children perform in a sadistic form of *The Hunger Games* involving Irish dancing, speech and drama, and a whole lot of recorder playing. It's brutal and there is no bigger threat to life and limb than the overzealous Feis mammy. Think *Dance Moms* does *Riverdance*.)

'Mammy, why can't Pammy drive and I sit shotgun?' Gemma whines from the back seat.

'Because daughter dearest, *Pammy* is not insured to drive my car, *Pammy* does not have her licence, and *Pammy* was also banned from driving when . . .' I stop myself because I realize that Gemma is intrigued at the thought of her granny being a badass bandit, and if I continue to tell the story of her famous DUI after crossing the border from Muff with a young Donegal farmer she swore she was in love with after only three days, I fear Gemma may prop her even higher on that pedestal she has placed her on. 'When never you mind,' I finish lamely.

'When what, Mammy? Finish your story, I hate when you do that!' complains Gemma.

'Aye,' laughs Pamela, 'finish your story, Tara love.'

'I'd rather not, Ma,' I tell her, 'I don't think that's one she needs to hear until she's a bit older.'

'Craic killer,' Gemma sniffs, and Pamela laughs.

'I'll tell you later,' Pamela says in a fair whisper, and I swear to the sweet Baby Jesus, I could swing for her – if I wasn't trying to be completely zen in the spirit of the perfect family Christmas.

'Cool, bestie,' Gemma says. 'How did my mammy get to be so embarrassing when you're so not?'

Car journeys with these two Mean Girls is hell. It feels like they are actually bullying me, but I'm not going to rise to the bait. Not today, Satan and Satan's spawn. Not today.

'We're at Jo's now,' I say, turning the car into the

childminder's driveway. I hope our arrival will be enough to kill their craic, or at least subdue it. 'Gemma, can you go in and grab Jax for me? Tell Jo I said hello and I'll see her tomorrow at drop-off.'

'Sure, I'll go too,' Pamela chimes in, as she takes off her seat belt and opens the door. I'm already dreading hearing what emotionally unintelligent or just downright rude thing she's going to say to Jo, but I let her go with Gemma anyway. Means I can sit here for a minute and shoot a few heartburn tablets, calming my urge to kick them both out of the car for good.

I'll apologize for her behaviour to Jo tomorrow. Maybe I'll bring some chocolates or something too. Or a bottle of wine. Or diamonds . . .

When Gemma and Pamela return, they are accompanied by Jax, who's holding a page covered, and I mean covered, in red and green glitter. Jax is also covered in the glitter and PVA glue; his face resembles an antique Christmas ornament that's been through six house moves, a few divorces and a fight with a one-eyed cat. He's delighted with himself.

'Cwistmas twee for you, Mammy,' Jax sing-songs proudly as Gemma buckles him into his car seat and he tries to stretch his tiny wee arm into the front to present it to me.

'Aww, darling.' I reach around with the grace of an elephant to retrieve it. 'This is the best Christmas tree drawing I've ever seen, Jax. Thank you so much,' I say, admiring his creation and wincing at the cascade of glitter falling all over my black leggings. I'm starting to look like a seven-year-old at her first school disco.

'Fwidge,' Jax shouts, and because I haven't the energy or agility to turn around to him twice, I look in my rear-view mirror and say, 'Of course, pet, this is definitely going on the fridge when we get home.'

'Yessss!' Jax grins, then he realizes he's got some glue on his fingers and starts to peel and pick at it, much to his delight. That's him distracted for another wee while at least.

'Here, Mammy. Can you hold that for me?' I say as I hand Pamela the glitter-bombed page and put the car in gear.

'Jesus Christ, Tara!' she squawks as yet more glitter rains from the card, 'My good Zara white trousers! Now I look like a bloody Christmas cake!' She drops her voice a bit – but certainly not enough. 'Can I not just throw this thing out the window? There are a hundred pictures at home and he's not going to remember this one, is he?'

I glare at her. She really doesn't know her grandchildren that well. Actually, she really doesn't know children at all. Of course he won't forget it! If that card doesn't go on my fridge you can bet your sweet ass he'll be telling some therapist about his horror show of a mother and granny in twenty-five years' time.

'No, Mammy, you cannot throw it out the window!' I bark, in as quiet a voice as possible so Jax can't hear. 'That is Jax's art, for me, and it is going on the fridge.' I glance in the rear-view mirror and see I have been singularly

219

unsuccessful in speaking so quietly that Jax can't hear me. His eyes are glossy and his bottom lip is trembling – he could go into a grade-A toddler meltdown at any second.

'Isn't that right, Jax?' I soothe. 'It's going right at the very front of the fridge.'

He nods his head and spits out a 'Bad Pammy.'

'Well, it's hardly a Vincent Van Goffey or whatever ye call yer man is it, it's just a mess of glitter and shite?' Pamela states matter-of-factly, and she's really, really pushing my buttons here, and Jax's, who begins to wail and kick his feet against her chair.

Gemma, meanwhile, is silent for once, which is strange because she's been Pamela's 'ride or die' lately. But if I know Gemma, and I do, she doesn't like anyone making her little brothers cry. That's a right she reserves totally for herself.

'Give it to me, Granny,' she says to Pamela, reaching into the front. The fact she has called her Granny and not Pammy isn't lost on me. No one messes with her brothers – not even her 'new bestie'.

'Look, Jax,' Gemma says as she shows her little brother that his Christmas creation is now safely in her possession. 'I'll keep it safe until we get home and then Mammy can put it on the fridge.'

Miraculously, this halts Jax's meltdown and makes him smile. 'Fank ooh, Memma,' he says almost in a whisper and goes back to contentedly picking the glue off his fingers.

The ten-minute journey to Nathan's school is eerily

quiet apart from the noise of Jax watching 'Baby Shark' on repeat on my phone. Gemma isn't talking incessantly to Pamela about the Kardashians, or her latest Shein order or about me and my inadequacy as a mother. In fact, she doesn't utter one word to her beloved Pammy, instead staring out of the window with a slight frown on her face.

While I like to see Pamela's true self start to peek through and the facade of 'World's Best Granny' begin to fade, I never want that to be at the cost of my children being upset. But here we are, maybe this is the only way she'll learn who Pamela is and how she was when I was a child.

Pamela's silence confirms that she knows she's slipped up, but you can't keep our Pammy down for long. After five minutes, she interrupts the quietness with, 'Here, that Jo girl doesn't half look like she needs a good wash does she, should she be around children, do ye think? She looks like one of them sex-trafficking girls.'

Luckily for my mother, and for everyone for that matter, we've just pulled into the car park at St Anne's College, meaning I don't need to acknowledge or reply to her ludicrous and possibly racist observation of Jax's child-minder. I'll deal with that later when I ask Gemma did her granny say something horrific to Jo's face.

Now, it's nativity time.

23

Once upon a time in Bethlehem . . .

Paul is waiting for us outside the school. He's wearing his overalls, his hair is all dishevelled and he has a smudge of oil on his cheek. Some women would scold their husband for turning up at the kids' school looking like that, but me, I want to climb this man, right now, like a tree. I feel the biggest, most inappropriate dose of the horn rush over me and I wonder if I could sneak him round the back of the school sheds for a quickie before the curtain rises. I feel myself blush as he gives me a peck on the cheek and I let out an involuntary gusty sigh.

'You all right, love?' my mother asks. I'm not about to tell her I want to ride the face off my husband right here and right now, so I mumble that the baby kicked. Paul can't be fooled though. He knows that sound well. That sound is usually my 'buck me now, big lad' sound. He gives me a cheeky smile and whispers 'later' in my ear, which just about turns my legs to jelly. I am weak for this man, which would be grand if we weren't surrounded by our family, in the foyer of a primary school, about to watch a gang of six-year-olds celebrate a virgin birth.

'Eughhh, can you two stop embarrassing yourselves, and me! You're in a school!' Gemma puffs, as if she is the grown-up and we are the teenagers.

'Are you OK, love?' Paul asks, and normally this would be when Gemma would transform into an angel and smile broadly at her daddy, but no, she doesn't.

'I just don't want to be late,' she sniffs, but given that I had to bribe her with extra phone time to get her to come along without a fuss, I'm not buying it. But we really don't want to miss the best seats, and I don't have time to pry any further.

'Paul,' I hear Pamela say. 'Could you not have got changed outta them grubby overalls to come to your son's play?'

'Ach, Pamela. We can't all look like an explosion in a glitter factory, can we?' he says with a smirk and she is lost for a comeback. Oh, Pamela can give it, but she can't take it.

'C'mon, Mammy,' I say. 'We don't want to miss the start.'

We are ushered by some very excited Primary 7 children down into the sports hall. Now, I've been here many times and sat through countless shows and concerts when Gemma was a pupil, but I do not recall it ever being this warm. When I say warm, I mean pure boiling. Forget it being December and freezing outside, this is on a par with a day on the beach in Santa Ponsa in August. I feel like two hobbits have just thrown a golden ring at me. Beads of sweat are trickling down my back, and between my boobs, and I'm pretty sure that my arse is sweating too. Trust me to go all out and insist on wearing my new, heavy, 100 per cent polyester Christmas maternity jumper to the show.

I look around to see if anyone else resembles the Wicked Witch of the West, currently melting into a puddle on the floor due to the heat, but it seems I'm alone. There are even people here wearing coats. What in the *Home Alone* is that all about?

I use the programme the overexcited Primary 7 pupils handed us earlier to fan myself, and I can feel sweat bead along my top lip. I'd probably be able to taste it by now, but thankfully the fact that I'm in need of a serious lip wax keeps it from entering my mouth. Would it be cooler if I just lay on the floor – they say heat rises, don't they?

'Mammy, stop overreacting,' Gemma hisses, watching my frantic fanning. 'It's not that warm. Oh my God . . .' She folds her arms – over her coat – and huffs back into her chair as if I've stripped off to my maternity knickers and am lathering myself in Ben & Jerry's ice cream to cool down instead of just sitting here minding my own business and sweating like a glassblower's hole.

'Gemma, my body temperature is up the left as it is without sitting here wearing this stupid Christmas jumper,'

I say with a whimper, and I think I would start crying if all the liquid in my body wasn't currently running down the crack of my arse in a pool of sweat. 'Give me a break, pet, please,' I plead.

'I told you not to wear it,' she counters. And she's right. She told me that Christmas jumpers were so 2020 and it's all about shirts this year, but did I listen? Abso-fecking-lutely not.

'It's pure fugly anyway,' she hisses, and as much as I love a well-timed *Mean Girls* quote, all I can think is 'not today, Regina George.'

'Love, why don't you just take the jumper off?' Paul asks, and of course I had considered this but it's not that simple.

'I'm wearing my jammy top underneath,' I say sheepishly, which of course garners me another 'Oh my Godddddah' from Gemma.

'No one is regretting that decision more than me, Gemma,' I hiss, and it's true. I hate the me that was too lazy to get dressed properly earlier. And I hate the me that ate custard (do not judge!) for breakfast and spilled some all down the front. The custard was amazing and I don't regret that for one second, but I do hate the me that didn't change after. The me who is now trapped in this plastic torture chamber cooking slowly in my own juices.

Thankfully I am distracted (sort of) by the dimming of lights and the sound of twenty-seven six-year-olds stomping onto the stage ready to regale us all with the story of the

First Christmas. I can't help but grin when I see Nathan walk proudly to his place and I'm sure I'd tear up if I wasn't in danger of serious dehydration at this stage.

The bells begin to jingle, and the piano starts to tinkle and the boys and girls stop waving to their mammies and daddies as their teacher encourages them to stand and smile and prepare to sing. This is my boy's moment and I'm hoping he's going to grab it with both hands and knock it out of the park.

He's taken his preparation for this moment as seriously as if he were rehearsing for his debut in *Hamilton* on the West End. Granted, he has been an annoying wee shite and we've all been singing the songs in our sleep, but I truly want him to shine like the star he is. There's a lot of me in my beautiful boy. He has that same love of performing that I had as a child. That's all I wanted when I was his age – and I felt so free on stage. But Pamela never supported me, so I'm determined that I won't make the same mistake with Nathan. I'll never tell him he's 'tone-deaf' or has the 'rhythm of a wardrobe' like Pamela told me.

I'll tell him he's a star and it's my job to help him shine.

The children start to sing – kind of hitting all the right notes but not necessarily in the right order. Within ten seconds one child messes up his words, one falls off the back bench, one sneezes and the snotters drip out of both nostrils right down her mouth onto the floor, but like a pro, she doesn't wipe. The show must go on! Then one child burps, and shouts 'scuse me', another begins scratching his private parts and another starts to sing so loudly that even Santa, all the way in the North Pole, can probably hear him. It's Nathan.

That's my boy!

But as the song continues he just gets louder, and louder and louder until we're hearing 'Jingle Bells' performed in a style best described as 'thrash metal'. Gemma is mortified, of course. Paul is giggling. Pamela is just shaking her head with her lips downturned and her eyes as dead as her soul. You'd think she was Simon Cowell and this was the fucking *X Factor* and not the Primary 2 nativity. I shudder at her expression, because I know it all too well. She used to give me the same look when she bothered to show up for any of my school shows. Normally though it was just my daddy, sitting on his own, and grinning with pride to see me. No matter the show, or my performance, he'd clap the loudest and give me a standing ovation. Oh God, I miss him so much.

My sadness for my daddy is mixed with my pride for Nathan, who is clearly living his absolute best life on stage. That's what I like to see: never do something half-arsed when you can go full arsed at it. I envy his confidence, which seems to be spilling out into Jax, who has now clambered up on his chair and is practically vibrating with excitement. He starts to sing with his brother, and just like Nathan, it is much too loud until all other noise in the room is drowned out by my two boys. Jax is now just shouting 'jingle bells' over and over again, until his face turns purple and a wee vein starts to protrude from his forehead.

I think everyone is relieved when the song ends and silence descends across the hall. It is time for Mary and Joseph to travel to Bethlehem to try and find a room for the night, meaning Nathan's moment is coming up very soon. But as Mary and Joseph pause before him, before he can deliver his one and only line, still vibing with the excitement of it all, Jax stands up and with extreme conviction, and volume, shouts:

'Nooooo! We do not have any woooooomm heeaaahhh.'

The room erupts into giggles and Jax is clearly completely lured with himself, waving at his adoring fans. But my eyes are on Nathan. He is devastated. He has been practising that line for five solid weeks and this had been his big solo moment, his time in the spotlight, on his own. My heart sinks as I see his lip wobble and all I can do is watch from my seat (where I am cooked to at least medium rare by now) as he starts to cry. But his tears soon turn to anger and I can see the rage building within him. This is not going to end well for anyone.

As if in slow motion, Nathan takes a deep breath and opens his mouth. 'I hate you, Jax!' he shouts. 'I hate you and I don't want Mammy to have another baby if it's going to be a wee dickhead like you!'

All eyes turn to the Family Gallagher as the room falls silent. Miss Rose is giving me the 'we'll talk about this later' look, and you could cut the tension with a knife.

That is until Jax replies, also at the top of his lungs, because clearly, I'm not humiliated enough:

'Dickhead! Dickhead! Dickhead!'

The audience can no longer hold back their laughter. Gemma is so mortified she has almost disappeared into her hoodie, her head bent forward so far, I swear she's going to pull a muscle in her back. Pamela is wearing the same horrified expression and in that moment, I can finally see the family resemblance in the pair of them. Luckily the music teacher, Mrs Campbell, very quickly reads the room and launches into a rousing rendition of 'Rudolph the Red-Nosed Reindeer', but Nathan refuses to sing. In fact he stomps to the side of the stage where he sits down, with his legs crossed and his head in his hands. I am heartbroken for him. All I want to do is scoop him up and make it all better, but I know I don't have the power to turn back time and undo Jax's scene-stealing moment.

Then a thought strikes me . . . A way in which I can, almost, make it better. How I can give him the moment he has rehearsed for. But I can't do it right away, so we just sit through the birth of the Baby Jesus, the arrival of the shepherds, and the arrival of the three wise men until the show is over and it is time to go home.

'Can you drop everyone back to the house?' I ask Paul. 'I'd like to take Nathan for a treat, see if I can cheer him up.'

'Of course, pet,' Paul says and kisses me on the top of my very sweaty head. 'You feel a wee bit clammy,' he says. 'Are you sure you're not coming down with something?'

'The only thing I'm coming down with is a severe dose of regret for wearing this jumper,' I tell him, already planning to strip it off the moment I get back to the car. Nathan won't mind that I have custard spilling down the front of my 'Santa, I can explain . . .' jammies. Especially not when I tell him I'm going to treat him to a Happy Meal on the way home, and maybe even stop in at Smyth's toy store to get him some Pokémon cards.

He is still sniffling as I strap him into his car seat. 'Will we get milkshakes?' I ask him, and he nods.

'OK, Mammy. I'm sorry for saying dickhead but Jax was a dickhead.'

Now I know it's not very nice to call your child names, but I can't deny the fact that Jax was indeed a wee dickhead during the school show. He's two – being a dickhead is part of his core identity, plus they don't even realize they're actually being dickheads at that age. We dress it up and call it the 'terrible twos' but only because 'the dickhead years' isn't as socially acceptable.

'He was, dote,' I soothe. 'He was very excited and it's just because he loves you so much and loves everything you do. But listen, I'm going to make it better. I promise. Now, let's go and get some chicken nuggets.'

230

24

Merry Kinkmas

Saturday, 17 December

A Happy Meal and two packets of Pokémon cards later, and Nathan was finally smiling again by the end of Thursday night. I'd told him stories about how I was just like him when I was his age and how all I ever wanted was to be on the stage and famous.

'Also, don't forget, pet,' I'd said, as we pulled away from the drive-through, 'Jax didn't mean to upset or upstage you. He idolizes you and wants to be just like you in every single way.' Nathan had nodded sombrely and by the time we were home, he was even able to give his brother a hug before bed that night – and everyone lived to tell the tale.

But I still wanted him to have his moment in the spot-light, and thankfully I know just the bunch of complete legends to make this happen. I fired up the Rebel Mums' WhatsApp group on Friday morning and after a few quick messages, plans were now well underway to get Nathan Gallagher, star in the making, on the stage again. And this time, Jax will remain home. Or we might gag him. Or sedate him, or something. I'll work it out.

I still can't quite believe how supportive the Rebel Mums continue to be – and how they've stepped up after my near breakdown at my baby shower. One or other of them has messaged nearly every day since, just checking in, and they've even been so lovely as to not mention Pamela's performance. More importantly, they are already arranging a post-baby shower for after the birth where I can drink, cry, dance and acclimatize to alcohol again after a very long, very dry nine months. I know it's the best thing for the baby – but taking a woman's coping mech-anism of both anti-anxiety medication AND alcohol from her for nine months while her body is invaded by another human is brutal!

This amazing group of women have also inundated me with offers to babysit and drawn up a rota to bring over hot dinners for the first two weeks. I've told them that's not necessary as the boys will only eat Potato Waffles and Turkey Dinosaurs at this stage – but they're insisting on making sure I'm looking after myself.

The Rebel Mums are incredible and have been so reas-suring, but though I could do with telling *someone*, I haven't told them about the Purple-Eyed Warrior. I suspect I'd get overwhelmed with many different opinions, so I'm keeping it away from them and reserving the conversation for my two longest life besties.

Which is exactly what I'm off to do now. It's Saturday and I'm finally meeting Amanda and Cat for lunch (assuming Cat doesn't ghost us again).

My stomach is in knots and I feel that familiar tightness of anxiety in my chest – and it's not just because I'm about to discuss what we think might actually be going on in Paul's mind but also because things have been so weird with Cat. Yes, she's been great since my SOS on Tuesday, but I still don't understand why she didn't make it to my baby shower.

Pushing open the door to Primrose on the Quay, I spy Cat sitting at a table sipping some water and looking at the menu. She looks as nervous as I feel and a wave of guilt washes over me. Yes, she let me down but it's the first time she ever has, if I'm honest. She's always been my go-to person and maybe I'm the one who needs to wise up and cut her a bit of slack.

'Well, big businesswoman, are ye well?' I say, and she stands up and pulls me into the biggest, loveliest, tightest hug. I will not cry, I tell myself. I will be a proper, decent, non-emotional wreck of a human, but I do hug her back tightly.

'I'm so sorry, Tara, I was sick. You know I would never miss anything like that usually,' she says, her voice laced with guilt. I can't help but notice that she looks pale and tired – almost drained.

'Shush,' I say with a smile, holding her shoulders in my

hands and looking directly into her eyes. 'I know you must have been sick or else you would have been there, Cat. You're always there for me. I just feel like you've been distant lately, and I've really missed you.' My voice cracks, but I pull it together like the 'fake it till you break it' badass I am. 'So I'm sorry too, for being an arse about it. It's your own fault though, love, because you're the best human being I know. I know I rely on you too much and don't think about the pressure you're under. So believe me, it's me who should be apologizing.'

She smiles, relief all over her face, but there's something else there too. I know this woman as well as I know myself and I know when she's hiding something. I'm about to demand that she spill the tea when Amanda bounces in wearing a black leather pencil skirt, four-inch black stilettos and a red silk blouse. She has the glow of a well-laid woman about her. Who could've known Sean had such hidden depths?

'Hi girls, happy nearly Christmas!' she says with a smile as she slides herself onto her chair so gracefully that I'm fully impressed. Who the fuck can look graceful sitting down while wearing a leather (OK, it's probably pleather, this is the anti-animal-cruelty queen, after all) pencil skirt?

'So what are we having?' she chirps, looking down at her menu.

'Whatever you're having,' Cat says, mimicking the iconic scene from *When Harry Met Sally*.

I look enviously at Amanda's blouse: she doesn't have

even a hint of a muffin top, and her skirt clings to her shape in a very sexy way. My shape is currently 'upturned bowl of jelly', and I don't so much have a muffin top as a loaf of bread top.

'Ah stop,' Amanda giggles, 'But I'm not going to lie. My sex life at the minute is incredible, Sean and I can't take our hands off each other. It's like when we first met, except now we know what we're doing,' she grins.

I eye Cat for her reaction, as she hasn't seen Amanda in full-on horn-bag sex guru mode, and I can't wait to see what she makes of it all.

'Look, Amanda,' Cat says with a laugh, 'I'm gonna be honest here, hearing you say that makes me feel like I've just walked in on my ma and da bucking, but I am happy for you. Like, totally delighted you've finally found your inner freak. Fair play to you, about damn time. Sláinte!' She raises her glass of water to us. Amanda and I haven't ordered yet, so we just nod a quick 'cheers' in response before signalling for the waitress. I, of course, am limited to soft drinks but Amanda orders a French Martini. Well, actually she orders two French Martinis telling Cat she'll just have to drink one. Cat nods noncommittally and mutters about feeling a bit fragile.

'I know this must be strange for you two,' Amanda says, stirring her drink with her straw. 'I know compared to you two, I was a bit of a – what did you call me again? Ah, "Frigid Brigid".'

'Ach no, we didn't,' Cat and I protest in unison.

'Yes, you did. All the time. And yes, I used to feel really

uncomfortable when you two talked about dildos and vaginas and all.'

Cat and I burst into a very immature giggle.

'She said vagina out loud!' I snort at Cat, remembering once again how beetroot red Amanda had turned when Cat had very loudly sing-songed the word vagina in this very restaurant just over nine months ago.

Amanda doesn't so much as bat an eyelid. 'My counsellor says that I am a late bloomer and that reinvention can happen at any time in our lives. And did you know that women in their mid thirties and forties are at their sexual prime? Statistically speaking, we're more likely to act out our fantasies at this age.'

'Well, you wee vixen, ye,' Cat smiles, 'I'm just delighted to see you smiling and finding out that your vagina actually works for more than procreating. Long may your freaky years last. But speaking of freaky years, we're here because we've been summoned to help our wee Tara. But before we get into reinventions and our Tara's current conundrum, let's order food.'

Five minutes later we've ordered enough to feed an army, and as soon as the waitress is out of earshot, I lean as far forward as my heavily pregnant tummy will allow, and place my elbows on the table to get as close as I can to the girls. Amanda might be OK with saying vagina at the top of her voice now, but I don't want the whole of Primrose to know that my husband wants to be spanked and gagged.

'So,' I say, 'you've both seen the picture. You both know

that Paul has been a bit distant and had been late from work a few times. And then Pamela showed up – fuck that was bad. Well, we had an argument and he said I was "draining" him.' I feel shame burn my cheeks but have to power on because if I stop now I'll start to cry, and I really don't want to cry.

'So, I'll admit, I have been a lot to deal with lately. There's always a drama in Tara land and I know I tend to get a wee bit self-centred.'

They nod; I'm not even offended because it's the truth. That said, these girls are the only people who would ever be able to agree with me and still walk away from the conversation with their teeth.

'And pregnant me is extra moody and needy. It can't be easy on him. So I started to put in some effort, doing a bit more with the kids and trying to create a bit more Christmas magic at home. You know how much I love Christmas.'

They nod.

'Anyway, long story short, we've been getting on better since I've gotten out of my latest "poor me" phase and enjoyed myself more at home, and we've have had sex more this week than in the last four months. It's not pretty or in any way sexy or sensual, but it's sex. The job gets done, and my libido is higher than the interest rate on my student loan.'

Amanda leans closer and says, 'So, what's the issue then? You're getting on better. You're riding each other senseless and your libido has woken up? I'd say that's a win all round?'

'The issue,' I say in a very matter-of-fact manner, 'is this fucking purple-eyed warrior. The thing, whatever it is, he bought from Dom Fun which looks to be a BDSM accessories seller. I asked him if he had any fetishes, but he said no. Well, actually he said I'm his fetish.'

'Awwww, now, that's the right answer. Well done, Paul!' Amanda says, and Cat nods in agreement.

'It *would* be the right answer if I hadn't found that damn shipping receipt which tells me in no uncertain terms there *is* something else going on. Something he's keeping secret from me – and we don't keep secrets from each other. I'm even honest with him about my online shopping. Well . . . most of the time anyway, Christmas online shopping obviously doesn't count. But does he think I'm some sort of prude who would be shocked? He knows I like a dirty little "Duke from *Bridgerton*" meme, so why would he think that? And then there's all the times he's been late and then there was this woman he was talking to at the Christmas light switch-on, but he said it was a customer and . . .'

I'm not taking sufficient breaths as I speak. My chest tightens and nausea swirls in the pit of my stomach. I begin to cry.

'Do you think he's having an affair?' I sob, voicing for the first time the fear that has been sitting on my shoulders since I found that fucking Amazon box.

Cat and Amanda hand me a napkin at the same time.

'No,' Cat says in a very reassuring voice as she rubs my shoulder. 'Paul Gallagher is not having an affair. I know this man, and I know you two. He would never, ever cheat on you, Tara, and not just because I would castrate him with a fucking butter knife if he did, but also because he loves you.' There's a wobble in her voice as she speaks.

'That's what I used to think,' I sniff. 'But that was before all the babies, and the stretch marks, the lack of sexual adventure, and the real life, and then there's all the easy availability of kinky shit online. Now I'm not so sure.'

Cat gently takes a piece of hair that's fallen out of my clasp at the side of my head and pops it back behind my ear. 'Look, Tara, you said it yourself, things have been tough. You're off your meds, and by your own admission you've never been as emotional as this during a pregnancy before. You have two crazy-ass boys and a teenager – who is an angel by the way, and I love her – but granted, can maybe, sometimes, test your patience. And then to put the shitty cherry on top of the shit cake, "Heeeeeere's Pammy!"'

I can't help but laugh at her awful Jack Nicholson in *The Shining* impression.

'It's Pamela, Tara. Holy shit! Of course Paul is annoyed she's back. He just wants to protect you from the witch. He's seen how much she's hurt you and let you down before. Remember the state you were in when she left while you were expecting Gemma? And here she is up to her old shite again with you ready to drop baby number four. No wonder he's been staying late at work, he's probably afraid he'll string her up.'

My crying starts to subside, thanks to Cat. She's right,

just like she always is. I have had a lot to deal with lately. And I've *been* a lot to deal with lately.

'But what do I do about this BDSM fetish thing?' I say, looking at both of them, desperately waiting for a response.

'I think it's likely Paul has developed a fetish,' Amanda says, pursing her lips together as if she's now officially a professor in all things kink. 'But what you need to realize is that a fetish isn't something to be afraid of. I mean, obviously you need to talk and explore your comfort zones and see if you can reach some sort of compromise with each other.'

'Do you think?' I ask incredulously.

'Oh for God's sake, Tara, it's perfectly healthy to explore your sexual desires and have a few leanings outside of the vanilla. Don't be kink-shaming the man. Maybe that's why he hasn't opened up to you? Maybe he's afraid you'll think he's some kind of pervert.'

Paul Gallagher is many things, but a pervert is not one of them. Surely he must be aware I'd never think of him that way?

'So you think he might be embarrassed?' I ask.

Amanda nods. 'Let's say, for argument's sake, his particular kink is being spanked by a leather-clad dominatrix. I'd say he might have a problem admitting that. This is Derry. Men here are only just getting used to admitting they have feelings in the first place, never mind wants and desires outside of the norm.'

Suddenly the thought of Paul being too embarrassed to talk to me makes me sad.

'OK, so what do I do?' I ask, again looking at them both for answers.

'Well, you have to remember that you are eight months pregnant,' Amanda says.

'And still able to have sex,' I remind her.

'Yes, I know, but maybe some of the things Paul is into right now aren't the most comfortable at the best of times never mind when you're a month away from giving birth?' Amanda says.

'Fuck that,' I say. 'Marriage is uncomfortable and full of challenges, and I'm sure Paul would do it for me, so I want to at least try and do something for him. Let him know I'm willing to explore the kinky side of life? Hook me up, girls. Where can I go to get kitted out with, ye know, external wear only, erm, rubber stuff.'

'Let's eat our lunch and I'll take you to where I get my wee bits and bobs,' Amanda says as casually as if we're talking about picking up arts and crafts materials for the wains.

'Tara, I'm all for supporting you,' Cat says, looking a wee bit green all of a sudden. 'Spicing up your sex life is still part of your "fuck-it" list, remember?' She stops and does a little dry heave and I don't think it's at the thought of my sex life getting spicy.

'Are you OK?' I ask.

'I was drinking tequila until three this morning,' Cat says and does another dry heave while covering her mouth. 'The smell of those oysters or whatever your woman behind us is eating has literally just turned my stomach.'

If I wasn't able to see Cat's stomach plummet and rise again through her facial expressions, I'd be worried she is bailing again, but she's not. It's clear she's genuinely sick, and the last thing I want to see after the recent Gallagher boke-fest is more boke.

'You don't look well,' I tell her. 'Go home and get to bed, you hallion. You can fill us in later about which poor soul of a man you were drinking tequila with into the wee hours.'

'Getting too old for the partying now are we, Granny Cat?' Amanda teases, clearly relishing her new role as party girl of the group.

'I hate to say it,' Cat says as she grabs her bag and coat, 'but I think you might be right, Amanda. But if you repeat that to a single soul, I'll post all your deepest darkest secrets on Facebook.' With that she gives a quick wave and heads off towards the door holding her mouth.

'There's our food now,' Amanda says as the door closes behind Cat and the waitress appears at our table. As she places three dishes in front of us, I realize today has just improved by 100 per cent, because not only do I get to eat my own lunch, I get to eat Cat's too. The baby needs it, after all.

25

Last-minute (sex) shopping

After lunch, or in my case, two lunches, we treat ourselves to a Christmas cookie before paying up to leave. As I edge out from the table, my belly is full but my heart is racing because Amanda's got a look in her eye that's making me feel as if I'm just about to be enlisted into some weird Sex Cult.

We nip over to Waterloo Street, a pedestrianized street in the centre of town teeming with bars and a variety of independent shops to suit all tastes. There is the Holy Shop, for all your God-fearing needs. The grunge shop for all your legal highs and dodgy weed-themed merch. And finally, of course, there's Naughty Peach, the sex shop for all your kinky needs.

I've never actually been in an 'adult shop'. The thing with living in Derry, and with the shop being close to the Holy Shop, is that you never know who might spot you popping in or out. Your great auntie Annie could be in town upgrading to the latest edition of *Rosary Beads* and see you carrying a bag full of beads of an altogether more intimate nature out of Naughty Peach. That would be a very awkward conversation I've no desire to have.

So, the closest thing from the 'sex-toy realm' that I've ever bought is a Rabbit vibrator, and that was purchased from a very reputable and tasteful website online. I even got it sent to Cat's house for fear the boys, or worse, Gemma would discover it. Irrespective of my delivery diversions, Nathan did find it in my bedside locker last year and had a complete meltdown as to why he couldn't play with the 'bunny'.

I told him it was Mammy's toy and only adults could play with them, and then swiftly bribed him with £20 worth of Robux if he promised never to tell his siblings. I found a new hiding place, and was incredibly relieved that Nathan didn't tell Gemma or Jax. Unfortunately for me, he did tell Miss Rose. In fact, he drew a picture of it during class when the children were asked to draw their parent's favourite toy when growing up. That was a fun phone call to have with Miss Rose while I was still at work. Paul found it hilarious, and it cost me another £20 worth of Robux to bribe Nathan to never talk about 'Mammy's bunny' in school again.

My heart is racing as I walk down the top of Waterloo Street and see Amanda waving like a lunatic. I'm sweating bricks here, terrified someone I know will see me – we should have come incognito. She continues waving and shouting 'Tara, yooohoo,' as if I'm legally blind and can't actually see her.

'Amanda, stop!' I whisper with urgency as I get closer to her.

'Aww, come on, Tara,' she laughs. 'This is totally normal, and we as women are now accepted as a gender who can embrace our sexuality and take pleasure in our own bodies.'

This! This from the woman who took a panic attack if there was a male sales assistant at the checkout in Boots when she was buying tampons, for feck sake!

As she pushes open the door, a little bell tinkles. I can't help but think of *It's a Wonderful Life* and that famous line about bells ringing and angels getting their wings. Maybe in this case, a bell ringing means an angel gets a new vibrator?

Is a bell really necessary? It's a small shop. There's no need to draw attention to the fact that I, an eight-month-pregnant woman with swollen ankles, and her newly sexually empowered friend have just entered the building.

'Hi,' says a smiley twenty-something guy with a closely shaved head, full neck tattoo, nose ring and a gauge piercing in each ear. Gemma would no doubt think he is a 'hottie' or whatever word teenagers use now to describe an 'absolute ride'. (I refuse to acknowledge that she may in fact use that phrase, even though I probably did at the same age without really knowing what I was on about.)

'Is there anything in particular you're looking for today?' the store assistant asks. I want to reply with: 'Yes, I'm looking for something fetishy, maybe rubber, a dominatrix outfit possibly, but it must be stretchy, like really stretchy, comfortable, maybe with a fleecy lining, not restrictive, possibly have built-in fans, maybe a few pockets for my heartburn meds and chocolate bars – oh, and a full brief, no thongs or G-strings or anything that wants to try and floss my ass crack or give me thrush.'

But I don't, I just shake my head and stay silent while Amanda confidently takes control. 'Oh, we're fine thank you,' she says. 'I can show her where everything is.'

He laughs and smiles at her. 'True enough, Manda. You probably do at this stage. Well look, just shout if you need anything.'

Manda? Besties with the sexy tattooed seller of sex goods? She knows where EVERYTHING is? How many times has this freaky bitch actually been in here?

I stand in bewilderment like I'm Frankie First Year, completely overwhelmed by the large selection of wall-to-wall vibrators, what I think are a more advanced form of sex toys, porn DVDs, posters, lubricants, chocolate genitalia, edible panties and . . .

'Role play and costumes,' Amanda says, louder than I'd have liked, taking me by the hand to the corner of the store decorated with wispy bits of lace, studded leather, sexy nurse costumes and a rack of crotchless panties. Even the word 'panties' gives me the dry bokes. Can we not just say knickers, or keep it real Derry style and say nags?

'Now let's see,' she says as she starts going through the

rail with such ease, you'd swear we were in Primark looking desperately for anything that's not a size six or cropped.

'Ah, perfect,' Amanda announces, grinning as she holds up what I can only describe as tangled strips of PVC to my bump.

'All right, *Manda*,' I interrupt. 'Hakuna your Tata, love! Don't scar my unborn wain before it's even born. Hold it up around my chest. Actually, on second thoughts, don't hold it up at all. What size is it?' It seems obvious to me that whatever the answer is, it won't be 'eight months pregnant' size.

'Let me see,' she says, looking for the label and before I know it, she is hollering to the man with the gaping earlobes. 'Bap,' she shouts, and I glare at her. She knows him well enough to call him by his name – and his nickname at that? 'Have you got this in XXL?'

'I'll check out the back,' he says, leaving us to continue mooching around the store, while my cheeks burn.

Amanda picks up a basket like she's in Tesco's getting groceries, and heads straight for the edible undies where she grabs two packs, then what I think are 'anal beads' (definitely not rosary-related), and then swiftly moves on to the lube aisle, examining the different types as if she were studying a wine cellar. 'Mint always give a great tingle,' she says, brandishing a bottle of lube like it's a trophy. She pops two of them in her basket, letting me know that's one for each of us.

'Oh Tara,' she says, moving further up the aisle. 'You'll be wanting one of these. This is the one I have. It's great.'

She pulls a whip out from the bottom shelf, below what I think are strap-ons but could be toilet plungers, I honestly don't know. Is plunger porn a thing? I'm afraid to ask. Maybe I'm the Frigid Brigid in this scenario.

'Sean loves it when I give him a wee whip or two, it lets him know that I can put him in his place. He loves to be dominated and a wee thwack on a bare arse really helps to emphasize your prowess, you know.'

No, I don't fucking know. If I whipped Paul Gallagher on the bare arse he'd probably cry or worse, laugh. The man's as soft as shite, he even makes me get the spiders out of the house. But there's a reason why I'm here: is that exactly the kind of thing he would like?

'OK, I'll take it,' I say reluctantly, and Amanda grins before heading off down another aisle, grabbing things as if she's in an episode of *Supermarket Sweep*. Things that I'm too afraid and frankly too nauseous to ask about.

At the DVD section there's a man with greasy black hair, dressed in a dated brown leather jacket, giving me the proper ick. He's given me the full up and down at least twice since I came in. Obviously, I've nothing against men being in a sex shop – each to their own – but the way he's looking at me is making my skin crawl. Hurry up to fuck, Bap or whatever your name is, so I can get out of this shop asap!

'Here we go,' the prodigal Bap returns, with the XXL 'costume' in his hand. Amanda gives it a quick look and declares that 'it will do'.

'Anything else today?' Bap asks, and that's Amanda's

cue to place her now full basket on the counter. 'Just these,' she says. 'Unless the Womanizer is back in stock?'

'Afraid not, Manda. Bloody Brexit has slowed our deliveries. We do have a different brand of clitoral stimulator . . .'

What might they think if I put my hands over my ears and shout, 'Can't hear you! Can't hear you!' Because the last thing I want to think about right now is Amanda's clitoris. Or anyone's clitoris. I don't even want to think about my own.

'I think I'll wait for the delivery,' Amanda says. 'This lot will do in the meantime. Here, hang on till I get my loyalty card.' Bap begins to bag up Amanda's kinky loot after being instructed to put the costume and the whip in separate bags. 'Now, this is my treat, Tara,' Amanda says, holding her debit card.

'No, Amanda, don't be silly,' I say, but she won't hear of it. She's gone full-on Mrs Doyle, relentlessly not taking no for an answer, so I give in. Anything to get us out of here quicker.

She hands me my bag and is delighted that she just got £5 off, thanks to her loyalty card.

And I thought I was sad getting excited about getting money off with my Clubcard points at Tesco. Maybe my priorities are all wrong.

As we turn to leave, the greasy brown leather jacket guy is standing behind me with a DVD waiting to pay. I avoid making eye contact and lower my head, but this means I'm now face to face with his DVD, *Pregnant Porn*

Party, featuring two heavily made-up, blonde, naked pregnant women holding their breasts to one another. I don't know whether I want to vomit or phone the police. No wonder he was staring at me.

I grab Amanda's arm and rush towards the door, but it opens from the outside as I go to grab the handle.

'Tara, um, ah, fancy seeing you here,' a familiar voice says.

Fuck.

It's Luke from work.

26

Craic that whip, girl

Of all the sex shops in all the world, he just so happens to walk into mine. Well, not mine. I don't own it. Of course.

'Oh, erm, hey Luke,' I stutter, aware that my face is turning as red as Santa's suit. I try to hide the bag containing my newly purchased costume and whip behind my back while praying for the ground to open up some sort of vortex and suck me right down into another realm right here and now.

'Doing some shopping?' he asks, eyebrow raised, as he nods behind me into the sex shop.

'I can explain,' I bluster, my mind racing to find a suitably believable explanation that won't paint me as a ho ho ho. Too much flirtation has gone under the bridge between Luke and me for this not to be awkward AF.

'Well . . . there's this friend of ours who's having her

251

hen do and erm . . . there's a theme.' I'm aware that the handle of the whip is poking out of the top of my bag screaming 'dirty dominatrix here'. 'It's erm . . . it's erm . . . it's Pussy in Boots!' I say triumphantly, instantly regretting my outburst. Pussy? Jesus! Could my brain not just have stuck with Puss? Or fecking say it was a Secret Santa present? (Of course that only comes to me now, after I've made a tit of myself.)

'No need to explain, Tara,' Luke says, amusement writ large across his face. 'It's none of my business.'

I wonder why he couldn't have just pretended not to see me as I came out of the sex shop then? If it was truly none of his business, that's what he should've done.

'I'm Amanda, I don't believe we've ever met.' A hand appears over my shoulder, outstretched as if she's an extra in *Bridgerton* waiting for the duke to kiss her creamy white skin, then ride her into the middle of next week.

'Hi Amanda, I'm Luke,' he says with his best fanny-flutter-inducing smile, as he takes her hand and gives it a shake. I watch with a mixture of jealousy and disgust as his eyes take in every inch of Amanda's sexy outfit from heel to head. 'Tell me, are you Tara's younger sister? Her niece maybe?' At this, Amanda giggles like a fucking sixteen-year-old schoolgirl. All right, Amanda, back in your basket there, girl.

'She's my friend,' I say. 'My very married friend. Who I went to school with and who is the same age as me.'

They both stare at me as if I'm the mad one and they are both grand, standing there practically salivating over each other. I do not back down. It's Amanda who breaks the silence.

'Well, it was lovely to meet you, Luke,' she purrs, 'but as Tara has pointed out, I'm very married and I'm also running late for picking my daughters up from horse-riding. So I'll have to run on.'

Before I can even pinch her in desperation to signal DO NOT LEAVE ME! she air-kisses my left cheek, and sashays down Waterloo Street, with Luke not taking his eyes off her as she does.

I know that look. He used to give me that look. That sexy, smouldering, hot . . . wait . . . what am I thinking! Any hint of attraction I felt for Luke was momentary, and well and truly buried when he stole a promotion out from under my nose.

'I must nip on too,' I say. 'You know what this time of year is like. So much to do. Have a great Christmas!' I turn to walk up the street, but I feel his hand at my elbow.

'Before you go, Tara,' Luke says, and I turn around to look at him. 'Look, I'm sorry I didn't get in touch to ask if you were OK, but I only have your work phone number, and as you left that in work, I didn't have any way to contact you. I thought it might be crossing a line to message you on Facebook or Instagram. Anyway, I hope you're all right after what happened with Handley.'

He looks sincere, but to be honest, I hadn't even thought, or cared for that matter about Luke contacting, or not contacting, me. It's not like we're friends outside of work. We're barely even friends *in* work. And he wants to know if I'm OK? Just what story has been doing the rounds at ToteTech about my early departure?

'I'm fine,' I say. 'But what exactly do you think happened with Handley?'

'Well, he said . . . erm . . . just that you wanted to finish up early because the pressure of the Langsworth project was affecting your mental health. He, erm . . . said he okayed some extra leave to support you.'

Luke can clearly see the look of indignation on my face because now he's blushing as if it was him who just blurted out 'Pussy in Boots'.

'Handley told you that?' I say, my voice tight, my blood pressure rising by the moment.

'Yeah,' Luke says, now unable to meet my eyes. 'At the handover meeting with the client. He asked me to take over as their account manager. You've saved my ass a few times I thought it only fair to help you out with Langsworth, and it's got great potential for upsell opportunities. I've got your back, Tara,' he says with a weak smile because he's a smart man. He knows I'm about three seconds from losing my shit very publicly.

I asked to leave early? Because of my mental health? And Handley, out of the goodness of his heart, okayed some extra leave for me? Not to even start on the fact he told this to the Langsworth team, who have always respected me, my work ethic and my professionalism. I've managed them for the last six years, ensuring they renew their contract with us every single year, resulting in some serious revenue for ToteTech. They trust in my ability absolutely. Or at least they did before that absolute rotten piece of dog shit, Handley, told them his version of events.

I want to launch into a rant about what actually happened with Handley and how he seems willing to break every HR regulation in the book regarding equality in the workplace and protecting my rights as a pregnant female employee. But I bite my tongue, because if I rant and rave now, I'm going to look like the madwoman Handley has painted me as. I need to be smart about how I deal with this and that means playing these cards very close to my chest for now.

'Well, look,' I say through gritted teeth. 'I appreciate that. But I really do have to go. Tell everyone on the team I said hello and I'll keep them posted about this one's arrival.' I nod to my stomach. 'Oh and Luke, I wouldn't try upselling anything additional to Langsworth, if I were you. They renew every year because we don't try and bleed them dry. Of course, you do you, but that would be my advice.' I turn and walk away.

I don't hear if Luke says thank you, or goodbye or anything because my heart is thumping loudly with rage and I can feel tears prick at my eyes. Assholes, what a bunch of fucking ASSHOLES!

I drive home listening to Kelis' scream-sing 'I hate you so much right now', and I feel every single lyric and every note in my very bones. When I get home I commit to leaving Kelis and my anger in the car. Because it is Christmas. I am on maternity leave and I can deal with

ToteTech and whatever is left of my professional reputation in the New Year.

I've more important things to be doing, like seducing my husband and making sure I still turn him on. Even though I'm pregnant, I still want to try and appreciate his sexual needs, wants and desires. Plus Amanda just spent the best part of two hundred quid on this gear so it would be a crying shame to let it go to waste.

With a bit of persuasion-slash-bullying ('but Mammyyyy I just need a wee bit of time with Paul before the wee one arrives, you know how it is'), Pamela reluctantly agrees to take the boys to the cinema to see the evening showing of *Elf*, on condition that Gemma manages any toilet-related issues, which to be honest, pretty much sums up about ninety per cent of all issues associated with Nathan and Jax.

I hide my bag of dodgy sex gear in our wardrobe and call Paul to come and help me with something. 'Do you think we should warn your mum that the boys like to loudly mimic any sounds they hear while in the public loos?' he asks.

I consider it for a moment, but no. 'Never worry about her,' I say. 'She can deal with it. Look, Paul, could you do me a favour and do the drop-off for them? I promise, if you do, I'll be waiting for you here when you get back . . .' I flutter my eyelashes in the hope it looks sexy and not as if I'm having a stroke.

'You going to get a wee nap?' Paul asks.

'What? No. I mean, I'll be here when you get back.

Naked. And waiting for you.' The spark in his eyes lets me know this mama still has it. I don't think I've seen him bundle up the boys and shove them and Pamela in the car so fast in my life.

After a quick shower, I lather myself in my favourite coconut body lotion then stand, naked, staring at the contraption Amanda convinced me to buy, wondering how in the Dita Von Teese I'm going to get this to fit my body.

I try one way, then another. Then I try a third time, but in every attempt I just end up giving myself a wedgie with a thick strip of PVC which couldn't possibly be, but seems to be, the crotch area.

Maybe if I start with the crotch area first, then hoist up the side straps, I might have more luck. I might even be able to manoeuvre the middle and upper costume straps over my swollen belly and even more swollen boobs.

I figure wrong, and I'm left sweating (not in a sexy way) and so out of breath I could steal a couple of puffs of Nathan's asthma inhaler. I'm also increasingly concerned that I might actually have dislocated my shoulder from trying to hoist the leg straps over my back instead of my thighs. I'm half in, half out of the damn thing, with bosoms tucked in, between-the-legs strap hoicked perilously high up my vagina, and just about screaming in pain and frustration when Paul walks in.

'Jesus Christ, Tara!' Paul says, standing in the doorway looking at me as if I've actually, finally, lost the plot. This is not a dress rehearsal or drill. This is full Tara insanity.

'I can't get it on properly,' I sniff, as the familiar lump in my throat signals an impeding cry is but seconds away. I close my eyes, swallow down my sobs and commit to what I have been trying to achieve. With tears running down my face, and the circulation now completely cut off to my labia, I stutter, 'But that's OK baby, I just wanted to show you that I am down for whatever . . . well, almost whatever and, erm . . . well, I heard you've been a very, very bad boy.'

As I call him a bad boy I lift the whip from the bed and attempt to crack it like the badass, sexy (still crying) dominatrix I am, but – much like I can imagine Paul's dick is at this moment – it just goes limp. Not one to be deterred, I try it again and this time, I aim it at the floor in front of Paul for maximum effect.

It cracks this time, oh yes, it cracks. But this time, it's off my poor husband's face.

'Oh my God Paul, I'm so sorry, are you OK?' I shriek, dropping the whip, and rushing towards Paul, who's holding his hands over his face and is evidently very much not OK.

'Aghhhh,' he moans, then he doesn't really say anything else for what seems like an eternity as he rocks back and forth. I can see he's using every ounce of his willpower not to swear at me.

'Let me see,' I say, gently tugging his palm from his face. I try not to scream when I see that Paul now looks a little like Sloth from *The Goonies*, with one eye blood-shot and really, really swollen.

'Oh my God, Paul, stay there! I'll go get some ice!' I head downstairs in my half-naked, pound shop Dita Von Teese state to grab ice from the freezer. One nipple is now pointing to the ground and the other to the sky and I don't think I've ever been so intimately acquainted with a piece of pleather.

When I return to our bedroom, out of breath, and looking like a Picasso painting of a pregnant prostitute, Paul is lying on the bed holding a wet towel to his eye.

'Here, love,' I say, 'wrap the towel around this ice and hold it to your eye. Oh my God, I am so soooooo sorry.'

And I am, I'm horrified. Why didn't I practise some whip-cracking before Operation Husband Seduction, and why the fuck am I still wearing this excruciating dominatrix contraption? Then again, I'm not actually sure how the fuck I'm going to get out of it. Maybe it's just a part of me now.

'I don't know what's worse, Tara,' Paul groans as he places the ice on his eye. 'Your whip-cracking abilities, or your random forms of seduction. Where the hell did all that come from?'

'I thought this is what you're into, Paul,' I say, and I can't keep the shake from my voice this time. 'I just wanted to show you that, pregnant or not, I can still be sexy and more than anything am willing to try out new things that you might be interested in.'

'Black eyes and my pregnant wife half tied up with duct tape?' He laughs. 'That's not my thing, love.'

'Look I know it's not a full dominatrix or BDSM

experience, but I just wanted to make an effort,' I say, feeling hurt by his laughter.

'Tara,' Paul says, looking at me with one eye and the other completely covered by my makeshift ice pack. 'You know I've never been into anything like that with you, and honestly, I never will be. It creeps me out a wee bit to be honest. I told you the other night. I just need *you*. You are what turns me on, so can you get any notions of me needing any sexual reawakening out of your head. I'm happy with our sex life.'

I'm speechless. I do an instant replay of his words. *I've never been into anything like that with you.* With. You.

It creeps me out, to be honest. Does that mean it creeps him out because . . . because it's me? Does he only want to do this stuff with someone else? *Is* there someone else?

I try to remove the pleather straps from around my waist but to no avail. I'm shaking from anger, shame, nausea and pure, utter disbelief. I can only imagine how horrible I look to him right now, trying to wrestle my way out of this creepy get-up. So I reach into my drawer, grab my scissors and cut each strap until the entire thing falls on the floor. I grab the remains of my failed seduction attire and the whip and push them hastily into the back of my wardrobe, then throw on my comfy maternity pants, a baggy hoodie, and Rudolph PJ bottoms before sliding my cankles into my fake UGGs.

'Where are you going?' Paul asks, and I can't actually speak yet so I fake a cough in order to gain myself a few seconds of some much-needed composure.

'I'm going to collect the guys at the cinema,' I say, avoiding any eye contact, which at least is made easier by Paul only having one functioning eye right now. 'You can't exactly drive with your eye,' I tell him. 'And well, you may as well get an early night to yourself. There's paracetamol in my bedside drawer there.'

'Ach, Tara, don't be like that,' Paul says, sitting up and taking my hand. 'Look, I'm sorry, it was just all really unexpected, I just wish you were more confident in yourself.'

'Me too, Paul,' I say with tears in my eyes, thinking that's too much to ask when I don't even know my own husband any more.

27

My very own Rebel Mum

Saturday night was, officially, the dark night of my soul. I lay on the sofa, covered in the boys' Christmas blankets, too wired to sleep but too exhausted to do anything productive. My brain would not switch off and stop thinking about my earlier humiliation with Paul, or how I almost blinded him. (Can you imagine, for one second, having to explain *that* at A&E?)

Paul had tried to call me back upstairs after I told him I was going to pick everyone up from the cinema. I'd ignored him and ended up sitting outside, in the cold, for forty-five minutes waiting for the movie to finish. I was so lost in my own thoughts I don't even remember driving there – just sitting in that damn car, with the engine running to keep warm.

Even when my darling family got into the car – the boys completely hyper, Pamela looking like she was fresh from the trenches, and Gemma looking relieved to be on her way home – I was still zoned out. I could hear them, of course – the boys weren't exactly subtle with their attempts at imitating the giant Coke burp produced by Buddy Elf in the movie – but it all felt a bit foggy. Nothing could pull me from my self-destructive thoughts.

I knew that I was going to have to address the earlier events of my failed seduction attempt with Paul, but I was scared to. Scared that if I pushed him to open up more, he would tell me that he *is* having an affair. Scared that if he *is* having an affair, that he's just choosing not to tell me right now because I'm heavily pregnant with his child. Or maybe because he's shit scared that Pamela will castrate him without thinking twice.

My mind jumped from one scenario to the next while, on autopilot, I got the boys their supper, changed them into their jammies and put them to bed.

Then it was just me, in the quietness of the house, looking at the twinkling lights on the Christmas tree and wondering what the fuck was happening in my life.

I didn't want to text Amanda or Cat because, if the truth be told, I was – and still am – humiliated by how badly things have gone. Thankfully Pamela retired for the night early, clearly traumatized by the boys and needing alone time to google Airbnbs nearby or cheap flights back to Spain. If she had spent too much time in my company without the distraction of the boys she would have twigged something was badly wrong, and I was not in the mood for a Pamela level interrogation. Gemma was holed up in her room, and it's not as if I could talk to her about it all anyway. There would be no, 'Hi love, I nearly blinded your daddy while trying to whip him because he's a very naughty boy.' I can already hear her 'OMG! You are like so embarrassingaahhh! You're wrecking my mental healthaaahhh!'

But I also knew I had feck all chance of falling asleep, so I headed for the sofa where I lay for hours, feeling completely confused and scared about what was going on with my husband and what that might mean for me. For us.

Paul would never do this to me, I told myself. Not *my* Paul. There must be a rational explanation for his distance, the late evenings, the new obsession with golf, not to mention the dominatrix accessory he bought off Amazon.

There had to be. But right then, I was fecked if I could think of it.

'Tara!' I hear Paul calling me, and for a second, I think it's a dream. Until, that is, I feel the familiar pang of neck pain which tells me that I have once again, fallen asleep on the sofa. That's two nights in a row now – ever since the big humiliation on Saturday. I just can't bring myself to go back to the scene of the crime properly yet, and I'm out of ideas of how to bring it up with Paul again.

'Tara, it's Monday morning, we've slept in!' Paul says as he rushes into the room. 'Did you sleep down here again? No alarm went off! Christ, where's the boys' lunch boxes? Can you get them dressed, and I'll do their lunches and defrost the car?'

I blink awake, look at him and see his eye is still red and swollen and I immediately wince. I've no time to think about it though, not as I haul my aching body off the sofa and up the stairs to wake our darling offspring.

Fortunately, Nathan has a Christmas party at school today, and Jax is making Christmas cupcakes with Jo. Without these events to look forward to, waking them up would be a total shitemare. 'Come on, boys!' I say, forcing Christmas cheer into my voice. 'There's another fun day ahead!'

Ten minutes later they are clean, dressed, in their coats and hats and scarves and straight out to the car where Paul has the heater blowing on full blast. I strap them in, give them both a kiss and a breakfast bar and tell them I love them more than 'Santa loves cookies'. Nathan tells me he loves me 'infinity plus a fousand' and Jax says he loves me 'more dan poo', which makes me laugh but also choke up a bit because my hormones are sky-high today.

When Paul walks down the path carrying a collection of lunch boxes and school bags, he hastily kisses me on the head and shouts, 'Bye, love.'

'Paul,' I start. 'I really am sorry about your eye.'

'It's nothing,' he says. 'And we really need to be going.' With that he is in the car and reversing down the driveway, leaving me standing in the sharp and frosty morning air. The trees in the garden are naked and stark and the grass is glistening with frosted tips. It's a perfect dry winter's morning and the smell of Christmas is in the air. I would be revelling in the beauty of it all if my head wasn't still monumentally up my hole.

I've never, ever, felt like this before. Not once in my fifteen years of marriage to Paul have I ever doubted his loyalty or our marriage. I'm trying my best to tell myself that I've no reason to doubt it now either. Call it denial, call it desperation, call it hormonal overload, but I refuse to think that Paul is having an affair. Nonetheless, we need to have a conversation about it because I can't deny that *something* is wrong.

Back inside, I click on the kettle to make myself a coffee. My anxiety levels are much too high to risk putting any caffeine in my system, so I'll have to rough it with a decaf. 'One for me as well, love,' Pamela croaks as she walks into the kitchen wearing a short black silk nighty and a dressing gown featuring a bright pink flamingo on the back. 'Jesus, love. Have you no heat on in this place? It would freeze the balls off a brass monkey,' she shivers.

'The heat is on full blast actually, Mother,' I tell her. 'Maybe if you were wearing more than whatever that is you have on you, you'd be a bit warmer. Do you not think that's a wee bit inappropriate?'

'You've a cheek,' she laughs, 'I was just in your room looking for a black top to wear with a cracker wee skirt I got yesterday in Dunnes and I found an interesting black leather number and a whip.' She raises an eyebrow.

'It . . . it was from Halloween,' I stutter and continue

making the coffee with my back to her so that she can't see my face. Pamela has always been able to suss out whether or not I'm telling the truth from the look on my face. 'I was dressed up as Puss in Boots. I must give that stuff back to Cat actually,' I say, grateful that I didn't say 'Pussy in Boots' this time because I've humiliated myself enough these last few days.

'Tara, love, turn around,' Pamela says, but her tone is different than usual. She's not goading, or mocking. I'd go so far as to say that she sounds concerned. So I turn around, and in that very moment I start to cry.

Pamela wraps her arms around me and pulls my head into her chest. I need this hug. God, I *really* need it. I sob for a minute before I feel myself instinctively pull away. I don't know why, but I don't want her to see any weakness in me. How fucked up is that?

'Tara,' she says gently. 'I look in your wardrobe nearly every day. I didn't bring enough winter clothes up with me, so I've been borrowing some of yours. I've never seen that in there before so don't be spinning me any "Halloween" line.'

She guides me to the kitchen table and we both sit down. 'This isn't an easy question for me to ask, but is Paul pushing you to dress up like that for him? Is he into all that submissive stuff? I've seen the *Fifty Shades* movies. I know some stuff, you know. And I know you think I don't know you but even I can see that he's changed since the last time I was here. All those late nights, and not being as loving or affectionate as he used to be with you.

I mean you two used to make me sick you were so loved up.' She says this with a small smile. I can't speak just now, my stomach is churning as much as I feel my heart breaking.

'Tara, is he forcing you to do stuff against your will? Because you know, that's illegal these days. And Jesus Christ, you're pregnant . . .'

I shake my head. 'Mammy, stop, look, no, he's not forcing me to do anything it's just—'

'You know I've half a mind to march down to that garage right now and give him a piece of my mind. I mean what kind of sicko—' Pamela interrupts.

'Mammy,' I say, this time more sternly. Whatever is going on with Paul, I can't have my mother thinking he's some kind of sex offender for God's sake! 'He is not a sicko and he is not forcing me to do anything. I swear. We've just been going through a wee rough patch, but it's going to be OK. Please don't mention it to him. We're working through it, I promise.' I'm not sure I sound as convinced as my words would indicate.

'Tara,' Pamela says, looking at me in a way I've never seen her look before, with empathy and even, if I'm not mistaken, love, 'I want you to know that just because you're married to someone, it doesn't mean that you have to stay with them, especially if you're unhappy.'

'I'm not unhappy, Mammy,' I hiss, because what she's just said, like many things she says, has hit a nerve. I think of my poor daddy – and his broken heart. I don't think he ever really recovered from that. 'Just because you left

Daddy when you were bored and some twenty-three-year-old caught your eye, doesn't mean that you're an expert in all things marriage. You don't know the meaning of marriage. It takes hard work, and commitment and sticking together during the boring times, knowing the good times will come again. There are highs and lows, struggles and triumphs, and how would you know about any of that? You jumped off at the first hurdle and never looked back. You don't know me, or Paul, or how we are together – what we mean to each other.'

She's finally silent and I should be relieved, but I'm not because she looks as if I've smacked her across the face. Yes, OK. That was harsh, but she needed to hear it. She walked away when the going got tough, so what does she know about working through your problems?

Pamela shakes her head slowly, and a tear rolls down her perma-tanned cheek. 'I never wanted to marry your daddy,' she says in a small voice, keeping her gaze downward. 'I met your father when I was eighteen. I was only a wain, Tara. Think about it. Eighteen is not much older than Gemma is. And yes things were different then. In those days you couldn't so much as hold a boy's hand without the Catholic Church and the entire fucking community guilting you into getting married, in case, God forbid, you got pregnant out of wedlock and brought shame on them. Or worse than that, they'd ship you off to the nuns in Marianvale up in Belfast, or down to one of the Magdalen Laundries in Dublin until your baby was born and taken from you. It might've been the seventies and eighties, Tara, but that carry-on was still going on then. I have friends who were shipped off and they were never the same when they came back. You know the kind of abuse that went on in those places. We were all terrified by it. So we'd had the fear of God, and the nuns, our parents, everyone drummed into us. Sex was sinful and shameful. I knew your daddy a wet week, and while we had a bit of craic for a few months, we were always more like friends. I should never, ever have married him. We were completely different people. I didn't even know who I was then. Who does when they're eighteen? I was trapped, Tara, trapped for life with a man I didn't and couldn't love, no matter how hard I tried. Not in the way he wanted or deserved anyway.'

As she looks at me with tears streaming down her face, my heart breaks. I never realized or even understood why she had an affair, or left him. I knew the shame inflicted by the Church in those days was bad, but I never made the connection between that and Pamela. She has always appeared so ballsy, I can't imagine her ever feeling compelled to conform to anyone or being an actual victim.

'I never wanted to be married, Tara. I'm not one of those women who dreamt of her wedding day when she was a wee girl. I never wanted to be tied down. But I did marry your daddy intending to do my best to make it work. I thought I'd change. Get used to it. Fall completely in love with him. But I only ever felt like a free spirit whose wings had been clipped. I love you so much, Tara, and I could never regret having you, but truth is, I'd never wanted children either. I wanted to be an air hostess, travelling the world on new adventures every day.'

My heart aches for my mother. This revelation makes everything so much clearer. She never wanted marriage, yet I thought she didn't want my father. She never wanted children, yet I thought she didn't want me.

I imagine society trying to do that to Gemma in a few years, and it makes me sick to my stomach. I suddenly understand why my mother is the way she is.

'But why didn't you just leave him?' I ask her, needing that last bit of closure. 'Daddy, I mean, why did you have to have an affair, why not just leave him rather than humiliate him in front of the entire town?'

'I didn't set out to humiliate him,' she says. 'Tara, I know how close you and your daddy were and I never wanted you to think badly of him. But I begged him for a divorce, time and time again. He always refused – said that he wouldn't have the shame of the Church on him, the shame of not being able to keep me as his wife, even though he knew how unhappy I was. Even though he knew we didn't love each other. He wanted to keep me even when I told him I felt like I was in prison. Well, eventually I had enough. Yes, the affair was wrong, but I just wanted to rebel. Against your father, my parents, the Church, the patriarchy, everyone. And you know what? I finally felt free. The only thing that broke my heart was leaving you. But I thought, one day, she'll understand. That you'd understand that we can be fearless, we can leave a marriage if we're truly unhappy, and we can be whatever the fuck we want to be.'

I blink back tears – my loud, proud, brave mother, all these years.

'I've tried to explain it to you a few times, but it was a tough conversation to have. We didn't have a connection, and I am so sorry for that, but I couldn't fake it. I had to be true to myself even if it was selfish. And you hated me and loved your daddy so much I didn't want to hurt your relationship with him. So I stayed quiet. But I see unhappiness in you here, and I need you to know it's OK to rebel.'

I'm speechless. My mother the rebel, stuck two fingers up to all of society's confines. I was so shielded from it all as a child that it's only now I can understand that she was never meant to be my mother, or anyone's mother. She was meant to be free.

28

I love him, actually

After my mother's honest revelation, we talk for two hours straight about how women in Ireland in the seventies and eighties had two choices: leave Ireland, or get married and have children.

She tells me some horror stories about the girls she knew who were sent away to the nuns in Belfast or Dublin. Teenage girls who had been taken advantage of, gotten pregnant, then were forced to carry their babies to full term before giving them up for adoption.

She also tells me stories of many affairs back in the day for which men were usually forgiven, but women cast out as whores. Women were denied basic rights because of their gender, marital rape wasn't laid down in law as a crime until 2003, and until the seventies, women couldn't keep their jobs in public service once they were married.

It's a stark reminder of how far we've come as a sex,

particularly in Ireland, but each change was hard fought. Yet I'd never viewed my mother as someone who was part of the rebellion.

'Mammy, if it was all so tough and this isn't the life you wanted – can I ask why you came back now?' I say. 'You want to get to know my wains. What's changed?'

'I'm not getting any younger, am I?' she says with a sad smile. 'I know I look amazing for my age but I'm starting to feel it, Tara. I've loved my years away. God knows I packed a lot of living into those times. But I think Javier and I splitting up made me evaluate what I want for the rest of my life. I'm ready to settle down now, I think. Not that I'm ready to join the full-blown blue-rinse granny brigade, but I want to try and be a better mother to you. And a better granny to your wains.'

'Well, I can drink to that,' I say, and I raise my decaf coffee in her honour.

'Drink to what?' Gemma says, and I don't know how long she's been standing at the kitchen door, but she has one eyebrow raised and isn't even looking at her phone.

'A family Christmas,' I say.

'And it's going to be the best one ever,' Pamela says, smiling at me reassuringly.

'Aye, class,' Gemma sniffs, clearly unimpressed. 'So, um, can I head into town this evening with Mia?' she asks sweetly as she reaches into the cupboard for a loaf of bread. My heart sinks. I know how this is going to go – and this time she'll have back up from 'Pammy'.

'Nope, Gemma, for the last time, you're grounded

until Friday,' I tell her, bracing myself for the incoming explosion.

I don't have to wait long. Gemma, it seems, has had enough of acting like a princess in front of Pammy, and has decided to show her true colours. 'Eughhh,' she screams, stomping her foot. 'Why are you so annoying? Like, seriously, would you ever get a grip and remember what it's like to be my age instead of being a sad boring witch all your life? I'm missing out on everything! I HATE you so much!' She completes her rant with a majestic firing of the loaf of bread at the wall, sending slices and crumbs everywhere.

Before I can open my mouth to respond, Pamela steps up, and steps in. 'Gemma!' she scolds. 'How *dare* you speak to your mother like that? You are grounded because you messed up. So take your oil! And after that bread firework display there, you'll be lucky not to get another week added on. Now pick up every piece of bread and apologize to your mammy, right now!'

I don't know who's more shocked, Gemma or me. Gemma blinks back tears before hurrying over to hug me and breaking into full-on sobs. 'I'm so sorry, Mammy, I've got my period, I didn't mean to call you a witch or sad, or boring, I'm just missing my friends but I'm still sorry. Swear.'

I can hardly believe it. Gemma hasn't apologized to me with any degree of sincerity in a long time, but here she is hugging me and telling me she was out of line. I glance over at Pamela, who gives me a wee nod and a smile.

'How about us three have a movie night tonight? I'll order pizza and we'll get some of that nice Ben & Jerry's Chocolate Fudge ice cream?' I say, warmed by the knowledge there are three generations of feisty, strong women in this room.

'Yes, please,' Gemma sniffs. 'I'll go make the beds upstairs.'

'OK love, thank you,' I tell her. 'I'll make you some breakfast and call when it's ready.'

Order is restored.

'Right,' Pamela says. 'This sitting about will be giving me varicose veins, I'm gonna nip into town, love, grab a few things for our wee movie night, oh and by the way . . . your sons last night . . .'

I'm already cringing as I ask her, 'What did they do?'

'Now, I'm not being funny love,' she says, which means she is about to offend me greatly, 'but those boys are feral. Jax put popcorn up his nose, pulled down his pants and ran up and down the aisle. Nathan asked at least three hundred and fifty-four questions, before he also decided to put popcorn up his nose. And they just talked, and screamed, and jumped mad for the entire film. Are they always like that?'

'Well, they have their moments,' I say, gathering the cups in front of us. 'Boys will be boys, they are wains. And yes, sometimes they get overexcited and go a bit wild but there is so much joy in how they live and love life. I've no time for the seen and not heard brigade. Yes, they embarrass me at times, but they're not wee for long. Before I know it,

276

they'll be teenagers, who will only speak to me when they want food, money or to get off their grounding early.'

'For what it's worth, I think you're an amazing mammy, Tara,' Pamela says, giving my arm an affectionate rub. 'You're a better mammy than I was or ever could be. I honestly don't know how you do it. I'd have been signed into some sort of facility years ago if . . .'

She stops herself before finishing her sentence. We both know where it was going anyway.

'It's OK, Mammy,' I reassure her. 'I get it. Motherhood is definitely not for the faint-hearted, but as much as there are days when I want to tear my hair out or drown myself in a gallon of wine, they really are my happiness. As is Paul. I do love him, Mammy, and he loves me. We married for the right reasons, I promise.'

'I'm happy for you,' she says, before standing up, leaving the kitchen and concluding the most surreal morning I think I've ever had in my entire life.

I sent a text to Paul to let him know of our plans to commandeer the living room for a girls-only movie night and that I'm setting up a boys-only movie night den for him, Nathan and Jax in our room.

I've made it look like the Wee Donkey actually made some popcorn while they were at school and set up a Christmas grotto on our bed, complete with fairy lights around the headboard, their Christmas blankets, candy canes and a chocolate Santa for each of them. *Arthur Christmas* is primed and ready to play.

The boys were ecstatic when they came home from school and wolfed down their dinner of chicken nuggets and chips as fast as they could so they could run upstairs and change into their festive PJs.

We girls have opted to watch the Christmas classic, *Love Actually*. Pamela has pulled the coffee table over beside the sofa and placed bowls with popcorn, Maltesers and some fancy crisps and dip on top. She bought herself a bottle of wine and even got some Shloer for Gemma and I, which we drink out of Prosecco glasses so I can at least pretend it's actual alcohol.

Paul and I haven't had the chance to chat much since he got home, which is the norm when the house is so busy, and the boys are next-level hyper. I was delighted to see the swelling around his eye seems to have gone down a fair bit, but I know I can't keep putting off talking about what happened on Saturday night. I just have no idea what I'm going to say to him. I only know I will lose it if he lies to me again.

Before they all disappear upstairs, I make sure they have everything they need, which includes pouring two large cups of juice. I'm not falling for the boys' claims that they are 'big boys' and that they can carry them upstairs their 'own selves'; I know how that particular story ends and it isn't well.

'Here, love,' I tell Paul. 'Can you carry those up with you for the boys?'

'OK,' he says, 'Will you grab my phone and my work

bag there and bring them up? OK boys, up we go, it's time for *Arthur Christmas* in the boys' den.'

'Of course,' I tell him, smiling as I listen to Nathan and Jax cheering as they reach the top of the stairs and see everything set up for them.

I grab Paul's bag and phone from the kitchen worktop. I'll be very clear. I am not snooping. I never usually look at his phone, but it lights up with a notification, and I instinctively look at the screen.

Ready for Friday night, Barbarian?

From a number with no name.

I don't know if the contents of my stomach are going to fall out of my ass or eject themselves through my oesophagus. Either way, I drop Paul's bag and phone and rush to the downstairs bathroom.

Ten minutes later and I'm still here, and still shaking like a toddler coming off a sugar rush. I've vomited twice, making sure to flush the toilet so no one could hear me. Gemma has called me three times to hurry up, but I asked her, my voice shaking, to give me a few more minutes. I'm in shock, complete and utter shock, and my heart is breaking into a million pieces. That bastard. 'Barbarian' eh? It all makes sense. Bastard! I want to run upstairs and confront him right now, but the boys are so happy and Gemma and Pamela have been so excited about our girly night.

'Mammy, come on,' Gemma whines, 'the movie is starting.' The last thing I want to do now is sit and watch a movie, but I won't let that bastard husband of mine ruin this, or any of these precious family moments, just because he's fucking about with some tramp.

As *Love Actually* plays, I'm unable to relax. Gemma and Pamela are heavily invested as it's their first time ever seeing this movie. I, on the other hand, have watched it at least ten times, all with Paul, which is its own heartbreak in this moment.

Pamela offers me Maltesers, but I refuse.

'My stomach isn't the best,' I apologize. 'Must have eaten too much at dinner.'

Thankfully she buys it. As I sip my Shloer, wishing I could substitute it for a proper emotion-numbing alcoholic beverage, arguably one of the most iconic Christmas movie moments of all time starts to play out on the screen.

Emma Thompson's character has just discovered that her husband, Alan Rickman, has bought a necklace for another woman and given her a Joni Mitchell CD, confirming her worst fear that Harry is having an affair.

As Emma Thompson sneaks off to her bedroom to play 'Both Sides Now' on her CD player, she begins to cry. And so do I. Gemma catches sight of me and rolls her eyes.

'C'mon, Mammy, you're so embarrassing.'

'Hormones,' I tell her. But it's not my hormones. It's heartache. A heartache that I hope she never knows or feels; one that I never want her to know about because Gemma idolizes her daddy. But what now? What will she think when she finds out he's a cheat and that he's broken our family?

How can I protect her from this, how can I protect all of them?

I am broken. My heart is shattered, just like Emma Thompson's is now, and just like her, I'm hiding the fact that I know the truth from my family, silently dying inside.

'Well, Jesus, if I wore a long skirt and had a haircut like that, I'd expect my husband to cheat on me too,' Pamela laughs, and so too does Gemma. But I don't. Emma should have been enough for Alan. Just like I should be enough for Paul.

29

The last Christmas

No matter how I try to rationalize it, my brain will not come to any other conclusion. My husband – the man I considered the love of my life – is cheating on me. He's off banging some sultry slut who doesn't look like a bag of spuds when she puts on her sexy bondage gear and calls him her 'barbarian', and then coming home to play at being the perfect family man.

The boys fell asleep watching the movie, as did Paul. That suited me. I don't want to breathe the same air as him, let alone lie in the same bed.

I couldn't face another night on the sofa though, so instead, I'm curled up in Nathan's single bed desperately trying to get some sleep. But it's no use. Even though I am exhausted beyond words, I haven't been able to shut my brain off long enough to drift into sleep. I've tossed and turned all night, swinging between agonizing heartache, which has me sobbing into a pillow so no one hears me, and an intense rage building up inside me so much I worry I might actually explode.

A part of me wants to hide away or bury all these feelings to try and get through Christmas for my children, especially this little monkey in my tummy. They deserve one last magical, family Christmas before their perfect world implodes.

That's what breaks me, even more than Paul's cheating. It's the thought of my children in a broken home, and this little unborn flump not knowing what it was like to have Mammy and Daddy in love and in the same house. I knew that agony as a child, and it's the last thing I want for my children.

When that particular heart-wrenching scenario gets too much to contemplate, I switch to wondering who the fuck the home-wrecking bitch is that's ruined my marriage, and my family.

Paul doesn't work with any women, but he fixes cars for a fair amount. And women love a bit of hunky mechanic, don't they? He's been hit on more times than the Credit Union for pre-Christmas loans. He's always laughed it off, or so I thought. Then it hits me. The woman at the Christmas light switch-on in town, pink bobble hat, blonde hair. He couldn't wait to get away from her when he saw me approach. It's her, isn't it? She was right there in front of me and I didn't catch on. I wonder if she knows

I'm pregnant? I wonder if she even cares. Is she pretty? Prettier than me? No doubt she's thinner, probably with perkier boobs and fewer stretch marks. And obviously she'll have fewer mental health issues and be less 'draining'. But she's not the woman he promised to love forever. She's not the mother of his children. She's not the woman he claims is his best friend.

I've always been enough for him in the past. Why am I not any more? Even if I say so myself, I'm a damn good mother, and a damn good wife. I'm not perfect, no one is, but I don't deserve to be cheated on. Where did we go wrong? Where did I go wrong? Was it my epic midlife crisis earlier this year? The one that resulted in me getting pregnant for the fourth time. Sure, this baby wasn't planned, and we will have to tighten our belts more, but that doesn't mean he or she isn't wanted and already loved. Or is it that a fourth pregnancy has finally pushed my body into not-one-bit-sexy territory? How many stretch marks is a stretch mark too many?

Marriage is supposed to be about loving each other through the good and the bad, and surely that includes hormonal mood swings and pregnancy farts. But maybe my husband is more traditional and old school than I ever thought and can't think of the mother of his children as a sexual being who gets a raging dose of horn and enjoys a good seeing to, and that's why he looks elsewhere for the kinky stuff.

Pamela is right. People don't have to stay in a marriage if they're unhappy, so why the fuck didn't Paul just tell me he was unhappy? Why did he have to deceive me? It's so incredibly unfair. If he had opened up to me, we could have worked it out before it went past the point of rescue. We could've gone to marriage counselling, or sex counselling like Amanda and Sean. I'd have worked at it. I'd have worked hard to make him happy, to make him love me, and want me again. But now it's too late.

I am in pieces, and even more insecure than ever before. Not only is this a reflection on him being unhappy and wanting something else, but it's a reflection on me as a person, as a wife, as a woman. He keeps telling me that our sex life is fine, so what else am I to think? And we'd said, once the baby was old enough to be left with a sitter, we'd rekindle the 'us' time properly.

I thought he was happy with how it was. Obviously, his hussy from whatever backstreet she crawled out of excites him more. No doubt she was the one who showed him BDSM and other filthy unimaginable things. I squeeze my eyes shut, as my stomach churns and my head spins.

No, I will not let him break me or my children. That bastard is not going to leave me in the gutter, pining after him. I am fucking class, and he is going to regret ever going elsewhere to get his end off.

That's it. Today, I choose anger. I am going to break his heart, just like he's broken mine. I want to expose him for the cheating, lying bastard that he is. And I can already think of a way to do it – a way he can't wriggle out of with lies and assurances that I'm the 'only fetish he's into'.

Hell hath no fury like a woman scorned, and you can

multiply that fury by about 1,000 per cent when the scorned woman is pregnant.

But I need help.

I send a text to Cat and Amanda.

SOS girls, if you love me, pick me up at 7pm on Friday night – I'll explain all then. Trying to process it myself now. PLEASE don't let me down.

I hit send, sure in myself that they'll be there for me.

Both reply within minutes. Amanda: Absolutely and categorically will be there x. and Cat with just three words: Heels, flats or DMs?

I think of her foot colliding with Paul's purple leather posing pouch.

DMs. Definitely DMs.

But for today, I have to pretend everything is normal. I need to focus on my beautiful children and making sure they come out of this shit show unscathed.

It's now 7 a.m. and I know there's no point in even attempting to sleep any more, so I head downstairs and tidy up our makeshift girls' den, returning it to its usual state. I pop on the kettle for a cup of decaf. I need to eat, but the thought of it is turning my stomach even more. I know if I don't, though, that I'll feel worse, so I slide a couple of slices of bread into the toaster, and nibble my way through, barely able to taste it.

I set up the Wee Donkey sitting on a chessboard opposite a Thor from the Avengers figurine. I pile up all of the chess pieces, scattering them around the elf, and I make a sign from white cardboard that says 'Cheater', placing it on the Wee Donkey's lap. I position Thor's arm so he's pointing straight at him, indicating that the Wee Donkey is a cheat. Yes, I'm being petty AF, but I'm teaching life lessons to my boys here. Cheating is never good.

I put some waffles in the toaster, slice some strawberries and pop the jar of Nutella (that I really need to replace soon and offer up a Hail Mary to my kids' dentist) on the table.

I pour two glasses of cold milk into the kids' *Elf* beakers and I get to making their lunches. Usually if I'm up this early, I'd make Paul's lunch too, but today, no chance.

That fucker can starve.

Sneaking into my bedroom, I try to get dressed as quietly as possible so I don't wake Paul. As I'm pulling up my black maternity joggers and slipping on my old running shoes, I hear, 'Is Arthur Christmas a real-life boy, Mammy?'

It's Nathan, who's lying on my side of the bed with Jax's leg on top of his head. Despite this, he looks so cosy and warm, his hair a gorgeous, bedheady mess of curls.

'I don't know, pet,' I whisper. 'Why do you ask?'

'Well,' he says, as he lifts Jax's leg from off his head and sits up, 'If he is real, den at means dat Santa has children, and if he has children, den at means dat he has sex.'

I cough and feel a little bit of the toast I barely swallowed in the first place threaten to come back up my throat. 'Erm . . . who told you that, son?' I ask, trying not to sound shocked or to laugh. I'm aware of Jax and Paul moving in the bed now, Nathan's excited chatter clearly waking them.

'Jason in school said dat you have to have sex to have children, and I don't know what sex is but I fink dat you know acuz you have children, and you have another children in your tummy just now.' And he's looking at me now in anticipation for my reply.

I don't know how I'm getting out of this one and after a night of no sleep I seem to have lost the ability to dodge all those Nathan-sized conversational bullets. 'Well . . . erm . . . you see,' I stutter, 'When a man and a woman . . . erm . . . it's really complicated actually . . . but . . . when two people love each other . . .' My voice trails off. I don't want to think about love this morning even more than I don't want to think about how to explain sex to a six-year-old.

'OK, boys,' Paul cuts in, 'Let's go see what the Wee Donkey did last night, will we?' And they bounce out of bed and run downstairs with Paul following them.

He saved me there, and normally I'd be so grateful, but this morning I'm not. This morning he's a prick. I head into the bathroom to brush my teeth and wash my face as I hear the boys scream 'Cheater! Cheater! Cheater!' over and over. I want to shout it a few times myself.

Glancing at my reflection in the mirror, I notice how

drained I am. There is no pregnant 'glow' here – just a pale, plump face with puffy eyes, swollen lips and a nose that's getting more bulbous by the day.

I feel ugly. I *look* ugly. No wonder Paul is having an affair, and that's before I even begin to dissect my flabby, stretched and saggy body . . . NO! No! I will not go into self-destruct mode, I tell myself. I am pregnant, I am thirty-six and this is my life.

I am me, and I should be enough.

I will be enough, for my children.

Because they are all that matters.

30

Who doesn't love a Christmas candle?

Thursday, 22 December

Everything aches. Most notably my jaw, from holding a fake smile on my face for the last two days. It's possible it looks a bit manic now, and I did catch my right eye twitching earlier. But for the most part I've managed to keep the Gallagher family Christmas on track, despite the fact every Christmas song has me running for the downstairs loo for a little weep. 'Last Christmas' had me cry-singing while cleaning the house yesterday and I have never felt more spiritually connected to George Michael in my life.

Today is a milestone in our Christmas preparation not only because it's the last day of term for Nathan but the last day Jax will be with Jo before the holidays. Thus begins the official Christmas countdown, with only three more sleeps until Santa arrives. And only one more sleep until I enact my plan to catch Paul red-handed, or purple-dildo'd or whatever the fuck it is.

When I drop Jax off at Jo's, I hand her a bottle of red wine and a card with a voucher inside for her favourite restaurant. If I could have, I would have spent more on her. I've said it before and I'll say it again, she really is the most amazing childminder I've ever known. And I'm not just saying that because I need to keep her sweet so she agrees to mind Baby Gallagher when the time comes.

Then it's Nathan's turn to be dropped off. What he doesn't know is that today I'll be making up for the nativity show fiasco and he *will* get his moment to shine. Even with all the stress in my life at the moment, this is bringing me so much joy and I am positively bursting with excitement about it. I can't wait to see his wee face when I tell him . . .

I give his hand an extra squeeze at the school gates, unable to contain the wave of love I feel for him. 'C'mon, pet,' I say. 'Let's go in for your last day!'

But Nathan stops me before I walk into the schoolyard, looking up at me all bright-eyed. My heart fills with more love than I ever thought possible.

'Mammy,' he says, 'you slept in my bed last night and I know you are very, very tired and I am a big boy now so I fink can walk down to the classroom myself.'

'OK baby . . . if you're sure?' I am simultaneously blown away by how empathic he is to my tiredness, proud of how he wants to make sure I'm OK, and properly emotional that he now thinks he is a big enough boy to walk to the classroom on his own.

'I am sure, Mammy,' he nods confidently. 'You have more grey hairs dan Granny Pammy so maybe you need more rest so that they go away and you look young like her. Oh and could you not call me baby outside of da house acuz I am a big boy now, 'member?'

'Sorry, son,' I say, that fake smile of mine getting faker than ever. The wee shite! I look older than Pamela? Jesus maybe I need to go to Majella the hairdresser too? If he wasn't my own son, I'd risk the hernia and drop-kick him down the playground right about now, but I won't. From the mouth of babes, eh?

'Can I at least give you a kiss?' I say, kneeling down in front of him, because I'm not taking no for an answer here, kid, I'm vulnerable after you just slagged off my grey hair and said I looked older than a sixty-two-year-old sun-worshipper.

'OK,' he says, looking around him to make sure none of his friends are watching. 'But only on the cheek, and make it quick.' He drives a hard bargain.

'OK,' I say, and plant a quick little peck on his cheek, taking a moment to breathe him in and savour the softness of his skin against mine. In a few years he'll be taller than me, and have a beard, and stinky man feet and, God forbid, have the power to break some girl's heart like his daddy has broken mine. I take a deep breath. 'Now, here's your lunch, your water bottle is in your schoolbag and here's a present for Miss Rose.'

'What is it?' he asks, peeking into the bag, no doubt checking if it's something he might like for himself instead.

'It's a candle, one of those expensive ones. So be careful not to drop it. Miss Rose will love it. Now off you go, or you'll be late and . . .'

'. . . Miss Rose will want to speak to you on the phone again,' he says with an eye-roll.

I nod. Miss Rose sure does love to make phone calls. 'Oh and Nathan . . .' I call. 'I've got a surprise for you after school, I'll pick you up right here!'

'Fanks, Mammy,' he says, and then he whispers, 'I love you,' and hops down the steps into school.

I love him too. More than he could ever fathom. Even if he is a wee shite sometimes.

With both boys now deposited, I can drop the fake smiling for a bit. I can even indulge in a well-deserved self-pity wallow in my car. It's only three more sleeps until Christmas Day. The children are fizzing with excitement. The air is crisp and cold. Christmas trees can be seen through every window, and the city streets are festooned with glittering lights. You can practically smell Christmas in the air – that mixture of chimney smoke, cinnamon and frosty mornings. I should be gearing up for a day filled with joy, happiness and laughter, but it won't be like that. Not for me, anyway. I will do whatever it takes to make sure the children enjoy every precious moment, it's going to be brutal.

I've been formulating a plan. These last couple of nights when I've barely slept, I've been trying to work out what my life will look like after I confront Paul 'the ballbag barbarian' about his betrayal.

What will it be like once I know who he's been sleeping with? Will he apologize? Will he even want to fight for us? Well, he'll be in for a shock if so. The time to fight was before he slipped his dick into some other woman.

I'll let Paul stay until the New Year. Then, even though I know it will break my children's hearts, he will just have to go. And I'll have to remember it's not me who did this breaking. Paul made his choices, and in doing so he's lost the best woman he could have ever had, and broken his family apart in doing so. I hope that hurts him every single day.

And I will come through this because I'm going to keep myself surrounded by strong women and show everyone, and my daughter especially, that I can rise in the face of adversity.

But I have many things to do between now and then – and for once I'm grateful to be so busy I'm in danger of meeting myself coming the other way.

Not only do I have Nathan's big onstage surprise this afternoon, I also have to show my face at the ToteTech Christmas Party at the Guildhall Taphouse later.

I had no intention of showing up to that party until meeting Luke outside the sex shop and his bombshell about Handley selling me down to the river to Langsworth, implying I wasn't up to the job any more due to my mental health.

I have no issue – none at all – in being open about my

mental health. I'm all about breaking the stigma. But I will not be lied about. Even through the worst of my struggles, I kept Langsworth on track and on our books.

I want to come face to face with that lying worm Handley and watch him squirm. He won't be expecting me to show up, and he'll have a hard time selling his 'Poor Tara and her mental health' line to the team when I rock up looking amazing (ish) with a fake smile painted on in Russian Red Mac lipstick.

For now though, I'm taking full advantage of a free morning without the boys to run a few messages in town. I've to pick the turkey from the butchers, get a few wee stocking fillers for the boys, and a present for Pamela.

I am a woman on a Christmas mission, determined that once I leave the madness of this city centre today, that is me officially done with Christmas shopping. Some people love the hustle and bustle of the shops at Christmas – I'd rather fart in my own spacesuit than stand in a queue for an hour to pay for a Dove shower gel set.

Which means standing in line at the jeweller's for twenty minutes has me on edge. I'm tempted to grab the first shiny thing that I see (that doesn't cost the sun, moon and stars, because let's be real here: maternity pay sucks) but I'm immediately entranced by the older gentleman with a white fluffy beard and a very dashing three-piece suit who offers to help me.

'Oh, my dear,' he says. 'It can't be easy, standing all that time. I know I find it tough and it's just buns and sweets that have made this belly of mine so big!' He laughs – it's more of a 'Ho, ho, ho' – and pats his tummy. Is this . . . is this Santa?

'Let me get you a chair,' he says, and while I'm a little embarrassed at the fuss, I'm also really quite emotional that he's being so thoughtful. And I do really, really want to sit down. He guides me to a quieter spot at the back of the shop and sits down opposite me. 'Now, are you sure I can't get you a glass of water or a cup of tea? You're carrying a very precious cargo there. More precious than anything I have in this shop anyway.'

I blink at him, wondering if I've just stepped into a scene from *Miracle on 34th Street*. 'Erm, a glass of water would be nice actually.'

'OK then. Now before I fetch your water, what can we help you with today? I can maybe bring some pieces for you to look at while you rest your feet there for a minute.'

I realize I am watching a master salesman at play here. But I don't *feel* as if I'm being manipulated. I feel as if I'm being drawn into a big Santa-sized hug.

'Well,' I say, 'I'm looking for something for my mother. We've had a difficult relationship,' I tell him, seemingly unable to stop vomiting the family's dirty laundry out of my mouth. But Santa doesn't judge and I keep going: 'She's lived away for a long time. Not in prison or anything,' I stutter. I can't have him thinking my ma was in the IRA or anything. 'In Spain. And well, she's just moved back and we're trying to understand each other a bit better. You see, she left when I was a child . . .'

The words spill out, one after the other, and Santa

doesn't stop me talking. He doesn't look at his pocket watch – because of course he has a pocket watch – or yawn, or make that 'wind it up' hand gesture. He just listens and nods and hands me a tissue when I find that I'm crying.

When I stop, he places his hand very gently on my knee. 'I think I have just the thing,' he tells me before disappearing and coming back with a small wooden box, and my glass of water.

'Now, this is a very special piece,' he tells me, opening the box to reveal a beautiful solid silver bracelet. 'Something tells me this would be perfect for your free spirit of a mother.' He takes the bracelet from the box and hands it to me. 'If you look in the middle, you'll see an engraving of a small aeroplane, and if you look inside you'll see a quote from Amelia Earhart herself.'

Being a proud Derry woman, I know only too well who Amelia Earhart is. The first woman to fly solo across the Atlantic, she completed that flight by landing on the outskirts of this very town in 1932. A proper she-ro and inspiration to many.

I read the inscription, 'Women, like men, should try to do the impossible.'

It's perfect. She wanted to be free, and she did it. Granted, she did it with a lot more decorum than Pamela did, but it took guts. For both women.

'I'll take it,' I tell Santa, choking back more tears, and he smiles.

'I knew we'd find the right thing! Now make sure you

enjoy your Christmas. And rest up!' I want to kiss him, but I don't want to get arrested for coming on to Santa, so I hug him a little instead.

Sometimes we all just need to believe in Santa for a little while. Or people that look like Santa and don't charge us for an impromptu counselling session in a jeweller's.

When I get home, I'm greeted by another Christmas miracle. Gemma and Pamela have been working through the mountain of laundry that I want to have done before the big day, and they have done a great job. These are the moments when I'm so grateful, not just for Gemma, but for Pamela, and the influence she's had on my terror of a teenager.

Without even knowing the turmoil I'm currently going through, they've stepped up and made my life easier. They've even agreed to go and pick Jax up from Jo so that I can take Nathan for his surprise moment on the stage without fear of another thunder-stealing moment from my youngest child.

The Rebel Mums have also been next-level amazing – rallying round to make today as magical as possible for Nathan. I can't believe I ever doubted that they cared about me or considered me an important part of their group.

To make my life easier, Eva, my original Rebel Mum pal, has agreed to pick me up and take me to get Nathan from school a little early. This means Pamela can have use of my car to get Jax. I'm kind of hoping she'll insist on cleaning it first. There is a well-worn method to my madness.

Eva picks me up, looking gorgeous as usual and smelling absolutely divine. I mean, I'm a straight woman, but Eva is undeniably gorgeous and sexy. And she makes it look so effortless.

'I love your perfume,' I tell her.

'Jo Malone,' she coos back. 'Tonka and Myrrh – thought it perfect for Christmas.'

OK, Eva wins. She event-coordinates her perfume with Christmas. If I didn't adore her, I could easily hate her.

We drive to Nathan's school and my mood is so light I'm almost – almost – distracted from the impending collapse of my marriage. All I want now is to give Nathan an afternoon to remember, so I put on my not-so-fake-this-time smile and walk to his classroom to collect him.

'Mrs Gallagher,' Miss Rose says, as I knock on her already opened classroom door. She has that look on her face. The look that says shit has gone down. I try to ignore it.

'Hi, Miss Rose,' I say. 'I'm just here to get Nathan a wee bit early. He has a . . . doctor's appointment.'

'Of course,' says Miss Rose, her smile broad and more fake than anything that has crossed my face. 'I would have had him ready to go if I'd received a note about his appointment.' If this woman was on *Mastermind*, her specialist subject would be passive aggression.

'Yes, well, we're only human,' I smile sweetly. 'And being the end of term, I figured you wouldn't be doing much work anyway.'

Miss Rose raises one eyebrow and takes a breath. 'Actually, can we have a quick word while Nathan puts the rest of his things in his school bag?'

I can't help it: I roll my eyes. Just a bit. Because what has this woman got her tinsel tits in a tangle about now? I follow her to her desk.

'Thank you for your present, Mrs Gallagher, but I don't think it's very appropriate for me to accept it. Let me just grab it for you.' With this, she reaches under her desk and grabs a large black bag. Quite frankly, I'm hella confused here.

'Erm . . . you think candles are inappropriate?' I say, wondering how a fancy candle can be considered an inappropriate gift.

'Oh, Nathan didn't give me a candle,' she says, with her lips pursed together and an expression that would curdle water. 'If you want to see what he did give me, I suggest you wait until you get to your car. And may I suggest keeping such items out of the way of little eyes and hands in the future, and maybe do a swift search of his bag in the mornings?'

I look at Nathan, and can see the gift bag containing the actual Yankee Candle I gave him to give to Miss Rose this morning stuffed under his desk.

He looks at me and blinks as if he has no idea what Miss Rose's problem could be. I need to get him out of there as quickly as possible before he makes whatever the hell is going on here worse.

'OK, Miss Rose, thank you. I'll keep that in mind. And,

you know, have a wonderful Christmas,' I say as I usher Nathan towards the door. 'I can see the real present he was meant to give you under his desk. It's just a wee something . . . well . . . it's a candle . . . but you already know that so erm . . . thanks and Happy Christmas.'

I rush out of the school with Nathan, clutching the black bag to my chest with one arm and holding his hand with the other. We get into Eva's car and I open the bag. Fuck!

'What's that?' asks Eva.

'It's a whip!' Nathan shouts excitedly. 'I found it in my mammy's wardrobe aside a black panther costume, and I fought it would be a cool present for Miss Rose.'

'He didn't,' says Eva, looking at me, and I can see she's dying to laugh.

'He did,' I say, and now I can't control my laughter, giving Eva the go-ahead to let hers out. Nathan joins in and we laugh the whole way to the community centre.

'Where are we, Mammy?' Nathan asks as Eva pulls into the car park.

'We, my sneaky wee rascal,' I say, taking off his seat belt and helping him out of the car, 'are here for your nativity. No Jax, no other children, no Miss Rose and thankfully, no whips.'

'My nativity?' he asks excitedly.

'Yes, pet! Me and my friends have been all been working really hard to give you the chance to say not just your line on stage, but the whole play, just like you wanted.'

Nathan gives me the biggest hug I think this child has

ever given me. He plants about twenty kisses on my face and randomly slaps my ass for good measure.

As we walk inside to the main hall, the stage is set and the Rebel Mums are all waiting for the show.

'My costume, Mammy, I can't do it without my costume!' Nathan shrieks in despair.

'Don't worry,' I reassure him. 'It's waiting backstage for you – let's go pop it on and give these guys the show of their lives.'

'I love you so much, Mammy,' Nathan says, and gives me another squidgy, shaky hug.

'I love you too, Nathan, more than infinity plus a million.'

31

You scumbag, you maggot

The Rebel Mums should really be renamed the Absolute Fecking Legend Mums. Not only did enough of them dress up to act with Nathan so he could deliver his line to real, live people, they even learned a couple of his songs, including 'Who's That Knocking at My Door' (still his favourite Christmas tune, though if I ever hear it again it will be too soon) and sang along. The rest of them sat as audience and clapped and cheered at his, frankly amazing, delivery of his line.

The pride was beaming off his face and I cried, of course, with happiness for him and for the wee girl I once was who so longed to get her own standing ovation one day. Well, it was mostly with happiness. It's hard to escape the impending doom for long.

After all, I have another non-cheating-husband-related mountain to climb before bed. Actually, I have a few mountains to climb and the first is transforming myself from a human Hoodie and Joggers into a sexy, sophisticated bombshell in time for the ToteTech party.

The thing with living in Derry is that this is a city where the women here are gorgeous. Some don't even leave the house to go to Tesco without full make-up and a fake tan. So you can imagine the level of utter ridieness that shows up at Christmas parties. Let's not forget I also work with the Ys – all in their twenties, none above a size ten, who get to spend their salaries on gorgeous clothes and make-up and not on Paw Patrol toys or Shein hauls like yours truly.

Looking in the mirror is quite depressing, especially given the fact I've barely slept in days. A wee inner voice screams at me, 'You can't polish a turd, Tara!' but I shake myself off. I may not be able to polish this particular turd, but I can roll it in glitter. I shower and dress in the frock I wore to my baby shower. It still looks good, despite the fact my stomach has expanded a lot in the short space between then and now. I curl my hair, do some soft, glam make-up with a hint of drama in the form of winged eyeliner. A red lip finishes the look and while I might not be able to compete with a gang of twenty-somethings in figure-hugging frocks and professionally applied make-up, I still look like one sexy mother.

Reminding myself I am capable, loveable and a good person, I kiss the boys and Gemma goodbye, leaving them to watch *The Nightmare Before Christmas* with Pamela. It's time for me to show Mr Handley, and all at ToteTech, that I am still very much a player in their game.

My positive affirmations last about as long as it takes me to get to the door of the Guildhall Taphouse, where I find myself on the brink of a full-on Tara panic-attack-special at the door. I can hear the noise from inside, see the huddles of smokers outside all dressed in their finery and in absolutely cracking form. For a lot of people, work is over for a few days and it is time to kick back and get festive AF, and they haven't wasted any time. Someone opens the door and a wave of heat, the kind that only comes when large groups of people are all gathered together in a small space drinking, singing and flirting when it's cold outside, hits me square in the face. Already I am sweating.

Breathe, I remind myself. In . . . and out . . . In and . . .

'Tara!' I hear a high-pitch squeal from inside as a hand appears above the crowd waving in my general direction. It's one of the Ys, of course, but since I can't see a face I have no idea who. I wave back, afraid to start walking towards the hand just in case it isn't one of the Ys and there is a different Tara in the room and I'm about to make a complete dick of myself.

Thankfully I see Amy push and nudge her way through the crowd, her smile gleaming white and her eyes as bright as someone who has been on the Prosecco since home time.

'Oh. Em. Gee,' she annunciates. 'You look ah-mazing. I couldn't believe it when I got your email to say you were going to come after all.' She gives me a huge hug before guiding me towards the back of the bar, where the entire ToteTech team are already clearly in full party mode. 'Look who's here!' she yells, to whoops and cheers from twenty-eight of the thirty people sat around a group of tables.

Two people are distinctly non-whoopy and non-cheery. If I was a betting woman, I'd say Luke is feeling deeply uncomfortable – perhaps because he's seen me with a bag loaded with sex gear. And Mr Handley's expression is a picture – somewhere between the deeply uncomfortable face that Luke wears, perhaps with a hint of 'scared shit-less' too. It's in his interest to have people believe he's scared of me. After all, my mental health is all over the place. Lord knows what I could be capable of. (Except doing my job, obviously.)

It's satisfying to watch him squirm a little, but I'm damned if I'm going to give him my attention. Not yet anyway. For now I want to catch up with my girls. All of a sudden, I feel maternal about them. Maybe it's because it won't be that long until Gemma is making her way in the world and I hope there will be someone there to take her under their wing.

I take a seat between Molly and Lucy, and Amy squeezes in opposite.

'It's so nice to see you,' Molly says, between sips of her strawberry daiquiri. 'The office isn't as much craic without you in it.'

'Not to mention, Handley seems to want to give all the good work to Luke and the other fellas,' Lucy says, her perfectly painted lips pouting.

'Girls!' Amy says. 'We said we'd not give out about work all night. And I'm sure Tara doesn't need to hear this.'

Actually, Tara does need to hear this. It's one thing that Handley was messing with me, but I'm about to go mama bear on him if I find out he's been messing the Ys around too. A drink is placed in front of me – one I didn't order and which looks like it contains the exact amount of alcohol I'd like to drink but can't. I start to protest.

'We ordered it for you,' Molly says. 'It has the best name! It's a Virgin Mary – how class is that? And very Christmassy too,' she nods.

'And Virgin as in non-alcoholic?' I ask.

'Of course,' Molly says. 'We have your back. Unlike some others.'

It's clear Molly isn't going to stop the work gossip soon, and that's OK with me. This just adds to my arsenal of information about that creepy fucker of a senior manager.

'C'mere,' she stage-whispers, and I lean a little closer, catching sight of Handley and Luke both staring in our direction – the fear now a little more evident on their faces.

'I know you're about to have your baby and all,' she says, 'and you probably don't give two shits about ToteTech right now, but you need to know the latest.'

'What?' I ask.

'Well, it's Langsworth. There's been a fuck-up.'

Amy nods from across the table and leans over. 'A BIG fuck-up. Major! Epic like.'

'Langsworth asked for Luke and Handley to send them

a proposal document on how they'd manage their account since you were gone,' Molly says.

'It did not go down well,' Amy adds.

'Like a shit in the swimming pool,' Lucy whispers.

'What did it say?' I ask, absolutely disgusted that Langsworth have been annoyed but delighted it wasn't me who annoyed them.

'All the upsell shit Handley tries to get us to do all the time. Totally different approach to you. I believe Langsworth's response included the phrase "consider which company might be best suited to our future needs".' Amy says, before knocking back a glass of Prosecco.

Holy shit. This is big. This is epic. This is . . . not my fault!

I must not gloat though. At the end of the day, it's my plan to go back to ToteTech, and Langsworth are not only one of my biggest accounts, but one of my favourites. I don't want to lose them.

'Oooh!' Lucy says. 'Langsworth are going to send you a big surprise when the baby is born! They wanted your address.'

'Lucy! You dick! Now it won't be a surprise!' Molly admonishes her.

'Ach, no. Sure, don't worry, I was secretly hoping they might. Look, girls, I really appreciate you telling me, and for always having my back.' I reach out and grasp their hands, all of us ending up clasped together in the middle of the table. Even with their high-pitched screams and extreme enthusiasm, these ladies have their hearts in the right place. I take a long drink of my Virgin Mary, which tastes a bit like tomato juice. I'll just have to pretend there's a wee vodka or two in there.

As we eat our gorgeous dinner, I think about Langsworth and how the shareholders will not be happy if Handley and Luke lose the account, although not too much because this is a nice evening. I'm enjoying living vicariously through the Ys. Watching them get drunk and hearing their stories, hearing how fucking uncomplicated life is for them – even if they don't appreciate that at all. They talk about their plans and the holidays they booked, and I can't help but think of how the majority of my twenties were spent raising Gemma and missing my mother so very desperately. I love that they have more opportunities than I did.

But as much as I'm enjoying it, there comes a time (about ten) when I know I need to head home and go to bed. But first I have a Christmas present I need to give Mr Lying Shithead Handley.

I look to the top of the table but he's not there. There's just Luke staring quite miserably into the bottom of a pint glass. The old me would've gone over to check he was OK and to offer buckets of reassurance, but the new me thinks he needs to learn that he does not know more about this job than the rest of us. I'd warned him outside the sex shop not to upsell to Langsworth, but he'd ignored me, no doubt because he thought he knew better than me, and the lure of some potential quick commission was obviously too much to ignore.

I leave him to his obvious misery and instead look for Handley so I can have a quiet word before I leave. That's when I spot that he's cornered Amy at the bar.

He's standing much too close for comfort and my stomach turns at the thought of what his hot whiskey breath (not that I've been watching, but he's had a few since I arrived) must feel like in her ear. He keeps slipping a hand to her waist, and she keeps shifting, to nudge it away. She looks deeply uncomfortable. I know that look. All women know that look. When some creep comes on strong but you have to decide if it's safe to knock him back or not. Will he call you names, hurt you, fuck up your career prospects?

I look back towards Molly and Lucy to see if they've noticed what's happening, but they're oblivious and in full-blown selfie mode. Which gives me an idea . . .

Taking my phone out, I select the video setting and look back across the bar just in time to see Handley's hand once again sliding around Amy's waist, and then slowly down to her ass – and I have it on film. I watch Amy once again twitch his hand away, and inwardly cheer her for not giving in to his advances, but when she tries to walk away, he grabs her by the wrist and pulls her back. A rage like none I have ever felt before fills me and I storm towards the bar.

'Get your hands off her,' I bark, loud enough that even the revellers launching into 'Fairytale of New York' beside us stop singing. 'How many times does she have to push your hand off her body before you get the message she is uncomfortable? I've been watching you repeatedly touching her while she tries to make you stop, probably too afraid to tell her boss to fuck off completely. But when she tries to walk away, you grab her by the wrist like she's your fucking property?'

I glance at Amy, who is crying as she steps towards me.

'I don't know what you're talking about, Tara,' Handley laughs, and I realize that, far from showing remorse, he genuinely sees nothing wrong in his actions. He has that sense of entitlement all too common in men who've cruised through life not caring to learn what women might think of them.

'We're talking about work here. Maybe you should head back to your family and leave us to it.'

'If you've only been talking about work then I'm sure you won't mind me showing the video of what just went down here to HR?' I say, impressed at how steady my voice sounds.

Even in the dimly lit bar I can see the colour drain from his face. 'I . . . erm . . . don't think you can film people without their permission,' he stutters.

'Oh I wasn't filming you,' I say. 'I was trying to take a selfie – you know us women, vain creatures and all – but it seems that I pressed the wrong button. Probably due to my tiny lady fingers and lack of male brain, and somehow I managed to catch you and Amy by accident. It's not like it was intentional or anything.' I shrug my shoulders, playing the role of the dumb blonde he seems to take me for.

'I mean, I would never try to intentionally rubbish someone's career. You know, like breaking any equality in the workplace rules, or telling clients that I'm suffering from a mental health crisis, or taking key accounts from me even though I have hit every single one of my targets. Tell me, Mr Handley, how *is* the Langsworth account doing in my absence?'

The bar is silent now, except for my voice, and in the background Kirsty MacColl singing about the NYPD choir.

All eyes are on me and Handley. I wait for him to speak but he just stands, open-mouthed like the absolute gobshite he is, trying to think of a way to lie his way out of this.

'Amy,' I say, 'do you want me to forward this video to HR?'

She blinks at me and for a tiny moment I wonder if she will bottle it. She's young, and scared and I understand that. But God, the Ys need to say 'enough now', or they will be dealing with this for the rest of their working lives.

'Yes,' she says, and her voice is strong. I resist the urge to punch the air.

'I think I'd like to talk to HR too,' Molly says, having come up behind us, now holding Amy's hand.

'And me,' says Lucy.

A few other voices join in from other female staff members and I want to cheer for them all. This is our #MeToo moment, and it is long overdue.

I stay with the Ys as Handley slams out of the bar, and once we're sure the coast is clear, they walk me to my car.

'Thank you,' Amy says, tearfully. 'I wanted to tell him to get lost, but I need my job. And who would believe me over him?'

I pull her into a hug. 'I believe you. I'm sorry I didn't speak up earlier – not just about his creepiness but about how he's kept us all back from progressing how we bloody well deserve to in the company. But it's going to change, girls. I know I'm on maternity leave and I've a new baby to factor into things, but I promise you things are going to change for the better in ToteTech.'

There are kisses and hugs and high-pitched squealing, which I allow just this once, and then I'm back in my car like the badass I am.

On the way home, I blast my Beyoncé Spotify playlist and sing louder than Nathan at his nativity. Some of these fools still don't know who run the world do they?

And Paul Gallagher is the next person who's going to learn that lesson the hard way.

32

Dashing through the snow

I've slept well, which is no mean feat, given I was curled up beside Jax all night. While his tiny, sleepy body makes for a great hot water bottle, his habit of star-fishing around the bed isn't usually conducive to a good sleep. All I can think is that I was just so tired I could've slept anywhere – except beside Paul. I'd come in from the ToteTech party on a high.

Handley is firmly in his place and I'm going to send the video on to HR, along with a detailed statement about his handling both of my pregnancy and of the Langsworth account. All being well, the Ys will also provide statements about his 'hands-on' approach to work. We're not excusing his behaviour any longer.

I was so wired with adrenaline when I got home I made

myself a cup of warm milk, which, if we're being honest, is disgusting, so I upgraded it to a hot chocolate with marshmallows and double cream.

Still unable to face being up close and personal with Paul, I had slipped under the covers with my baby boy Jax and watched him sleep for a while as my mind tried to quiet itself. He looked so tiny there, beside me. His face still has so many babyish features and I wonder how he's going to react to not being the baby in the family any more. I kissed the top of his head and whispered that he will always be my baby before drifting off.

I only wake up when one of his toes finds its way up my nose hours later. Having removed it, I grab my phone from where I left it on the floor: it's half eight. In mammy time that's such an epic lie-in that it might as well be one in the afternoon. I can't quite get over how rested I feel.

But then I remember that today is the day my 'barbarian' is going to get caught with his loincloth around his ankles (or whatever barbarians wear these days, I'm not up on period-BDSM fashions), and that familiar knot of anxiety starts to tighten in the pit of my stomach.

I text Cat and Amanda, checking they're still on for tonight. They both reply almost immediately, asking if they need to bring anything and what they should wear. I'm not sure what to tell them because I'm not sure where we'll be following Paul to. Will it be his dirt bird's house? A seedy hotel? A sex dungeon with a live orgy in full flow? Shaking some very disturbing mental images out of my head, I tell them just to bring themselves, some chocolate (because I'm going to need it) and to wear something warm. It seems a fair bet.

Scrolling through my messages I see Paul has sent me a text to say he is 'going for a few pints' after work. So that's what he's calling doing the dirty these days? I also see he texted me a few times last night checking if A) I was OK, B) if I had punched Handley in the face yet, and C) that I knew to drive carefully because there was a black ice warning. A pang of sadness washes over me that this is how we've communicated over the last twenty-four hours. In ordinary times, he would have been picking me up from the ToteTech party, we'd have stopped at the chippy on the way home, and we'd have laughed our heads off at what went down with Handley over a shared bag of chips eaten out of the paper in front of the fire.

But then I push the sadness away. Today is not a day for sadness. Today is a day for going full Beyoncé in *Lemonade* and battering some metaphorical cars with metaphorical baseball bats. Well, it will be. After I get up and feed the wains, do the laundry and light the fire. I just have to make it through the day without killing anyone. Today will be a day of least resistance. If the children want something, they get it. If Gemma wants to go out, she can. Anything to keep things calm because there is only so much crazy any house can take and I'm carrying that load for today.

Over lunch, Pamela asks me if everything is OK.

'Of course, Mammy. I'm just very pregnant and very tired.'

She raises one eyebrow as if to say, 'Aye right, now tell me the truth', so I distract her with a blow-by-blow account of what went down last night with Handley. I even show her the video.

'Well, he's a sleazy wee fucker,' she exclaims. 'Good for you, Tara. Looking out for yourself, and those girls.'

'Those girls' have been texting all morning. They are absolutely dying with hangovers but said this is still the 'best day at work ever'. Luke, it appears, has phoned in sick. Handley has been shut in his office all day and any time he has emerged to get a coffee or go to the bathroom he has kept his eyes downward and not made eye contact. They have already started drafting their statements for HR.

We watch *Home Alone* in the afternoon, which I start to think is a bad idea when Nathan asks if it's too late to ask Santa for 'some new fings'.

'What kind of fing – I mean things?' I ask him.

'Uhm, just some marbles for the stairs and sticky glue for the floor and rope to tie up heavy fings so they hit the burgleeurrs in the face when they bust down the door,' he says. With visions of me being mistaken for a 'burgleeurr' and getting an iron up the bake, I tell him that sadly, yes, it is much too late for Santa to change his list.

'He'll already be packing his sleigh up, pet,' I tell him. Thankfully he shrugs and says he will get those 'fings' for his birthday instead. I don't argue. I just hope this is the one time in his life when he forgets something he said months before.

By 7 p.m., I am in full-on heightened anxiety mode. I jump when my phone pings with a message from Cat.

We're outside, ya wee international woman of mystery.

Here I go. Time for the moment of truth! Fuck, have I time for a quick vomit? No, Tara, just breathe . . . breathe.

I kiss the kids and tell them to be good for their granny, who thinks I'm just going for a brief pre-Christmas get-together with the girls. And then I walk slowly down the driveway to Cat's car and get into the back seat.

'OK, girls, we're going undercover,' I say, as I strap myself in.

'Tara, are you serious? Cat says with a laugh. But she stops when she notices the despair in my face and the tears surfacing in my eyes. 'We thought that text you sent was just an elaborate way to get us all together or get you an hour out of the house for some adult conversation. What's going on?'

'Paul's . . . Paul's having an affair,' I say, and I choke back the lump in my throat, hardly able to believe these words are coming out of my mouth. 'I've found evidence, so now we're going to catch him in the act. Head to the garage and turn your lights off when you get to the corner. He'll be finishing up on his last job now. Then we're going to follow him.'

'Holy shit,' says Amanda, looking at Cat.

'Fuck,' says Cat, looking at Amanda, then back at me in her rear-view mirror.

As Cat drives towards the garage, I sense I'm not the only one who's nervous. Amanda hasn't shut up since we left my drive about how marriages need spice, and how they can survive infidelity. She's throwing questions at me that I'm too wired to answer. But she still doesn't seem to get the hint and jabbers on and on about how transformative counselling can be.

Instead of smashing her head off the windscreen like part of me wants to, I just let her ramble, I don't care what she's read or what sex doctor or philanthropist has regurgitated this absolute bullshit to her. Sean didn't cheat on her. They just grew stale. That can be fixed. Cheating is a whole other ballgame.

We stop a few cars back from the garage and Cat turns the lights off as planned. We each stay silent until we hear the clatter of the garage shutter being pulled down. I think I might actually boke, but instead I just grab Amanda's hand and squeeze it tightly. Thankfully she doesn't speak. I *so* want to be wrong. I so want to see him head for pints with the lads just like he said. I want to laugh about this and just how wrong I got it. But I watch him look around, before getting into his car and starting the engine.

I might not know much about how the male brain works, but I do know that you don't take a car to a piss-up. Paul would never drive with so much as a half pint in him, so there's no way he is heading for drinks. For a moment, I'm stunned into silence. Then I almost jump the height of myself when Amanda shouts, 'After him! Don't lose him!'

We follow Paul over the Foyle Bridge into Derry's Waterside and then off a slip road into a dark and winding country road. Not only is it dark and very winding, it's also badly laid and has more bumps than an old B2K song. There's bugger all chances the gritters have been up here, so the risk of us hitting ice is high. This risk grows even higher when snow begins to fall in fat flakes covering the windscreen almost as quickly as the wipers can clear it. Cat has to slow down. We lose sight of Paul's tail lights, leading Amanda to start screaming at Cat, 'You're losing him, you're losing him!'

'It's snowing for fuck sake, Amanda, and those bumps are turning my stomach, I have to slow down,' she says, her voice tight.

I know she's right about needing to slow down, but we can't have come this far to lose him now. I can't go through Christmas without knowing what he's really up to.

'Can you speed up even a wee bit, Cat?' I plead and glance up at the rear-view mirror where I can see her face, drained of all colour, her lips pursed tightly.

'I'll try, Tara,' she says through gritted teeth. 'But I'm not losing any of our lives over the sake of Paul fucking Gallagher, OK?'

She speeds up just a little and we spot Paul's car in the distance. Clearly he has had to slow down too.

The snow begins to ease and we watch as he turns up another windy, bumpy, rough road.

'Jesus, Mary and St Joseph,' Cat mutters.

'Keep going,' I say, my voice now raised from the adrenaline pumping through my veins.

'C'mon, Cat, put the foot down!' Amanda shouts, and you'd swear this is the most excitement she's had in her whole entire life. So much for her sexual reinvention being a high.

'Stay on him, Cat,' I plead, and I'm on the edge of my seat as we turn up the even windier bend.

'That's it, Cat, floor her, flooooor her,' Amanda screams like a seventeen-year-old culchie at the rally races. At this point it feels like we're in a rollercoaster and not Cat's Audi TT, and even I'm starting to feel a bit queasy.

We climb over the brow of one last hill and start hurtling down the steepest, most windy hill of them all when suddenly Cat slams on the brakes, bringing us to a dead stop. No sooner has she pulled on the handbrake when she pulls open her door and projectile vomits over the ground, her legs and her feet.

'You can't stop now,' Amanda shouts, ignoring the fountain of puke escaping our friend's mouth. 'We've almost got him.'

'Cat, please,' I plead. 'Can you go on? I know you're probably hungover, but we're going to lose him.'

'I'm not hungover,' Cat mutters. 'Jesus Christ, I'm pregnant.' And she unleashes another stream of sick over the ground.

'What?!' Amanda and I screech in unison.

'I am pregnant,' Cat says, and she bursts into tears. 'I'm

321

six weeks pregnant,' she sniffs, 'I wanted to tell you both, but then I wasn't sure if I wanted to keep it, but now I know I do, I really do, but you fuckers bring me out on this cheater chase and . . .'

'Cat,' I say, unbuckling my belt and wrapping my arm around her seat. 'So this is why you avoided the baby shower? And have been really distant? I'm so selfish, Cat. I should have picked up on it . . .'

'How on earth would you?' Cat says, 'You know me – president of the no-baby-thank-you-very-much camp. Totally against the wee vagina goblins . . . but, this is different, somehow. I can't explain it, but I had to get my head around it.'

'And you're happy?' I ask. 'You're happy with your decision? You're doing it because this is what you want and not because this is what you think you should do?' I think of my mother – how her wings were clipped by convention. I don't want Cat to ever feel that way, and I don't want Cat's baby to ever feel anything less than loved.

'It's what I want,' she sniffs, through a watery smile. 'I could do without the boking, and the sore boobs – what the actual fuck is that about? They hurt when someone so much as looks at them! Can't say I'm looking forward to pushing it out of my vagina either, but aye . . . Aye, this is very much what I want.'

'Well then congratulations, my gorgeous friend.' I squeeze her as tightly as I can, considering there's a car seat between us. 'I'm really happy for you. And I'll help you in whatever way I can.' Tears spring to my eyes as I think of Cat – my

Cat – becoming a mammy for the first time. Cat never does anything by halves so I know instinctively she will be an amazing mother.

'Who's the daddy?' Amanda asks, in her usual, naive way.

'That's irrelevant, Amanda,' I say (even if I really want to know too). 'Cat will tell us as and when – and if – she wants. What matters is that we are here to support you, Cat, always . . . and you are going to be the coolest mammy ever,' I add, tears now spilling down my cheeks.

Amanda sniffs as Cat and I continue to cry, and then she claps her hands in the manner of a primary school teacher calling a room to order. 'Ladies, this is lovely and we're very, very happy for you, Cat, but we've got a cheating bastard to catch and there's a chance we can catch him. The thing with snow is that cars leave tracks in it. I think we can still get him. I'll drive. Cat, get into the back with Tara.'

As Cat climbs into the back the smell of the vomit on her legs and shoes turns my stomach but I stay strong and crack the window a wee bit for the fresh air.

'It's not the first time we've been covered in each other's vomit.' Cat laughs, 'And it won't be the last.'

'You two are disgusting,' Amanda scolds, and I can almost see her giving herself a pep talk inside her head. She may be the new sex queen in the group but she's not known for her cool driving skills – more likely to drive like an eighty-five-year-old out for a Sunday run in the car than someone hell-bent on reaching a destination quickly.

'But you love us,' I say.

'Of course I do,' Amanda smiles. 'Now let's go pop some caps in some asses.'

Christ, she thinks she's in some Hollywood police chase.

33

We Three Queens . . .

At the top of the next hill there stands a house. A gorgeous new build that I could only dream of – one that no doubt has all sorts of fancy extras like more than one shower, a utility room, and probably even a purpose-built pantry. Gemma would die.

But it's not my house, even if it is my husband's car parked outside, along with two others. The momentary feeling of triumph at having successfully followed him to his destination is lost in seconds when I realize that now I have to confront him. There is no getting around this. I squeeze Cat's hand tightly, unsure if I'm going to be able to go through with this.

'You've got this, Tara,' she says. 'You deserve to know exactly what's been going on and to get closure. I know it's hard, but better to know the truth.'

I nod because I'm afraid to speak.

'OK girls,' Amanda says. 'We're here at Ground Zero. What's the story now? How're we doing this?'

I take a deep breath, while examining the terrain. If we're going to be in stealth-attack mode, we need to at least adopt some of the lingo. 'Right,' I say. 'We sneak up to the front door. The lights appear to be off at the front of the house, so hopefully no one is in any of those rooms and they won't see us. If it's open, we go on in.'

'Are you sure?' Amanda asks. 'Is that not a wee bit like breaking in?'

'No breaking involved,' I say. 'We'll say we knocked but no one answered. It'll be grand.' I don't sound convinced.

'And if the door is closed?' Cat asks.

'We stakeout here and wait for him to come out,' I say assertively, fixing my hair as if that will distract whoever Paul is riding from my gargantuan stomach, and the fact my clothes are now flecked with Cat's sick. 'I want to do that whole "when they go low, we go high" thing. Keep our cool. No hysterics or violence. Plus we've two pregnant ladies amongst us. We're taking no chances. I just want him to know that I've caught him, that his dirty little secret is out and it's up to me who I expose that to and when.

'As for whatever tramp is in there under him,' I add. 'I just want to look her in the eyes and ask her if she's happy now that she's wrecked my family, and had an affair with my husband while I'm eight months pregnant.'

'OK, but could I give her just one good bitch-slap and then run out?' Cat asks.

'No hitting, Cat,' I scold her, as if I'm talking to Jax and Nathan about the dangers of being too rough when they're play-fighting. 'Let's walk out of there with our heads held high. I'm sure as shit that's what I'm going to do.'

'We ready?' Amanda asks, taking off her seat belt.

'Ready,' I say.

'Born ready,' Cat chimes in. We exit the car and I can only imagine what we look like. We're not Charlie's Angels, that's for sure, more Charlie and the Chocolate Factory's Rejects. Cat holds my hand and gives it a tight reassuring squeeze. Amanda begins a ridiculous attempt at a stealth walk and I'm starting to think she genuinely thinks she's an undercover cop here.

'I'll check the door – you two wait here and then I'll give the signal,' she whispers, and she runs to the door crouching like the Hunchback of Notre Dame. Before we can ask what the 'signal' is, I see her turn the handle, look back at us, clasp her hands around her mouth and make a strange 'Cuckoo' sound. Ah, *that* signal.

Cat and I storm up the driveway to the door. 'On three?' Amanda whispers, and I nod. 'Three, two, one . . . !' The door opens into a beautiful hall and I can see a door to the rear of the house open, light streaming from it.

'In there!' I whisper, just as a male voice is heard cheering.

'Ah, I'm going to make you pay for that! You're going to get such a spanking!!'

My eyes open wide. Cat's eyes open wide. Amanda is practically peeing herself with excitement. 'It's a *man*!'

327

she says, as if we're not talking about my husband having an affair and she hasn't just uncovered that he appears to be getting his BDSM kinks with a very throaty-voiced bloke.

Well, that's the point when my shit is finally lost. Enough. Just enough. Has he been lying to me all this time? Is he bisexual? (I mean, that wouldn't in theory bother me, but cheating is cheating and that very much bothers me a LOT.) I storm down the hall, sneakiness forgotten, mentally trying to prepare myself for what I'm going to see next.

'Paul Gallagher, you've gone too far this time!' I shout, turning into the room and . . .

'Tara, what are you doing here?' Paul asks, his face a picture of confusion and, maybe, a little shame. 'And what the fuck is all over your legs?'

The room is silent. My husband is seated at an antique mahogany dining table with five other men, who I've never seen before. There are no whips, or leather thongs (thank Christ). Instead they appear to be in the middle of playing some sort of board game – but it's not Monopoly, or the Game of Life or anything I've seen before for that matter.

Amanda jumps in front of me shouting, 'We're here to catch you in the act, you bas . . . erm . . . ahh . . . is that a board game?'

'What act?' Paul says, looking embarrassed and confused.

'The affair, Paul,' I say, although there is much less conviction in my voice now. 'I found the shipping label for your dirty little purple warrior thing. I saw the text from your mistress calling you "Barbarian".'

'She knows everything, so don't try to lie!' Amanda says, crossing her arms in front of her, adopting a total power pose. I, on the other hand, am adopting a 'want the ground to swallow me whole' pose but I've committed to my anger and I can't just run away.

'Aw Jesus, Tara. Is this what all that madness has been about? You think I'm having some sort of kinky affair?' Paul asks, as the other men let out little sniggers.

'But . . . the . . . purple warrior thing and the barbarians and . . .'

'Tara, this is a LARP club. There's no sex. Jesus. You really thought—'

'This is a what now club? Cat interjects.

'Did you bring everyone you know? Are your ma and the wains going to walk in next?' Paul asks.

'No,' I say, my voice smaller now. 'It's just the girls. For support.'

'Oh hey, everyone,' Cat adds, looking around at the table of men who range from early forties to late fifties, and each have their own particularly nerd-inspired style. Paul, definitely the youngest among them, looks like a bit of a misfit.

'A LARP club? What's a LARP club?' I ask.

'LARP,' a gentleman with a short crew cut and thick-lensed glasses replies, 'stands for Live Action Role Play. It's a combination of re-enactment, storytelling and gaming, we LARP with Dungeons and Dragons. Although, technically speaking, we'd dress up for actual LARPing but a few of us are still waiting for our costumes so . . .'

A snigger bursts out of Cat and I yank her arm, once again reprimanding her for behaving like a child.

'I wanted to tell you, Tara,' Paul says, ignoring Cat's giggling. 'I did, but I didn't want you to think I was weird – no offence, fellas.' The other men shrug as if they are well used to being called weird and they don't give a damn about it.

'I didn't want you to think I was spending time away from you and the kids just to play board games, but it's more than that. I've always wanted to try it, and when Bob from work hooked me up with these guys, I finally felt like I had something of my own. And it's great. Real escapism. You have your girls,' he says, nodding to Cat and Amanda, 'I suppose this is my version of that.'

'What about the purple-eyed warrior bag?' I ask.

'It's for my dice,' Paul tells me, and holds up a little black leather pouch with a purple dragon eye on the front. 'It's a Dungeons and Dragons themed dice bag. Did you really think it was something . . . sexual?' A couple of the men are openly laughing now and I feel my face colour.

'Well . . . maybe,' I say. 'And the text calling you Barbarian and asking if you were ready for tonight?' I whimper.

'That's his Dungeons and Dragons name,' a skinny man in his mid fifties pipes up. 'Hi, I'm Dragonborn.' And this sets Cat off in another peal of laughter. Amanda too.

'Girls!' I shout. 'Please can you wait in the car?'

'Yes, ma'am,' Cat says as she throws a military salute. 'Bye, Barbarian . . . I mean Paul.' And she ushers Amanda to the door, the pair of them still creasing themselves.

'Wait, but . . . so . . . is he having an affair with all those geeky men?' I hear Amanda ask Cat on the way out.

'No, Amanda,' Cat teases. 'Not everyone has sex on the brain like you. I'll explain to you in the car.'

'Paul,' I whisper, and I wave him over to me, away from his new LARP buddies, or whatever the hell he calls them. 'So this is your thing now? You haven't been having an affair?' I say, relief warring with embarrassment within.

'Yes,' Paul says. 'Jesus, Tara, did you honestly think I was having an affair?' He's wounded. I pull him into the hall and close the door so the lads can't hear us talk.

'I did, Paul,' I say, finally giving in to the tears. 'Between the purple warrior thingy, the text calling you Barbarian, the late nights and general distance between us lately – yes, I really thought you were having an affair. My heart has been breaking into a million pieces and I'm just so relieved, but sooo mortified, and I'm so, so sorry. I'm sorry for never making you feel safe enough to be able to tell me what gave you joy outside of our marriage. I can't say it's not a surprise or feels a little out of character for you and . . . well, it's borderline weird, if you ask me, but, if you enjoy it that's all that matters. I'm glad you've found your tribe.'

'I'm sorry I didn't tell you. I've felt so selfish taking time to myself, it's just been—'

'Draining,' I interrupt, and he nods his head. And there and then I know exactly what he means. I couldn't agree with him more.

Life *is* draining sometimes, especially when you have a teenager, two young boys, another baby on the way, a hormonal, volatile wife like me, oh, and the addition of a new lodger in the form of Pamela.

'I get it,' I tell him. 'I understand all of it. I understand you, and I love you so much. Hopefully you still love me too even though I've just made a complete arse of myself in front of your new friends.'

He smiles. 'Do you not know that I love you by now, Tara Gallagher? I always will. Even all the messy, dramatic parts. You wouldn't be you without them. And I promise you, no more secrets.'

'Deal,' I say, and I lean in to give him a hug.

'Love, no offence,' he says, pushing me away gently, 'but you stink, and I'm guessing that's either the remnants of a cottage cheese accident all over you or you boked over yourself again.'

'Long story,' I smile, not taking any offence to him not wanting to hug me right now. Hell, if I could get away from me and morph into someone else's body to get away from the stench and the embarrassment of my antics right now, I would.

'Go back to your game,' I say. 'I'll see you at home when you're finished.'

*

Cat, Amanda and I laugh the whole way home. The windows are cracked the full way down and the freezing air is finally starting to reduce the smell of Cat's stomach contents from the car. We are baltic, but our spirits could not be higher. The fact that these two never once questioned my motive but joined me in trying to catch Paul having an affair tonight is a blessing.

Amanda is high-as-a-kite giddy. She got a real rush from the whole thing. Granted, she's a bit out there at times and bores the fucking skull off me with her psychobabble, but she was there for me tonight in a way that I'm grateful for beyond words. I really need to start praising her more, especially now that she's found this new lease of confidence and zest for adventure.

And then there's Cat. My BFF from when we were wee. I feel downright awful for not twigging that she was pregnant.

I should have known that, like Paul, she's always been a constant. They've always been there to pick up the pieces. Every breakdown, meltdown, crisis and fiasco, they've been there. And I hate how I doubted their loyalty for even a second.

And now Cat's pregnant. What in the actual fudge. Cat! Pregnant! If there's one thing I'm an expert at, it's all things Mammy. This is my chance to finally be able to give her sound advice and guide her through every stage of the journey.

Yes, this is my jam, and I know in my heart that this

is going to bring us even closer together. Our babies are going to grow up together, imagine!

As we pull up outside my house, I lean forward in between Cat and Amanda.

'Girls,' I say, 'I fucking love you both. Thank you for always being there for me, now, it's time for me to do the same for you both.'

'Houl yer whisht, would ye,' Cat says. 'Look, I'm just glad that Paul's not acting the dirt bird.'

'Me too,' I say with feeling. 'Thank you again, I shall bid you adieu.' I open my door. 'And wishing you both the happiest of Christmases! Let's all grab lunch the day after Boxing Day – we can swap presents then?'

'Sounds good,' Cat smiles.

'I'll have to check my diary, but sure I'll let you both know on WhatsApp,' Amanda says, pulling me into a hug before getting back into the car to drive off. I stand and watch them leave, waving the whole time.

God, I'm a lucky woman.

But I'm also a freezing, stinking, disgusting woman.

It's time to shower, then I'll get the wains to bed, and wait up for Paul.

34

There's snow place like home

Dear Reader, I did not wait up for Paul. I was a fool to think that was ever going to happen. I intended to, of course. As I kissed our boys goodnight, it was still in my thoughts. When I sat and held Gemma's hand and let her feel her baby brother or sister kicking, I was already thinking about what I would say to him.

I planned all my conversation points as I showered, feeling the tension wash away down the drain along with all the soap suds and sick. Paul wasn't cheating. I was not going to have to arrange a hit on him after all. There would be no broken home. No devastated children. No bleak Christmas trying to make everything feel normal when it so clearly wasn't. Just us. Our family.

I was planning to tell Paul just how much I appreciate

335

him, and all he does for us, but first I thought I'd just lie down a wee minute, towel still wrapped around me, and air dry for a bit before putting my jammies on. I really was exhausted. So exhausted in fact that the next thing I was aware of was Bing Crosby crooning 'White Christmas' from my morning alarm.

I open my eyes and there is Paul, fast asleep and snoring beside me. There's a duvet covering me at least, which is something to be grateful for. I don't even want to think about the questions I'd have to answer if Nathan walked in to see a naked me at eight months pregnant. He's still struggling with the concept that I don't have a penis.

The house is silent, which is perfect. There is so much to do today that I need to get started before the children wake up. I like to have all my prep for the big day done by three so that I can spend the rest of Christmas Eve just relaxing with my family and soaking up the magic of Santa's imminent arrival. We'll order takeaway (because I'll be doing enough cooking tomorrow), curl up in our matching Christmas jammies and watch *The Muppet Christmas Carol* together. I've even bought an extra pair of festive PJs for Pamela. (Hers say 'Dear Santa, Define Naughty' across the front, which I think she might appreciate.)

It's going to be strange having my mother with us for Christmas – but I'm no longer dreading it. After last night, I'm grateful for every single member of my family. Even the borderline insane ones.

And I'm particularly grateful for my mother today because she will be taking the boys, and Gemma, to the panto – which is quite remarkable, given that she is still traumatized by her cinema trip. I must remind her not to feed them too much sugar, although something tells me that's not a mistake she'll be making again in a hurry.

I pull on my PJs and wrap myself in my big fluffy cardigan and peek out the window, wondering if the snow that was trying its best to lie last night has succeeded. We all dream of a white Christmas after all – especially when we have finished running around town and can just close the door and watch it from inside the house.

And it's like a Christmas miracle.

Nothing ever fully prepares you for the beauty of a fresh snowfall, when it's still dark outside and everything has taken on a hazy glow thanks to the street lights. Everything is covered in a blanket of sparkling white. Large snowflakes, fluffy and full, are still drifting from the sky. There are coloured lights twinkling in some of our neighbours' gardens, giving the whole scene a real 'Christmas card' feeling. It fills my heart with joy as much now as it did when I was a child and I'm almost tempted to wake the boys to tell them. But also I'm not completely off my head: I let them sleep. The snow is so deep there's no doubt it will still be there when they do wake up.

As I stand, entranced by the beauty of it all, gently rubbing my tummy as this little miracle in waiting gives me a good kicking, I hear an engine roar nearby.

It's our neighbours, the Johnstons, who seem to be trying but failing to move their car out of the driveway.

Shite!

Does this mean Pamela won't be able to take the kids to the panto after all? If the roads are treacherous, I can't expect her to drive. Granted, it's probably only four inches of snow at the most, but us Derry folk are not acclimatized – or skilled, for that matter – in driving in the snow. Give us torrential rain and a flood any day, yup, not a problem, but snow as heavy as this pretty much means everything shuts down.

'Paul,' I say, just loud enough to wake him but not loud enough to wake the whole house. 'It snowed last night, come see.'

He yawns and stretches his arms up high, then arches his back before swinging his legs out of the side of the bed. He is wearing nothing but boxers and he's sporting a sexy bedhead of hair. He walks over to the window and wraps his strong arms around my waist, pressing his chest against my back. He leans his head around my shoulder and gently plants a kiss on my neck.

'Good morning, my beautiful crazy lady,' he whispers into my ear, and I'm immediately distracted from worrying about the children and Pamela.

'Crazy lady, indeed?' I ask, sinking back against him, both of us still looking out the window.

'Yes,' he says, turning me around to face him. 'But good crazy . . . most of the time,' he smiles, before kneeling down to kiss my swollen belly. 'And it's only going to get crazier soon.'

'I'm so sorry I doubted you, Paul,' I whisper, and I'm

about to dive into a complete retrospective of the how and why I thought he was having an affair but, before I can, he stands back up and leans in to kiss me.

'Tara,' he whispers, 'you have no need to be sorry. If I had been honest with you from the start about the LARP club, none of this would have happened. I got over-whelmed with everything – work, life, the kids – and just needed an escape. It's kinda like you and the Rebel Mums, but geekier, I suppose. I just kept thinking how I had nothing of my own outside of family life that made me happy. But I was afraid that if I told you that I needed something more you'd have taken it personally and it would've hurt you. You *have* been a little more emotion-ally unstable lately . . .'

He's not wrong, and now I feel shit. This poor man has been my rock and dedicated his life to me and our family. He's had to deal with my breakdowns, my meltdowns, my midlife crisis, and has never once made me feel bad about any of it. But how shit am I as a wife, if he felt that he couldn't be honest with me about how *he* was feeling for fear I would kick off?

And what's worse is that I probably would've kicked off. Life has been a struggle without my anti-anxiety medication. So in the midst of the madness with the boys, Gemma's rebellion, being pregnant and then Pamela arriving on the scene, if he'd told me he was staying out late to play board games with strangers, I probably would have strung him up.

This makes me incredibly selfish. He deserves time to

himself too, he deserves happiness outside of our family. Finding the Rebel Mums gave me an outlet where I could have fun and recharge before coming back home to be a better wife and mother. He just wants and needs the same. I should've understood that more than anyone and made him feel supported and comfortable enough to tell me what he needed.

'You don't have to explain anything, Paul,' I say as I stroke the side of his face. 'I've been a total and utter selfish bitch.'

He shakes his head, but I give him a look.

'Seriously, Paul, let's not lie about this. I'm a fecking nightmare at times.'

He laughs.

'We're both at an age now where we realize that family life and marriage alone isn't going to keep us fulfilled,' I say, realizing the fairy tale we were all sold of 'happily ever after' never went back twenty years later to see how Cinderella and her prince were coping three kids later. 'Neither of us needs to get offended by the other needing a wee bit more. If you're happy, I'm happy, and that means that our children will be happy. This baby coming is going to turn our family life up another notch, so we need to make sure that we're both getting enough time to do our own thing, together as a couple, but also alone, and with other people.'

'That's exactly it, Tara,' Paul says, smiling. 'That is exactly what we need to do, and I know we can do it. But to be fair, if this is my midlife crisis, it's been pretty timid compared to yours, so technically, I win.'

'I'll give you this one,' I say laughing, 'But I think it's more a third of our lives crisis. Come our late forties, you might be the one dyeing your hair pink and joining a Rebel Dads motorcycle club or something, so I wouldn't get too cocky.'

'Rebel Dads motorcycle club? I like the sound of that! How good would I look in a leather motorcycle jacket?' he teases.

'Will you get Barbarian stitched on the back?' I reply with a grin.

'Most definitely,' he laughs. 'I love you, Tara, and if I ever seem distant again, please pull me on it. I've never been one to talk about my feelings, but as long as I know you're there for me, I'll open up.'

'I've got you,' I say. 'What is it with men and bundling everything up inside? Be more like me, let it all out, ya gotta let the crazy out or it'll eat you up.'

'I think there's only room for one Tara in this relationship, but let's see how we go,' he says.

'Come here, Barbarian,' I tease, and I pull him in for a snog. 'Your morning breath stinks,' I say mid kiss.

'As does yours,' he replies.

'Is that sex?' a small voice shouts from the doorway. It's Nathan, and I hear Jax shuffle close behind.

'No, this is not sex, you wee rascal!' I laugh, holding out my hand to him. 'But do you want to see something really special?'

Nathan runs over and I lift him up onto my hip. Christ, he's getting heavy. It strikes me that he really won't be my little boy for much longer. It makes seizing the moment all that more important. Paul grabs Jax up into his arms and we bring them both over to the window.

'It snowwwwwwwwed,' screams Nathan, in a voice that makes Buddy the Elf look calm and in control.

'Snow, snow, snow!' shrieks Jax, and the look on their faces is just priceless. Imagine waking up on Christmas Eve to see that it's snowed and knowing that Santa is coming to bring you presents in just one more sleep. They are ecstatic. Cue the Christmas Eve hyperness in 3 . . . 2 . . . 1 . . .

'Can we go make a snowman now?' Nathan shouts, jumping out of my arms.

'Yayyy pwease!' cries Jax, who is already gesturing Paul that he wants down to join Nathan in his happy snow dance.

'Boys, you know it's Christmas Eve, so Mammy and Daddy have a lot to do this morning, but how about we wake Pamela and Gemma and see if they'll take you out?' I say, already aware there's a chance this will make me public enemy number one with both my mother and daughter.

They erupt in a unison of 'yay's and rush towards Gemma's room.

'Paul,' I whisper, 'we're going to have to wait until they're asleep tonight to get the presents down from the loft. Pamela will never be able to drive to the panto in that.'

'I'll sort all that. You get yourself into the kitchen and

I'll take the boys outside to make snowmen. Pamela can help you with the cooking, and how about we let Gemma go see the girls today. I'll keep them all as busy as possible.'

'Deal,' I say, and we share another soft kiss.

'Eughhh, like seriously, youse are disgustin',' a voice bellows from the door. 'The gremlins want me to take them out into the snow, at this time of the morning!' Gemma continues. 'Are they serious? It's still dark! What's wrong with you two? Like, can youse not take them? They are actually your children, ye know?'

'Happy Christmas Eve, cheerful daughter,' I say with a bright smile. 'Guess what?'

'Whatuhhhh?' she groans.

'Your grounding is officially over. Here's your phone. Why don't you go text Mia and the girls and go have a snow-day or take pictures of the snow for Snapchat or something?'

'Really, Mammy?' She runs up to Paul and me and gives us an excited hug. 'Thank you so much, besties,' she shrieks, then she grabs her phone and skips off to her room.

'Pammy said her head is too sore, she is going back to bed,' Nathan says, walking into the room looking disappointed, as Jax follows behind. 'She smells yucky too.' That's because Pamela is, more than likely, hanging like a bat. I vaguely remember hearing her clash in at around 2 a.m. this morning, so maybe it's best we let her sleep. Don't wake the beast, etc.

It also means I'll be free of her critiquing when I'm preparing the Christmas dinner.

'It's OK, boys,' Paul says. 'I'm going to take you out. Now let's all get wrapped up in warm clothes, grab our gloves, hats and scarves, and head out there and make the best snowman in the entire street!'

'Yayyyy!' they scream. As they run towards their room with Paul in tow, I hear Nathan ask, 'Can Santa fly in the snow? What if he can't get here tonight?'

'Don't worry. Santa is extra brilliant at flying in the snow,' Paul says, 'sure, the North Pole is covered in it.'

'Oh yeah,' says Nathan, 'Fank God.'

35

Twas the night before Christmas

I've peeled the spuds, carrots and parsnips, and have them sitting in pots of cold water along with a pot of Brussel sprouts or 'russel prouts' as Nathan calls them, ready to be boiled tomorrow.

I've brined my turkey and got it in the oven on a low heat along with two pans of my own home-made stuffing, complete with mixed herbs, breadcrumbs, sausage meat and a little bit of cranberry.

My ham has been glazed in honey and adorned with cloves. My gravy stock is done and currently chilling beside the window. I've chopped up all my soup veg and added it to a large pot with stock and a shin of beef. I have pigs in blankets and Yorkshire puddings in the freezer, ready to be air-fried just before dinner. (Air fryer, by the way, best purchase of my life!) A Black Forest gateau is defrosting in the fridge, alongside a Christmas pudding and a trifle that I unashamedly bought and did not make from scratch.

There is an assortment of cheese and biscuits for tomorrow evening, a tin of Quality Street and a tin of Roses.

The smell of power-packed cloves, mixed herbs and home-made beef and vegetable soup is drifting mercilessly throughout the house. The excited screams and laughter of the boys outside paired with the sound of Mariah Carey belting out 'All I Want for Christmas' on the living room TV is almost euphoric.

I nip upstairs to make a start on wrapping Gemma's presents before she gets back from Mia's. Pamela is still sound asleep, which I can't actually believe is possible with the racket I've just made in the kitchen and the noise from the boys outside in the garden. But it means I can wrap her present too, and Paul's, as long as he doesn't come inside in the next ten minutes.

I take out an old gym bag from my wardrobe containing all the gifts I've bought over the last few months. As soon as Amazon or anyone delivered a parcel containing a present for any of my loved ones, I immediately brought it upstairs and hid it away in my gym bag – the perfect hiding place, considering how little use it's had recently.

Any Jax- or Nathan-related gifts have to be hidden in less accessible places because those two wee rascals can sniff out a present quicker than I can sniff out any of Paul's hidden chocolate stash. And believe me, that's fast. This year that inaccessible place has been the loft, and

Paul has become the designated present hider – given that loft ladders and pregnant tummies don't go together well.

I genuinely can't remember half of the stuff I've ordered at this stage and have to push down the fear that I might have forgotten something vitally important. It's too late to do anything about it anyway.

I spend half an hour wrapping presents, hoping that Pamela, Paul and Gemma will love all the gifts I've got for them. As I wrap up tops from Shein and a pair of Jordans for Gemma, I think back to when she was wee and how I used to love picking out all the gorgeous girly toys for her. Time really does go too fast. I find myself crying again. My hormones are on overdrive today. Or maybe it's because I'm just a really, really lucky mama.

As I pop the wrapped presents back in the wardrobe, I start to feel a few twinges in my belly. This is probably the baby telling me to slow the fuck down and stop jumping about so he or she can sleep. To be fair, the poor wee thing hasn't felt me move about this much in probably the guts of three months. OK, Baby Gallagher, I'll rest now for a wee while, no need to be sending the Braxton Hicks patrol out in force. I give my tummy a rub, and yes, of course, that sets me crying again.

But it isn't long until my sniffs are completely drowned out by the noise of the boys bombing in through the front door, both crying hysterically. I wipe my eyes, hoist myself out of bed and make my way downstairs.

'What's the matter, boys?' I ask.

'My hands are spiky sore,' Nathan wails.

'Ouch ouch ouuuuuch,' Jax cries.

'Frostbite,' Paul says, dusting his boots on the mat and closing the front door.

'Come upstairs with Mammy and I'll run the warm tap and Daddy will help me get you into your cosy jammies,' I say, but they're still screaming as if they both in fact have spikes impaled in their hands.

'Oh,' I say excitedly, realizing that in all the excitement about the snow, they never asked about the Wee Donkey, or even noticed his absence for that matter because, yes, today is the day I've been waiting for all December. The day the Wee Donkey fucks off for another year. Joy to the world!

Before I'd gone to shower last night I'd done my final set-up of the year. I'd positioned two personalized Christmas Eve books and two pairs of matching flannel pyjamas for the boys on the fireplace with a note that read:

Dear Nathan and Jax,

Thank you for letting me stay in your home again this year and for my awesome new name! I have loved making you smile and I hope that Santa brings you everything that you want.

I've left you both a special book to read before bed, and some cosy jammies.

I have to leave now to make my way to the North Pole to help Santa pack up his sleigh, but I'll be

sure to tell him what great, funny, a wee bit crazy
but definitely nice boys you both are.

Happy Christmas,

Love, the Wee Donkey

'I think the Wee Donkey has left a present for you both, look over at the fireplace,' I tell them, and their tears stop almost instantly as they rush over to see the note, their new books and new jammies.

'What does the note say, Daddy?' Nathan asks, and as Paul reads it out, he looks up at me and smiles lovingly and I wink back in return. I take my crown as the Queen of Christmas Magic, and he knows it.

The boys are delighted at their gifts from their favourite elf, but also a bit sad that he's gone back home to the North Pole for another year.

'Don't be sad,' I say, kneeling down and wrapping my arms around them both. 'Maybe the Wee Donkey has his own family to go back and see, and Santa really needs his help tonight.' This seems to appease them, and so Paul and I usher them upstairs and decide that it's time for an early warm bath and jammies to help warm them up.

'My mouth is watering with the smell coming from the kitchen,' Paul says, walking behind me up the stairs, and before I can respond with a smart 'Well did you expect anything less,' I'm stopped in my tracks by another belly twinge. It's enough to make me wince.

'What's wrong?' Paul says, his voice laced with worry.

'Nothing,' I tell him. Because it *is* nothing. This is my

fourth time on this particular rodeo and I know the difference between Braxton Hicks and the real deal by now. 'The baby is just giving out because I've been moving about more than usual today.'

'Right,' Paul says in an authoritarian tone. 'You, into bed for a lie-down, I'll bath these two and get them into their jammies, then I'll bring you up a cup of tea and some shortbread.'

'Thanks, love,' I say. I don't need asking twice. My ankles are starting to swell like balloons and I am tired.

Paul is true to his word and wakes me a whole two hours later, with a cup of tea and some shortbread. The boys have been doing some Christmas crafts and he has even tidied up after them. Gemma is home and has actually agreed to wear her pair of matching pyjamas: our very own Christmas miracle. Already the light outside is starting to fade, I grab a quick shower and get my new (maternity, of course) red tartan flannel jammies on, as well as the fluffiest socks I can find.

As I come downstairs I'm hit with a waft of different scents. The mixed herbs from my stuffing and the honey and cloves from the ham make me salivate with hunger. The smell of a cinnamon candle combined with the smoky scent of the blazing fire makes me feel warm, cosy and positively Christmassy AF.

The boys are cuddled up on the sofa in their snowman jammies with Paul watching *The Polar Express*. Pamela is sitting on the armchair beside the window looking like death warmed up. When I ask her if she's OK, she simply mutters 'Never again', before asking me to pour her 'a wee Baileys' since it's Christmas.

Gemma is on the armchair opposite on her phone looking like the cat that got the cream. She grins at me as I walk past – only for a second though. She has a lot of time to make up for with that phone.

Thankfully the nap I took has put a stop to any Braxton Hicks, so I pop out to the kitchen and check on my dinner prep. It's all going perfectly.

As it starts to get dark outside and more snow begins to fall we snuggle up to watch *The Muppet Christmas Carol*. I've had to abandon all hopes of a night off cooking as the roads are all but impassable now, but I thank the wee Baby Jesus that I have some pizzas in the freezer and everyone is happy with a picnic on the living room floor. Old me would have flipped her tits that her plans for a takeaway were scuppered – but the new me, the me who is determined to be grateful for all the joy in her life – stays remarkably calm. It's still absolutely perfect. In fact this entire day has been absolutely perfect.

Just after seven, when we've laid out a plate of treats for Santa and the reindeers, Paul and I take the boys to bed. I cuddle with Nathan and Paul cuddles with Jax, as we take turns to read out their personalized Christmas Eve stories. We kiss them goodnight, and after we close their door we hang about outside for a few minutes, just to be sure they're asleep. After a few footsteps and a few little giggles, the room goes silent. When we open the door again ten minutes later, they're both tucked up in

Jax's bed with their arms around each other, sound asleep. It's enough to set me off again.

'Right, Paul,' I whisper, through my tears. 'I'll stay here and man the door, you and Gemma get everything down from the loft.'

'Yes, sir,' Paul whispers and gives me a salute before heading downstairs to fetch Gemma. To my surprise, Gemma is excited – enthusiastic even – about her new role in helping keep the Christmas magic alive for her little brothers. It's the first year we've brought her in for this bit, and I can tell she's enjoying feeling like one of the adults. She's grinning as she climbs the stairs, which does nothing to stop me from crying. She's helping us to become Santa. It's another stark reminder of how she's not my wee Gemma any more. But I'm equally as proud as I am sad because, despite her angst towards me, she really is the best big sister my boys, and this little baby, could ever wish for.

'Are you really cryin'?' she whispers.

'Ach, it's just you're getting so grown-up,' I mumble.

'Oh my godddduh, Mammy. Wise up!' She's not embarrassed or annoyed though – this is as close as my eldest child gets to affection these days. She smiles, and hugs me before stepping back. 'Seriously though, stop being a gack and crying. You're going to wake the boys.'

36

Santa's been!

Sunday, 25 December

'Mammmmmmmeeeeee, Daddddddeeeeee, it's Christmas morning!' shrieks Nathan, and his voice is in the highest pitch that I've ever heard.

'Kissmass, it's kissmass!' I hear Jax shout, and there follows a thunder of feet as two exceptionally hyper and definitely very awake little boys run down the hall towards our room.

Bing Crosby hasn't sung yet, so I know it's early. When I look at the clock, it's just gone six. We only got to bed at one after spending hours setting up the children's presents, trying to find the batteries I'd hidden 'somewhere safe', and Paul almost losing the head while trying to set up the camera for Nathan so it would be ready for him to record his first YouTube video.

But regardless of how tired we feel, the excitement of the boys is infectious and I can't wait to see their faces when they see what Santa has delivered. This is what it's all about for me – all the hard work all year, saving and hiding presents – this moment when our children get to live that wee bit of Christmas magic and truly believe in Santa.

Of course, the boys' excited shouting has also woken Pamela and Gemma, who emerge from their rooms looking as if they are both still half asleep. I brace myself for a rant from my beautiful daughter about it being too early, and for Pamela to make some passive-aggressive comment about children being made to wait until a 'decent hour' – but despite their obvious exhaustion they both seem to be caught up in a little of the magic too. My tummy tightens into a ball of excitement. I promise myself I will not cry because my eyes are still puffy from all the crying I did over everything yesterday. Hormones have a lot to answer for. Last night I cried as Paul drank the milk that had been left out for Santa, because it was 'just so nice of him not to let it go to waste'.

Seriously, like.

Gemma, delighted with her new role, sneaks down the stairs first, as we all wait on the landing. The boys watch with bated breath as she opens the living room door, peeks in and calls back to the boys, 'He's been!' sending them both catapulting at a dangerous speed down the stairs. What can only be described as chaos follows as they shout and scream with delight upon seeing cars and trucks, and their favourite toy characters positioned in a pile for each of them alongside a name-tagged stocking filled with sweets and chocolates. Nathan is practically hyperventilating with excitement at his YouTuber kit and is flat out practising his 'Hey guys!' intro voice.

Paul is on hand with extra batteries and instruction manuals to make sure everything is working properly. I'm on hand with my trusty black bag, intercepting any excited throws of wrapping paper or packaging before they even hit the ground. We're a well-oiled machine when it comes to Christmas morning, and I'm reminded again that Paul and I, while not perfect by any means, make a good team. Everyone in this house, even Pamela, makes a good team.

I can see Gemma champing at the bit to look through her presents, and I'm impressed that she's waiting until the madness of the boys has passed before diving into her own.

'Go on, Gemma,' I say, nodding towards the pile of gifts on the armchair for her and earning a huge, genuine, grin in return. She may not be as hyper as her brothers, but that doesn't mean she is any less excited. To my delight, she declares each present 'class' as she opens them. When she uncovers the Nike Jordans, Paul and I are rewarded with big hugs, which I enjoy every second of. But nothing quite prepares me for her reaction to her final present – a much-coveted iPhone (bought second-hand because we're not made of money).

'A new iPhone!' she screams, 'Oh my God, I can't

believe you actually got me it, even after my behaviour this year.'

'You didn't really think Santa would leave you a bag of coal, did you?' Paul asks, pulling her into a hug.

And she starts to sob, which makes me sob. 'I promise I'm going to be better, Mammy and Daddy,' she says, clutching the phone in her hands in disbelief.

'That's what we're hoping,' I say with a smile.

Paul and I exchange our presents and while he loves his watch, and I love the new necklace he got me, we both know that the joy of our children right now is the biggest gift we could ever give to each other. We also know that we're coming out of this year even stronger, with a new understanding and a promise to be more supportive and empathetic about each other's needs. That's not the kind of gift money can buy.

Pamela hands me a card and in exchange I pass over her present. The card is a voucher for a night away in one of the most expensive spa hotels in Ireland. Inside she's left a message that reads,

To Tara,
I know I've a lot of making up to do, but
let me start by watching the kids for a
night while you and Paul head away.
Thank you for letting me back in.
Love,
Pamela

She also hands Paul a present, which he opens and bursts out laughing.

'Boxers, Pamela?' he asks.

'Aye well, that day I arrived you were wearing a pair that looked like they were gonna walk off ye, so I thought you could be doing with some new ones, especially if youse are going for a night away,' she says with a wink, and I realize some things – like her brutal honesty – are never going to change about Pamela.

Then it's time to watch her unwrap her present. Butterflies flutter in my tummy while I wait for her reaction. It's a soppy gift and we haven't been soppy towards each other in well . . . never. Pamela opens the bracelet, blinking away tears.

'Read the inscription on the back, Mammy.'

As she does, two heavy tears fall down her cheeks and she stands up and walks over to me, pulling me into a hug.

'Tara,' she sobs, 'this means so much. I don't think I'll honestly be able to tell you how much. It's perfect. Absolutely perfect.'

And now, of course, I'm crying again too as we embrace each other and sob into each other's shoulders.

As she pulls me into the tightest hug I feel a pop somewhere deep inside me. It's a pop I remember well. The pop of doom. My tummy tightens again but not with anticipation, I now realize: it's a fucking contraction.

A gush of water expels itself from my body, splashing onto the floor.

'Mammy!' Gemma says. 'Have you just peed yourself again?'

'No love,' I say, as what is very definitely a contraction shoots up my back and across my stomach. 'I think my waters have just broken.'

'Jesus, I'll ring an ambulance,' Paul shouts, and he runs upstairs to grab his phone. 'I'll never be able to get you there in the snow.'

'There's no need to panic,' I tell him, as I myself fight the urge to panic. 'You know labour lasts for hours. We've loads of time.'

'Tara love, just sit down now and breathe deep breaths, it's going to be OK,' Pamela says, and she guides me towards the sofa, asking Gemma to bring a couple of towels.

'Mammy, the baby's not coming just yet,' I tell her.

'I know,' she says, 'They're for the sofa. You don't want to be leaking all over that. It'll be ruined.' Fair point.

When Gemma comes back, she is scared. So scared in fact she has put her new iPhone down. Nathan is looking at me with puzzlement, and I'm sure a little fear too. Jax is thankfully more interested in his Paw Patrol toys, but he does stop playing long enough to declare, 'It's OK, Mammy, we all have ackydents sometimes.'

But this isn't an accident. This is the real deal, and as another contraction hits, uncomfortably close to the last one, I have to hold in every bad word in my vocabulary. Jesus, but those motherfuckers hurt like a bastard.

I don't want to traumatize the children.

'Mammy,' I whisper, grabbing her hand as she lays towels over the sofa. 'Will you help me upstairs? I have a feeling this baby isn't waiting for me to get to hospital or for an ambulance to arrive.'

'I want to come with you,' Gemma says, her face pale with worry. 'I'll help you up, Pammy can watch the boys.'

Pamela looks to me for guidance and I nod.

'OK love,' she tells Gemma. 'But you have to promise to call me if you need me?'

Gemma nods solemnly as she guides me towards the stairs. Thankfully the contraction has now passed and I'm able to climb them without having to hang on to anyone. But I've no sooner reached the top when another contraction begins, bringing me to my knees and onto the floor.

'The operator said the snow is holding response time up, she's going to stay on the line,' Paul says, looking panicked as he pops the operator on speaker.

As the contraction eases, I allow Paul and Gemma to get me seated at the side of the bed, but before they've even lifted off my slippers to move my legs and hoist me onto my back, another contraction starts.

'Tara that's not even two minutes apart, love.' Paul repeats this to the operator, who I can hear telling Paul to go and get towels and a wet cloth in the bathroom. As he does, Gemma pulls my hair back into a scrunchie, and sits beside me holding my hand.

'Just breathe, Mammy,' she says, as I close my eyes

against the wave of pain in my middle. When did she become so sensible?

As the contraction subsides, and Paul returns following all the instructions given to him by the operator, I realize this baby really is coming, and now. The urge to push is kicking in and I am powerless to stop it.

'Gemma,' I pant, and I look directly in her eyes, 'this baby is coming now, and I might scream a little, but don't be scared, OK?' She nods, but I can see she is scared, how could she not be?

As another contraction shoots through my back and around my stomach I feel the most intense pressure as the urge to push takes over. 'I neeeeeed . . . To . . . Push . . .' I pant and it's Paul's turn to go pale, and I see sweat beading on his forehead.

'You can do this,' the operator says, and I'm not sure if she's talking to me, to Paul or to both of us. She instructs him, very calmly, to remove my underwear and to have a look to see if the baby's head is visible yet.

To his credit, he does what he's told and he does not faint or boke at the sight of my dilated cervix and stretched va-jayjay.

'I . . . erm . . . I think there's a head,' he says. 'There's a lot of hair.'

Now is not the time to comment on the upkeep of my pubic region!

'Yep, definitely a head,' he says, with a tiny wobble in his voice, as I bear down again.

Gemma moves herself up the bed and sits behind me

(praise Jesus, or she might never recover), dabbing the cold cloth on my face and watching on in a mixture of horror and fascination.

I push with every contraction, and I try as best as I can not to scream because I know it will scare Gemma, and the boys downstairs, but there are times there is nothing else for it but to let rip – probably also around the time my perineum is letting rip. I often wondered how these women who swear by hypnobirthing and the crazy Scientology loon-bags go through labour without making as much as a peep. Anyone who manages not to scream during the 'ring of fire' stage of labour is superhuman or super-drugged-up. Me, I'm a screamer. And not a pretty one.

I grip Gemma's hands so tightly I'm afraid I'm hurting her, but also find it impossible to stop. I hear her voice in my ear: 'You're doing it, Mammy. Keep going!' and I try to lock into that. To lock into the reality that I am so close to meeting our new baby.

'The head's out!' I hear Paul shout, as excited as if he's just scored the winning goal in the FA Cup Final and I focus on what the operator is saying, and on Paul guiding this new wee life into the world and on my daughter – my beautiful firstborn – in my ear crying now.

'Oh Mammy! You've done it, Mammy!'

With one last gentle push I feel the release of my baby coming into the world, and when I open my eyes there, in my husband's arms, covered in mucus and blood, and screaming just like their mammy was a minute ago, is our baby.

'It's a girl,' Paul says, and a tear rolls down his cheek. Gemma wriggles out from behind me as I slump back on the pillows, exhausted. I watch as my firstborn helps her daddy wrap my newborn in a towel to keep warm. My heart is bursting. My new daughter in the arms of the man who will forever be her first love, while my eldest daughter – always a daddy's girl – looks on in wonder.

The bedroom door crashes open and two paramedics rush in. 'Looks like you didn't need us at all,' says the first one with a smile.

'I don't know about that,' Paul says, wiping the sweat from his brow. 'I for one am glad you're here.'

'I think you deserve a cup of a tea after that,' the second very smiley paramedic says, a Santa hat perched on her curls.

'I'll go and make tea for everyone,' Gemma declares, and I smile with pride.

'OK, Tara. We'll get you all sorted, and get a wee look at this one. Then we can take you up to the hospital and the midwives can get a wee look at you both, or if you prefer we can see if one of the community midwives can pop in and see you here?'

'I don't have to go to hospital?' I ask, dreading the thought of leaving my family on Christmas Day.

'Not unless we find anything to be concerned about, or you really, really want to,' the Santa hat paramedic says with a wry smile.

'I think I'd like to stay here if I can,' I say. 'I don't think there's anywhere else I'd like to be today.'

'Let's get a wee look at you then,' Santa Hat says, smiling as she sits at the end of the bed.

Thankfully, everything with me is just as it should be. The cord is cut, the placenta healthy. The tearing I was sure I felt is little more than a graze and, perhaps most importantly, my new daughter is perfect. A community midwife is en route to check her over just to be extra sure, but there is no reason for me to leave the cosiness of my family home.

The paramedics even help Paul change our bed while I get a quick shower to freshen up. I can't tell you how amazing the fresh sheets feel as I'm guided back under them, and handed my beautiful baby to nurse.

Her eyes try to focus, and as she looks up at me I see so much potential in her already. So much joy and love: she's going to have the most magical life.

'She's so beautiful,' I hear Gemma say from the doorway as she brings me in some tea and toast. 'Can I hold her?' she asks, blinking away tears of her own.

'Of course, darling,' I say. She places the tea and toast on my bedside table, and sits beside me, making a crook in her arms for the baby to rest in.

'Be careful with her head,' I say, and Gemma looks at me as if I've offended her.

'I've been watching TikToks about babies, so I know how to hold then, bestie. Chill your boots!'

I can't help but smile. I've just had a glimpse of what a protective force to be reckoned with this big sister will be.

'Why don't you bring the boys and Pamela up now?' I ask Paul, and he smiles and bolts downstairs with more enthusiasm than the boys did earlier when they were dying to find their Christmas presents.

Nathan bounces into the room holding his camera, and climbs up beside me to give me the biggest hug. Gemma hands the baby back to me and Nathan gives his baby sister the softest kiss on the top of her head before launching into a hundred questions.

'So will we call the baby Jesus acuz it's Christmas? And where is the donkeys? Are the people from the ambliance the wise men here, cos I fink one of them is a girl? Does the baby want a share of my Wotsits? Can I hold the baby? But then who is the innkeeper? Wow, it must be really me acuz dis is my house! Does the baby want to play wif my Avengers?'

We're all laughing, but Jax just cuddles into Pamela, a little overwhelmed by everything around him. She gently strokes his hair and reassures him that his mammy is fine and his new baby sister is going to be a good baby and not take all his toys, and I can actually see the moment he relaxes in her arms.

But I can also see that Pamela is longing to get closer to this baby herself and get a wee hold of her youngest granddaughter. Sweet Lord, she just might turn into the maternal type after all this time; Pammy may actually have found her way. Sure, she'll always be a bit wild, but there's nothing wrong with walking your own path.

'Right,' the Santa hat paramedic says. 'I think we can

leave you all here for now. The midwife will be here later, and obviously we're only a phone call away. Happy Christmas to all of you. What a very lucky baby to be surrounded by so much love.'

37

All is calm, far from shite

Night has fallen and my heart could not be more full if it tried. I'm on the sofa, propped up with pillows with the most beautiful newborn I think I've ever seen in my arms, fast asleep.

The day has certainly not been what we planned, but it has been perfect.

Sure we didn't have dinner until gone six, and because Paul and Pamela cooked it, it wasn't quite up to my standard, but to be honest, I'm on such a natural high I wouldn't have cared if they'd served me beans on toast.

After dinner, as Pamela nursed her youngest grandchild, Nathan asked another question – one we knew was coming.

'So what is the baby's name?' Nathan asks. 'Can we call it Thor?'

'*It* is a *she*,' I correct him, 'And your daddy and I have decided that the baby's godmother should name her.'

'Is that like a fairy godmother?' Nathan asks.

'Kinda,' I reply.

'Who's the godmother?' asks Pamela, and I turn to Gemma, who's snuggled with her head on my shoulder.

'It's Gemma,' I say with a smile and a lump in my throat.

'Really, Mammy?' she asks, sitting bolt upright.

'Really,' I say. 'Your daddy and I couldn't think of anyone better.' And I give her hand a squeeze before asking, 'So, what's her name?'

'Amelia?' she says, looking at Pamela and then back to me.

'It's perfect,' I say. And it is, just like Gemma, and just like today.

Perfect.

After the boys have gone to bed, the snow begins to fall again. The fire is crackling, the lights on the garland and the tree are glistening, Paul is snoozing on the armchair, having brought down all our baby things from the attic. Pamela is on her phone, and Gemma is still stuck to my side as we both stare at Baby Amelia asleep in her Moses basket.

If this time last year, someone told me I'd be cosied up on Christmas Day with all my family, including a new baby daughter and my estranged mother, I'd have told them to go and jump back on their magic carpet. But here I am. A full belly and an even fuller heart, with another gorgeous daughter, two happy content boys, a husband who still loves me even though I can be selfish and crazy, and a mother who I now look at in a whole new light.

367

I can feel my priorities changing once again.

And though I don't want to dwell on it now, that also applies to my work. Yes, I always wanted to keep my career and raise a family at the same time, but over the last few weeks, my desire to work in project management, and, in particular, for ToteTech has significantly decreased. Even though we have enough evidence to make sure Handley is held to rights for his behaviour, there's something about the corporate environment that doesn't appeal so much any more.

Maybe it's seeing how everyone's life is changing. Cat is about to become a mum. Amanda is reinventing herself as some sort of sex guru. My mother is putting the ghosts of her past to rest and settling into her role of doting 'Pammy', and even Paul is finding a new hobby to distract him. Maybe they're all showing me that life is for the living. We might be able to get shot of Handley, but there will be another Handley waiting in the wings. There always is.

Do I fight it, or do I find something else that really makes my heart sing?

It's a lot to think about, and thankfully I have months of maternity leave to do so.

But one thing I'm no longer scared of is rebelling and choosing my own path. I'm going to show my daughters they can be whoever they want to be and that plot twists aren't always a bad thing. I'm gonna take a leaf out of Pamela's book, and Amelia Earhart's.

As that thought crosses my mind, I glance over at

Pamela, who's scrolling her phone, proudly wearing her new bracelet. She's also wearing the sneakiest smile across her lips.

'What's got you smiling like that?' I ask her.

'Oh just Tinder, love, I got a few wee matches.'

My ma is on Tinder!? Holy fuck.

A Christmas Glossary
of Derry/Irish terms

Boggin': filthy, dirty, grubby, unclean. Can be used to refer to toddlers after they've eaten their Christmas dinner with their hands.

Catch yourself on: come on now, be smarter.

Christmas cupboard: where sweet treats are stored in the run-up to Christmas and must not, under any circumstances, be touched until Christmas Day.

Cool your jets: calm down.

Cracker: used as a term of praise, as in 'That's a cracker Christmas jumper you have on ye.'

Craic: fun, banter, enjoyment. Can also be used to describe a situation e.g. 'This parenting craic' meaning, this parenting situation.

Dose: an insufferable human being.

Dose of the horn: a strong urge for sex.

Go away and take your face for a shite: please leave me alone and go and have a stern word with yourself.

Jesus, Mary and the wee donkey: a term usually used in despair, e.g. when someone's raided the Christmas cupboard.

Lured: happy or delighted, prefixed with the word 'pure' emphasizes how much e.g. 'I am pure lured I got to have a lie-in today.'

Quare: Great. E.g. 'That's a quare day for drying the clothes on the line.'

Shite the tights: someone of a nervous disposition.

Sláinte: Irish for cheers when taking a drink (usually of the alcoholic variety).

Taking the hand: not being serious.

Acknowledgements

Thank you once again to the team at HarperCollins for giving me the opportunity to bring Tara and her tumultuous family back to life once again, especially at Christmas, my favourite time of the year. In particular, thanks to my editor, Martha Ashby, who believed I could do this again and encouraged me to push my limits. And to my fellow Derry writer, Claire Allan, my mentor, who trusted me to deliver on time, kept me sane, helped me to grow more in confidence as a writer and not once questioned my method or creativity.

To my husband who once again had to man the fort, work his own job, keep the children alive and entertained and ensure I was taking enough breaks. I love you.

To Ava and Alfie, for whom I do everything. My two crazies. I hope I make you half as proud as you two make me.

To Jody and Amy at A3 for being my cheerleaders, bringing positive energy always and helping this mama to grow and conquer outside of her comfort zone.

To my mammy for being my biggest fan, my creative

inspiration and for always, always believing in me. Just to be clear, Pamela is in no way based on you. ☺

And to you, the reader, for picking up this book, for supporting me in the most incredible way possible. I might not be able to thank you in person, but I sure hope I can put a smile on your face and make you feel like you're not alone. Thank you for appreciating my madness.

If you loved Tara's story, why not go back to the beginning of her hilarious escapades in Serena Terry's first *Sunday Times* bestselling novel?

From *Sunday Times* bestselling author and TikTok sensation @MammyBanter

Available now